# DRAGONWATCH
## RETURN OF THE DRAGON SLAYERS

ALSO BY BRANDON MULL

SERIES:
Fablehaven
The Candy Shop War
Beyonders
Five Kingdoms
Dragonwatch

BOOKS:
*The Caretaker's Guide to Fablehaven*
*Fablehaven Book of Imagination*
*Spirit Animals: Wild Born*
*Smarter Than a Monster*
*Legend of the Dragon Slayer*

# DRAGONWATCH
## RETURN OF THE DRAGON SLAYERS

# BRANDON MULL

ILLUSTRATED BY
BRANDON DORMAN

SHADOW
MOUNTAIN

© 2021 Brandon Mull

All rights reserved. No part of this book may be reproduced in any form or by any means without permission in writing from the publisher, Shadow Mountain®, at permissions@shadowmountain.com. The views expressed herein are the responsibility of the author and do not necessarily represent the position of Shadow Mountain.

Visit us at shadowmountain.com

Library of Congress Cataloging-in-Publication Data

(CIP data on file)
ISBN 978-1-62972-930-5

Printed in the United States of America     7/2021
Lake Book Manufacturing, Inc., Melrose Park, IL

10   9   8   7   6   5   4   3   2   1

*To Calvin—MY tiny hero!*

*And to Emily Watts,*
*who has helped me since the start.*

# Contents

| | | |
|---|---|---|
| Chapter 1 | Refugees | 1 |
| Chapter 2 | Escape | 11 |
| Chapter 3 | Devastation | 20 |
| Chapter 4 | Solitude | 31 |
| Chapter 5 | Mayor | 44 |
| Chapter 6 | Showdown | 55 |
| Chapter 7 | Pillagers | 64 |
| Chapter 8 | Divide and Conquer | 78 |
| Chapter 9 | Pool | 90 |
| Chapter 10 | Divining | 103 |
| Chapter 11 | Celebration | 110 |
| Chapter 12 | Stratos | 124 |
| Chapter 13 | Giants | 133 |
| Chapter 14 | Captured | 145 |
| Chapter 15 | Ethershard | 156 |
| Chapter 16 | Giant King | 164 |
| Chapter 17 | Lizelle | 175 |
| Chapter 18 | Vision | 185 |
| Chapter 19 | Wounded | 200 |
| Chapter 20 | Radiance | 215 |
| Chapter 21 | Flight | 228 |

# CONTENTS

CHAPTER 22    Tower . . . . . . . . . . . . . . . . . . . . . . . . 238

CHAPTER 23    Diverging . . . . . . . . . . . . . . . . . . . . . 250

CHAPTER 24    Talizar . . . . . . . . . . . . . . . . . . . . . . . 264

CHAPTER 25    Second Try . . . . . . . . . . . . . . . . . . . . 274

CHAPTER 26    Bernice . . . . . . . . . . . . . . . . . . . . . . . 285

CHAPTER 27    Muster . . . . . . . . . . . . . . . . . . . . . . . 299

CHAPTER 28    Magdalena . . . . . . . . . . . . . . . . . . . . 304

CHAPTER 29    Duel . . . . . . . . . . . . . . . . . . . . . . . . 321

CHAPTER 30    Batoosa . . . . . . . . . . . . . . . . . . . . . . 335

CHAPTER 31    Homecoming . . . . . . . . . . . . . . . . . . 347

CHAPTER 32    Miguel . . . . . . . . . . . . . . . . . . . . . . . 360

CHAPTER 33    Scheming . . . . . . . . . . . . . . . . . . . . . 370

CHAPTER 34    Gerwin . . . . . . . . . . . . . . . . . . . . . . 380

CHAPTER 35    Traveler . . . . . . . . . . . . . . . . . . . . . . 395

CHAPTER 36    Campfire . . . . . . . . . . . . . . . . . . . . . 405

CHAPTER 37    Prison . . . . . . . . . . . . . . . . . . . . . . . 410

CHAPTER 38    Vez Radim . . . . . . . . . . . . . . . . . . . . 427

CHAPTER 39    Delivery . . . . . . . . . . . . . . . . . . . . . . 439

CHAPTER 40    Nadia . . . . . . . . . . . . . . . . . . . . . . . 455

CHAPTER 41    Fairview . . . . . . . . . . . . . . . . . . . . . . 471

CHAPTER 42    Mission . . . . . . . . . . . . . . . . . . . . . . 486

CHAPTER 43    Source . . . . . . . . . . . . . . . . . . . . . . . 500

CHAPTER 44    Alderfairy . . . . . . . . . . . . . . . . . . . . . 512

CHAPTER 45    Dragon Storm . . . . . . . . . . . . . . . . . . 522

CHAPTER 46    Ethergem . . . . . . . . . . . . . . . . . . . . . 541

CHAPTER 47    Reinforcements . . . . . . . . . . . . . . . . . 553

# Contents

Chapter 48    Ronodin . . . . . . . . . . . . . . . . . . . . . . . 572

Chapter 49    Healer . . . . . . . . . . . . . . . . . . . . . . . . 586

Chapter 50    New Beginnings . . . . . . . . . . . . . . . . . 599

Acknowledgments . . . . . . . . . . . . . . . . 608

Note to Readers . . . . . . . . . . . . . . . . . 610

Reading Guide . . . . . . . . . . . . . . . . . . 612

# CHAPTER ONE

# Refugees

For the first time since he had arrived at the Museum of Gigantic Achievement, Knox heard no sounds of dragons wreaking havoc above. No buildings collapsing. No primordial roars. Only silence.

Protected by an iron door, the dim room occupied a corner of the lowest level of the museum. The mismatched furnishings looked like they consisted of the surplus from diverse displays showing giant civilization over time. A huge board against one wall showcased taxidermied animals—horse, cow, elk, tiger, boar—pinned and labeled like insects. Off to one side, a young giant girl cut the final pieces of an apple, feeding the wedges to a younger giant boy, who accepted the bites of food around his whimpering.

A matronly giant with her hair bound in a scarf, a massive infant cradled in one arm, stared upward hopefully.

Trickles of dust no longer sifted through the cracks in the ceiling. The woman was tasked with caring for the eight giant children in the room and the ailing, elderly giant on the bed while the city was under attack. Knox, Tess, and the two satyrs, Newel and Doren, were doing their best to share the space without ending up taxidermied themselves.

"Are the dragons taking a break from trashing the town?" Newel asked.

"Setting a trap, more likely," Doren said. "Hoping to lure careless satyrs topside."

"I'm not sure we're a priority," Knox said. "If they knew we were down here, they could get to us easy enough."

"Watch your tongues," the matronly giant whispered. "Many dragons have excellent hearing. They hunt best in stillness."

"She makes a valid point," Doren whispered.

Newel shook his head. He spoke quietly. "Sounded like the whole museum came down. The demolition might be over. We're beneath a pile of rubble."

"I'm hungry, Nesha," Dirk, an eight-year-old giant, said. Knox was barely taller than the boy's knees.

"Tighten your belt, lad," the matronly giant replied. "I'm no magician. We already ate what we brought. There wasn't time to gather much."

"Don't get any funny ideas about us," Doren said warily. "We're guests of the queen. Plus, we're gamey."

"They won't eat us," Tess said from where she stood by a four-year-old female giant three times her height. "We're friends."

"The wyrms will come for us," croaked the old giant on the bed. "They have a score to settle, mark my words. They'll ferret us out one by one."

"Shut your trap," Nesha said. "You'll frighten the children."

Propping himself up on one elbow, the old giant gave a wheezy chuckle. "No use coddling them now. Their folks are dead, and they'll soon follow. Our days of feasting are over. The hour of becoming the meal has arrived."

A couple of the giant kids began to cry.

"You shush," Nesha scolded, flinging a wooden salt-shaker at him. "Now you've done it. If the dragons didn't hear us before, they do now."

The old giant flopped back on his pillow. "Bah. Best to have it over and done with. We played with fire longer than we should have. We all knew what we were doing. It's time to get burned."

Knox shuddered. It had been ugly up in the streets.

Knox had expected to find the city secure when he, Tess, and the satyrs arrived at Humburgh through the queen's passage from Terastios. Humburgh should have been under the protection of Humbuggle and his Wizenstone. Instead, the sky giants guarding the Humburgh side of the passage informed them that the defenses had mysteriously crumbled. Humburgh, particularly the section of the city called Big Side, where the giants dwelled, was under attack.

A giant guard named Morgana had been dispatched to take Knox, Tess, Newel, and Doren to a safe room within the thick walls of the museum. After placing the four of them in a cage for transport, she had carried them outside, the cage tucked in her arm like a football clutched by a running back.

When Morgana exited to the street, a two-headed dragon armored with jagged purple scales glided overhead, just above the rooftops, widespread wings momentarily blocking the sunlight. The pair of heads sent a deluge of fire and lightning onto the street, and Morgana had ducked into a recessed doorway, raising a huge rectangular shield to deflect the conflagration. After the dragon passed, Morgana proceeded across red-hot cobblestones, passing windows that had exploded inward, a blazing vegetable cart, and a pair of charred giant corpses.

As Morgana ran, Knox became petrified with overpowering dragon fear, Tess clinging to his waist. Immobilized inside the transport cage, they had absorbed the sights and sounds of battle. Dragons snarled, buildings buckled, fire crackled, and thunder boomed. Giants shouted orders and bellowed challenges. Smoke hazed the air, but through it, Knox could see dragons strafing Big Side with acid, flame, and lightning. Dozens of dragons approached in the distance.

After dodging around a corner, they found a greenish gold dragon harnessed and bridled to pull a wagon. The dragon wrenched against the harness, twisting and bucking, trying to break free as the driver of the wagon, a broad giant with a bushy beard, flogged the creature liberally. Leather creaked and wood splintered as the dragon struggled, rocking the wagon from side to side while the giant driver cracked his whip.

An enraged maroon dragon with black markings swooped in from one side, and a gray, speckled dragon attacked from the other. The maroon dragon bit off the arm holding the whip, then sprayed the giant with an exhalation of orange gel that made him fall from the wagon, screaming and tearing at his skin. The speckled dragon destroyed the restraints, freeing the greenish gold dragon, who turned and pounced on the driver as he attempted to rise.

Knox looked away as the dragons converged to feed.

The giants seemed panicked and unprepared against the deadly fury of the attackers. Knox glimpsed a few giants staunchly fighting the dragons, including one who shot a dragon out of the sky with a colossal bow. He noticed an orange dragon dead in the street, back broken, wings crumpled. But he saw many slain giants, and others cowering among the rubble or furtively peering from windows.

The giants were formidable, but Knox could see that the attack was going to be a massacre. The magical barriers Humbuggle had put in place around the city would have prevented an attack from outside, but clearly those barriers had failed. And the giants, who had grown to view the dragons like domesticated animals, seemed shocked by their unbridled power and fury.

The Museum of Gigantic Achievement was a grand stone building crowned by three domes with statues of mighty giants, arms upraised, serving as pillars. The marble façade was blackened in places, and the charred remnants of flags and banners dripped bright embers. Avoiding the stairs that led to the main lobby, Morgana had used a side entrance and raced down a flight of stairs, along a hall, and then to the iron door where the safe room was located. After a shouted conversation through the door, Morgana had left her charges in Nesha's care.

Sword drawn, Morgana had swiftly departed, and a horrible clamor had continued from above ever since.

Until now.

"I think it's over," Knox said quietly. "The dragons don't need to be subtle."

Doren held up a finger. "Unless they decided it's easier to let the stragglers come to them than to dig for us in the rubble."

"Go have a look if you can't keep still," the old giant suggested from his bed. "Better you than any of us."

Dirk tugged on Nesha's skirt. "I don't want the dragons to eat the little goatboy."

"I'm not holding anyone captive," Nesha said. "The satyrs have minds of their own."

"I'll pop my head up," Newel said, crossing to the door. "If trouble lies in wait, I'll hurry back."

"And lead them right to us," the old giant griped. "Once you're out, stay out."

"Pipe down," Nesha said. "This is my nursery. You're here as a courtesy, not to bark orders."

"I could crush the lot of you," the old giant griped, ending with a fit of coughing.

"Don't mind him," Nesha said. "I'd like to know what

the quiet means. Check it out if that suits you. Don't lead trouble to us or I'll make sure you're squished good and flat. If you survive undetected, return and report."

"If I were in my prime, nobody would be hiding," the old giant claimed. "I'd tie those dragons in knots."

"Be glad you're down here," Nesha said. "I'll wager plenty of brave giants met their end today."

The old giant gave a snort. "What brave giants are left? That was my father's generation. Mark my words, we had it coming, and it came, and none of us were giant enough to stop it."

"I'll be right back," Newel said.

"Be careful," Knox said.

"I've got a knack for dodging trouble," Newel assured.

"And dragon fear fries my thinking," Doren whispered. "I don't perceive any right now. Based on that, I'd bet my horns they've gone."

Newel unfastened the latch he could reach. The door was more than ten times his height, with locking mechanisms at various intervals. Nesha crossed to the door, unbarred it, and slid aside a huge bolt.

"We need a secret knock," Knox said.

Rapping his knuckles against his palm, Newel did two slow taps, then, after a pause, three quick ones.

"That will serve," Nesha said.

"What about a knock for if you're under duress?" Knox said.

"Clever, that one," Doren said. "They don't call him Knox for nothing."

Newel gave his palm an experimental tap, then followed it with five rapid smacks.

"If you're under duress, don't come back," Nesha hissed. She hauled the heavy door open a little, and Newel slipped out.

"I'll wait outside," Doren offered. "Just so I can better hear what happens up top."

Nesha closed the door behind Doren, then rebarred and rebolted it.

"Don't worry," Dirk announced to the room. "I'll fight the dragons."

Tess moved close to her brother. "They'll be okay," she said.

"Sure," Knox said, one hand on the object hidden beneath his shirt. Only he knew that he secretly carried the Giant Queen's crown.

Knox, Tess, and the satyrs had witnessed the moment when the Giant Queen was struck down by Celebrant and a mob of dragons. Her enormous crown had been left on the floor of the throne room, unnoticed as the dragons continued to raze Terastios. Hoping it would help their cause, Knox had gone back for the crown, and when he reached for it, the crown had shrunk to a size that would fit on his head.

Knox had kept the crown hidden since then. In the commotion of getting away, the others had barely registered his absence.

Were the dragons aware the crown was missing? Was anyone looking for it? Had any giants at Terastios survived?

Could the crown have been forgotten?

Knox wrestled over what he should do with the crown. Did he have a responsibility to return it to the giants? Might there be a reward? It was probably needed for when they selected their next monarch. How did that work exactly? What if possession of the crown determined the ruler?

If Knox put on the crown, would he become the Giant King? Might he even transform into a giant? Or at least be filled with tremendous power?

What if the giants had to obey him? Could he unite the giants against the dragons? What if he used the crown to help win the dragon war? This attack had caught the giants unprepared. There had to be survivors. With the right leadership, the giants might still have a major impact against the dragons.

Then again, what if as soon as he tried to wear the crown, Knox was labeled a traitor and a thief? Was there a chance the giants might take revenge against him for the death of their queen?

Keeping the crown might be a liability. If he hid the crown in an unlikely place and walked away, he could always return for it. Or he could forget he had ever known anything about it, ditch the responsibility.

There came two slow knocks on the door, and then three quick ones. Nesha undid the locks and opened the door enough for the satyrs to slip inside.

"All clear," Newel reported. "The way up is choked with rubble, but it can be navigated. Might be harder going for you giants. I wriggled through some tight spots."

"Did we drive them off?" Nesha asked.

"The skies are empty," Newel said. "I felt no twinge of dragon fear. Big Side is leveled and scorched. The rest of Humburgh is damaged but mostly standing."

"Tried to tell you," the old giant griped. "This is the end of the road for us."

"For you, maybe," Nesha spat. "Any giants moving about?"

"Not yet," Newel said. "Hopefully others are hiding."

The silence that followed did not feel hopeful.

"What if the dragons come back?" Tess asked.

"They'll roast you and eat you," the old giant predicted.

"We should take advantage of the lull," Newel said. "See what we can learn over in Small Town."

"You're free to leave as you please," Nesha said. "But if you venture out into the open, don't return."

"Good riddance," the old giant grumbled. "Let us mourn in peace."

"Do you need protection?" Dirk asked.

"We'll manage," Doren said. "You're needed here to help watch the young ones."

"Let's go," Knox said. "I want to find out what happened."

# CHAPTER TWO

# Escape

Seth examined the dungeon corridor by the maroon light of his blade. The radiance was a darker red than when Seth had previously wielded Vasilis, but he supposed that made sense. Since his last time carrying the fabled sword, he had served as an agent of darkness, and the experience made a visible difference to the energy his nature projected.

A glance over his shoulder showed his oversized, misshapen shadow on the uneven wall, made extra strange by his wings. He could not see far in either direction because the corridor turned sharply. The other cells within view were empty, though he could sense entities elsewhere in the dungeon. The wraith at his side remained a cold presence, the humanoid shape absorbing light rather than reflecting it.

Thanks to the vitality flowing from the sword, for the first time since he had regained his memories, Seth's mind felt sharp and clear. This jailbreak suddenly seemed less daunting, as did the idea of defeating anything that got in his way, but Seth wanted to remain wary of overconfidence. Based on the instructions received from Morisant, Seth knew that Vasilis magnified whatever was inside of him, and experience had shown that some aspects of his nature were dangerous. The sword had led previous wielders to ruin.

Torchlight became visible from up ahead. Though he heard no footfalls, he could see that somebody was approaching. In these close confines, if the guard was a dragon, it would be in human form. Seth considered retreating along the corridor, but realized if he backtracked, his empty cell would soon be discovered and an alarm would be raised. He had to take care of the guard—quietly, if possible.

Deciding to shade walk, Seth found it unusually easy to access his power, and realized that must be another benefit of the sword. He crouched and quietly advanced to the next bend in the corridor as the torchlight approached, still hearing no footsteps. Crouched in the shadows, he would be virtually undetectable. Hopefully the guard would stroll past him, which would allow Seth to attack him from behind. Seth motioned for Whiner to step against the wall, and the wraith complied.

Treading silently, the guard strode into view and stopped. Clutching a torch in one hand, the woman had cruel, harsh features, her body sheathed in dark gray plumage, with vulture wings gathered behind her back like a shawl. She glared directly at Seth.

"Return to your cage," the guard uttered in a garbled voice that seemed to overlap itself.

His cover blown, Seth stood up, holding Vasilis out warily. "Back off. I don't want to harm you."

The woman bared a mouthful of pointed teeth. "I need no quarter from you, human. Return to your cage lest I devour you."

"Get her, Whiner," Seth said.

*I will not come off victorious against a Siberian harpy,* Whiner communicated directly to Seth's mind.

"You wish to cower behind a wraith?" the harpy asked, a touch of amusement in the question.

"I don't want to hurt you," Seth said, even as Vasilis tugged him toward the feathery woman.

"Test yourself against me, if you wish," the harpy invited, the fingers of one hand hooking into claws, wicked talons gleaming in the torchlight. "I am an artist. You will not die swiftly."

"I'll be fine," Seth said. "You'll end up looking like modern art."

The harpy hissed at him. "Come taste the reward of defiance."

Effortlessly connecting with the dark source of his power within, Seth willed coldness into the torch, and it snuffed out. By the deep red light of Vasilis, Seth saw Whiner rush at the harpy. Dropping her darkened torch, spinning like a whirlwind, the harpy dug her talons into the wraith's sides and hurled it down the corridor.

The ferocious creature turned in Seth's direction,

feathers fanning out, and a gust of foul wind streamed over him as she lunged in his direction. Vasilis pulled him toward her, the blade jerking in his grasp, drawn to intercept each swipe of her talons, every clangorous impact shedding sparks. The harpy shrieked like an eagle as Seth lopped off one plumy arm just below the elbow. His feet shuffled to keep up with the sword as he stepped in and cut her down with a diagonal slash across her torso, the blade flashing brilliantly. The harpy lay motionless on the dungeon floor, red-hot cinders smoldering in the wound, the smell of burnt feathers polluting the air.

Rage and elation flooded through Seth as he stood over the fallen creature. Sheathing the sword helped Seth tamp down the wild emotions, but he still had to pace for a moment, convulsively clenching his fists, before turning his attention up the corridor.

"Whiner, are you all right?"

*Damaged but not destroyed*, the wraith replied. *I attempted to fulfill your command.*

The passage was so dark with the torch extinguished that Seth drew his sword again. An extra dose of courage and confidence coursed into him with Vasilis in his grasp. "I didn't think a creature like that harpy could harm you," Seth said.

*Harpies can torment almost anyone*, the wraith replied. *I sense other harpies in the vicinity. Do not underestimate them.*

"I'll watch out," Seth said.

*Must you use the title "Whiner"?* the wraith asked.

"It's just a joke," Seth said. "When I first met you, all you talked about was how cold and hungry you were."

*That condition remains,* the wraith said. *When we met, I had been in isolation for a long while. My sense of self had degenerated. The witches helped revive me.*

"I can give you a better nickname," Seth said.

*It would be appreciated,* the wraith replied.

"How about Witchprize?" Seth asked.

*Would you want that title?* the wraith asked.

"Or just Prize," Seth offered.

*Very well,* the wraith accepted.

"Glad I finally caught up to your high standards," Seth said. "Do you know the way out of here?"

*I do,* Prize replied. *You will be grateful for your wings.*

"Lead the way," Seth said.

The corridor wound past a few empty cells before ending at a gated archway. Seth stopped short and backed away before edging forward. A chilly breeze wafted through the bars, the starry night visible beyond.

"I assumed we were deep underground," Seth said.

*The opposite is true,* Prize replied as Seth walked to the archway and peered at the long drop below.

"A dragon put me to sleep before I arrived here," Seth said. "Its breath knocked me out instantly."

*Your cell was located high within an enormous pinnacle of rock,* Prize explained.

From where Seth stood, forehead pressed against the cold bars, craggy mountain peaks created jagged shapes in the moonlight, most of them considerably lower than his current vantage. The rock face fell away below him in a sheer drop and continued steeply above. "How did you get up here?"

*It was a long climb,* Prize conveyed.

"Are there stairs up the middle?"

*No stairs. No ladders. This portion of the prison contains only eleven cells.*

"But I could sense other presences in here," Seth said.

*There are many unconnected sections to this towering dungeon,* Prize replied. *Separate clusters of cells. All are primarily accessible by flight.*

"Or to a good climber," Seth acknowledged.

The wraith held up a small pouch. *A gift from the Singing Sisters. Place this silt in a pool of water and you can communicate with them.*

"Can't wait to reconnect," Seth said, accepting the pouch.

*The Sisters are wise,* Prize replied. *Until you fulfill their task, your fate is in their hands.*

"Assembling the pieces of the Ethergem is an impossible job. I'm not sure I want them prescribing how I do it."

*We must flee before other harpies become aware of us,* Prize urged.

Flexing his astrid wings, Seth knew that more than harpies awaited him in the night sky. The dragons would not want him to escape. "I can't leave without the Unforgiving Blade."

*But you have Vasilis,* Prize expressed.

"The Unforgiving Blade is too powerful," Seth said. "Celebrant already has every advantage. I can't hand him this one as well. I won't leave the Unforgiving Blade behind. I have to find it."

*I can sense the blade,* Prize told him. *The weapon shares a deep connection to the Void.*

"Can you take me to it?" Seth asked.

*I would be a slow guide,* Prize replied. *The blade is above us.*

"In a higher cell?"

*Inside Solitude Keep.*

"Where is that?"

*Atop this pinnacle.*

"Is it the main castle of Soaring Cliffs?"

*I know it is where the caretaker resided.*

"Can you climb to it?"

*Eventually.*

Seth knew he had no time to spare. "Can I carry you?"

*You must avoid direct contact with me or I will drain your life force.*

"Can't you control yourself? Suppress the draining for a time?"

*Feeding on life is my nature, as inevitable as your heartbeat is for you. I exercise control every moment I do not prey on you.*

"You want to eat me right now?"

*I crave your warmth and vitality.*

"I need to find safer friends," Seth muttered. "Can you dangle from something? How heavy are you?"

*I am lighter than I appear,* Prize communicated. *I saw a possible solution.*

The wraith moved away, and Seth gripped the bars of

the gate, closing his eyes. He could sense the simple locking mechanism, and a minor effort of will clicked it open. Seth took a step back from the archway, crouching and using his shade-walking ability to cloak himself.

"Calvin, are you ready?" Seth whispered. "I'll need your eyes and ears. We don't want a dragon sneaking up on us."

"As a nipsie, I'm always paying attention," Calvin said, poking his head out of Seth's pocket. "At this size, almost anything can be a predator. I'm here for you. Not all of your friends are wraiths, you know."

The Tiny Hero had stood by Seth through many adventures, before and after he had lost his memories. Smaller than one of Seth's fingers, Calvin was nevertheless reliable in dangerous situations.

"Wraiths are the friends I deserve," Seth muttered. "I've worked with darkness too much, for too long."

"You lost your memories," Calvin said. "And you had dark guides deliberately deceiving you. Even so, you ended up resisting darkness rather than embracing it."

"My powers are dark," Seth whispered. "I can wield weapons that good people can't even touch. Look at Vasilis."

"It is dark red," Calvin conceded. "But it's fiery, and flames are full of light. You'll overcome the shadows."

"I'm a shadow charmer," Seth said, "not a shadow conqueror."

"Don't sell yourself short," Calvin said. "That remains to be seen."

From the darkness beyond the archway came the heavy downbeats of enormous wings. Seth put a finger to his lips and, staying low, withdrew from the gate. The ponderous beats had space between them, like the strokes of oars. Seth kept still, braced for disaster, until the whooshing rhythm gradually receded, the creature flying higher and farther away.

"Dragon?" Calvin asked in his quietest whisper.

"Something big," Seth replied with minimal volume. "We won't be alone out there."

"The moon is fairly bright tonight," Calvin whispered. "Might be smart to study the lay of the land. We want to get a sense for what we're up against."

Seth slithered to the gate on his stomach, then watched in silence from a prone position. He could not see much in the night sky, but he occasionally heard the flap of wings coming from unpredictable directions. Sometimes he heard clusters of tinier fluttering, and little squeaks that might have come from bats or mice. Down on the distant ground, he saw a dark, shaggy shape cross a light expanse of rocks before vanishing into a stand of trees.

"Lots of traffic out there," Seth finally whispered.

"We'll want to gain altitude fast," Calvin said. "Are you sure we need to retrieve the Unforgiving Blade?"

"If we don't, the dragons will find a way to use it," Seth said. "It's very powerful. It was hidden for a reason."

Prize returned, bringing an icier chill to the air. The wraith dragged a metal chain. *This will serve.*

Seth offered a grim smile. "Dodging harpies in the night with a wraith dangling below me as we fly to a castle full of dragons. What could go wrong?"

# CHAPTER THREE

# Devastation

Flying barely higher than the treetops, Kendra saw three major columns of smoke rising from the city of Humburgh, along with numerous lesser fumes. The closer she approached, clutched in Raxtus's claws, the more clearly she recognized scorched walls, fallen towers, and crushed buildings.

Raxtus flew with his form disguised, rendering him nearly invisible. Even being held in the dragon's front claws, Kendra could see him only as a shimmer in the air above her. Merek soared nearby, golden astrid wings spread wide, occasionally flapping.

Kendra's feet skimmed along just above the ground as they approached the city, weeds whipping her shins, before landing just outside the battered wall, near a collapsed section where blackened blocks of masonry fanned outward.

Raxtus folded his wings and hunkered down, blending with the singed rubble.

"What happened here?" Kendra exclaimed. "I thought Humburgh was supposed to be protected."

"Humbuggle's magical defenses must have failed," Merek said.

"Does that mean Seth got the Wizenstone?" Kendra asked.

"Hard to be sure," Merek said. "But it certainly implies Humbuggle's power has been shaken."

"Do you think we'll find him here?" Kendra asked.

"Seth?" Merek checked. "It's a possibility, if cutting the harp strings summoned him to Humbuggle."

"I'm worried about Knox and Tess," Kendra said.

"We passed Terastios on our way here," Merek said. "We all witnessed the same scene. The fortress was leveled."

"They would not have been primary targets," Serena, the nipsie, said from Merek's pocket. "Hopefully they escaped."

"I didn't notice any sign of them around the ruins," Raxtus said. "Hopefully no other dragons did either."

"All will eventually come to light," Merek said. "Let's enter Humburgh and learn what we can. Much now depends upon who possesses the Wizenstone, and on what happened to Seth."

Kendra faced Raxtus. "Where will you be?"

"I'll stay here, unless I'm discovered," Raxtus replied. "The survivors in Humburgh don't want to see a dragon right now, not even a little glittery one. If my cover gets blown, I won't stray far, probably to the west. Go find your brother."

"I have an idea where we can start," Merek said. "Follow me."

Kendra scrambled after Merek over the remnants of the toppled wall. He could have continued to fly, but instead he kept his wings folded behind his back. The depth of the debris increased the closer they got to the wall. Kendra advanced using her hands nearly as much as her feet to scramble over the uneven mounds.

"Humburgh is a big town," Kendra observed.

"You wouldn't know at a glance, but some of the size is hidden," Merek said. "Accessed through the town square, a vast colosseum stands on an island within a pocket dimension. I trained gladiators there for decades."

"I wonder if it survived," Kendra said. "The town got hit hard."

"Not as thoroughly as Terastios," Merek replied.

Kendra felt impressed by the diverse and elaborate architecture within Humburgh, what remained made more visible by sightlines created by fallen buildings. Many structures were three or four stories tall, topped by gables, spires, domes, cupolas, and chimneys. The streets of Humburgh were mostly deserted. Those who had ventured from behind their doors moved furtively and cast uneasy glances toward the sky. Kendra noticed a few centaurs, a couple of ogres, some dwarfs, and several humans.

"How did you meet Seth?" Kendra asked.

"He found me," Merek said. "Restored my memory,

actually. He somehow befriended my memories while looking for his. They existed as a separate entity, thanks to some power of Humbuggle's. After I awoke to my true character, I abandoned my role in the Games and joined Seth in his quest to win the Wizenstone."

"I'm glad Seth wasn't alone," Kendra said.

"I hope we can find him," Merek said, leaning to look through a shattered wall into a newly exposed basement. "*Something* happened here."

"Everyone is hiding for a reason," Serena said. "The protection the Wizenstone provided must be gone. Which would mean Humbuggle no longer has the Wizenstone. This sort of thing has never happened on his watch."

They traversed a narrow alley, then came out into a broad street with a crater in the middle, as if a bomb had recently detonated there. Merek increased his pace to catch up to a dwarf with a reddish-brown beard.

"Good sir," Merek said. "A moment of your time."

"Got my own troubles," the dwarf grumbled, altering course to distance himself from Merek.

"Isn't Humburgh protected?" Merek asked. "What happened here?"

"You must be a heavy sleeper," the dwarf muttered, bowing his head and moving away more purposefully.

Merek jogged over to a centaur who was searching through a pile of partly burned boards. "Noble friend," Merek greeted. "Could you tell me what has occurred here?"

"What are you supposed to be?" the centaur asked. "A ramshackle angel? Where were you during the attack?"

Merek turned away from the centaur and continued along the street. Kendra ran several paces to catch up.

"I could not help overhearing," said an old woman with a long beak of a nose, her head wrapped in a shawl. Kendra noticed that her skin had a greenish tint, and there were boils on her hands. "Could you really have missed the festivities?"

"We just got back to town," Merek said. "How was Humburgh attacked?"

She gave a dry cackle. "A magical disaster, followed by a physical one. The magic sustaining Humburgh is undone. And dragons attacked soon after. Big Side got the worst of it. Then the dragons left. Where they went, or when they'll be back, who can say?"

"The sleeping giants awoke and turned the tide of the attack," Merek informed her. "I expect the dragons won't return anytime soon."

The old woman gave an exasperated sigh. "You feed me lies in exchange for true tidings?"

"We saw the giants wake," Merek said. "Believe it or not."

Merek walked briskly away, and Kendra stayed with him. They passed down more streets, including one where an inn had been pulverized. Several goblins hunted for prizes among the corpses.

Merek attempted no further conversations with anyone they passed. He strode purposefully until they reached a row of townhomes with the roofs torn off. A few moments after Merek knocked on a door, a satyr answered. He wore a long red vest with gold buttons and had a pencil perched on one ear. Brass binoculars dangled by a strap around his neck.

"Hello, Virgil," Merek said.

"Merek!" the satyr said brightly. "You're alive! Who is your new lady friend?"

"Kendra Sorenson," Merek said.

"Seth's sister?" Virgil asked. "I see zero resemblance. You two look unharmed. How is Seth?"

"That's what we want to know," Kendra said.

"Calvin was with him," Serena said.

"Hi, Serena," Virgil said.

"I should have stayed with him," Serena lamented. "He doesn't have as much experience as I do at surviving extreme situations."

"Calvin does really well," Kendra said. "You'd be proud of him."

"Have you heard anything?" Merek asked Virgil.

"Not directly about Seth," the satyr replied. "Were you here for the attack?"

"We arrived only minutes ago," Merek said.

Virgil raised the binoculars to his eyes and swept the sky. Then he stepped back into his home. "Come inside, just in case, before we get a second wave."

Merek and Kendra entered his cluttered living room. An overturned bookshelf had crushed a small table and left a sprawling mess of volumes on the floor. Kendra noticed a painting in progress on an easel and several canvases stacked against the walls.

"I doubt you'll see a second wave anytime soon," Merek

said. "We watched from Beacon Hill as the titan Garocles awoke, along with the sleeping giants, and drove the dragons away."

"Are you serious?" Virgil asked.

"The titan was enormous," Kendra said.

"We're living in a time of wonders," Virgil said. "And you have wings."

"It's been eventful," Merek said, flexing his wings. "We obtained the Harp of Ages, and Seth cut the strings with the Unforgiving Blade."

"You succeeded," Virgil said, amazed.

"Seth disappeared after cutting the final string," Merek said. "Presumably he was taken to Humbuggle, along with Calvin."

"That fits," Virgil said. "Humbuggle must have lost possession of the Wizenstone. The Games are over, Merek. The pocket dimension collapsed. The square was flooded with refugee gladiators. The magical secrets of Humburgh came undone all at once. Even before the dragons arrived, multiple buildings toppled, and several structures changed in appearance, some becoming visible for the first time."

"That must have been when the defenses went down," Serena said.

"The dragons arrived like a typhoon," Virgil said. "There was no place to hide. Entire city blocks were demolished in seconds. One of the dragons collided with our townhomes and swept away the attic. My bedroom now has a panoramic view of the stars. Makes a satyr glad he is renting."

"Parts of the city still burn," Merek said.

Virgil sighed weightily. "I hope somebody cares enough to put them out. I'm afraid Humburgh has become obsolete."

"What do you mean?" Merek asked.

"What happens to a mining town when the ore runs out?" Virgil asked. "The draw to Humburgh has always been the Games. Now the Games are over, along with the magic that made this town unique and secure."

"You predict an exodus," Merek said.

Virgil shrugged, turning to Kendra. "You were with Seth at Stormguard Castle. You met Humbuggle. You sent the Wizenstone away?"

"Yes," Kendra said.

"Then you realize, winning at Stormguard Castle and sending the stone away had no effect on Humburgh. The Games here continued uninterrupted, and the town remained undisturbed. Now the pocket dimensions have been turned inside out and the magic upholding the town has vanished. Whatever happened, I suspect Humbuggle finally lost the stone."

"Could Seth have it?" Merek asked.

"I can only guess," Virgil said. "If he won the Game, that seems the most likely conclusion. If he is wielding the Wizenstone, he has access to enormous power and is also in mortal danger. That is too much power for any one person. If he found a way to own the stone without wielding it, he might stand a chance. But many will seek to take it from him, including the dragons."

"We have to find him," Kendra said. "Could he be nearby?"

Virgil shrugged. "Humburgh is Humbuggle's seat of power. The showdown likely happened in town. The dragons may have also been after the Wizenstone. All I can report with confidence is that Humbuggle lost it. When did you last see Seth?"

"When he cut the last harp string," Kendra said, "the sleeping giants awoke and Seth vanished."

Virgil rubbed the crown of his head, eyes roving the room, then straying to the window. "Be careful what you wish for."

"What do you mean?" Kendra asked.

Virgil picked up a loose sheaf of papers crisscrossed with notes and drawings, then let them scatter to the floor. "I devoted my life to the study of the Games, with the far-fetched hope of helping a champion win them one day. That goal is now accomplished. I played a role in it. And on the same day the Games are finally won, I find the town I know and love ravaged, the life I have lived irretrievably lost, and myself unemployed. I'm a scholar of a subject that has become irrelevant. Beware of summiting a mountain without a plan for where to travel next."

"So much has changed so quickly," Kendra said. "Some of what you built your life around is gone. But don't let a success become a failure. You helped Seth win the Games, and you became an expert about Humbuggle and the Wizenstone. There is still much you can do."

Virgil gave a weak smile. "I'm not a champion, Kendra.

I was only ever a student of bravery. I never stepped into the arena. I was content to watch others square off against monsters in the ring."

"There are many ways to fight," Merek said. "Seth might never have found me without your assistance. I prepared many combatants in the Games. On the arena floor, my training spilled much more blood than any single weapon. The arm that swings the sword is only part of it. Knowing where and how to swing can be everything. You are more than you realize."

Virgil rubbed a forefinger against the tip of one horn. "I guess going to the meeting with Isadore involved risk. And I do know more about Humbuggle and the Wizenstone than most."

"Kendra is right," Merek said. "You'd be a huge advantage to us in the struggle against the dragons. What has happened to Humburgh is tragic, but it is only a hint of things to come if the dragons remain unchecked. This war must be won, or our ability to live anywhere in this world may be lost."

"I suppose I'm in shock," Virgil murmured.

"Right now, we need to learn what happened to Seth and the Wizenstone," Merek said.

"And Calvin," Serena added.

Virgil gave a small nod. "I might be able to help."

"And I need to figure out what happened to my cousins," Kendra said. "Knox and Tess. Do you know them?"

"They are friends with a couple of rowdy satyrs," Virgil said.

"Yes," Kendra said.

"Last I understood, they had returned to Terastios," Virgil said.

"Terastios has been destroyed," Merek said.

Virgil winced. "Let's hope they got out in time. Satyrs can be quite adept at avoiding battle, and the attention of the dragons would have been on the giants. As to your question about Seth, one place to investigate comes to mind. Let's go find out if Humbuggle's manor still stands."

# CHAPTER FOUR

# Solitude

The wraith dangling from the chain beneath Seth significantly reduced his mobility, especially as he attempted to gain altitude. Gone were the effortless turns and swoops of unencumbered flight he had enjoyed before coming to Soaring Cliffs. His metallic wings labored steadily to climb as he struggled to compensate for the weight of the wraith pendulating beneath him. Seth wondered if this was how a ship might flounder at sea with the anchor lowered.

Seth used his concentration to cloak himself as he flew. If shade walking was a thing, why not shade flying? He needed to avoid the notice of the other creatures in flight around him. Most forms he glimpsed seemed relatively small, but occasionally, some distance away, large patches of stars were blotted out by amorphous shapes.

Solitude Keep rose from the top of the towering stone pinnacle that held the dungeons. The closely grouped collection of walls, towers, terraces, and balconies forming the castle stretched vertically to significantly extend the pinnacle's summit. Portions of the forbidding stone complex overhung the edge, the projecting structures cantilevered or otherwise supported by heavy buttresses, struts, and trusses angling up from the cliff face.

Seth made for the underside of the largest overhang, teeth gritted, muscles straining, wings tenaciously beating the cool night air. The wraith seemed to be increasing in weight.

"You're getting wobbly," Calvin said quietly.

"Tired," Seth whispered. "It's too heavy."

"Just make it to those trusses," Calvin said. "You can rest there."

"Trying," Seth replied.

The links of the chain digging into his palms, Seth's wings labored to lift him into what looked like the underside of a dock reinforced with intersecting timbers. He deposited Prize on a stout beam and then flew to a slightly higher perch, where he slumped on his hands and knees to rest, wings folded about him like a cloak. Panting, Seth flexed his hands where the pressure of the chain had left painful grooves.

He heard rustling in the dimness around him. Despite the bright moon, scant light reached the underside of the overhang, but Seth could perceive a multitude of shapes shifting in the gloom.

"We're not alone," Calvin whispered.

*Gargoyles*, Prize transmitted.

Though Seth had seen pictures of gargoyles on old cathedrals, he knew little about them as living creatures. He slid Vasilis slightly from its scabbard, throwing deep red highlights over the scene. It looked like he was roosting in the midst of a colony of giant misshapen bats. His muscles tensed, and it took an effort to resist crying out. Gargoyles huddled on much of the available space atop the surrounding supports, and many others dangled upside down. The faces were foul and bestial, often with teeth projecting beyond their lips and short, crooked horns sprouting from their foreheads. Extremely lean bodies left their wiry musculature grotesquely pronounced, and most of their forms were contorted in one way or another.

The nearest gargoyle to Seth, only a few feet away on the same timber, turned to face him. The brute was hairier than most, with an exaggerated underbite and a strangely prominent rib cage. He smelled like a monkey house.

"Why . . . you . . . here?" the gargoyle asked in a crude, guttural voice.

"Just resting," Seth said, aware that he was not speaking English. "I'm a friend."

The gargoyle snorted and shook his batlike wings. "Our friend . . . dead."

"What friend?"

"Sang Rou."

The other gargoyles stirred at the name, and baleful eyes turned toward Seth. He tried not to dwell on their jutting fangs or their sharp claws. The words *Sang Rou* were echoed by several other voices.

Seth did not know the name. "What happened?"

The gargoyle cowered a bit. "Wyrms come . . . Sang Rou . . . no come. Sang Rou gone."

"Sang Rou . . . Sang Rou," others murmured.

"Was Sang Rou the caretaker?" Seth asked.

"Sang Rou . . . speak . . . us," the gargoyle expressed haltingly. "Sang Rou . . . know . . . words."

"Sang Rou . . . Sang Rou . . . Sang Rou," others jabbered. Some flew from one roost to another, leathery wings flapping.

Seth considered himself lucky that Vasilis remained only partway drawn. He worried the wrong move might place him at the center of a swarm of attackers. The majority were larger than him. "I'm Seth. I'm on your side. I'm going to find out what the wyrms are doing."

The gargoyle growled, a primal utterance that made Seth tighten his hold of Vasilis. "Wyrms . . . hunt . . . us. No more . . . walls. Only . . . hide."

"Did you used to perch on the castle walls?" Seth asked.

The question sent a ripple of motion through the crowded colony, accompanied by guttural chattering and an occasional growl. Wood creaked as the gargoyles shifted.

The nearest gargoyle swiped at his nostrils with a hairy wrist. "We . . . high . . . before. See so much. Now under."

"I'm going to spy on the wyrms," Seth said.

The gargoyle tucked his head, covering his eyes with

one hand while chewing on the other. "Safer . . . hide. Better . . . hide."

"Not for me," Seth said. "Good luck."

Snapping Vasilis back into the scabbard, Seth flew off the timber where he had been crouching. Pulling the chain taut, he lifted Prize off the beam where the wraith had waited. Seth lost some altitude as he flew out from under the patio, then resumed his arduous ascent.

When Seth rose above the overhang, he saw that it held stables. Above him, a sinuous body stirred, winding among the battlements atop a soaring wall. The long Chinese dragon had a head like a crocodile. The creature was not yet gazing his way, but Seth knew those sharp eyes would spot him soon.

The stable on the projecting platform looked dark and quiet, so he glided toward it and landed with Prize beside the door. It was slightly ajar. Seth eased it open and stepped inside.

"What else is in here?" he whispered.

*We are alone*, Prize responded directly to his mind.

Once the wraith had entered, Seth quietly closed the door. He could make out a dry dung heap in the nearest stall. "What was kept here?"

*Winged mounts*, Prize replied. *Griffins, mostly. Some hippogriffs and others.*

"How can you tell?" Seth asked.

*Droppings, smell, residual energy*, Prize explained. *They were here until a few weeks ago.*

"They probably cleared out when the sanctuary fell,"

Seth said. He crept over to a window and gazed up at the keep. "Can you sense the Unforgiving Blade?"

*The blade resides in a high room within the castle*, Prize confirmed.

"Up one of the towers?" Seth asked.

*Not that high*, Prize clarified. *The object you desire awaits within the top level of the central building.*

"Will we have to fly over the walls?" Seth asked.

*Unless you wish to pass through the main gate.*

"A dragon is watching."

*Courage will be required.*

"Is there something here we can use to disguise ourselves?" Seth asked, looking around the dim stable. "Or will shade walking be enough?"

From somewhere below rose a chorus of jarring shrieks. The discordant screeches set Seth's teeth on edge.

*The harpies are raising the alarm*, Prize warned. *They have discovered your escape and are swarming this way.*

Seth raced out the stable door and leaped into the air. The chain pulled taut and he climbed with all his might, flying upward toward the castle wall, heedless of the dragon above. The overlapping shrieks grew louder as the harpies came nearer. Peering up, Seth noticed the crocodile dragon staring into the night in the direction of the screeching. Seth concentrated on cloaking himself with his shade-walking power while his wings toiled.

As Seth crested the wall, the head of the crocodile dragon jerked in his direction. Scales glimmered in the moonlight as a shiver traveled the length of the tubular body, like a wave gliding along a jump rope. Having over-topped the wall, Seth flapped hard toward the castle, losing some altitude to gain speed.

"Here it comes," Calvin warned from his pocket.

The dragon sprang from the battlements and rocketed toward them, elongated jaws widening. Seth felt a potent surge of dragon fear and steeled himself against the paralysis it could instill. Recognizing that he had no hope of outrunning the dragon, Seth dropped the chain and drew Vasilis. Prize plunged out of view into the courtyard below.

The sword flared bright in his hand, instantly dispelling any shred of dragon fear. Instead, Seth felt emboldened, and he soared to meet the dragon, unencumbered by the wraith, the sword pulling him along. He became lost in an intense rush, the crimson blade blazing ever brighter as the dragon neared.

The crocodilian jaws gaped eagerly, showing long rows of triangular teeth. At the last moment, Seth dipped and swung Vasilis, the blade cleaving through the dragon's lower jaw, unhindered by scales and bone, leaving the dragon with a colossal overbite.

The dragon tried to veer away, serpentine body curling, but could not get clear before Vasilis slashed along the flank, hot ichor fountaining from a glowing red wound. The dragon fled, diving, but Seth gave chase. He wanted to end the fight while his enemy was flustered.

The wounded dragon flew erratically, zigzagging and corkscrewing, and Seth attempted to follow, swerving and darting, until he anticipated a turn, which brought him to a point in space just behind the head of the dragon. His blade hacked through the top of the dragon's neck almost to the hilt, and the magnificent beast fell in a limp tumble, like a thrown snake.

As Seth hovered in the sudden stillness, a thrill of ecstasy overtook him. He had survived the dragon! Not only that, he had slain it in midair! Harpy shrieks continued to shrill from a distance. As sizzling blood steamed off his sword, Seth realized how brightly the blade was blazing, and sheathed Vasilis.

Engaging his senses, Seth detected Prize in a courtyard down below. He landed beside the wraith on a shadowy lawn edged by twisty trees. "Are you all right?" Seth whispered.

*A fall is not my preferred means of travel,* Prize conveyed, still clutching the chain. *But it caused little harm.*

"The Unforgiving Blade is in the castle above us?" Seth asked.

*How can you sense me and not perceive the blade?* Prize asked.

Pausing, Seth engaged his shadow senses. He drew Vasilis to increase his connection to his power. Seth swiftly recognized wraiths and other undead presences in the dungeons below, but he sensed nothing he could recognize as the dark sword.

"How does it feel?" Seth asked.

*The castle is protected by spells,* Prize expressed. *But nothing can fully hide the pull of the Void present within the Unforgiving Blade.*

"Does the blade feel like a wraith?"

*A wraith is sentient,* Prize explained. *The blade has no mind to engage with. Seek out the pure essence of the Void.*

Seth remembered when he had first encountered the Unforgiving Blade, how he had felt drawn to it and was nearly pulled into the darkness that encased it. He might have drowned in that endless oblivion without help from Merek. Suddenly Seth became aware of a similar darkness in the castle, drawing his attention like a magnet. How had he missed it? Now that he knew what to look for, he suspected he could identify that steady concentration of darkness anywhere.

"I feel it," Seth said.

*Then you no longer need me,* Prize resolved. *Go. I will find my way back to the Sisters.*

Seth could hear the harpies screeching from beyond the castle walls. Their wails emanated from all directions, as if they were circling Solitude Keep. Seth assumed they could not enter the castle grounds, because not a single one had come over the wall. "The harpies are swarming. Be careful."

*I will endure,* Prize said, dropping the chain. *Go.*

Seth knew it would not be long before more dragons came to intercept him. Once word spread that he had escaped the dungeon, the manhunt would escalate, and efforts to protect the Unforgiving Blade would increase. He had to hurry.

"'Bye," Seth said, keeping Vasilis unsheathed as he jumped, wings propelling a steep climb. It was so much easier to fly without a dangling wraith! Holding the magic sword made his wings feel supercharged.

Seth alighted on one of the castle's higher balconies and sheathed his sword to douse the light. The squalling harpies filled the night with grating cries. With the sword sheathed, connecting to his power no longer felt effortless, but, crouching and exerting his will, Seth started shade walking. Gently testing the handle to the door leading in from the balcony, he found it unlocked and crept into a dim bedroom. With the door closed, he could only faintly hear the clamor of the harpies.

Missing the confidence Vasilis gave him, Seth fingered the hilt of the sword. Enough moonlight spilled into the room to reveal that the bed was empty. Seth hurried to the far side of the room and out into a long hall.

The castle was oddly still and dark. Could it be deserted? The previous occupants had either fled or perished. How many dragons would have chosen to stay here after overthrowing the caretaker? They would have to assume human shape. Would they have invited others to dwell here? Goblins or minotaurs or somebody? It was hard for Seth to imagine many dragons remaining in a castle built to human scale.

The hall was too dark to navigate swiftly, so Seth drew Vasilis. With the tips of his wings brushing the walls, Seth soared down the length of the hall, landing at the foot of a narrow, winding stairway. The stairway was too cramped for flight, but Seth could feel the Unforgiving Blade somewhere above him, so he charged up the corkscrewing steps two at a time.

A locked door at the top halted his progress momentarily, but, accessing his power, Seth swiftly disengaged the lock. His swordlight revealed a corridor narrower than the one below. Seth could feel that he was on the same level as the Unforgiving Blade. It was down this corridor and off to the right. Why had he met no guards yet?

If Celebrant was off fighting a war, he may have left only a skeleton crew at Soaring Cliffs.

Seth ran down the corridor. He stopped in front of an iron door. Without trying the handle, he could sense that it was locked, both mechanically and magically.

"Is it in there?" Calvin asked quietly.

Seth nodded. Tightening his grip on Vasilis, Seth placed a palm flat against the door, bowed his head, and summoned his power. The mechanisms protecting the door resisted. Leaning against the iron surface, breath coming in ragged gasps, Seth heaved with all his will. Vasilis flared brighter, and all at once the locking mechanisms released. After taking a moment to wipe perspiration from his brow and steady himself, Seth opened the door.

The tenebrous room beyond had no windows and no other door. By the crimson swordlight, Seth saw the Unforgiving Blade dangling from a rope at the center of the room, tip pointing down. The sleek blade reflected no light, seeming instead like an absence. Seth supposed that since the blade could not be sheathed, hanging it from the ceiling by the hilt was a sensible way to store it.

"You found it," Calvin said as Seth entered the room. "Careful not to cut yourself."

"The wound would never heal," Seth said. "I remember."

"Is that your satchel?" Calvin asked.

Seth tore his attention from the Unforgiving Blade to notice makeshift cubbies against one wall holding various belongings, including cloaks, coats, hats, weapons, and satchels. A leather messenger bag leaned against the side of one cubby. Seth hurried over to the bag, picked it up, and opened it. "It's mine. And my stuff is here."

"Including the pieces of the Wizenstone?" Calvin asked.

"Including those," Seth said, fingering the two halves.

"Good!" Calvin explained. "Now we just need the stone from the Dragon King's crown, the stone from the Giant Queen's crown, the stone from the Demon King's crown, and the Ethershard, and you will have all the pieces of the Ethergem."

Seth sighed. "More likely I'll die trying. But at least Celebrant won't have an extra weapon in his arsenal." He crossed to the Unforgiving Blade and cut the line connected to the hilt. The blade dropped, plunging into the stone floor up to the hilt.

"Now, that is a sharp knife," Calvin said.

Seth crouched and picked up the Unforgiving Blade. Vasilis blazed in his other hand, but the dark blade reflected nothing. Seth stared at the perfect blackness, absorbed by the fathomless depths. It was as though reality had parted to reveal the nothingness beneath.

"Seth," Calvin said. "Snap out of it."

Seth wrenched his gaze away from the dark blade. As he did, he found that Vasilis had dimmed to a darker red than ever. Blinking to clear his vision, Seth swished both blades through the air. "We should go."

He stepped out into the corridor and was confronted by two men to his left, and a man and a woman to his right. Both couples stood several paces away. They carried weapons and looked determined to bar his way.

"You could have fled," one of the men to the left said—the tallest, with broad shoulders and long, blond hair. He had a rather long face with chiseled features. "Instead you came for the blade. And you found it swiftly."

"I'll leave just as fast if you get out of the way," Seth said.

The blond man shook his head. "My father would not approve. Dead or alive, you will make a fine trophy."

# CHAPTER FIVE

# Mayor

The outer fence of Humbuggle's manor had been violently trampled, wrought iron twisted like spaghetti. Huge sections of hedgerows were flattened or uprooted. The grand fountain had been smashed—chunks of marble and partially recognizable fragments of statuary lay heaped half drowned in the basin. A grove of smoldering trees near the house were carbonized down to fuming poles. One of the great pillars sheltering the porch looked like a broken tusk. A gray film of soot muted the entire estate.

"It must have been lovely," Kendra said as they crunched along what remained of the pebbly path leading to the front steps.

"Up until today it was immaculate," Virgil said. "Yet the manor still stands. Much of Humburgh cannot make that claim."

"I saw a face in an upper window," Merek said. "Ducked away as soon as I saw it."

"Since the manor survived, you can bet the staff is inside," Serena said. "Humbuggle's servants were extremely dedicated."

"How long were you there?" Kendra asked.

"A couple of years," Serena said. "Not everyone knew me. Nipsies understand the value in hiding from big folk. But several members of the staff associated me with Isadore, who had a questionable reputation. If you don't mind, I want to lie low. I'd rather not be seen in your company."

When Kendra reached the front steps, the front door opened. An older woman glowered out at them, wearing a matronly outfit, left arm in a sling, her hair singed on one side. "No visitors this week," she announced in an authoritative voice. "Be on your way."

"Is Humbuggle here?" Kendra asked.

The matron scowled. "The lord of this manor goes where he pleases and answers to none, least of all you."

"Has he noticed that his city lies in shambles?" Merek asked.

The woman frowned into the distance, eyes roving. "What's that to him? He invited nobody here and promised them nothing. They came of their own accord and they reap what they sow, same as the rest of us." The woman began to shut the door.

"Humbuggle knows me," Kendra insisted.

The matron paused with the door mostly closed. "He knows everyone in this town."

"He'll want to talk to me," Kendra pressed.

"Why might that be?"

"My brother won the Wizenstone from him," Kendra said.

The woman huffed and shook her head. "I've heard some whoppers in my day, but that takes the cake. Be on your way now."

"Ask Humbuggle, or else risk his displeasure," Merek said. "Her brother is Seth Sorenson. This is Kendra Sorenson."

"You're telling me the Games are over?" the matron asked acerbically.

"Look around," Virgil said. "The defenses are down. The pocket dimensions have collapsed. The arena is gone."

"Says you," the woman spat.

"Go see for yourself," Virgil said. "Or send someone. Have none of you ventured out since the attack?"

"The Games have ended," Kendra said.

The matron narrowed her eyes and shook her head. "You don't know Humbuggle. Schemes within schemes within schemes, he has. This is all part of the smokescreen. Another trick. Another test."

"The kind of trick where he lets dragons destroy the city?" Kendra exclaimed.

A tall man in a somber suit appeared behind the woman and whispered something in her ear. Her expression changed, eyes widening. She pulled the door open and stepped aside.

"It appears your audience is desired after all," the woman said. "You may pass. Baynard will escort you."

The interior of the manor showed none of the hardship experienced without. The opulent furniture and décor were in a state of order and cleanliness possible only through the steadfast attention of a dedicated staff. Floors gleamed, brass shone, flowers bloomed, glass was nearly invisible. All was tidy and polished. Only the soot on the exterior of the windowpanes betrayed the devastation the town had faced.

The solemn butler led them without making eye contact or conversation. One of his jacket sleeves was torn, but otherwise he looked impeccable, down to the gloss of his shoes.

Baynard opened a door to a sumptuous study. Heavy curtains were drawn over the windows, and shelves of dark wood supported books and curiosities from floor to ceiling on two walls. In one corner, a bulky suit of armor posed as if clutching a halberd. A dormant fireplace sat with logs ready. Behind a heavy desk of rich, reddish wood sat a dwarf with a forked beard. He was wearing spectacles as he studied an open tome.

"Thank you, Baynard," Humbuggle said. "That will be all."

The butler departed, shutting the door.

Humbuggle closed his book and removed his spectacles. "Welcome to my humble home. A pleasure to see you again, Merek. And, of course, Kendra. Along with my old friend Virgil. And Serena, tucked away."

"We have questions," Merek said.

"Everyone always does," Humbuggle said. "Virgil, you look as if you've seen a ghost."

"It's you," Virgil mouthed, hardly making a sound.

"In the flesh," Humbuggle agreed. He slid off his chair and came around the desk.

"How well do you know me?" Virgil asked.

"We've met many times, though I was in disguise. You paid sharp attention all along. Would you care to guess who I was?"

Virgil cleared his throat. "I'm not sure. Maybe the old flower woman on the corner leading into the plaza?"

"I wasn't Midge," Humbuggle said. "She was genuine. But as a disguise she would have served my purposes well— she saw nearly everyone come and go, and she took an interest in many while also merging with the background. An astute observation, as expected."

"When did we meet?" Virgil asked.

"You knew me most often as Dante the briar troll," Humbuggle said, altering his voice to match.

"No," Virgil said. "That was you? Every time?"

The dwarf spread his hands in a kind of shrug. "One of my many personas. You engaged with me more than most. Thank you for guiding Seth in the proper direction."

"Did Seth beat you?" Kendra asked. "Did he get the Wizenstone?"

"You set an important example for him at Stormguard Castle, Kendra," Humbuggle said. "It was useful for him to see that obtaining the stone was not necessarily the best way to win."

"Where is Seth now?" Merek asked.

"I see you've sprouted wings since we last met," Humbuggle said. "You might be the finest trainer we ever had."

"I was your prisoner," Merek said. "You stole my memories and enslaved me."

"I most certainly did not," Humbuggle said. "Words have meanings—choose yours with care. You forfeited those memories in your quest to take my stone. I helped restore them to you. As Dante, I sent Seth to retrieve what you lost."

"You caused me great harm, and in the end helped a little," Merek said. "I suppose I knew you in the Games?"

"Most often as Driggs," Humbuggle said.

"Ah," Merek said. "You oriented me when I began."

"I have also been many gladiators," Humbuggle said. "I love a good death scene."

"You fought in your own Games?" Kendra asked.

"I seemed to fight, yes," Humbuggle said. "And I appeared to die many times. Anything to entertain."

"Your city lies in ruins," Merek said.

"A house of cards is bound to topple," Humbuggle said. "It was a city built with borrowed power, its bricks mortared with ambition and greed."

"Where is the Wizenstone now?" Virgil asked.

Humbuggle lowered his voice. "Can you three keep a secret?"

All three responded in the affirmative.

"So can I," Humbuggle whispered. He pantomimed locking his lips and tossing the key aside.

"Really?" Kendra scolded. "You let us in here and now you're not telling us anything? Where is Seth? We saved Titan Valley. You owe us."

Humbuggle cocked his head, his face puzzled. "I thought it was the titan who drove the dragons away."

"After we woke him," Kendra said.

"And how did you wake him?" Humbuggle inquired.

"Seth cut the strings of the Harp of Ages," Kendra said.

Humbuggle assumed an innocent expression. "And who gave him that task?"

Kendra paused. "You did."

"You're welcome for the rescue of Titan Valley," Humbuggle said with a little bow. "It was my pleasure."

"Seth did the work," Kendra said.

"Let's call it a team effort," Humbuggle said. "Semantics get tedious."

"What will you do now?" Virgil asked.

"Me?" Humbuggle asked. "Really?" He went and dragged a little suitcase out from behind his desk, laid it flat, and clipped it open. "As mayor of Humburgh, I will pronounce the township unincorporated." He grabbed some papers from his desk and placed them in the suitcase. "Then I intend to hit the road."

"What about this home?" Kendra asked. "Your staff?"

Humbuggle looked up from packing. "I have good people here. Some are strong in magic. They all have their uses. They kept the dragons at bay during the attack and drove off a rogue giant who sought me. They kept my house intact. But they are all here to win the Games. And the Games are over."

"So you lost the Wizenstone?" Virgil asked.

"Kendra's brother cleaved it with the Unforgiving Blade," Humbuggle said. "He has the remnants."

"The Wizenstone was destroyed?" Merek asked.

"And now, for the first time in a great while, I am free," Humbuggle said. "Every possession is a burden—life will teach you that if you pay attention. I now wield less power, but I feel much lighter." Standing on his toes, the dwarf raised both hands over his head and stretched.

"Where is my brother?" Kendra asked.

"Pushy, pushy," Humbuggle chided. "Give a dwarf the chance to speak. I admitted you for a reason."

"Why?" Kendra asked.

"I was no slouch before I claimed the Wizenstone," Humbuggle said, twisting at the waist and holding the stretch. "I made plenty of mischief without it, helped kingdoms rise and fall. This dragon war concerns me." He twisted the other way.

"Now that they tried to burn down your house?" Kendra asked.

Humbuggle waved a dismissive hand. "My real estate here has become a bad investment. When Seth broke the Wizenstone, this town was doomed—if not by dragons, then by giants. To enjoy my freedom, I need a world where I can live. The dragon war places that in jeopardy."

"Don't tell me you intend to help us?" Merek asked.

Humbuggle took a small jar from his desk and placed it

in the suitcase. "You slayers created this mess. Dragons don't naturally collaborate. There was never meant to be a dragon army! Concertedly hunting them made them band together. And then confining them to sanctuaries allowed a shared unrest to ferment over the centuries. The previous dragon war was nothing compared to the avalanche Celebrant has set in motion. Prognosticators often err in forecasting the end of the world—but this time there is a real chance of it."

"What can we do?" Virgil asked.

"Don't seek to bridle the uncontrollable," Humbuggle said. "The brief season of quiet you produce will not be worth the explosion that follows."

"You think we should let dragons overrun the world?" Kendra asked.

"At this stage, we must do our best to stem the tide," Humbuggle said. "In a fight for survival, you do what it takes to live on. Learn as you go. Your brother is learning plenty."

"Is he?" Kendra asked.

"From the best teacher," Humbuggle said.

"Who?" Kendra asked. "You?"

Humbuggle laughed uproariously. "No, silly girl. The best teacher is pain."

Kendra worried what Humbuggle might be implying. "Is Seth hurt?"

"More than anyone can measure," Humbuggle said. "His memories were restored, which meant he had to confront actions that disgusted him. Some lessons are learned only through suffering."

"Where is he?" Kendra asked.

"I lost track of your brother after Celebrant captured him," Humbuggle said.

"Celebrant has him?" Kendra asked.

"The Dragon King caught up to him shortly after Seth destroyed the Wizenstone," Humbuggle said. "Having just regained his memories, your brother was in no condition to put up a fight. He departed in Celebrant's custody and could be anywhere by now, if in fact he still lives."

Kendra ached inside. "Did Celebrant harm him?"

"Celebrant took him captive," Humbuggle said. "I watched in secret. If the Dragon King meant to kill your brother, he had the opportunity."

"Any clue where they went?" Kendra asked.

"Far from here, I suspect," Humbuggle said.

"What about my cousins?" Kendra asked. "Knox and Tess?"

"They were at Terastios, I believe," Humbuggle said. "By all reports, Terastios was demolished and the Giant Queen perished, which does not bode well for your relatives, or for the satyrs accompanying them."

Kendra staggered and felt Merek steady her. "What should we do?"

"That is for you to decide," Humbuggle said. "I gifted you some information it might have taken you a long time to learn. You came with questions, and I gave freely. I hope it helps against the dragons. We all stand to lose if the dragons reign supreme."

"Why not help us?" Merek asked.

"I just did," Humbuggle said. "Under these conditions,

any demon would do the same. We have no love for dragons. We learned long ago that they cannot be harnessed
without misfortune for whoever holds the reins."

Humbuggle crossed to the door.

"You're leaving?" Kendra asked.

"As should you," Humbuggle suggested. "Without the
Giant Queen, this sanctuary is at the center of a power vacuum. Get clear until after the dust settles. You can take a
moment to deliberate in this room. I'll leave orders for my
staff to let you depart in peace. But I can't promise they will
hold to my orders much longer. Good luck."

Humbuggle opened the door, stepped out, and closed it.

"He just gets to waltz out of here?" Kendra asked.

"I'm not sure what more he could do for us," Merek said.
He turned to the satyr. "I assume he was telling the truth?"

"I think so," Virgil said. "Humbuggle can be deceptive,
but I'm not aware of any outright lies. Doubtless he had his
own reasons for what he chose to share. He always does."

"I agree," Merek said. "He knew nothing definitive
about Knox and Tess. Do we start by seeking them?"

"Terastios is demolished," Kendra said. "Could you fly
around Humburgh? Have a look?"

"Let's see what we can find," Merek said.

"I'll watch as Merek flies," Serena said.

"Virgil and I will search on the ground," Kendra said.

"What about your brother?" Virgil asked.

"We don't know where to start," Kendra said. "For now,
Seth is on his own."

# CHAPTER SIX

# Showdown

L ay down the swords, and I may spare your life," the
blond man said.

"Who is your father?" Seth asked.

"Celebrant, of course," the blond man said. "I am
Tamryn, his eldest. Lay down your swords."

"If I set them down, how will I use them to kill you?"
Seth asked.

Tamryn flashed a dangerous smile. "You clearly don't
understand your predicament."

"I take it all you guys are dragons," Seth said.

"You're surrounded," Tamryn said. "Your escape has
failed. I was offering you a chance to live."

Seth glanced back to make sure nobody was sneaking
up from behind. "Is that the offer you made to Sang Rou?"

Tamryn chuckled. "Sang Rou? The gamekeeper? He

died screaming. Put down your weapons or you will join him."

"You just want me to give up my advantage," Seth said.

Tamryn shrugged. "If you would rather die in combat, I will gladly oblige."

"Get out of my way, and I'll spare you," Seth said.

Tamryn smirked. "You are alone, friendless, in the halls of your enemy. The four of us are more than enough to deal with you. Dozens of harpies await out there, along with a host of other loyal guardians, not to mention many dragons."

"I know there's a dead dragon outside," Seth said.

"You got in a lucky blow against Pershanka."

"With the crocodile head?" Seth checked. "I cut off its jaw, then slaughtered it as it tried to flee."

"Your sword surprised her," Tamryn said.

"I'm full of surprises," Seth said.

"I'm running out of patience," Tamryn said.

"Have you any notion whom you are addressing?" the man beside Tamryn asked. He was stouter than Tamryn, with a crooked nose and fleshy cheeks, and he held a heavy spear. "This is the master of this sanctuary, the firstborn of Celebrant, and heir to his crown."

Seth stared at the tall, blond warrior. He kept Vasilis trained on him and the Unforgiving Blade pointed behind. "Heir? I thought the crown had to be earned through combat."

"Heir apparent," Tamryn said. "Other dragons have

challenged Father, but when the time comes to truly unseat him, most dragons understand it will be my duty."

"I guess most dragons are wrong," Seth said.

"Why would that be?" Tamryn asked.

"Because you're not getting out of my way," Seth replied.

Tamryn gave a small chuckle. "You really are determined to die."

Vasilis tugged Seth forward, power and confidence flowing into him. But Seth resisted. Just because the sword always wanted to fight did not make it the smartest choice. If the four attacked together, who knew if he could fend them off? Seth tried to stall them. "Where is your dad?"

"Finishing a war," Tamryn said.

"He left you behind?" Seth asked.

"I guard our prisoners," Tamryn said. "You were left alive in case you could be used as a bargaining chip. But who needs to bargain in a war we have nearly won?"

"Come try me, Tamryn," Seth said. "You alone."

"You've already been defeated," Tamryn said. "You are our prisoner because you were taken. There is no honor in giving up my advantage."

Seth held out the Unforgiving Blade. "You're right to be afraid. Let me show you how I made Velrog beg for death."

"You exaggerate to the point of absurdity," Tamryn scoffed, drawing his sword.

"This was a day or two ago," Seth said. "He was the third guardian of the dragon temple at Titan Valley."

"Preposterous," Tamryn blurted.

Seth smiled. "Come find out. Just you, if you know so much."

"Hilzog, dispose of him," Tamryn ordered, motioning toward Seth. The bald man beside Tamryn shifted from one foot to the other.

"It's okay, Hilzog," Seth said. "I'll kill you cleanly."

Hilzog charged forward, spear held ready.

"Behind you," Calvin warned.

A quick glance over his shoulder showed the woman dashing toward Seth from behind, brandishing a sword. When in flight, Seth had learned to trust the inherent expertise of his astrid wings. Vasilis had a similar native competence. Seth had felt the weapon pull him along and guide his strokes every time he wielded it, but in this moment of duress, Seth deliberately yielded to the instincts of the sword as never before.

Impelled by Vasilis, Seth raced forward, allowing him to reach Hilzog before the woman caught up from behind. As the spear thrust toward him, Seth twisted to avoid the tip and deftly hacked off the spearhead. Still charging, Hilzog lowered his shoulder, but Seth sprang sideways, and the edge of Vasilis met Hilzog instead, ending his life with a deep slash across the torso.

Seth whipped around to confront the woman, using Vasilis to block her first swing, then chopping her sword down to the hilt with a swipe from the Unforgiving Blade. She seemed astonished to have only a hilt in her grasp, and Seth ran her through with Vasilis before she could recover.

Seth turned to face Tamryn and found him watching,

sword ready. Seth's wings stiffened into a shape that shielded him from behind, and he felt something ping sharply against them. A glance back showed the man holding the crossbow he had just fired. Seth returned his gaze to Tamryn.

"Get out of my way," Seth demanded. "Call off your other clown."

"Let's take this outside," Tamryn called, turning and running down the hall. The other man sprinted in the opposite direction.

"They would rather fight as dragons," Calvin surmised.

Seth nodded, unsure which way to run.

Windows awaited at each end of the hallway. Tamryn crashed through one window, and the guy with the crossbow smashed through the opposing one. The gaping mouth of a dragon promptly appeared outside the window through which Tamryn had jumped, and Seth shoved open the nearest door and lunged into a room as fire gushed down the hall behind him. Seth slammed the door against the searing heat and retreated to the leaded window on the far side of the room.

Seth threw open the window and then ducked aside, in case a dragon was waiting. A few quick peeks revealed stillness outside, shadowy parapets silvered by moonlight. The roar of fire continued in the adjoining hall, gouts of flame lapping under the door. Seth sheathed Vasilis to douse the light and leave a hand free. There would be no sheathing the other blade.

Tucking his wings, Seth sprang headfirst through the open window, falling some distance before spreading his wings and swooping out of his descent. He could hear the harpies wailing as they circled the pinnacle, and he saw the large shapes of dragons flying toward the castle from multiple directions. Floral scents wafted up from the courtyard below.

He focused on cloaking himself as he darted over the wall and then plunged to take refuge beneath the overhang where he had encountered the gargoyles. In the night above him, a dragon roared.

"I need a favor," Seth announced.

The shapes of the gargoyles shifted in the dimness, wings rippling.

"The sky is too empty," Seth said. "I need a distraction. The dragons evicted you from your normal roosts. The harpies are trying to replace you. I've come to stir things up. The dragons won't rule here long. I've already slain three of them. It's time for you to fly."

"Dragons . . . bite us . . . burn us . . . when fly," one of the gargoyles lamented.

"Hunt us . . . like vermin," another gargoyle said.

"Do you know what else the dragons did?" Seth asked. "They killed Sang Rou!"

"Sang Rou!" many of the gargoyles lamented.

"Tamryn the son of Celebrant boasted that Sang Rou died screaming," Seth said.

Gargoyles began striking the timbers supporting the overhang.

"Filthy wyrms!" a gargoyle cried.

"Sang Rou!" the gargoyles yelled.

"Show the dragons they can't get away with it," Seth

said. "Fly wildly! Don't let them catch you. Can't you still fly?"

"We still fly," a gargoyle said.

"Better . . . than birds," another replied.

"Better than bats," a third voice added.

"Prove it!" Seth challenged. "Go! Fly! Tell the other gargoyles to fly! Help me get away, and I will stop the dragons. Sang Rou must be avenged!"

"Sang Rou!" the gargoyles sang out.

A gargoyle dropped from the ceiling, spread his wings, and flapped away. As if his decision granted permission, a flood of gargoyles descended from the beams and from beneath the overhang. Seth joined the flock, hoping his golden wings wouldn't stand out too much.

Most of the gargoyles curved up and to the left. A lesser portion swerved up and to the right. A few glided downward.

Seth angled downward, trending away from the pinnacle, using the descent to create extreme speed. Above and behind him dragons roared, and a plume of fire temporarily brightened the night.

The dragons were no longer hunting a single mosquito. They were trying to track a mosquito through a swarm of flies.

As cool wind washed over him, Seth held the Unforgiving Blade away from his body. He would have to remain alert in order to avoid cutting himself with the impossibly keen edge. He couldn't afford an injury that would never heal.

His wings swerved hard to the left, and a harpy streaked

by just ahead of him, flailing claws whooshing near the side of his head. Had Seth not abruptly altered his course, the harpy would have plowed into him from above.

"We have you now," the harpy exulted. "Come, sisters."

Seth took evasive action, rolling, plunging, changing direction. The harpy stayed on his tail, and Seth glimpsed others converging.

As the harpy closed in directly behind him, Seth slowed and spun, swiping with the Unforgiving Blade, and the edge slashed across her shoulders. With a strangled hybrid between a scream and a hiss, the harpy peeled away, hands clutching the wound.

"Nightbringer," the harpy cried in a language Seth could barely recognize. "He has Nightbringer."

The other harpies who had taken up the pursuit veered away. Seth suspected it was a trick and continued to fly at top speed, complete with evasive maneuvers. After several minutes, having changed course multiple times, he began to fly with less desperation. Studying the night around him, he saw that he was apparently alone.

Seth focused on using his camouflaging abilities to blend with the darkness. The jibbering of the gargoyles, the shrieks of the harpies, and the occasional bellows of the dragons faded above and behind him. He skimmed along ridgelines and treetops alone, weighed down by two blades of great importance, an anonymous shape in the darkness, lost in an unknown wilderness, uncertain of what course he should follow.

# CHAPTER SEVEN

# Pillagers

Are the dragons really gone?" Knox said, turning in a slow circle, looking beyond the damaged city to the clear skies.

"Looks that way," Doren said, hopscotching to avoid the rubble in the street. "But if we're wrong, we die. It doesn't take an army of dragons to eat us. One would do the job."

"They were winning," Newel said, winging a stone side-arm down an ally. "Why give up the attack?"

"They flattened Big Side," Tess said. "Maybe that was why they came."

Knox glanced back at Big Side. The portion of the city reserved for giants had once loomed high above the rest. Now only select remnants remained standing—a crooked chimney, a steepled archway, the intersection of two ragged walls. Most had collapsed into mounds of blackened rubble.

"You may be right," Newel said. "The dragons must have accomplished their aims and left. I feel no dragon fear. But who can say when they might return?"

"What a compelling scent," Doren said, sniffing the air, then picking up his pace to a run.

The quiet street they were following into Small Town ended at a square with statues of dancing dryads at the center. At the far side of a horse trough, Doren paused beside an abandoned cart. He opened a wooden lid to reveal a bin full of baked apples. Closing his eyes, the satyr inhaled the aroma.

"You keep away!" a dwarf called from the doorway to a townhouse. He stomped forward, carrying a bulging sack over one shoulder, and clutching a hand ax. His black, braided mustache hung halfway down his stocky chest.

"I have to know how they taste," Doren said. "We'll pay."

"I'm not open," the dwarf declared.

"Leaving town?" Newel asked.

"Mind your business," the dwarf snapped.

"You wouldn't want these fine delicacies to go to waste!" Doren exclaimed.

The dwarf returned to his door, locked it, and started marching away up the street. "You want the apples? Take the apples! Run the cart if it pleases you."

"I take it the Games are canceled for today?" Doren called.

Turning back toward them, the dwarf harrumphed. "Where've you been? The coliseum collapsed. The Games are over. This town is finished." The dwarf waved a disgusted hand and tramped up the street.

"Why's he so angry?" Tess asked.

Newel surveyed the square. "Folks are tense. Looks like a lot of them are leaving town. See the guy with the rolled-up tapestry? And the lady with the birdcages? They're taking their favorite belongings."

Doren munched an apple. "I like the cinnamon," he reported. "Could be warmer." He held up another apple inquiringly. Knox held out his hands and caught the baked apple Doren lobbed his way.

"Are we kinda stealing these?" Tess asked.

"He gave them to us," Newel said. "Rule number one for life on the road? Eat when you can." He snatched an apple for himself and handed one to Tess.

"It's also rule number one when off the road," Doren said. "Or in a tent. Under a bridge. Anywhere, really."

Knox took a bite of his apple, finding it softer than he expected, and more flavorful. He watched double doors open across the square. A group of goblins rushed out, two of them carrying a trunk between them. "You're right about people leaving."

As Newel chewed his apple, Doren tapped him on the shoulder. "What's the trouble with a ghost town?"

"The ghosts?" Newel asked.

"I mean an abandoned town," Doren restated. "What's the problem?"

"Everything is closed?" Knox tried.

Doren shook his head. "It's been picked over. The best loot is gone."

Newel tapped the side of his nose and pointed at Doren, considering the square anew. "But we're here at the start of the panic. The city is just starting to empty."

"Humburgh is old news," Doren said. "The reason people came here is no more. The defenses are clearly down. If the dragons don't return to pillage the town, the giants will."

"We're here ahead of the pillagers," Newel said, eyes shining.

"The exodus is just beginning," Doren said.

"You want to loot the town?" Knox asked, wiping his lips on his sleeve.

"What's the best kind of treasure?" Doren asked.

"Gold?" Knox attempted. "Diamonds?"

"Magic wands?" Tess proposed.

"Unguarded treasure," Doren said. "Hands down, neglected spoils top all others. High yield for low hassle."

Newel glanced at Knox and Tess. "We have a responsibility to the kids."

"We sure do," Doren said. "We have to teach them how to keep their wits about them in emergencies. How to prosper when others panic. Think about their futures. A little treasure can go a long way."

"How will we carry the treasure?" Knox asked.

"Some we can wear," Tess said. "Like necklaces."

Newel rubbed his hands together, looking around and speaking in a low voice. "Big town like this? Doesn't have to be about quantity—we should focus on quality. Portable wealth. The kind of prizes you kids mentioned. Magical items. Precious metals. Jewelry."

"The sky is the limit," Doren said. "We might find weapons that could help in the war."

Knox could not avoid thinking of the crown in his possession. There was probably no bigger treasure in all of Titan Valley. But to mention it could potentially end his ownership, so he kept quiet.

"What if the dragons come back?" Tess asked.

Doren shrugged. "We hide or flee. Same as we would do without treasure. Would you rather flee rich or poor?"

Tess smiled. "Rich."

"A lot more fun to be had when you're rich," Newel said. "Less starving, for example."

"Are you sure this isn't stealing?" Tess asked.

"Think about it," Newel said. "If you find a treasure at the bottom of the ocean inside a sunken ship, who does it belong to?"

"Well, nobody anymore," Tess said. "Whoever finds it."

"Is this why people have children?" Newel asked. "I feel like a proud father!"

"We can look for Kendra and Seth as we go," Doren said. "Try to reconnect."

"Where do we pillage first?" Knox asked.

"That's the spirit," Newel said, clapping Knox on the back.

"Someplace with valuables?" Knox mused. "Like a bank? Or a jewelry store?"

"Good thinking," Doren said. "But those places might still have security this early in the exodus. We might have more luck with fancy private residences."

"I've dreamed of having a tavern to myself," Newel mused. "Everyone gone. Just me in there, with all that defenseless food and drink."

Doren licked his lips. "You're speaking to my stomach more than my brain, and you have my stomach's attention. You don't suppose Humburgh has a McDonald's? Or a Taco Bell?"

"Now you're just toying with my hopes and dreams," Newel said.

"Think of it," Doren said. "Endless rows of crunchy tacos, just for us. Specialty burritos. Fountain drinks."

"I like the nachos," Tess said.

"Stay focused," Knox said. "This town is medieval. There's no fast food around. But after we get out of here, you can buy a lot of hamburgers with gold."

"The kid has a point," Newel said.

"And if we don't win the war, there might not be any fast food anywhere," Knox said.

Both satyrs sobered up immediately.

Newel turned in a slow circle, scrutinizing the square. "I wish I knew this town better," he said.

"Should we try Arena Plaza?" Doren asked.

Newel shook his head. "That's the most obvious place in town. And probably a disaster after the coliseum collapsed."

"If the rubble spilled out of the pocket dimension, Arena Plaza would be buried," Doren said.

"I'm not sure exactly how it works," Newel said. "But there could be a horde of angry gladiators."

"Would the Humburgh Mystery House hold treasure?" Doren wondered.

Newel shrugged. "Might be worth a shot. It was heavily protected by magic. If those safeguards have unraveled, who knows what we might find?"

"Do you know where to go?" Knox asked.

"To the west, I think," Newel said, pointing down an avenue. "We'll adjust our course as needed."

"Anyone else want another apple?" Doren asked, taking one more from the bin.

"I'm going to hold out for something meatier," Knox said.

Doren started munching his third apple as they walked. The closer they got to the edge of town, the more crowded the streets became. Wagons dominated the center of the main thoroughfares, forcing those on foot to hug the margins. Almost everyone clutched possessions, bundles of food, or bulging sacks. Some people had loaded items into handcarts or wheelbarrows. Some had pets with them. All the traffic was flowing out of the city.

Newel led Knox and the others around a city block that was still burning, the fire finally low after having consumed most of the available fuel. Near the expiring flames, Knox breathed through his shirt, using the material to filter fumes out of the air. Tess consistently coughed, her eyes red-rimmed and watery.

The individuals heading out of town looked beleaguered.

A group of goblins powdered with dust and ash combined their efforts to push an overloaded wagon. An ogre toted a barrel over one shoulder, moderate to severe burns defacing much of his body. A troll with a splinted leg hobbled along using a mop as a crutch.

Newel increased his pace to a hasty trot. After a moment, Knox realized Newel had spotted a satyr. The satyr looked like a teenager, with light brown fur on his legs, little nubs instead of horns, and a wispy mustache. A bandage was wound about his forehead.

"Hoy, lad, give me a moment," Newel called.

The young satyr backed up against the wall of an emporium to avoid the flow of refugees. "What is it?" the satyr asked, glancing at Doren, then taking in Knox and Tess.

"I'm Newel; this is Doren."

"Charmed," the kid replied, checking the sky. "I'm Rory."

"We're looking for the Humburgh Mystery House," Newel said.

Rory chuckled. "Sightseeing, are you? The Games are over, you know."

"We have business there," Newel said.

"Are you sure about that?" Rory asked. "Most business in Humburgh is history. When a ship is sinking, even the rats know to jump overboard. Use the lull, mates. No promises how long it will last."

"I hear you," Newel said. "But we're meeting someone."

"More humans?" Rory asked.

"Something like that," Newel said.

"What have satyrs come to?" Rory lamented. "This town makes folk behave unnaturally. Our kind were never meant to be nannies. Don't matter what they're paying you."

"We have our reasons," Doren said.

"You're new here," Rory said.

"True enough," Newel replied.

"Elsewise you wouldn't need help with the obvious," Rory said. "Whatever preys on this town next will show no mercy. You overshot the Mystery House." He pointed down the nearest alley. "Head that way until you reach the main road. Then you'll have to push against the crowd. Good luck with that."

"Thanks for the pointers," Newel said. "One question about this migration. What happens if you're out in the open when the dragons return?"

Rory shrugged. "I let them eat the slow groups while I skirt the edges and find cover. Better than getting cornered in this rattrap."

"Where is everyone headed?" Doren asked.

"Depends who you ask," Rory replied, casting antsy looks at the crowd and the sky. "There are no safe harbors to match what Humburgh has been. A lot of folks hope to flee Titan Valley. Short term? Some will make for the sky giant garrison. Some will go to the southern villages, or over to Milford. A few might try their luck with the valley giants. Anyone with a brain will head to the woods."

"Are there satyrs in the woods?" Doren asked.

"At Titan Valley our kind mainly keep to Humburgh," Rory said. "The woods are full of trolls and giants. Some demons. But the woods offer more cover than overrun villages. I'm off."

Rory hurried away without looking back.

"Will we go to the woods too?" Tess asked.

"If it comes to that," Newel said.

"What about the trolls and the demons?" Tess asked.

"We'll avoid them," Doren said. "Satyrs are pros at staying alive, especially in the woods. Here are some of the basics: Always let someone else be the hero. Always sleep somewhere uncomfortable."

"Why?" Tess asked.

"It's better to wake up fast than to sleep well," Newel said.

"And always bring along others who are slower than you," Doren finished.

"I'm slower than you," Knox said.

"Normally that would make you the insurance policy," Doren said. "Not to worry, we've got your back. I'm sure we can find somebody slower."

"Rory might have a point about taking advantage of the lull," Newel said. "We could use the time to get to the woods."

"That wasn't Rory talking," Doren said. "That was panic. While he takes advantage of the lull, we'll take advantage of the panic."

"Trying to outrun dragons across open plains sounds like lining up for execution," Knox said.

"It does have that stink to it," Newel admitted.

From back the way they had come, a terrible wailing

broke out, harsh enough to make them all flinch. As the caterwauling continued, faces in the crowd craned to see what was generating the sound. First, a few people started running; then, within seconds, the weary procession in the street escalated into a stampede.

Newel seized Knox by the arm and hauled him into a nearby alley, perpendicular to the stampede. Doren carried Tess. Behind them, the desperate wailing continued, and people in the frightened crowd began to collide and fall, some getting trampled.

"No use looking back," Doren said. "We're safe for now."

Knox glanced back at the pandemonium on the street. A couple of dwarfs and a troll also took refuge at the mouth of the alley.

"What is making that racket?" Knox asked.

"I hope never to know," Newel said.

"Doesn't sound like a dragon," Tess said.

"Not a human, either," Doren said. "Or a satyr."

"We're getting farther from the screams as we go," Knox said.

"Hopefully the folks on the streets ahead won't be as spooked," Newel said.

They continued in the direction Rory had pointed, crossing a few minor streets and mostly sticking to alleyways. When they reached the next major boulevard, the wailing could no longer be heard. Along the thoroughfare, refugees were exiting the city in droves, wagons making slow progress amid the throng.

"This must be the main road," Doren observed. "Time to swim upstream."

"Knox, keep behind me," Newel said.

"I'll take Tess piggyback again," Doren said, crouching.

Knox stayed dutifully behind Newel as they advanced against the press. The crowd seemed irritated to encounter anyone going the opposite direction. All of the handcarts were loaded. Some were stacked with possessions; others held bodies, some old, some injured, a few apparently dead. Knox kept his eyes on Newel's hoofs, striving to ignore the rest of the scene.

"Pardon me," Newel repeated over and over. "Coming through. Beg your pardon. Family emergency."

Doren followed, carrying Tess, her arms crossed in front of his neck.

They passed a stretch of buildings reduced to smoldering embers on the right. Again Knox put his shirt over his nose and mouth to filter the foul air. They continued for several blocks before Newel cornered another satyr.

"Oi, mate, Humburgh Mystery House?" Newel asked.

"You're going the wrong way," the satyr said. He had black fur on his legs and a narrow beard that followed his jawline. "It's a block behind you."

Newel reversed course, staying with the new satyr. Knox appreciated no longer pushing upstream against the throng.

"Tumbled down," the satyr said, pointing to a jumble of debris. "Doesn't look like it burned. Several of the most magical buildings collapsed once Humbuggle's power no longer sustained them."

Diverging from the helpful satyr, Newel led the little group out of the crowd, onto the heaps of rubble. Knox had vaguely noticed the collapsed building when they passed. As he now looked more closely, he saw that the debris was eccentric. Weather vanes projected from the haphazard piles, alongside taxidermied bears, grandfather clocks, cast-iron bathtubs, and enormous painted portraits. The building materials were mostly dark wood and stone, interspersed with bright flashes of wallpaper and exotic carpets.

Newel led them farther from the busy avenue, back out of sight amid the wreckage. "Looks like the Mystery House was turned inside out and smashed to bits," he said.

"Anybody want a stuffed grizzly bear?" Knox asked, fingering a furry ear.

"Course I do," Doren said. "Transporting it is the problem."

"There are legitimate treasures in this mess," Newel said.

"And it would take legitimate hard work to reach them," Doren said. "No thank you."

"We need to be fast, right?" Tess asked.

"Why are we the only people doing this?" Knox said. "Maybe looting is a bad idea."

"Don't lose the vision," Doren said. "This is the peak rush out of town. Before long it will be like shopping with an unlimited credit card."

"Unless it turns into dragons eating the crazies who stayed behind," Knox said.

"Where would you run?" asked a deep, ponderous voice behind them.

Stiffening with startled fright, Knox rigidly turned around.

A peculiar giant faced him—a hulking, thickset brute with red, barklike skin and a head like that of a rhinoceros minus the horn. Gashes on one shoulder bled down the right side of his body. Looking up, Knox took a step back. The creature could clearly kill him with a punch.

"Pardon our intrusion," Doren said hurriedly. "Is this private property?"

"I mean you no harm," the giant said.

"That's very reasonable of you," Doren replied, still speaking rapidly. "Times being what they are, we should realize we're all on the same team."

"You think you're here to plunder," the giant said. "But fate may have a grander design."

"What?" Doren asked, waving away the statement. "Who needs plunder at a time like this? We were trying to avoid the crowds."

"Were you indeed?" the giant asked calmly.

"We were also hoping to find abandoned stuff," Tess said.

"And I was hoping to find you," the giant said. "We are approaching one of the great hinge points of history, and you four have roles to play. I am called the Diviner, and I suspect that we should talk."

# CHAPTER EIGHT

# Divide and Conquer

Kendra and Virgil sat on a low bench with their backs to a boutique art gallery. Looking over her shoulder through the panoramic window behind her, Kendra could see stunning arrangements of blown glass, gloppy paintings on the walls, and stately sculptures in marble and bronze. Most of the subjects were trolls or dwarfs, though others were abstract.

"Beautiful, right?" Virgil commented, following her gaze into the gallery.

"Lots of trolls," Kendra said.

Virgil gave a little chuckle. "The trolls purchase art. Especially paintings and statues of themselves. Artists have to eat."

"Are dwarfs big customers too?" Kendra asked.

"Not as much as the trolls," Virgil said. "But dwarfs run

this gallery." Sighing, the satyr turned to face the street. "There was plenty of sophistication in Humburgh. A lot to love. It went beyond art and food and performers. Mysteries, Kendra. Puzzles within puzzles. This town was a masterpiece of interwoven secrets. I wish I could know how many hidden spaces went undiscovered, how many ingenious clues were never noticed, how many treasures went unclaimed."

"Perhaps Humburgh will survive," Kendra said.

Virgil shook his head. "I don't see how. It's hard to make art with giants beating down your door. Let alone dragons tearing off your roof. This town was perilous, and the Games were barbarous, but it was also surprisingly safe, especially if you respected the rules. Humbuggle provided protection, and the Games powered our economy."

Merek landed in the middle of the nearest intersection. The refugees moving along the street altered their routes to give him space.

Virgil waved. "Over here."

Springing back into the air, Merek spread his wings and soared to the front of the gallery, taking a few steps to slow his momentum upon landing. Perspiration dampened his hair, and a gray mixture of ash and dust clung to him.

"Any sign of Knox or Tess?" Kendra asked.

"Sadly, no," Merek said. "Though I must confess it is hard to assess the town from the air. I had many arrows shot at me, and more than a few rocks thrown my way. All eyes are to the sky right now, and though I don't consider myself very dragonlike, anything airborne is currently suspect."

"Kill first, ask questions second," Virgil said.

"I flew from rooftop to rooftop, using steeples and chimneys for cover," Merek said. "It was either that or fly so high I couldn't distinguish the people below me. I swept the entire town, but if your cousins were in a building or on the move, I could have missed them."

Kendra frowned. "It's impossible to know. They could be hiding behind one of the doors across the street. Or nowhere near Humburgh."

"One thing is certain," Serena said. "Humburgh is emptying. The main roadways out of town are packed. Before long, this town will be mostly deserted."

"But the titan drove off the dragons," Kendra said. "Most of Small Town is still standing. Aren't they fleeing after the battle has been won?"

"The magical protections are gone," Virgil said. "Outside the domain of the sky giants, this is the richest city in Titan Valley. Humburgh was defended by Humbuggle from the start. The citizens here have never coexisted with giants unprotected. Even if the dragons don't return, the sky giants or some of the lesser giant tribes will soon arrive to raid and pillage. Our physical defenses are no match for them."

"But what will all of these—" Kendra began before her words were interrupted by a terrible wailing coming from a couple of streets over, desperate and alarming. Kendra clamped her hands over her ears. "What is that?"

"I'm not sure," Merek said.

"Me neither," Virgil said.

Even with her ears covered, Kendra could clearly hear

the horrid cries. "Let's hope my cousins aren't involved!" she exclaimed.

"Maybe we should find out," Merek said, taking a running start to fly toward the caterwauling.

Kendra and Virgil followed on foot, both keeping their ears covered. Merek glided no higher than the second stories of the nearby buildings, soaring straight down the street before swooping around a corner. Everyone they passed was scurrying away from the wailing. As they drew nearer to the source of the outbursts, the ground vibrated with the intense keening.

Virgil paused at the next corner. Standing on one hoof, he pointed with the other at a partially collapsed building down the block. The style of the damaged building made Kendra think of an old Spanish mission—rounded corners with curves in the façade, coated in dull yellow plaster. The wailing emanated from somewhere within.

Virgil led the way up the deserted street. Other pedestrians were visible only in the distance. As Kendra approached the partly crumpled building, the caterwauling ceased. Keeping her hands over her ears, Kendra glanced at Virgil, waiting for the outcries to resume, but the silence stretched on.

"I don't see Merek," Virgil said.

"Could he have gagged the screamer?" Kendra asked. "Or killed it? The wailing stopped so abruptly."

"I can only guess," Virgil said. "Let's hope the quiet is a favorable sign."

"What was this building?" Kendra asked.

"Secretive," Virgil said. "Trolls only. I've always been curious to know what happens inside."

"Now is your chance," she said.

One of the double doors at the front of the structure hung askew, but it squealed open when Virgil pulled. With buckled walls, sagging ceilings, splintered beams, and missing blocks, the portion of the building that had not collapsed looked like it might tumble down at any moment. Kendra hesitated, wondering if it was smart to proceed.

A heavy iron chandelier occupied the middle of the entryway, having shattered the tile floor when it fell. Virgil walked around the wrought-iron obstacle, stopping when some timbers creaked overhead and a few pebbles pattered to the floor.

"I'm worried if we sneeze it will all come down," Kendra said quietly.

Watching the ceiling, Virgil stamped a hoof. "I'm no expert, but if it hasn't fallen yet, hopefully we'll be all right."

Merek appeared at the end of the hall. "It's less stable where you're standing than deeper inside."

Virgil and Kendra hurried toward the winged Dragon Slayer.

"Any sign of my cousins?" Kendra asked.

"There's only a demon here," Merek said. He kept a level gaze trained on Kendra. "She wants to speak with you."

"With me?" Kendra asked.

"She told me she could sense you," Merek said. "Both your inner light and the mark you carry."

"What was with the yelling?" Kendra asked.

"The demon awoke to find herself crushed beneath a pile of rubble," Merek said. "I believe she was lamenting her fate."

"Will she survive?" Virgil asked.

"I don't think so," Merek said. "I think she means to help you, Kendra, but I'm no expert on demons."

"They are treacherous," Kendra said.

"That much I know," Merek replied. "I think this one is about to expire."

"Why did she stop screaming?" Virgil asked.

"She stopped when I showed up," Merek said. "She was lost in hysterics, not expecting anyone to answer her cries. My arrival seemed to shock her out of her panic."

"Lead the way," Kendra said.

Merek guided them deeper into the building. The farther they proceeded, the less damage Kendra noticed. Merek held a torch as they descended flagstone stairs into a basement, then progressed along a corridor with a barrel-vaulted ceiling that ended where it had caved in.

From beneath the jumble of dusty masonry, an arm reached out, slender and gray, but on a scale to match an ogre more than a human. Quills the length of toothpicks bristled along the back of the arm from the wrist to where it disappeared from view. Beside the arm a large head lay bowed, crested with longer quills, pinned to the floor at the neck by a huge stone slab. The head shifted as they approached, and yellow eyes with slitted pupils stared up at Kendra.

"You came," the female demon said in a harsh whisper. Kendra wondered if her voice was ragged from the wailing.

"You want to talk to me?" Kendra asked.

"You are she who slew Gorgrog," the demon said. "You are Kendra Sorenson."

"I am," Kendra said. "You're hurt."

"I am beyond hurt," the demon said. "Fate can be wicked. I was trapped here for many long years. On the day the bonds that held me were loosed, as I fled, my prison fell upon me."

"Can we help?" Kendra asked.

"Attempting to free me would only hasten my demise," the demon said.

"Do you have a name?" Kendra asked.

"I am Raisha," the demon said. "The trolls enslaved me and used me to gain knowledge."

"You were screaming," Kendra said. "Are you in pain?"

"Very little physical pain," Raisha said. "My pain runs deeper. My captors escaped my vengeance. My kind have been imprisoned, marginalized. The demise of any demon is a tragedy. We live in such a way that the worlds to come are . . . not pleasant."

"I'm sorry, Raisha," Kendra said.

"You were marked . . . by Jubaya . . . an old acquaintance," Raisha said, speaking haltingly.

"Yes," Kendra said.

"We demons . . . want reparations," Raisha whispered. "I . . . share . . . in this desire."

"What do you mean?" Kendra asked.

"Kill the Dragon King," Raisha said, panting.

"We're in a war with the dragons," Kendra said.

"Celebrant is the aberration," Raisha whispered. "You slew our king . . . slay theirs. And neutralize . . . his son . . . Tamryn . . . who could perpetuate the same cycle."

"I'll try," Kendra said.

"Celebrant . . . taught dragons to behave . . . like humans . . . or demons. Combining. Scheming. Going to war. That must end. Stamp him out. Erase his ways."

"I hear you," Kendra said.

"Don't poke . . . the snake. Don't reason with it. Cut off . . . the head."

"You might be right," Kendra said.

Raisha gave a strangled cry, eyes shut. Her breaths came in shallow gasps. She opened one eye. "I am right. None . . . understand . . . power dynamics . . . like demons. Ask any demon. Or anyone wise."

"I'll fight him with all I have," Kendra said.

"Liar," Raisha whispered through gritted teeth. "You have . . . access to help. Yet you ignore it. Talizar. Batoosa. Vez Radim. Real help. Expert help. Our interests . . . coincide. Why spurn aid?"

"I guess I have ignored some possible help," Kendra admitted.

"Talizar . . . at Wyrmroost. Batoosa . . . at . . . the . . . Starlit Shrine. Vez Radim . . . at Selona . . . in the former home . . . of the vampire."

"You have lots of knowledge?" Kendra asked.

"Had," Raisha said with a rattling wheeze. "Past tense. Dying."

"What do you know about Ronodin?" Kendra asked.

The demon gave a small grin, dark fluid leaking from the faltering smile. "Dark unicorn. Conquered . . . the fairies . . . at last."

"Is he a demon?" Kendra asked.

Raisha grunted in disgust. "No. Too chaotic. No loyalties."

"Too chaotic to be a demon?" Kendra muttered to herself. "How can I stop him?"

"Doesn't belong . . . with that crown," Raisha said, struggling to speak. "Incongruent. Won't last. Horrible timing. Could destroy much . . . including help . . . you need."

"Does he have a weakness?" Kendra asked.

The demon gave a strangled cough, expelling flecks of black gunk. "No . . . real . . . allies. He can be useful . . . but also works . . . against . . . anyone. Kill Celebrant." Raisha inhaled in a series of little gasps but seemed unable to exhale. Her eyes grew wide and desperate. "Find demons," she whispered, little more than mouthing the words. Then her head slumped. The quills on her head and arms fell flat.

"She's gone," Merek said.

Kendra blinked back tears. The demon had almost certainly harmed others, betrayed innocents, and even caused wars in the course of her life. But it was hard to watch anyone suffer and die. Especially since the demon seemed to be trying to help her in the end.

"That was intense," Kendra said with a shuddering breath.

"I vote we exit," Virgil said, "before we get buried with her."

Merek led the way out. Kendra heard wood groaning. Somewhere bricks fell. The whole world seemed like this retreat for trolls—wounded and on the brink of collapse.

After they walked around the fallen chandelier and out to the street, the avenue remained deserted. The distant crowds seemed sparser and farther away.

"What now?" Virgil asked.

"We need to get involved in the war," Kendra said.

"Is that all?" Virgil asked.

"I need to find the other Dragon Slayers," Merek said. "My brother and sisters will be powerful assets."

"What about King Konrad?" Kendra asked.

Merek scowled. "Father vanished a long time ago. I believe he yet lives, but he hasn't been seen for three times longer than the rest of us. We'll search for him, too, of course, but I'm worried the war could end long before we find him. This hunt will be a challenge. Will you join me?"

"I have another mission first," Kendra said. "Raisha got me thinking."

"You're not going after Celebrant?" Virgil asked.

"I will, but not yet," Kendra said. "It was what she said about Ronodin. How he has no allies."

"Meaning what?" Virgil wondered.

"I do have allies," Kendra said. "Powerful ones, who

were always there for me. And now they're in trouble. They need me. And I need them. We all do."

"Are you talking about the Fairy Queen?" Merek asked.

"Yes," Kendra said. "And her son, Bracken."

Virgil whistled. "That's ambitious. How would you get to the Fairy Realm?"

"Raxtus," Kendra said. "He'll know a way."

"I must find my siblings," Merek said.

"I'll stay with you," Serena said.

"I'll appreciate the extra eyes," Merek said.

"Sounds good," Kendra said. "I'll catch up and help when I can."

"With these wings, I'll have an advantage I've never known," Merek said.

"Could you do me one favor?" Kendra asked.

"Name it," Merek said.

"Fly back toward the Dragon Temple," Kendra said. "Find Tanu, Vanessa, and Warren. Tell them where I'm going. And tell them we need to find Knox, Tess, Newel, and Doren. I can't leave without somebody following up on my cousins."

"I can help with the cousins," Virgil said, raising a hand. "I want to be of service."

"I have something else in mind for you," Kendra said. "Want to come with me to the Fairy Realm?"

"Me?" Virgil asked.

"It'll be dangerous," Kendra cautioned. "But the outcome is critical. Everything depends on it. Some satyrs go there, right?"

"Those satyrs are a little more . . . devout than I have been," Virgil said. "But technically she is my queen too."

"Raxtus can carry two," Kendra said. "I could use your help."

Virgil glanced around. He cleared his throat and straightened his shirt. "Not much left for me here. It would be a grand adventure, beyond the scope of anything I have considered. Sure, Kendra. Why not?"

# CHAPTER NINE

# Pool

Seth leaned closer to the fire. The warmth felt comforting against the chill of the night. He knew dawn had to be coming, but he still saw no light on the horizon. After the moon had set, the firmament had become saturated with stars, though he could no longer see them as well with the flames ruining his night vision.

After hours of flying, hopeful he was not being pursued, Seth had finally landed on a forested slope, below an outcrop. He had gathered wood, and Calvin had started it burning. The rushed flight of his escape had left his wings exhausted, which had forced him to take a break.

The Unforgiving Blade rested nearby. Seth had discovered that if he carefully set down the flat side of the blade flush against the ground, the long knife would remain as he placed it. If the edge or tip of the blade turned downward, the blade would sink into the earth, with only the hilt poking out. At the moment, the blade was a strip of pure darkness, tapering to a point, reflecting no firelight.

"The harpies seemed stunned by that sword," Seth said.

"They scattered after you wounded one of them," Calvin replied. "I didn't see any of them trying to find us after that."

"The one I cut called it Nightbringer," Seth said. "She spoke in some harpy language. She sounded afraid."

"Harpies are expert tormentors," Calvin said. "They're used to dealing out suffering. They wanted no part of the Unforgiving Blade. Too much of their own medicine."

"Do you think the harpies know which way I went?" Seth asked. "We changed direction a lot."

"Harpies could hunt you better than hounds if they really wanted to find you," Calvin said. "I suspect the risks were too much for them. But we have to stay ready. Who knows whether that could change? Dragons or harpies could show up anytime. Or who knows what else?"

Seth listened to the fire crackling. The night seemed too calm for a dragon to appear. Maybe that was his fatigue talking. At some level, he knew Calvin was right.

Seth's gaze returned to the Unforgiving Blade. Harpies had fled from it. Dragons feared it. Not the same way they might fear Kendra wielding Vasilis. Not as though the forces of good had come for retribution. This was no weapon of light. It was a weapon connected to the Void, a weapon that inflicted permanent wounds. Its victims died in ugly ways. It had chopped the Wizenstone in half. This blade had been hidden in an obscure reliquary, heavily guarded by tricks and traps.

And Seth had brought it back into the world. If it fell into the wrong hands, terrible harm would follow. What if Kendra, or any good person, ended up with wounds that never healed?

Seth flexed his fingers. Who could say whether his weren't also the wrong hands? Better than some, probably, but he had caused plenty of damage. He would be foolish to trust himself with a weapon of such darkness.

How could he get rid of it? Ditch it in the woods? Bury it? Toss it into the sea?

Prize had sensed the blade. If a wraith could sense it, what else might be drawn to it? To abandon the blade could be a step away from handing it to an evil wielder.

For now he had to keep it—until he could find a safe place to abandon it.

"What are you thinking?" Calvin asked.

"I wish I knew what to do with the Unforgiving Blade," Seth said.

"You might need it," Calvin said. "You have a lot of danger ahead."

"I'm worried that blade increases the danger," Seth said. "I already have Vasilis."

"One step at a time?" Calvin asked. "Where do we go from here?"

"Do you even know where we are?" Seth asked.

"Somewhere outside of Soaring Cliffs," Calvin said. "A forest in Asia?"

"It's tough when the closest guess we have is a continent," Seth said.

"I'm no cartographer, but I think Soaring Cliffs is someplace in the Himalayas," Calvin said. "We've flown a good distance from where we started. Maybe we're in Nepal? India? Bangladesh?"

"Nice to narrow it down," Seth said.

"We'll figure it out," Calvin said.

"I have a huge job ahead of me," Seth said. "I made a bargain with the Singing Sisters. I don't think it's fair to drag you along."

"Are you testing me?" Calvin asked. "I swore to serve you. And your mission could help solve the nipsie curse."

"Could it?" Seth asked.

"We were cursed because we helped steal the Ethergem," Calvin said. "Gathering the pieces might help."

"But we're gathering them for witches," Seth said.

Calvin shrugged. "We can worry about that when we succeed."

Seth gazed into the wooded dimness beyond the radiance of the campfire. "I set us down near a pond. Maybe I should use the silt Prize gave me. Contact the Singing Sisters."

"You sound hesitant," Calvin said.

"I don't want them running the show," Seth said. "I'm tired of other people telling me what to do. I'm sick of running errands for bad guys."

"Do we know the Singing Sisters are evil?" Calvin asked.

"They're not a choral group," Seth said. "They're definitely dangerous. They can be helpful, but they ask for a lot in return. Patton guided me toward them in an emergency, so he must trust them somewhat."

"Could they tell you where we are?"

"Worth a try." Seth stood up, staggering a little.

"Whoa. Are you okay?"

"Head rush. I'm wiped out."

"It was a long flight," Calvin said.

"The wings have their own energy," Seth said. "It isn't limitless. When I push extra hard, I feel it." Seth massaged his temples. "My exhaustion feels more than physical. Like I haven't slept in days, even though I rested plenty in the dungeon."

"You're under a lot of stress," Calvin said.

"Who isn't these days?" Seth said. "I'll be right back." He glanced at the Unforgiving Blade. Should he hold it for safekeeping? He would only be a few paces away, and Calvin was watching. If the witches saw the blade, they might want it. Probably better to keep it out of the conversation.

Seth walked over to the pool he had noticed from the sky. It was separated from a larger pond by a marshy area. The hard mud at the edge of the pool let Seth stand right by the water. If the night were much colder, the water would freeze. Fortunately, he was back in the northern hemisphere, so it was summertime, even though he suspected he remained at a high altitude.

The pool beautifully mirrored the abundant stars above, though Seth could only barely make out his own reflection.

He hoped it wasn't too dark for communication to occur. Opening the pouch Prize had given him, Seth removed a pinch of fine-grained silt. He sprinkled the silt into the pool, hoping there was no accompanying incantation the wraith had failed to mention.

Immediately the stars in the pool vanished, and the water became agitated. A fetid stench arose. The water smoothed and brightened, and Seth found three older women peering at him, as if reflected in the water. One had narrow features, one had lost most of her hair, and the third was unusually flabby. They were crowded together as if holding hands in a circle. Though he could not see their arms, Seth knew their hands were fused together at the wrists. They stared up from the pool, but the perspective made it feel like they were looking down at him.

"Is that him?" asked Orna, the balding one.

"It's so dim," said Berna, narrow features squinting. "Gromlet! More light!"

"We sent the wraith with the silt," Wilna said. "Who else would reach out to us in this fashion?"

"The wraith found me," Seth reported.

The pool brightened, casting extra light onto Seth and letting him see the conjoined sisters in clearer detail.

"So it is," Berna acknowledged.

"The boy is maturing," Orna noted appreciatively.

"Show us the Sword of Light and Darkness," Wilna said.

Seth drew Vasilis, and his weariness melted away. Its crimson light bled into the water.

"He has experienced pain," Berna said.

"And partaken of darkness," Orna added.

"The boy wavers," Wilna pronounced.

"The boy broke out of prison and killed three dragons," Seth said. "I'm not giving up. Can you tell me where I am?"

"On the outskirts of the Soaring Cliffs sanctuary," Berna said.

"Am I beyond the borders of the sanctuary?" Seth asked.

"Yes," Orna replied. "In Nepal."

"The more relevant question might be, where are you going?" Wilna said.

Seth sheathed Vasilis, and his weariness returned. He felt even more tired than before he had drawn it, and he wondered if the sword was responsible for his exhaustion. His mind felt cloudier without it in his grasp, and he considered taking it out again, but refrained. He didn't want to become dependent on it.

"Do you hear us, Seth?" Berna asked, leaning toward him.

"I was just thinking," Seth said. "I'm not sure what my next move should be."

"The wraith is no longer with you," Orna said.

"I left Prize behind," Seth explained. "I had to fly fast."

"Your wings look striking," Orna gushed. "Very noble."

"Decorum, sister," Berna scolded.

"You named our wraith?" Wilna asked.

"It's short for Witchprize," Seth said.

Wilna sniffed. "I suppose that is appropriate."

"Wilna likes it," Orna whispered loudly.

"You gave me five tasks in one," Seth said.

"You owed us a favor," Berna said.

"Bringing the pieces of the Ethergem to us is a single request," Orna said, "though it has multiple components."

"We could have let you rot in prison," Wilna said.

"How did you know I was there?" Seth asked. "How did Prize find me so quickly?"

"We check in on you, child," Berna said.

"The wraith, Prize, used the paths of the Underking," Orna said.

"We are not casual in debt collection," Wilna intoned.

"There is a lot going on right now," Seth said. "Did you know I lost my memories? Do you know about the dragon war?"

The sisters looked at one another and burst into cackling laughter.

"Who warned you that a storm of dragons was coming?" Orna asked. "Have you forgotten so quickly?"

"We know more than you ever will," Berna said.

Seth glowered. "Then you know there are more important things to do right now than collecting pieces of a fancy rock."

"Have you any fragments of the Ethergem already in your possession?" Wilna asked.

"The two halves of the Wizenstone," Seth said.

"An admirable start," Orna said, nodding to her sisters.

"He has scarcely begun," Wilna muttered.

"Do not forget that we see both deep and far," Berna said. "This task may benefit all, ere it is done."

"You speak too freely," Wilna hissed.

"Can you see the future?" Seth asked. "Do you know how this ends?"

"The magical world is in disarray," Berna said. "The scales are unbalanced."

"The full fury of the storm will be unleashed," Orna said.

"We do not surrender secrets freely," Wilna chided.

"The boy is on an errand for us," Berna said. "He must know enough to succeed."

"He need know only that if he deviates from his task, the covenant knife will claim him," Wilna said.

"There are diverse ways to inspire obedience," Berna said.

"Few yearn to see the dragons victorious," Orna said.

"Are you telling me that gathering the pieces of the Ethergem will help us win the war?" Seth asked.

"Should you succeed, all shall prosper," Berna said.

"All save the dragons," Orna added.

"What will you do with the pieces of the Ethergem?" Seth asked.

All three sisters burst into wild cackles.

"Our purposes are our own," Wilna said as sobriety returned.

"We do not deal in Source magic," Orna said.

"Quiet, sister," Berna said.

"Do we look like fairies?" Orna asked with a snicker.

"Enough, Orna," Wilna demanded.

"How do you suggest I get the gem from the Dragon

King's crown?" Seth asked. "Wouldn't we have to win the war first?"

"Coming events are clouded," Berna said. "There is too much tumult, like peering into a sandstorm. But the dragons will prevail unless the stone is taken from Celebrant before the war ends."

"I will reveal more to focus your intent," Wilna said. "Should you fail to complete our task, the war will be lost."

Orna scowled. "And you accuse me of divulging too much?"

"What if you're taking advantage of me to get the pieces?" Seth asked. "How do I know I can trust you with them?"

The witches cackled a third time.

"He is Patton all over again," Orna said.

"We must help him survive simply for the comedy," Berna said.

"It's far too late to question this partnership," Wilna declared. "Where do you intend to begin?"

Seth rubbed his eyes. "I don't know where to find Celebrant. Getting the crown from the new demon prison will be even harder."

"Two of the fragments you require are still at Titan Valley," Berna said. "You are on the same side of the world as that sanctuary."

"The Giant Queen has fallen," Orna declared. "Her crown is at large."

"The Ethershard remains at Stratos," Wilna said.

"I guess I start there?" Seth asked.

"That would be wise," Berna approved.

"Waste no time," Orna urged.

"You must prevail," Wilna said.

"How do I navigate back there?" Seth asked.

"Fetch the remnants of the Wizenstone," Wilna said. "Quickly."

Seth knew they were in his knapsack back at the campfire. "One moment."

He walked over to the modest fire.

"How is it going?" Calvin asked as Seth rummaged in his knapsack.

"They told me that collecting the pieces of the Ethergem will help win the dragon war," Seth said. "They might just be trying to convince me to prioritize what they want." He removed the two halves of the Wizenstone. Though their inner glow was gone, they sparkled in the firelight.

"Why do they want the pieces?" Calvin asked.

"They're not very open," Seth said. "Supposedly getting the pieces will help the war. But maybe the Sisters mean to destroy the world in some new way."

"We won't let that happen," Calvin said.

"Really?" Seth asked. "With my track record, I'll start a cataclysm and end up as the sole survivor."

Seth walked back to the pool.

"We're not trying to rule the world," Berna said.

"Or destroy it," Orna said.

"Your interests and ours are more aligned than you realize," Wilna said.

"You were eavesdropping?" Seth asked.

"You were only ten paces away," Berna said.

"You weren't even whispering," Orna added.

"Who gave you the weapon that slew Graulas, Nagi Luna, and the Demon King?" Wilna asked. "Did that cause a demon apocalypse? Or avert one?"

"I hear you," Seth said. "We couldn't have stopped the demons without you. And Patton recommended you."

"Look to Patton's example," Berna said. "It's hard to accomplish greatness without proper orientation."

"I've had a lot of misorienting lately," Seth said.

"Surely we haven't misoriented you," Orna said. "Tested and challenged you, perhaps."

"You helped me find Vasilis and stop the demons," Seth agreed.

"We restored Vasilis to you again," Wilna said. "And now we claim the service you owe us. Hold the Wizenstone in the pool."

Seth crouched and submerged the Wizenstone in the cold water.

"Keep it there for a moment," Berna said.

The three witches closed their eyes. For a moment, the pool shone like liquid light.

"You may withdraw the stone," Wilna said, opening her eyes.

"The remnants of the Wizenstone will now sympathize with its sister stones," Orna said.

"Held in an outstretched arm, it will glow if aimed at one of the other stones," Berna said. "You may also feel a slight vibration as you draw near."

"The stone in the crown of the Demon King will evoke a blue glow as deep as midnight," Wilna said. "You may see that one better under daylight. The Dragon King's stone should produce a white glow. The Giant Queen's jewel will prompt a red glow. And the Ethershard will instigate a prismatic shine."

"I forgot my dictionary," Seth said. "What's prismatic?"

"Rainbow," Orna said.

"Travel swiftly," Berna encouraged. "Let's hope you are not already too late."

"Do not turn aside for other matters," Wilna warned. "Our knife will not hesitate to collect what you owe us."

The light in the pool went out, and once more the surface of the water reflected the stars. Stepping away from the pond, Seth held out half of the Wizenstone, slowly turning until the crystalline hemisphere softly glowed red. Little rainbows of light also flickered inside. At this distance, the Giant Queen's crown and the Ethergem appeared to be in the same direction.

He was lost somewhere in Nepal.

The dragons wanted him dead.

The witches required their bounty.

At least the Wizenstone gave him a course to follow.

Where else was he supposed to go?

# CHAPTER TEN

# Divining

C ome this way," the Diviner invited, guiding Knox, Tess, Newel, and Doren to where four chairs awaited in a semicircle, shielded from onlookers on the street by heaps of rubble.

"He had them ready for us," Tess exclaimed.

"What if he holds conferences with his meals?" Doren asked. "When are you going to grind our bones into bread?"

"I am one of the Kurut Oi," the Diviner explained. "More commonly we are called the gentle giants. I abstain from violence, and I eat no flesh."

"That's a really big vegan," Knox murmured.

"What do you want with us?" Tess asked.

"That partly depends on you," the Diviner said. He sat down cross-legged, facing the four chairs. "Please be seated."

The foursome accepted the invitation. Two of the chairs

looked like they belonged at a dinner table, another was a wide armchair, and the smallest was fashioned from bamboo. Knox claimed the armchair. Tess ended up on the bamboo seat.

"You're called the Diviner," Newel said. "Does that mean you find things?"

"Yes," the Diviner said. Leaning forward, he produced a tuning fork and flicked it with his fingernail. "Keep still," the giant said. He placed the humming fork beside Doren's left ear, then swept it over his head to the right one. He repeated the process with the others. Knox was mildly surprised at how much louder the tuning fork sounded when it vibrated beside his ear.

"Are you helping us find the right pitch?" Newel asked, humming to match the tone of the tuning fork.

"I'm learning about you," the Diviner said. "I lack my ideal setting, and I have lost many of my tools, but I can still discern much."

"I need to find my cousins," Knox said. "Kendra and Seth."

"I've actually met your cousin Seth," the Diviner said. "We spoke not long ago."

"You know Seth?" Tess asked. "Do you know where he is?"

"You can ask his friend," the Diviner said, turning to stare at rumpled tapestry partly buried under broken bricks. "Come out, little one."

The tapestry shifted and a portly little troll emerged, with a rather large head and stubby limbs. "How you know I here?" the short troll asked.

"I pay attention," the Diviner said.

"Who's this guy?" Doren asked.

"Me Hermo," the troll said.

"A hermit troll?" Newel asked.

"Tell them about Seth," the Diviner coaxed. "These are his cousins and his friends."

Hermo spat on the ground. "Seth gone. Went far. No use fishy."

"How do you know Seth?" Tess asked.

Hermo folded his arms. "He my friend. He lost me."

"May I?" the Diviner asked, holding out the tuning fork.

Hermo waved him away. "No tricks. No magic. Me follow goatboys and cousins already. Find Seth."

"Were you following us?" Newel asked.

"Me on walk," Hermo said. "Find you. Go same direction."

"What does the chime show you?" Knox asked the giant.

"Truth resonates," the Diviner said. "I seek what actually is, what actually was, and what actually will be. Simple truths are obscured by deception and illusion and often missed through inattention."

"Sounds deep," Newel said.

"Is it the kind of deep with a practical side?" Doren asked.

"Little is more practical than knowing truth," the Diviner said.

"How about the truth of where treasure is hidden?" Doren asked.

"We are all wanderers in this world," the Diviner said.

"We create a home, forgetting it is temporary. We possess an item, forgetting this state will not endure. We dwell in a dimension of beginnings and endings. We embark on journeys, presuming to know what we seek, while the wise are always finding. I do help the worthy find treasure, though you and I may define the term differently."

"I see," Doren said, steepling his fingers. "In your definition, does treasure jingle? Does it shine? Is it expensive?"

"What you most value is your treasure," the Diviner said.

"Giant talk and talk," Hermo said. "Me know how find treasure."

"You acted like you have a message for us," Knox said to the Diviner. "What did you want to share?"

"Your cousin Seth is far away but will return," the Diviner said. "Your cousin Kendra is near but will depart."

"Can we find Kendra before she leaves?" Tess asked.

"Doubtful, little one," the Diviner said. "Even if you could, it would cause delays for all."

"And you know this by waving around a tuning fork?" Knox asked.

"The fork heightens my perceptions," the Diviner said.

"This sounds like fortune cookie nonsense," Knox said. "I've never liked this kind of thing. What's my favorite color? What number am I thinking of? What's my destiny?"

"Manners, Knox," Doren said through a brittle smile.

"I require none to believe me," the Diviner said. "Most feel more comfortable living in denial."

"Is the best use of time in an emergency to have our palms read?" Knox said.

"You are free to go where you choose, Knox," the Diviner said. "I know about your secret. Do with it as you will."

Knox froze. "My secret?"

"The one in your possession," the Diviner said. "You claim to have no favorite color, but it is bright orange. The number you wanted me to guess was seven. Your destiny is complicated, but you do possess potential for greatness. I won't tell your secret. It is for you to disclose as you see fit."

"Are you keeping secrets from us?" Tess asked her brother.

"We all have secrets," Knox said.

"Is he right about the color?" Newel wondered.

"Psychics have their little tricks," Knox said.

"The number too?" Doren checked.

"Seven is the obvious choice," Knox replied.

"The valley giants already march to raid Humburgh," the Diviner said. "They have steadfastly honored whoever wore the crown. Some of the hill giant tribes draw near as well. As do many ogres. Those of you who want gold and jewels should hurry. Be prepared to defend what you claim."

"He is sucking the fun out of this," Doren grumbled.

"What about me?" Tess asked, raising her hand.

"You are drawn to light, little one," the Diviner said. "Your perceptions are keen. Use that to the advantage of all around you. Escape to Selona. Resist the storm there."

Newel gave a chuckle. "Easier said than done. Selona is a legendary realm. Who knows where to find it?"

"Follow the guidance of those privy to the secret," the Diviner said.

"Aren't you supposed to find things?" Newel asked. "Why don't you tell us how to get there?"

The giant smiled. "Stay your course, take it one step at a time, and watch for opportunities to arise. First you need to help Seth."

"How?" Doren asked.

The giant stared directly at Knox. "Aid him in his quest. Beware of claiming that which is not yours, and of discarding that which is precious."

"This is deteriorating into riddles," Newel said.

"I think he has issues with looting," Doren said.

The Diviner stood. "Loot. Hide. Flee. Fight. It all involves risk. My time here is done."

"Where will you go?" Tess asked.

"Back to my clan," the giant said. "After a long absence."

"How can we win the dragon war?" Knox asked.

"There are various ways to help," the Diviner said. "I will not fight, nor will my clan. But we shall do what we can. I wish I could see more, and farther, but the coming storm is chaotic indeed." He produced a coin and tossed it to Knox, who caught it.

"What's this?" Knox asked, holding it up. "Is it made of jade?"

"The coin marks you as a friend to giants," the Diviner said. "The service you are performing for us remains incomplete." He held out a hand, palm downward. "I bestow this status freely."

Knox felt a tingle in his chest.

The giant turned and strode away.

"I like his style," Newel said. "Very mysterious."

"He could add some showmanship," Doren said. "Some smoke bombs. Snakes in cages. Maybe an exotic hat."

"Wouldn't a psychic have gotten out of town before the attack?" Knox asked.

"It would have been nice to hear about some prime loot," Doren said. "But I'm glad to know Seth is heading our way."

"Assuming he's right," Knox said, fingering the crown hidden beneath his shirt.

"Him blowhard," Hermo said. "Me find loot. What you want?"

"Are we still after treasure?" Newel asked. "Knowing the giants are coming?"

"We already suspected that," Doren said. "I say we still look around. It beats roaming an open plain or cowering in a cellar. Hermo, how are you at finding gold?"

The little troll gave a snort. "It easy."

"Do you already have a lot?" Doren asked.

Hermo shook a finger. "Gold make problem. Too much gold is too much problem."

"Knox, you haven't told us your secret," Tess implored.

"It's private," Knox said. "I'm with Doren. Let's find some problems."

# CHAPTER ELEVEN

# Celebration

W e're landing soon," Raxtus announced.

Kendra snapped awake, her torso gripped by one of the dragon's front claws. Glancing to one side, she saw Virgil at the end of the other foreleg. Wind streamed against her face as the dry prairie below drew nearer, lit by the rosy brightness of the rising sun.

"You fell asleep," Virgil called. He was relatively near, but the steady wind in her ears made it hard to hear him.

"I guess I did," Kendra replied loudly. "Are we inside Obsidian Waste?"

"And approaching the fairy shrine," Raxtus reported with a nod.

"I'm not sure you get it," Virgil said. "You fell asleep while soaring at high speeds, suspended in midair by the claw of a dragon."

Kendra smiled. "I guess I was really tired!"

"It's so nonchalant," Virgil said. "A move only a seasoned adventurer could pull off. I have not encountered a level of fatigue that allows for napping during dragon flight."

"It helps that I trust Raxtus," Kendra said.

"Satyrs are not part of my diet," Raxtus inserted. "You could have slept too."

"You carried us the whole way without rest?" Kendra asked. "You crossed most of a continent while I snoozed!"

"You're brimming with magical energy, Kendra," Raxtus said. "Carrying you is easier than flying solo."

Back at Titan Valley, Raxtus had shown great willingness when Kendra had asked him to take her to the Fairy Realm. He also reminded her that the way to the Fairy Realm from Titan Valley had been sealed. Of the three magical preserves nearest to Titan Valley, Raxtus suspected that Obsidian Waste in Australia was the most likely to remain free from his father's influence. It wasn't a dragon sanctuary, but it had an accessible portal to the Fairy Realm.

After bidding Merek farewell, Kendra had left the Dragon Slayer behind, flying away from Titan Valley over the ocean with the sinking sun. She missed Merek's stalwart presence but was glad he was working to help her cousins and to find the other Dragon Slayers.

Kendra felt tingles as Raxtus dipped downward. A bluff appeared up ahead, beside a bend in a winding river, the water tainted orange. Slowing his glide, Raxtus set down Kendra and Virgil between the river and the bluff, then landed a few yards beyond them.

"Orange water?" Virgil questioned.

"A gift from the Rainbow Serpent," Raxtus said. "The color of the river varies, but the water is always clean. We'll find the shrine halfway up the cliff face, inside a narrow cleft."

"It looks unclimbable," Kendra said. "Why did we stop flying?"

"See the bulges on the cliff?" Raxtus said. "Those are beehives."

"Those hives are massive," Kendra said.

"The bees are the size of sparrows, and they fiercely protect the shrine," Raxtus said.

"I don't like beestings," Virgil confessed.

"Does anyone like them?" Raxtus asked. "These particular stings pack a wallop. It wouldn't take many to kill a person."

"If the Fairy Queen had invited me, she would calm them," Kendra said.

"If only she were free," Raxtus said. "Ronodin runs the Fairy Realm now. If he knew I had permission to enter and exit at will, I'm sure he'd block my access. But my arrangement with the Fairy Queen was not highly publicized. Let's hope the dark unicorn isn't aware."

"Ronodin tends to figure out more than anyone would suspect," Kendra said. "We'll find out soon enough."

"How will we get to the shrine?" Virgil asked.

"No matter how we approach, the bees are in our way," Raxtus said. "I may be able to help. The stingers can't pierce my scales. And my breath should calm the bees. I'll be back soon."

His iridescent wings spread wide and Raxtus took off, heaving dust in all directions. Kendra turned her head and covered her eyes with one arm until the air cleared.

"How did you befriend a dragon?" Virgil asked quietly.

"Raxtus is an outcast," Kendra said. "Fairies rescued his egg from a cockatrice. They ended up hatching him and raising him. He turned out all small and sparkly and was ridiculed."

"But his father is Celebrant?" Virgil asked.

"Yeah," Kendra said. "His mom died, so his only motherly figure besides the fairies is his stepmom. His dad tried to recruit him to harm Dragonwatch, but in the end, Raxtus chose to help us instead. Now he lives in exile. He's tougher than he looks. Those scales of his are almost unbreakable."

"You have a bow but no arrows," Virgil noticed.

"It's called a bow of plenty," Kendra said. "I've had it since Wyrmroost. When I pull the string back, an arrow appears, up to three hundred every day. I can also shoot a bunch simultaneously."

"Who refills it for a new day?" Virgil asked.

"I don't know how the magic works," Kendra admitted.

"Remarkable," Virgil said.

"I also have a sack of gales," Kendra said, patting the sack tucked into her belt. "It looks empty, but open the mouth, and wind pours out. Great for messing with dragons in flight."

They watched Raxtus glide along the face of the cliff, spraying glittery exhalations over the hives. He made several passes, thoroughly gassing his targets. As Raxtus soared back to them, Virgil stripped off his vest and dropped it on the ground. He had a slender build, with a little tuft of hair in the center of his chest.

"Trying to cool off?" Kendra asked.

"No," Virgil said, swinging his arms awkwardly. "Part of my job on this mission is to blend in, right? See what I can learn from the natives? The satyrs in the Fairy Realm prefer the natural look. No shirts or vests." He handed over his brass binoculars. "You can keep these if you like."

"Are you sure?" Kendra asked. "These are nice."

"I'd rather not look like a tourist," Virgil said, folding his arms. He glanced down at himself. "I wish I had more chest hair. They're liable to tease me. My back is bald as an egg."

"You look great," Kendra encouraged, hanging the binoculars around her neck. "Very wild."

"It's a challenge to act fun-loving and frivolous when you're nervous," Virgil said. "I'll do my best."

Raxtus landed nearby. "We should hurry. The bees will remain sedated for only a short while."

"Let's go," Kendra said.

"You're ditching the vest?" Raxtus asked.

"It was one of my favorites," Virgil said. "But I don't want to stand out."

"Good thinking," Raxtus said, seizing Kendra with one claw and Virgil with the other. "The satyrs in the Fairy Realm aren't very civilized." He launched into the air.

Kendra enjoyed the sensation of rising like a kite above the river. Raxtus tilted and they angled toward the cliff.

"The opening is smaller than I remembered," Raxtus

said. "You two will have to squeeze. I don't stand a chance in my dragon shape. No laughing."

"Why would we laugh?" Virgil asked.

"You'll see," Raxtus said.

Raxtus slowed as he approached a vertical fissure near the center of the cliff. Brown beehives clumped like huge bunches of grapes at either side of the narrow opening. Water trickled from the base of the gap and other water percolated from dozens of tiny holes. Raxtus deftly placed Kendra in the cleft, followed by Virgil. Kendra had to climb up a little and then turn sideways to scoot into the gap. She edged forward as quickly as she could, the rough stone scraping her skin and snagging her jeans. Only the urgency of her situation compelled her to keep forcing her way forward.

She reached a section where the walls became so close she could barely inhale. Blowing the air from her lungs, Kendra squirmed past the narrowest place, and the cavity widened into a broad, rounded chamber with a pool at the bottom. White fish with feathery fins circled in the clear water. Atop an angular stone poking out of the glassy pond stood a tiny clay statue of a fairy with a simple wooden bowl beside it.

"Now I'm doubly glad I left the vest," Virgil said, brushing grime off his torso. "I'm not sure I could have wriggled through with it on. Blimey, it's dark in here."

"Dark is perfect right now," Raxtus said, flitting easily through the crack, his voice high-pitched because his body was currently about a foot tall. He looked like a male fairy in his teens, with metallic wings and spindly limbs. Since Kendra could see in the dark, he was not hidden from her.

"Any chance of the bees following us in here?" Virgil asked. "It feels sacred."

"This is definitely hallowed ground," Raxtus said. "Perhaps that keeps them out." He reverted to his dragon shape beside the pool, filling much of the available space in the cavity. "This is where we cross over. Moment of truth. Are you both sure you want to do this?"

"I am," Kendra said.

"Sure enough," Virgil said.

"I'll do my best to protect you, but there are no guarantees," Raxtus said. "With Ronodin in charge, we won't have many friends there. Our best protection will be camouflage. Keep quiet and think invisible thoughts. Who knows how well guarded this entrance will be on the other side?"

"Let's do it," Kendra said.

Raxtus grasped Kendra with one claw, Virgil with the other, and plunged downward into the shallow pool. After passing through the surface of the water, instead of striking the bottom, Kendra found herself rising from a pond on a mountainside. The bright, sunless sky was a deep, unnatural blue. Even from Kendra's close proximity, Raxtus seemed nearly invisible, his body warping light just enough to hint at his shape. The fairy dragon landed behind a group of boulders, out of sight except from directly above. Kendra faintly heard rollicking music, pipes and harps, and the murmur of far-off conversation.

She waited silently beside Virgil, her hair and clothes

dry in spite of having passed through water. Raxtus was visible only as a shimmer beside her, an odd distortion in the air that gently rippled when he moved.

"So far, so good," Raxtus said. "Normally these entrances cannot be used except with permission from the sovereign. There are no guards posted at this one."

"Do I hear music?" Virgil asked.

"There appears to be a festival of some sort at the base of the slope," Raxtus said. "We might want to check it out, see what we can learn. There are satyrs among them. This could be your moment, Virgil."

The satyr cupped his hands and blew into them, then rubbed his shoulders. "I'm not very comfortable at parties, but I'm game to try."

"I see naiads and dryads," Raxtus said knowingly.

"Please don't taunt me," Virgil said. "I'm nervous enough. What if they ask me for a melody?"

"Can't you play the pipes?" Raxtus asked.

"Not all satyrs are photocopies of one another," Virgil said. "We have different strengths."

"You're an unfamiliar satyr," Raxtus said. "They will take interest in you. They may hand you an instrument and want a tune, especially since they are celebrating."

Virgil shook his head, staring at the ground. "This is a poor idea. I'm a bookworm. I'm a painter. I watch the stars. On a pipe? The best I can manage is 'Row, Row, Row Your Boat.'"

"Make jokes, turn cartwheels, get into a wrestle," Raxtus encouraged.

"You sound like my dad," Virgil said. "It came so easily to him."

"Can you do this?" Kendra asked. "Should we look for information another way?"

Virgil clenched his jaw. "This is a relatively safe way to gather some knowledge. I'll fake it as best I can. I know a few dance steps."

Kendra craned to peer beyond the boulders. "The last time I was here, there were fires. It looks like they've gone out. I don't see any smoke."

"Me neither," Raxtus confirmed.

"The Fairy Realm doesn't seem war-torn," Kendra said. "Satyrs and nymphs are partying? What's the deal?"

"Stay down," Raxtus cautioned. "You must not be seen. There does seem to be considerable merriment. We need reconnaissance. I'm too conspicuous to make inquiries, and Kendra is a mortal."

"I can do this," Virgil said, straightening. "I'm playing a role to gather research."

"There are plenty of trees around the clearing," Raxtus said. "I'll set us down in the grove. If nobody notices our approach, we'll hide while Virgil socializes."

"And if somebody notices you?" Virgil asked.

"We fly away until I lose them," Raxtus said. "There's no profit in waiting. Come on."

Kendra gave a nod, and Raxtus lifted her and Virgil into the air. As they swooped down the mountainside, Raxtus shielded them from view with his nearly invisible wings and body as best he could. He landed on soft heather at the edge of a stately grove of birches and poplars. Kendra ran into the undergrowth beneath the elegant trees, noticing how generously the foliage was laden with fragrant berries and blossoms, more like an extravagant garden than wildland.

Kendra crouched behind a shrub brightened by colorful flowers shaped like starbursts, and Raxtus hunkered down beside her, nearly undetectable. The lively piping and boisterous conversations were much louder. As Kendra shifted her position, she glimpsed a clearing through the trees where tall dryads clad in gossamer gowns danced gracefully with capering satyrs. Up a gentle slope from the dancing, a buffet table laden with rich food attracted considerable attention as well.

"Here goes nothing," Virgil muttered. He circled off to one side, then tromped noisily through the undergrowth over to the feast.

Kendra plucked a plump boysenberry from a slender limb and popped it in her mouth. It was perfectly ripe, juicy and sweet, so she gathered others.

A pair of human-sized fairies intercepted Virgil as he approached the celebration, ushering him over to a table. While talking to them, he stuffed himself with nuts. Then a dryad approached, and the fairies moved away.

While Virgil mingled, Kendra noticed some bell-shaped yellow berries above her. She reached for some after Raxtus affirmed that they were edible. The berries awakened hunger inside of Kendra, and she found herself savoring the aromas wafting over from the feast on the long table.

After some time, she saw Virgil theatrically juggling three pears while attempting a little jig. He almost lost control of them a few times, but, rushing around, managed to avoid dropping any—until a larger, hairier, more muscular satyr tackled him from behind. They tussled on the ground, rolling out of view.

"How rough do satyrs get?" Kendra whispered.

"Looks like acceptance to me," Raxtus said. "See, he's back on his feet."

Kendra relaxed as Virgil continued to mingle. Eventually she lost sight of the satyr, until Virgil showed up beside them again. He had a couple of leaves in his hair and grass stains on his chest.

"There you are," Kendra said. "I was starting to worry."

"I tried not to rush it," Virgil said.

"How did it go?" Kendra asked.

"Satyrs are roughnecks," Virgil said, wiping his lips on the back of his arm. "I got grass in my mouth. I hate that."

"Did you make some friends?" Kendra whispered.

"They wondered why nobody knew me," Virgil said. "I explained that I usually like to lie low, but the food smelled too good."

"What else?" Raxtus asked.

"Ronodin is in charge," Virgil said. "He ordered a fortnight of revelry to celebrate his coronation."

Kendra frowned. "I hate it when he's clever."

"The move earned him popularity with the satyrs and the nymphs," Virgil said.

"Is Ronodin at the palace?" Kendra asked.

"I'm not sure," Virgil said. "I didn't want to ask too

many questions. But it seems clear the fairies are overseeing this celebration."

"Ronodin directly controls the fairies?" Kendra asked.

"For as long as he wears the crown," Raxtus verified.

Kendra smiled at Virgil. "Did they try to get a song out of you?"

"I juggled instead," Virgil said. "Oh, I almost forgot." He held out a linen napkin to Kendra. "I smuggled you some hard-boiled eggs and a couple tarts. Figured you could use breakfast."

"That was so thoughtful," Kendra said, biting into one of the eggs. It felt good to taste something more substantial than berries.

*Kendra.* The word entered her mind as if spoken.

Her head whipped around. "Who said that?" she asked with a gasp.

"Said what?" Virgil whispered.

*Above you,* the male voice in her mind directed.

Looking up and to one side, she saw a large golden owl in a tree, staring down at her with a human face. The bland features wore a neutral expression, the eyes regarding her somberly.

*You're in your owl shape?* Kendra thought to him.

*We astrids went into hiding,* the gilded owl communicated. *We remain loyal to our king, not the queen's crown. Ronodin cannot track or influence us in this form. You must depart the Fairy Realm now or face capture.*

*What?* Kendra transmitted.

*Bracken sent me,* the voice informed her. *They are coming for you. If you do not flee the Fairy Realm immediately, you will be apprehended.*

*Bracken knows I'm here?* Kendra asked.

*More importantly, Ronodin knows you're here,* the astrid emphasized. *He felt you and the dragon enter, as did we. He has dispatched troops to capture you.*

Virgil stared at Kendra curiously. "Are you communicating with that astrid?" he whispered.

"Yes, just a second," Kendra whispered. *I need to find Bracken. Do you know where he is?*

*The son of our king is being held at the palace,* the astrid conveyed. *Ronodin presides there. And you will be taken there shortly unless you abscond.*

Kendra's mind raced. There was no time to plan. She had to rely on instinct. "Raxtus, you need to escape."

"Excuse me?" the dragon said.

"Ronodin knows we're here," Kendra said. "He has sent troops to apprehend us. You have to go."

"Shouldn't we all go?" Raxtus asked.

Kendra waved away the statement. "Virgil, yes. But I'm staying. They'll take me to Ronodin, and that's where I want to be."

"Kendra," Raxtus said reasonably, "why not live to fight another day? We'll get help and try again."

"What would we do?" Kendra asked. "How are we supposed to overpower Ronodin here? With him wearing the crown? My strongest allies are his prisoners. I'm staying. But you should go. Find Seth. Help him. Or find my cousins. Please. Before it's too late."

"I'm staying too," Virgil said, backing away. "I can blend in here, lie low, and then try to come help you."

"You're both crazy," Raxtus said.

*Here they come*, the astrid warned, taking flight.

"Go," Kendra insisted.

Virgil ran.

Warrior fairies dropped through the branches, clutching spears, bows, and slender swords. They wore light, snug armor and had the limber musculature of professional ballerinas. All were taller than Kendra and emitted light in darker hues than Kendra remembered being common. A fairy with Asian features landed near Virgil and clotheslined him with an outstretched arm, leaving him sprawled on the forest floor.

Barely visible, Raxtus sprang from hiding and crashed upward through branches on his way to the sky. A stern fairy with dark bobbed hair pointed her slightly curved sword in his direction. "Lenore, Faline, Minerva—after him."

Three fairies leaped into action, wings and armor flashing as they pursued the swift shimmer. After taking Kendra's bow, strong hands gripped both of her arms and forced her to face the commander.

"Not much fight in this one," sneered the fairy on her right.

"She's brimming with energy, though," noted the fairy on her left.

"Kendra Sorenson," greeted the coldly beautiful fairy with the dark bobbed hair. "You are now a prisoner of the Fairy Realm."

# CHAPTER TWELVE

# Stratos

Isn't there supposed to be a distracter spell protecting Titan Valley?" Seth asked, flying along a couple thousand feet above the corrugated blue of the Pacific Ocean. Up ahead, a rugged coastline awaited.

"Yeah, our attention should already be diverted from the island," Calvin said. "Something must have happened to the Giant Queen. Why else would their defenses be down?"

"Without the spell, will the rest of the world discover Titan Valley?" Seth asked. "Are New Zealanders about to notice their biggest island?"

"If they haven't drunk the milk, the high concentration of magical creatures at Titan Valley should still divert any casual attention."

"Good thing I have my walrus butter with me," Seth said. "I could be flying blind."

"At least you won't have to summon the leviathan to get inside the sanctuary," Calvin said.

"One less thing to worry about."

"The lack of defenses might mean the dragons are in control," Calvin said.

"It seemed like Celebrant was retreating when he left with us," Seth said.

"Possibly," Calvin said. "He might have left other dragons behind to mop up while he moved on to new conquests."

"We need to stay ready for anything," Seth acknowledged.

"How are your wings?" Calvin asked.

"Tired, but not exhausted," Seth said.

"We've come thousands of miles," Calvin said.

"My wings don't get fully depleted unless we're going at maximum speed," Seth said. "They know how to use the winds, even headwinds, to do some of the work."

"Don't headwinds push you in the wrong direction?"

"You can use them for lift, then trim your wings and dive. You can fly into headwinds at an angle, or sort of zigzag. I never knew there were so many textures and subtle currents in the sky. It's hard to explain, but the wings make it feel really natural if I rely on their instincts."

"It will feel good to stand on solid ground again," Calvin said.

"Especially if nothing attacks us."

The previous morning, Seth had flown over lush jungles, catching glimpses of primitive villages and ruined temples, as well as aerial views of modern cities. After sleeping for a few hours on a quiet beach in Vietnam, he had set out over the ocean, passing some large islands as the light failed. In darkness, he continued over empty expanses of the Pacific, with only the glow of the broken Wizenstone to guide him.

Now the sun was climbing toward noon, and as he landed atop a sea cliff, Seth realized that with these wings he could fly anywhere on Earth. He had made it from the Himalayas to New Zealand in a day and a half.

"Well done, Seth," Calvin cheered.

"I could have flown farther, though now that I'm on the ground, I feel ready to drop."

"Do you need to rest?"

"Not yet," Seth said. "We have a decision to make." He held out half of the Wizenstone, adjusting the direction until it glowed red. "That way will take us to the Giant Queen's crown." He swiveled his arm and the red glow went away, replaced by a rainbow shine. "Or else we can go toward the Ethershard."

"The two destinations no longer overlap," Calvin said.

"They haven't for a while," Seth said. "I've been using the red light to guide me, so we may be a little closer to the crown than the Ethershard. But really, we could head for either one first."

"The crown might be more heavily guarded," Calvin said.

"I worried the dragons might have swiped the crown," Seth said. "But it still seems to be here someplace. Which might mean the sky giants protected it. After the dragon attack, I expect the giants are taking extra precautions. But who knows?"

"Somebody typically wears a crown," Calvin said. "It isn't kept in storage. But the Ethershard could be in a more secure place, like a vault."

"After all that happened, either could be in a vault," Seth said. "All we know for sure is they're not being kept together. They're in two different directions."

Seth set the Unforgiving Blade aside and sat down. It felt good to lean back and watch the waves below roll in and crash against the angular rocks. The air smelled wet and salty, and the breeze ruffled the tall grass along the clifftops.

Calvin scrambled over to the brink of the cliff. "Don't get too cozy," the Tiny Hero reported. "We've got giants heading this way."

"Really?" Seth asked. "Already?"

"Three of them," Calvin said.

Seth scooted to the edge of the cliff. The shirtless, bare-footed giants were double-timing it up a steep trail from the shore. They had glaringly large hands and feet, and the tops of their heads were abnormally flat. Seth estimated they were about four times his height. All had weapons, and two also carried nets.

"Think those nets are meant for us?" Seth asked.

"Hard to fish from the top of a cliff," Calvin said. "They probably saw us fly in. It's a clear day."

Seth picked up the Unforgiving Blade. "At least I have wings." He placed Calvin in a pocket.

"Time to choose," Calvin said.

Holding out half of the Wizenstone, Seth pointed it in the red direction. Then he swiveled it to rainbow shine. "We don't have the facts we need. But since the Ethershard is the smallest piece, let's guess they're guarding it less than the larger one."

"Sounds reasonable," Calvin said.

Seth took flight, enjoying the rush of acceleration. "Hopefully the dragon attacks left the giants disorganized."

"Hopefully they rely on locks more than guards," Calvin replied.

"I like locks," Seth said. "I'm not sensing any undead. Sometimes I can get help from them. Or at least info."

"I can gather intelligence for you," Calvin said. "Compared to the giants, I'm microscopic."

"I may take you up on that," Seth said.

Fires no longer raged at Titan Valley, but huge swaths of the countryside had burned. Forests had been reduced to spent matchsticks, and fields had been scorched into life-less swiddens. The sky was mostly clear, with no sign of the Perennial Storm, but the scars from the dragon attack would clearly mar the landscape for years to come.

Holding to the course dictated by the rainbow shimmer of the Wizenstone, Seth soared over a colossal giantess resting on her side. She had a stocky build and wore the home-spun attire of a peasant. Seth gained altitude as he flew over her, hoping to stay out of reach in case she stood, but it was hard to judge just how high he needed to climb because, even lying down, she outmeasured some of the surrounding hills. But Seth's concerns proved unnecessary, for the immense woman did not stir.

"I guess the sleeping giants are back in dreamland," Seth said.

"Looks that way," Calvin said. "It was a shock to see them up and active as we flew away with Celebrant. I wonder how long before they look like mountains again?"

Seth glanced back at the slumbering giantess, trying to imagine how she would appear after enough dirt and foliage accumulated for her to be mistaken for a landform. "Do you think they will ever reawaken?"

"I expect they take their signals from the titan," Calvin said. "But who knows?"

Seth flew over a ruined village. The enormous, primitive huts had been charred almost beyond recognition. Seth noticed oversized, blackened skeletons splayed on the scorched earth. Not far beyond, Seth glided over the remnants of a stone bridge that had collapsed into a ravine.

He also crossed miles of wild country untouched by dragon fire. He got an eagle's view of wooded slopes, surging rivers, grassy valleys, and craggy mountains.

"At least the fires didn't spread everywhere," Seth said. "Based on our view from Beacon Hill, I thought the whole island might be torched by now."

"The ground was wet from the storm," Calvin said. "That must have helped. And maybe the sleeping giants took action to limit the spread."

"I'm glad a lot of the wilderness survived," Seth said. "It

would be hard to rebuild a sanctuary on top of cinders and charcoal."

An especially tall, sheer range of sawtooth mountains came into view up ahead. The closer Seth drew to the mountains, the more familiar they seemed. As he ascended in preparation to fly over them, a gap in the chain became visible, and he realized he was looking at Terastios, which he had spotted from Beacon Hill immediately before severing the harp strings.

The gigantic fortress had been replaced by a desolate crater, the remnants inside fused into tenebrous slag. Deformed stones were scattered for miles around, as if flung by a vast explosion. A squad of sky giants scoured the pulverized ruins—digging in the crater, sifting the ashes, overturning stones. At one edge of the site, a solitary giant added part of a rib cage to a grisly pit of seared bones, apparently a mass grave.

One giant pointed up at Seth, followed by others turning their attention skyward. As the sky giants scrambled for bows and slings, Seth veered away from them at maximum speed. Though several arrows took flight, none came close to him. His evasive action put him on a course diagonal to where he wanted to go, but Seth knew he could correct his trajectory later.

On the far side of the sawtooth range, Seth aimed the Wizenstone at his destination, and a gentle vibration accompanied the rainbow glow. Assuming that meant he was close, and not wanting to get spotted by more giants, Seth flew nearer to the ground. He promptly discovered that the trees on this side of the mountain were monumental in scale, making him feel like he had shrunk to the size of a swallow. The shrinking illusion was compounded when he saw a brown bear bigger than a semitruck.

"Where are we?" Seth asked.

"Everything is humongous," Calvin said. "Look at those flowers! And that crow! We must be in Stratos. Or what remains of it, after it fell to the ground."

Seth remembered the story he had heard from Isadore about the kingdom of the sky giants that used to float up in the atmosphere. When the Ethergem had been stolen, the kingdom had crashed at the edge of this island, with much of it lost to the sea.

After some time weaving among the gargantuan trunks, Seth rose up above the treetops. Beyond the forest, he saw gigantic farms, complete with titanic livestock and enormous barns. The Wizenstone was leading Seth directly toward the oversized town visible beyond the farms.

"Looks like the town survived the dragons," Seth said.

He flew low and fast over the fields, skimming the water in irrigation ditches, zooming along the deepest furrows, and staying beneath the height of any crops he encountered. He gave the farmhouses a wide berth and avoided roads. At one point, he passed a giant cow that reminded him of Viola back at Fablehaven.

Eventually, Seth landed beside a towering oak at the outskirts of the town and nestled into a fork between massive, gnarled roots. The Wizenstone was now steadily vibrating in his hand, the rainbow sparkles bright even in the daylight.

"I think we're close," Seth whispered. "But I can't have the giants spotting me and getting alarmed. This might be the right time for you to go see what you can learn."

Calvin saluted up at him. "I won't disappoint you."

"It will be a long way for you to go on foot," Seth said.

"Let me worry about that," Calvin said. "You need some rest. You're getting circles under your eyes."

Seth glanced at the oak looming above him. "Maybe I'll look for a spot where I can nest up in the branches. Take a nap."

"Do that. I got plenty of rest while you were flying. I'll return with word about the Ethershard."

Seth held out half of the Wizenstone, feeling it vibrate. "That is your heading."

"Got it," Calvin said, extending an arm to track the line Seth was showing him. "Get some sleep."

As Calvin took off at a run, Seth leaned back against the tree root. Was he really about to get some rest while somebody else shouldered a share of the hard work? He found his eyes drooping but forced himself to stand. Though it was quiet now, if he slept on the ground, he would be too vulnerable to giant critters.

Seth flew up until he found a thick limb that afforded him plenty of room to lie down without coming too close to an edge. The grooved bark was not terribly comfortable, but he barely had time to be bothered by it before he fell fast asleep.

# CHAPTER THIRTEEN

# Giants

"Gold this way," Hermo said, hustling along the empty street. "Plenty good food too."

"We've found enough gold," Tess said.

Knox rolled his eyes. "Can you ever find enough gold?"

"When you have more than you can carry," Tess said.

"You can always hide some," Doren said. "Come back for it later."

"How about when you have enough to cover your expenses?" Tess tried. "Like for the rest of your life?"

"That's hard to judge," Doren said. "Expenses increase as you upgrade your lifestyle. It's always prudent to set some aside in case of disasters. And satyrs live a long time."

It was the middle of the day, the street was empty of life, and no sounds carried from out of view. Occasionally Knox had caught a glimpse of somebody else—perhaps peering through a window, or breaking down a door, or hurrying across a street. Humburgh had been mostly deserted for over three days now. Knox and his companions explored a silent town, entering newly abandoned shops and residences.

"We can still find gold in more portable forms," Knox pointed out. "Coins, or jewelry. Treasure you can wear. And we have yet to find any magical weapons."

"Plenty of standard weapons, though," Doren said, twirling his trident.

"What do you know about wielding a trident?" Newel asked.

"It's a tournament town," Doren exclaimed. "The trident is a classic gladiator armament."

"Seems more like a merman weapon to me," Newel grumbled.

"What about your bow?" Doren scoffed. "A town full of weapons and you only chose a bow and arrows."

"You want me to fight giants up close?" Newel asked. "Get pounded into pulp?"

"A trident lets you poke from a distance," Doren countered.

"If we end up fighting giants, I'm pretty sure we all lose," Knox said.

"You still grabbed a sword and a helmet," Doren said.

Knox patted the sword sheathed at his side. "Mostly in case other looters bother us. I won't be going after any giants with it."

"I chose knives," Tess said. "And I hope to never use them."

"Hiding better to survive," Hermo stated. "Fighters die. We here now."

The hermit troll stopped in front of a rundown eatery with grimy windows. The battered signboard out front dubbed it The Dizzy Goblin.

"This place looks sketchy," Knox said.

"We better not be here for goblin food," Doren said. "Their taste buds work backwards."

"This fake," Hermo said. "You see."

The little troll opened the door. Low stools surrounded round, shabby tables. Several keys were missing from the dilapidated piano. Gauzy cobwebs clotted the high corners of the drab room.

"This place needs an exterminator," Newel said.

"These cobwebs predated the attack," Doren said. "The grime too."

"Hermo hasn't been wrong yet," Tess reminded everyone.

Hermo gave a pleased grunt. "This way." The hermit troll led them across the room and through a wallpapered door behind the piano into a cramped wooden hallway. He paused to face a dusty painting depicting a lush mountain valley complemented by harmonious Asian architecture. He simultaneously pressed two nailheads in a splintery wallboard beneath the painting, and a secret door swung open with a soft click. "Good place downstairs."

"I never doubted him," Doren said.

"How do you find these hideouts?" Newel asked. "Are you scouting while we sleep?"

"Trade secret," Hermo said, leading the way down a carpeted stairway with a wrought-iron banister. At the bottom they found a long, cozy room with a coffered ceiling. Big game trophies decorated the walls, the lifelike heads ferocious—a polar bear, a lion, a cape buffalo, a walrus, a tiger, and a hippopotamus. Several high-backed booths offered private dining, and a long marble bar presented the option to mingle.

A lone woman sat at the bar, middle-aged, with an air of sophistication that matched her surroundings. A tall, empty glass sat in front of her beside an empty plate.

"Yeah, I'm still here," the woman said. "We're closed, we don't serve kids, and nobody gets in without a reservation."

Newel made a point to peer around the vacant room. "You don't look very busy."

"That's what happens when we're closed," the woman said.

"Did you hear about the dragon attack?" Doren asked.

At this the woman laughed warmly. "You five are too much. I've never set eyes on such mismatched scalawags in all my days. Come inside, if you must. Welcome to Shangri-La, the finest taphouse in Humburgh."

"You work here?" Knox asked.

"I own the joint," the woman said. "I guess we can relax the rules since we have no witnesses."

"Are you alone down here?" Tess asked.

"I just finished a banana daquiri," the woman replied.

"This chapter in my life is over, but I'm not quite ready to turn the page. Any giants up top yet?"

"Not that we've seen," Newel said. "Supposedly the valley giants are coming. And others."

"They'll come, all right," the woman said, rising from her stool. "Won't be pretty when they do. Why are you waiting around?"

"We're looking for my cousin," Tess said.

"Why not?" the woman asked. "Can't say my reasons are any better. I'm Dagny."

Tess and the others gave their names.

"Are you going to try to skewer me with that trident?" Dagny asked.

"What?" Doren asked. "This? No, it's for self-defense."

"None of you are Humbuggle in disguise?" Dagny asked, searching their eyes.

"We're not in disguise," Tess said.

"I'd like to give that munchkin a piece of my mind," Dagny said. "We were counting on him! Some of us made lives here! I don't know any of you. New to town?"

"Pretty much," Knox said.

"Then how in the world did you find me?" Dagny asked.

"The troll is the mastermind," Newel said.

"Me find gold and food," Hermo said.

Dagny smiled. "Treasure hunters, are you? Help yourselves. I have more than I need of both."

"Is she serious?" Doren whispered to Newel.

"Absolutely," Dagny said. "Head around the bar into the kitchen. You'll find bread, cheese, cured meat, fruit, nuts—or you can fire up the grill if you don't mind cooking."

Hermo led Newel and Doren into the kitchen. Knox and Tess lingered by Dagny.

"How do a couple of mortal kids get mixed up with satyrs and a hermit troll?" Dagny asked.

"We got separated from the people who brought us here," Knox said.

"It's been an easy week to get separated," Dagny said. "Who brings kids to Humburgh?"

"We're fighting in the dragon war," Knox said.

"Hence the weapons," Dagny said, gesturing at his sword.

"Are you just going to stay here?" Tess asked.

"Not forever," Dagny said. "I'm not waiting for any cousins. My cousins are long gone."

"Did they die?" Tess asked.

"They flew away," Dagny said. "You're new to town, so none of you have heard the rumors that I'm a dragon."

"Wait, are you?" Tess asked.

Dagny stared at the bar, running a finger along the rim of her glass. "I was." She looked up at the kids. "I am."

"And you didn't leave with the others?" Knox asked.

Dagny gave a rueful smile. "I don't want to be a bloated, disgusting reptile. I've been living as a human in Humburgh for many years, and I immensely prefer the mortal lifestyle."

"Are you a wizard?" Tess asked.

"I wish," Dagny said. "This is my human avatar. The path to becoming a wizard has been lost."

"Dromadus did it," Tess said. "Not long ago, he became the wizard Andromadus."

"Dromadus?" Dagny asked. "Really? The former king?"

"He's a powerful wizard now," Knox confirmed.

Dagny shook her head. "Had I known he held that knowledge, I would have sought him out before his transformation. The way cannot be taught by a wizard. Only by another dragon."

"I heard stories of wizards teaching other dragons how to change," Knox said.

"If so, they taught them before their own transformations, or had the help of a dragon to share the knowledge. Archadius figured it out first, and he instructed others before he formalized the metamorphosis, back when he was Archanon."

"You don't have a collar," Tess said.

"I haven't been a slave for decades," Dagny said. "I escaped that bondage and began living like a free human. I opened Shangri-La many years ago, and I've run it ever since."

"When was the last time you changed into a dragon?" Knox asked.

"Before I was a slave," Dagny said. "Dragons think differently than people do. I don't want to risk the attractions my old form might hold if I revert to that shape. I don't want to give my lizard brain a chance to restructure my thinking. I have to protect my humanity."

Newel and Doren came back in bearing bread, cheese, sausage, lettuce, tomatoes, cuts of meat, smoked salmon, a jar of pickles, several types of mustard, and a few avocados. They piled the edibles on the bar.

"Sandwiches," Newel announced. "Dig in."

Doren approached Dagny. "The hermit troll is fiddling with your strongbox."

"Let him take what he wants," Dagny said. "If it doesn't go to him, the giants will seize it. Speaking of which, what is your plan for when the big fellas arrive?"

"We'll hide," Knox said. "Hermo will help us."

"Me best hider," the hermit troll said as he waddled out from the back room, both hands loaded with coins.

"We can lie low in town better than out on the plains," Newel said. "We have to wait for their cousin somewhere."

"We're eating well," Knox said. "We sleep in comfy beds."

"New ones every night," Doren added.

"It won't last," Dagny said. "You have a lot of faith in this cousin showing up. But he or she better hurry or you will all be running for your lives."

"His name is Seth," Knox said. "A giant called the Diviner told us to wait for him."

"The Diviner?" Dagny asked. "You really are a peculiar lot." She started slicing a loaf of bread.

Everyone except Dagny made sandwiches. Hermo went heavy on the sausages and smoked salmon and used the hottest mustard. Tess had cheese and avocado on hers. Knox opted for meat and cheese with honey mustard and ate a sausage on the side. The satyrs put everything on theirs.

Dagny disappeared into the back and returned with

flagons of water and apple cider. The diners drank appreciatively.

Hermo paused with a pickle halfway devoured and raised a stubby finger. "Hush," he ordered. Then he closed his eyes and sniffed the air. Quietly he whispered, "Giants coming."

"Are you sure?" Dagny whispered.

"Many outside," Hermo said. "Know we here. They smell you."

Dagny rushed over to a periscope on one side of the bar, the brass tube disappearing up into the ceiling. She looked into the eyepiece and swiveled the handles.

"The troll is right," Dagny said. "It's quite a squad." She pulled away from the eyepiece. "I have a secret way out."

"They know," Hermo said. "Somebody coming."

They heard the hidden door open and boots on the stairs. Dagny hefted a crossbow from behind the bar. A muscular troll clomped into view, taller than any of them. He had a head like a turtle, with a flat snout and tiny teeth, and his scaly body was quite muscular. He stopped when he saw the crossbow trained on him and raised one hand, waving a white handkerchief with the other.

"I'm unarmed," the troll said. "No use slaying the messenger."

"Could be just the thing to brighten my day," Dagny said, one eye shut, crossbow steady. "This taphouse is closed."

"I'm just a mouthpiece," the troll said. "This is your sole warning. The giants will burn you out if you don't come up."

"What giants?" Dagny asked.

"I represent Runder Khan of the valley giants," the troll said.

"The biggest clan," Dagny said. "What terms do they offer?"

"Come up now and you get a clean death," the troll said. "Harm me, or try to escape, and they will make it hurt."

"I have food and money," Dagny said.

"Humburgh is overflowing with food and money for the taking," the troll replied.

"Not food like mine," Dagny said. "Spicy pickled eggs, soursop tarts, beetle hash—"

"Beetle hash?" the troll interrupted, licking the lipless rim of his mouth.

"Why not tell the giants you only found corpses down here?" Dagny suggested.

"They can smell you're alive," the troll said. "Three humans and two satyrs. Nobody can smell a hermit troll."

Hermo gave a little salute.

Dagny looked at Knox and Tess. "What do you say?"

"I guess we head up," Knox said.

"Brave boy," Dagny said. "And right answer, by the way."

"You'll come?" the messenger troll asked.

"All but Hermo," Knox said. "Can you keep quiet about him?"

"Fine with me," the troll said. "Best leave your weapons."

Dagny nodded, setting down her crossbow. Knox

unstrapped his sword and placed it on the bar. The others followed suit.

Walking up the stairs behind the heavy-footed troll, Knox fingered the coin in his pocket. His other hand clutched the crown under his shirt. Might Dagny transform into a dragon and bail them out? Would she be willing? Could a dragon overpower a bunch of valley giants? How big were they?

They followed the troll through the shabby tavern and out to the street. At least twenty giants awaited. Knox stood barely taller than their knees. Smudged with grime, the dusty brutes wore skins and carried primitive weapons—clubs and axes fashioned from wood and stone. Most had slender braids in their long hair and beards.

A giant in a bronze helm stepped forward. His lightly dented helmet was the only piece of real armor in view.

"You came up good," the giant said, his words accented. "Runder grant you quick deaths."

"Wait, Runder Khan," Knox cried, holding up his coin. "We're giant friends."

Runder scowled. "You speak Jiganti?" His voice no longer had an accent.

"Yes," Knox said, though he was unaware he was speaking another language.

"That status is unusual," the giant said. "Show me the coin."

Stepping forward, Knox held up his hand as high as he could. Runder crouched forward, squinting speculatively.

"Where did you unearth such a token?" Runder asked. "Are you a grave robber?"

"It was given to me by one of the Kurut Oi," Knox said.

This caused murmuring among many of the giants. Runder straightened and scratched his beard. "What would one of the Kurut Oi see in a pipsqueak like you?"

"That's for him to know and you to find out," Knox said.

"Perhaps you are a giant friend," Runder conceded. "But the others are not."

"The others are my family and friends," Knox said, returning the coin to his pocket.

"I will spare you, in deference to the Kurut Oi," Runder said. "Your family and friends will serve as appetizers."

Knox glanced at Dagny. She wasn't turning into a dragon. Figuring it was up to him, Knox pulled out the crown and placed it on his head. He felt a mild tingle, but he did not transform into a ten-story giant, as he had hoped.

"You will not harm my friends," Knox said. "And you will start showing me the respect I deserve. Because I am your king."

# CHAPTER FOURTEEN

# Captured

The royal palace of the Fairy Realm seemed more like a miraculous accident of nature than a constructed edifice. The delicate towers could have grown like trees, the walls may well have erupted from the earth in response to tectonic forces, the networks of interior rooms and hallways might have been sculpted and polished by wind or water. The smooth contours of the palace had few sharp edges or corners—they flowed without interruption, lacking doors and gates.

The warrior fairies toted Kendra through a lofty, rounded window into labyrinthine passages. Kendra had freely walked similar halls as a guest of the Fairy Queen before coming to Titan Valley. Of all the potential dangers she had envisioned back then, Kendra had never imagined she would return to the palace as a prisoner. The Fairy Queen and her realm had always seemed untouchably safe, apart from the rest of the world.

The entourage of fairies flew aggressively through the passageways, clutching Kendra between them, zipping around bends and up or down the sloping ramps that substituted for stairs. At length they dodged around a freestanding screen and zoomed past a cluster of guards to deposit Kendra on a floor as smooth and glossy as a river stone.

Ronodin, clad in black, stood halfway across the room, preparing to throw a dart at a scarred dartboard hanging about ten paces away on the wall. The Fairy Queen's crown hung casually from his belt. Looking relaxed, Ronodin turned and gave Kendra a smug smile. "Well done," he said, addressing the fairies. "This one can be squirrelly. What about the dragon?"

The fairy with the dark bobbed hair spoke. "He eluded our pursuit."

Ronodin tossed a dart. It hit just outside the bull's-eye. "Any idea where he went?"

"Back through the portal to Obsidian Waste," the fairy reported.

Ronodin gave a little shrug. "No great loss. And the other companion?"

"A satyr," the fairy reported. "We have him in custody."

"I see," Ronodin said. He tossed another dart. This struck near the center of the bull's-eye. "Feed him to the sharks."

"No!" Kendra shouted.

Ronodin smirked and chuckled. "We don't have sharks.

Treat him as an honored prisoner for now. Leave us. Keep everyone out of earshot, but come quickly if I summon you."

The fairy put a fist over her chest and gave a swift little bow. Then she turned and flew out of the room with her companions.

Ronodin tossed a final dart. It almost completely missed the target, hitting just within the outer edge. "How can I have two great tosses, then miss so badly with the third? Why not a perfect throw every time?"

"Maybe you need more practice," Kendra said.

Ronodin placed a fist over his chest and gave a little bow. "Did you like the signature bow? I made that up. I want to give the fairies a more military edge."

"Where'd you find the cheap dartboard?" Kendra asked.

Ronodin strode to the dartboard and retrieved the darts. "I've had it for years. I practiced with these very darts in my humble apartment in Amsterdam, back when I was living lean. And now? The same target hangs in my fairyland palace." Ronodin paced away from the board and turned, a dart in his hand.

"Is this why you became Fairy King?" Kendra asked. "To throw darts?"

Ronodin shrugged. "I can also use them for self-defense. I'm going to let you in on a little secret. I'm not very popular here."

"Shocker," Kendra said.

Facing the dartboard, Ronodin looked at her from the corners of his eyes and gave a smirk. "Acceptance takes time. During this period of transition, it is wise to lie low."

He tossed a dart, and it landed a few inches directly below the bull's-eye.

"And to sponsor parties throughout the land?" Kendra asked.

"If life is good, few care who sits on the throne. Satyrs especially feel that way. Many of the nymphs too. The fairies would kill me if they could, but the crown prevents it. Their feelings will change as they acclimate to my leadership."

"It's a crown of light, Ronodin," Kendra said. "You're the dark unicorn. Is it comfortable? Do you really think this can last?"

Holding a dart ready, he turned to face her. "Ever since I was banished from the Fairy Realm, I knew one day this crown would be mine. Nobody would have predicted my success. It did not seem likely. And yet, here I am."

"Is this what you wanted all along?" Kendra asked.

"It's part of what I wanted," Ronodin said. "It has been a long-standing goal, one I chose to keep private. Talking about certain ambitions has a way of deflating them. You invite naysayers to plant doubts, and you give enemies a chance to undermine you."

"You stole the crown," Kendra said. "What next?"

"Now I do what any monarch does," Ronodin said. "I hold my throne, and I explore what I can accomplish with my kingdom. Plenty to keep me busy."

"Are you aware there is a war going on?" Kendra asked.

"Don't forget who you're with," Ronodin replied. "I

caused the war. I laid the logs out, added kindling, and applied a match to the tinder."

"And now you'll just hide out here?" Kendra asked.

"While my rivals destroy one another?" Ronodin asked. "I fail to see the downside."

"The dragons will destroy the world," Kendra said.

"They'll try," Ronodin said. "They are already wreaking havoc in the magical community. Upsetting the power dynamics. If Celebrant has his way, he will conquer all of humanity, massacre most of them, and keep a small sample on human sanctuaries, as pets."

"That's sick."

"It's payback. And it raises questions. What would a dragon war against the mortals look like? Will the humans even see dragons? Or will it look like violent acts of nature—whirlwinds and storms? If the dragons destroy the Sovereign Skull, then attack humanity with enough persistence, they could feasibly destroy the barrier between mortals and magic, allowing all to view their true forms. Can you imagine how humankind would respond? It has been a long time since dragons attacked mortals in force. How will dragons fare against human technology? Against machine guns and tanks, fighter jets and missiles? Against the atomic bomb? The battles will be fascinating."

"Millions would die," Kendra said. "Billions."

Balling his fists, Ronodin shivered theatrically. "I adore chaos." He flung two darts at once. One hit the board; the other clicked against the wall and fell to the floor.

"Being a true king is the opposite of chaos," Kendra said. "I can't think of anything more orderly."

Ronodin held up a finger in protest. "Unless you are the ruler of your enemy's kingdom. The captain's traditional job is to keep everything shipshape. But what happens if the captain deliberately runs the boat aground? Nobody inhabits a stronger position to promote chaos than a king."

"What exactly do you hope to accomplish?" Kendra asked.

Ronodin approached her. "You see, Kendra, this is why we need private conversations. So I can enjoy your audacious questions without needing to tap dance for bystanders. Why should I share goals that you would endeavor to obstruct? Why not maintain the element of surprise? But enough small talk. We both know what you really want to ask."

"Which is what?" Kendra asked.

Ronodin rolled his eyes. "We know why you came here. What you really want to know. You already saved him once."

Kendra was scared to ask. Ronodin seemed too happy to answer.

"He isn't dead," Ronodin said. "Is that what has your tongue tied?"

"Where is Bracken?" Kendra asked, relieved to hear he was alive.

"There we go!" Ronodin exclaimed. "My celebrated cousin. You two bested me in the Under Realm. I don't enjoy defeat, and I seldom face it, but I'm realistic enough to admit when I'm beaten. You two thwarted me because you had a surprise." He placed both hands on the crown. "This glittering piece of headgear! This talisman of fairydom! You shouldn't have had it, shouldn't have been allowed to bring it there, but somehow you did, and you triumphed. Why did you return it to the queen?"

"I had borrowed it," Kendra said. "It served its purpose."

"You could have done so much more with it," Ronodin said.

"Maybe," Kendra allowed.

"If you had kept it, I might not have it now."

"Enjoy it while it lasts," Kendra said.

Ronodin chuckled and nodded. "Here is what matters: I get a do-over. Bracken is imprisoned again. As before, you've come to his aid. But who has the crown this time?"

"You do," she said quietly.

"I have what?" Ronodin asked, playing dumb.

Kendra sighed. "You have the Fairy Queen's crown."

Ronodin pointed at her. "If I got cell service here, that would be my ringtone! You repeating that sentence."

"Stop gloating," Kendra said.

"I can't help smiling," Ronodin said. "You made it so easy. I would have handsomely paid a mercenary to deliver you to me. Raxtus did that for free. Did you really just show up here without a plan?"

"I have plenty of plans," Kendra said. "And you can't imagine what Seth is up to right now. I came here for Bracken."

"Is this helping him?" Ronodin asked.

"I guess that depends on you," Kendra said.

Ronodin blinked. "Do you expect to rely on my mercy?"

"There is no advantage to destroying me," Kendra said. "I'm fighting the dragons, and I'm asking for your help."

Ronodin shook his head. "Pathetic."

"You and I have a relationship," Kendra said. "Too much is happening. There is no time to beat you with force."

"You're right about that," Ronodin said. "Your power move has always been to get help from the Fairy Queen. Who is now my prisoner. I thought it felt good to have Bracken in a cage. That was nothing compared to watching him realize that I have his mother incarcerated. My know-it-all aunt. Sometimes life grants special moments for a person to truly relish."

"Can I try your darts?" Kendra asked.

"That depends on whether you plan to hurl them at me," Ronodin said.

"I won't," Kendra said.

"I seem to recall diverse fruit flying in my direction," Ronodin said.

"I promise," Kendra said.

Ronodin gestured toward the dartboard. Kendra retrieved the two from the target and one from the floor. She pocketed one of the darts, then paced away from the board, turned, and deliberately missed the dartboard with her first toss.

"New to darts?" Ronodin asked.

"Bad idea," Kendra said, flinging the other dart aside, hoping it looked like she had discarded both.

"Watch your temper," Ronodin said, amused.

"Why do you hate Bracken so much?" Kendra asked.

"He is finally getting a taste of what I dined on for years," Ronodin said. "Do you know how long I was an outcast, Kendra?"

"What happened?" Kendra asked.

"It's complicated," Ronodin muttered. "You'll get a different tale depending on who you ask. All I wanted was to be my own kind of unicorn. And that was too much."

"You went dark," Kendra said. "Did you think you could do that and still belong in a realm of light?"

"Who possesses the crown?"

"But do you really belong here?"

Ronodin straightened. "I guess that remains to be seen. If I don't fit the realm, why not make the realm fit me?"

"Good luck," Kendra said.

"I'm getting bored," Ronodin complained. "And that is saying a lot, considering how alone I have been. You want Bracken free?"

"What do you think?"

"Very well. Stay here as my consort. When you turn eighteen, we will be married."

Kendra felt thunderstruck. "Marry me?"

"I want Bracken to watch you choose me," Ronodin said. "That would gratify me enough to release him."

"No, Ronodin," Kendra said. "Ew. No."

"You liked me when we first met," Ronodin said with a charming smile.

"I did," Kendra said. "You stepped in when the cyclops

was bothering me. But then you kidnapped my brother and my boyfriend. And you helped Celebrant get free. You've hurt the people I love most and endangered everything I care about."

"Nobody is perfect," Ronodin said. "With the right woman in my life, who knows?"

"I'm sixteen," Kendra said.

"What is that supposed to mean to me? I'm a unicorn. I belong more to eternity than to time. Years hold little relevance to me. What is the difference between sixteen and six hundred? A few moments, as far as I'm concerned. A slightly longer blip."

"You're ancient," Kendra said.

Ronodin spread his arms wide. "I'm ageless. I have no age. I'm outside of time. There is no comparison between us that makes sense. I'm both younger and older than you."

"However old you are, I'll never be your girlfriend or your wife," Kendra said.

"Then Bracken stays where he is," Ronodin said. "And you are my newest prisoner. Tell me about the satyr. What's he like?"

"He's great," Kendra said. "Weirdly smart and studious for a satyr. Be nice to him."

"Isn't suspense delicious?" Ronodin asked. "An educated satyr . . . you keep strange company."

"Can I please see Bracken?" Kendra asked.

"Sorry, no," Ronodin said.

"Don't hold us here," Kendra said. "Let us meet our fate against the dragons."

Ronodin sighed. "I don't mind *you* fighting the dragons. The war has become lopsided in their favor, and I tend to root for the underdog. But I adore having Bracken as my prisoner. If you are willing to depart without him, I might be willing to negotiate your release, assuming we can arrive at agreeable conditions."

"If you want to give the dragons trouble, release Bracken as well," Kendra said. "We're short on allies."

Ronodin shook his head. "Whatever else happens, my cousin stays. Chin up. You're fairykind. You've left many of those perks on the table. Figure out how to use what you've got."

"I'm not leaving without Bracken," Kendra said.

"Never say never," Ronodin chided. "You could have done worse. You could have tried to fight me. I may not be merciful, but I've always preferred a deal to a duel. I know the perfect cellmate for you." He closed his eyes. "I just called my guards. It was nice to catch up. Enjoy your stay. And Kendra?"

"Yes?"

"Please leave behind that third dart."

# CHAPTER FIFTEEN

# Ethershard

W ake up!" a voice whispered loudly in Seth's ear.

Seth jerked, disoriented. He was lying beneath a starry sky, resting on a surface furrowed with unusual grooves, enfolded by wings that were a peculiar blend of feathery and metallic.

"Giants!" the voice continued.

Seth snapped to full alertness, hand going to the hilt of Vasilis. The Unforgiving Blade lay nearby, where he had left it. The Tiny Hero stood beside his ear.

"Are we in danger?" Seth whispered.

"Not yet," Calvin said. "You were sleeping heavily. If a giant owl had come along, you would have awakened in its beak."

Sitting up, Seth swept crust from the corners of his eyes. "You're back. What time is it?"

"Well after sundown," Calvin said. "It took longer than I expected."

"Seemed fast to me," Seth said.

"The distance wasn't so bad," Calvin said. "I whistled up a tern. Not the giant variety. They venture into giant land sometimes."

"Why are you so good at befriending birds?" Seth asked. "Are your pockets full of birdseed?"

"Haven't you guessed?" Calvin asked. "It's my knack. I was born with an affinity for woodland animals."

"Can you speak to them?" Seth asked.

"We don't have conversations," Calvin said. "All but the largest and most fierce respond to me. I can ask for favors, give simple instructions. The tern dropped me off on this branch."

"What did you find out?" Seth asked.

Calvin drew his little sword and swished it through the air. "Where would you imagine the giants keep the Ethershard?"

"An underground vault? The top of a giant tower?"

Calvin smirked. "It's on a raised platform in the middle of the town square."

"Seriously?" Seth asked. "Just out in the open?"

"Out in the open surrounded by giants," Calvin said. "The whole town protects it. Plus official guards."

"Tell me everything," Seth said.

"The shard itself rests in the middle of a cauldron of fire," Calvin said.

"A giant cauldron?"

"Yes, with magical flames. An everlasting fire that burns intensely hot."

"Putting out fires is a specialty," Seth said, flexing his fingers.

"Two iron statues stand near the cauldron," Calvin said. "I'd be shocked if they're not magical. And two giant guards are posted there as well. Massive sky giants."

"I can fly," Seth said. "If I cool the flames, I bet I can swoop in and out before they know what happened."

"They probably have other magical safeguards," Calvin cautioned. "The Ethershard can't be as vulnerable as it looks."

"The dragons just attacked," Seth said. "The sanctuary used to have more protections. There may never be a better time to do this."

"If we take our time, watch and listen for a few days, we can learn more about what obstacles await."

"The longer we wait, the more time they have to rebuild their defenses," Seth argued. "Besides, we have so much else to do and not enough time."

Calvin knelt and stabbed his sword down into the bark of the oak. "I will obey whatever commands you give."

"I think we should go now," Seth said. "Use the cover of darkness. Act before they have more time to recover."

Calvin arose. "Then that is our plan."

Seth picked up Calvin in one hand and the Unforgiving Blade in the other. After pocketing Calvin, Seth leaped from the oversized branch and dodged through limbs and leaves until he flew in the unobstructed night. The giant town up ahead still had lights in some of the windows, and streetlamps interrupted pockets of shadow. Seth took out half of the Wizenstone, and rainbow light glittered as he pointed it toward the town square, the semispherical stone buzzing eagerly.

"We're glowing like a firefly," Calvin scolded. "I know the way."

Seth returned the stone to a pocket and stayed on the heading the glow had suggested. He flew over enormous outlying farmhouses, veering around the smoke from the chimneys. A couple of dogs barked up at him. A wall encircled the town that was low compared to the giants, but huge for a regular human.

"Make for the belfry," Calvin suggested.

Seth altered his course slightly and soon landed on the window ledge of a bell tower that seemed high as a mountain and commanded a clear view of the square below. The public space was the brightest area in town, with plentiful freestanding streetlamps, and other torches and lanterns affixed to the surrounding businesses. Seth noticed the headquarters of the town watch, a barbershop, a general store, a cobbler, and a toy store with an adjoining confectionery.

On a raised platform at the center of the square, the fiery cauldron stood on clawed feet, the likeness of a grinning face etched into the bulging black surface. The flames crowning the cauldron were the brightest in the square, rippling with hints of every color in the rainbow. The iron statues flanking the platform had heads like vultures, and their hunched bodies bristled with blades and barbs. The grotesque duo looked more suited for a house of horrors than a city center. Three sky giants were positioned around the platform: one at attention, the other two leaning on their polearms. An empty cage big enough for a sky giant loomed to one side of the platform. A smaller, cubical cage hung suspended at the height of the giants' heads.

"Three giants?" Seth whispered, conscientiously using his power to shade walk.

"They added one," Calvin apologized.

"What's with the cages?" Seth asked.

"Beats me," Calvin said. "Maybe for public punishments?"

"Why the smaller one?" Seth asked.

"For pets?" Calvin guessed. "Or humans? There is a third one, much smaller. You could only see it if we were closer."

"How much smaller?" Seth asked.

"More on my scale," Calvin said.

"Nipsies originally stole the Ethergem," Seth said. "Maybe the tiny cage is to remind everyone. Are you sure the Ethershard is in the cauldron's fire?"

"You have to get close to see it," Calvin said. "I had a good look. It's in there."

"What if it's a phony?" Seth asked.

"It looked legitimate," Calvin said. "I guess I can't be sure. But it's a lot of trouble to protect a decoy."

Seth produced half of the Wizenstone. Cupping it to shield the light, he pointed it at the cauldron and felt it vibrate insistently. "Checks out."

"Are we really doing this tonight?" Calvin asked. "There could be other variables—unseen barriers, secret guardians."

"I don't see an advantage to waiting," Seth said.

"I can keep snooping," Calvin said. "The giants might be extra vigilant because of the recent dragon attack."

"They'll stay extra vigilant," Seth said. "But they'll get more prepared."

"We're doing this," Calvin muttered. "Right now?"

"The giants are going to hate us," Seth said. "Aside from the stone in the Giant Queen's crown, this is what remains of their precious Ethergem."

"We're going to be unpopular with a lot of powerful beings before your quest is through," Calvin said.

Seth nodded. "I'm already unpopular with the people who matter to me. Let's steal the bacon."

"Are you sure you can handle the flames?" Calvin asked. "I think they're enchanted."

"The hot coals in the crypt back at Crescent Lagoon were magical too," Seth said. "Only firewalkers were supposed to cross. I chilled the coals and wrapped myself in coldness. I'll try a mix like that. Do you want to wait up here? Just in case?"

"No," Calvin asserted. "I'm with you."

"We'll fly through it so fast, we'll hardly feel it," Seth said. "Hold on."

Seth leaped from the belfry and tucked his wings to fall fast and gain speed. As he adjusted his angle of descent and streaked toward the cauldron, he stopped focusing on shade walking and tried to douse the flames. He focused his power, but the fire in the cauldron felt slippery and unreceptive. Pushing hard, Seth summoned enough cold and darkness to extinguish the blaze, but as the frigid blast washed over the target, the fire burned uninterrupted.

Could the flames be an illusion? If so, the illusion included heat—he could sense it. The cauldron drew rapidly nearer. Seth changed tactics, cloaking himself in cold, the sudden chill bringing his senses to even sharper alertness. He readied himself to pour on the cold when he reached the fire and peered ahead, searching for the Ethershard within the colorful blaze.

One of the giant guards pointed at him as he passed them. They were too late unless he failed to snatch the Ethergem on his first pass. The flames came up fast, and he slowed a little, not wanting to fumble the grab. He could see the crystalline shard at the center of the fire, and he increased the cocoon of cold around himself as he entered the flames.

With a flash, the multihued fire vanished, and Seth tried to swerve before he rammed into a wall of iron bars at full speed. He almost succeeded in turning, but instead he struck the bars wings first, jolting his entire frame. Seth rebounded to the floor of a cage and rolled to a stop.

Stunned, his entire body smarting, Seth tried to make sense of what had happened. The cuboid cage had a solid floor and ceiling, with closely spaced bars on all sides. The cage was suspended in the air, and he could see the flaming cauldron down below. An alarm blared, and the giant guards pointed at Seth.

He was inside one of the cages he had viewed from the belfry.

Somehow the flames had teleported him into it!

Feeling a stripe of pain along his leg, Seth looked down and realized his thigh was cut and bleeding. The Unforgiving Blade was no longer in his hand. Only the hilt of the weapon was visible on the floor of the cage, the blade having cleaved through the metal.

He must have sliced himself with the blade when he crashed into the wall of the cage.

The wound would never heal.

And giants were rushing to apprehend him.

Seth picked up the Unforgiving Blade, slashed through the tops of the bars on one side of the cage, then made a low return stroke. Eight or nine of the bars tumbled away, leaving a large gap through which he flew.

Giants roared in anger as Seth soared straight up into the night as fast as he could, wings thrashing, the alarm blaring behind him. As lights came on around town, Seth raced toward the stars.

# CHAPTER SIXTEEN

# Giant King

Knox sat upon an improvised throne in Crossroads Plaza, basking in the light of several bonfires stoked by valley giants. A wooden stage had been repurposed as a dais, and a long table was brought, so that Knox sat side by side with Tess, the satyrs, and Dagny. Knox's throne looked built for an ogre, and it had been heaped with so many cushions that he was too high to properly eat from the table.

A bloody haunch of venison sat before him, leg attached down to the hoof, much of the hide still in place. The offering had been brought to him raw, and when he asked for it to be cooked, it was returned to him singed along one edge and partially dipped in ashes, but still disgustingly rare. Knox had cut off some slimy pieces and slipped them under the table, hoping not to offend his enormous attendants. The satyrs and Dagny had surreptitiously collected more suitable food and smuggled some to Knox and Tess, while they all did their best to ignore the undercooked deer parts and the spitted raccoons.

Knox was unsure of the hour, but suspected it was nearing midnight, when Runder came before the grandstand and raised both hands high. The revelry quieted as all eyes regarded the leader of the valley giants.

"Venerable king," Runder said, addressing Knox. "We trust you have enjoyed making merry with us in honor of your coronation."

Knox raised a mug, feeling small as he gazed up at Runder from his oversized chair. "I will never look at deer the same way again," he said.

"Giants have huge appetites," Runder said. "Never has it been so simple to feed one of our monarchs. You'll be interested to learn that the scuffling with the hill giants has ceased. After some persuasion from their superiors—" here a mighty cheer from his fellow valley giants interrupted Runder for a moment "—their representative, Spurlip Mawn, has arrived to vow his loyalty to you."

A giant more than a full head shorter than Runder hobbled forward, using a ladder as a crutch. He was bare chested, with numerous scrapes and bruises marring his torso. One eye was swollen shut under a bloated top lid.

"We hill giants are glad the crown survived," Spurlip Mawn said. "Though humans are inferior to us in every way, I see that the crown is on a human head, and for now you are the king of all giants."

"Does the boy have your allegiance?" Runder inquired.

"Aye," Spurlip Mawn said.

"Together with the allegiance of all hill giants?" Runder pressed.

"Aye," Spurlip Mawn repeated.

"Then why not kneel to demonstrate your fealty?" Runder asked.

"Kneel to a human?" Spurlip Mawn asked, pain in his voice.

"Kneel to the crown," Runder grumbled, one hand tightening into a fist.

Repositioning the ladder, the hill giant gingerly bent down to his knees. "Shall I grovel and kiss his feet?" Spurlip Mawn asked.

"Only if his majesty commands it," Runder said, extending a hand toward Knox.

"You can get up," Knox said, pleased to see the huge leader display such humility. "Thank you for your loyalty."

Spurlip Mawn used the ladder for leverage as he rose. "Am I free to go now?" he asked.

Runder kicked him hard in the rear end, which sent him stumbling. "Get out of here. And cause no more trouble, or we'll put an end to you."

"You're making fools of us," Spurlip Mawn complained.

"We must respect the value of our crown," Runder said. "Leave before your breath puts out the fires."

The hill giant hobbled away.

Facing Knox, Runder dropped to one knee. "I will also formally pledge my services to the crown, together with the loyalty of the valley giants."

"Thank you," Knox said.

Runder rose and spread his arms wide. "Midnight has come and gone, has it not?"

"It has!" affirmed a throaty voice.

"Meaning," Runder continued, "with your coronation feasted, and with pledges made, this hour marks the commencement of your first official day as king of all giants."

"So it does!" called another voice.

"According to tradition," Runder said, "a new king cannot be challenged for the crown until one moon cycle after his coronation."

"Such is the law," a hearty voice affirmed.

Runder held up a fist. "Therefore, I stake my claim to challenge you in twenty-eight days' time, when the moon returns to the same shape as tonight, for the crown and the title of king of all giants." The other giants yawped and cheered.

Knox looked to Newel, who shrugged, then over to Doren, who mouthed, "I don't understand much Jiganti."

"What say you of this challenge?" Runder asked. The giants grew silent, awaiting an answer.

Knox straightened in his seat. "I accept," he pronounced boldly.

The valley giants cheered with full-throated jubilation. Some beat on their chests or stomped their hefty feet.

"The king has spoken," Runder told the others. "A contest is ordained."

Newel leaned close to Knox. "What did you accept?"

"A challenge for the crown," Knox replied.

"Tonight?" Newel asked.

"In a month," Knox said. "A lunar cycle. Sounds like they can't do it sooner."

"This might have been his plan ever since you put on the crown," Doren said, leaning in from the other side. "Play along with a wimpy king, then challenge him for the throne."

"Wimpy?" Knox asked, offended.

"Compared to a giant?" Doren asked.

"Could you have turned down the contest?" Newel asked.

"Why would I?" Knox said. "I can take him."

"Do you think so?" Newel asked. "Take a good long look at him, and then go find a mirror."

"I think that crown is going to his head," Doren murmured.

"I have this under control," Knox said.

"I guess you bought some time," Newel said.

"Not just time," Doren said. "Nobody ever made me raccoon on a stick!"

"By the way," Newel said. "How is it you failed to mention having picked up the Giant Queen's crown?"

"A king has his secrets," Knox said.

"Where did you hide it?" Newel asked.

"Under my shirt, mostly," Knox said.

"We were searching for treasure," Doren said. "You never thought to mention your acquisition of the most valuable item at Titan Valley? It's worth more than the combined riches of Humburgh!"

"I was weighed down by the responsibility," Knox said. "I thought about getting rid of the crown. I didn't realize how natural the role would feel once I put it on."

"You picked the right time to use it," Newel said. "But I'm still not sure how we'll get out of this."

"It won't look great on our childcare résumé," Doren said. "While under our supervision, Knox became king of the giants and was then crushed to a pulp."

"Your majesty," Runder called, approaching the grandstand. "An admirer wishes to make your acquaintance."

The satyrs pulled away from Knox. "I will allow it," Knox said. "Another giant?"

"Someone on your scale," Runder said. "A powerful mystic known to my people. The wizard Isadore."

Runder stepped aside to reveal a slender, dark-haired woman in a stylish gown. She swept forward and gave a deep curtsy. "Felicitations, your majesty."

"Thank you," Knox said. He noticed she remained in a crouch with her head down. "You may rise."

Isadore straightened and smiled deferentially. "You are the first human to wear that crown. It suits you. Few could have predicted this development. I have cultivated relationships with the giants of Titan Valley over many years, and I would love to see you have a prosperous reign. Perhaps I could be of some assistance."

"A king does need advisers," Knox said.

"Who are your companions?" Isadore asked.

"This is Tess, Newel, Doren, and Dagny," Knox said.

Isadore arched an eyebrow. "I trust you know Dagny's true nature?"

"Yes," Knox said. "Why don't you join us for the rest of the feast?"

"I would be honored," Isadore said with another curtsy.

Knox waved her forward. Isadore ascended the grand-stand and Doren helped her move a chair to sit down opposite Knox, with her back to the giants, becoming the only person on that side of the table. She pointed a finger at each of the four corners of the grandstand, then twirled that finger in the air. Immediately the boisterous giants fell silent. Knox could still see the faces of the valley giants laughing and calling to one another, but no sound reached him.

"We deserve some privacy, don't you agree?" Isadore asked.

"The giants can't hear us?" Knox asked.

"And we can better hear one another," Isadore said.

"Watch out for the deer," Tess warned. "It's like the giants thought they were feeding tigers."

"I'm not squeamish about eating flesh tartare," Isadore said, making no move to eat anything.

"I see you're still in town, Isadore," Dagny greeted.

"Perhaps not much longer," Isadore said.

"She is a true wizard," Dagny informed the table. "A former dragon working for Humbuggle."

"None of us work for Humbuggle anymore," Isadore said. "He closed up the manor and departed. You didn't elect to join your kind, Dagny? I have long wondered why you embedded yourself among the commoners here." Isadore used a fork to take a tiny bite of deer meat.

"I sometimes suspected you might be Humbuggle in disguise," Dagny said.

"Sorry to disappoint," Isadore said, chewing daintily. "Where do the rest of you hail from?"

"Texas," Tess said.

"And his majesty?" Isadore asked.

"Best state in the world," Knox said.

"What about the satyrs?" Isadore said. "Not local, I presume?"

"Visiting with the kids, ma'am," Newel said, imitating a rural Texas accent.

"Charming," Isadore said. "The Giant Queen seemed fully in control of Titan Valley until you arrived on the scene. I expect the battle where you wrested it from her would have been impressive to behold."

"Let's just say it was a tough fight and I walked away with the prize," Knox asserted. He had used similar language when Runder had inquired. He wanted to make it sound like he had fought the Giant Queen fair and square without overtly lying.

"Was this before or after the dragons attacked?" Isadore pursued.

"It happened amidst the confusion," Knox said.

"I see," Isadore said, dabbing her lips with a napkin. "Revolutions do tend to occur during periods of upheaval. I wonder what the sky giants will have to say about it?"

"They may not yet know," Knox said.

"Word reached me swiftly," Isadore said. "Tidings like these travel on wings."

"There will be trouble from them," Dagny said.

"Runder already issued a challenge," Knox said. "Nobody can fight me before him."

Isadore smoothed an eyebrow. "That depends on whether the sky giants accept your coronation. If those scoundrels label your possession of the crown as an act of thievery, one of them could challenge you immediately."

"There goes our month," Doren muttered.

"I hate to agree with Isadore, but she may be right," Dagny said. "Your claim to the crown is tenuous at best. Unless you can retain it through combat, you will not wear the crown long."

"Whoever issues a challenge has to go through me," Knox said. "If it comes to it, the crown may have powers for me to draw upon."

"Possibly," Isadore said. "If you permit me to examine it, I could tell you more."

"Unwise," Dagny said.

"Certainly not here," Isadore agreed. "Behind closed doors."

Knox leaned forward to reply but was interrupted by a heavy thump on the stage that caused all heads to turn. Knox gaped in amazement as he recognized Seth, with golden wings, rising from a crouch just beyond the end of the table. Seth slipped a glowing stone into his pocket.

"Hey, cousin," Seth said. "Nice hat."

"Seth!" Tess cried. "You have wings!"

"You!" Isadore exclaimed, gripping the arms of her chair.

Seth held up a dark short sword. "Why is she here? She's bad news."

"Intruder!" Runder bellowed. "How did you access the royal dais?"

"He's family," Knox called. "He has my permission."

Runder gave a nod and turned away.

"Good to see you, Seth," Newel called. "Is your leg all right?"

"It's been better," Seth said.

"Nice entrance," Doren approved.

"He broke my veil of silence," Isadore said, rising from her seat.

"I'm going to break more than that unless you get out of here," Seth said.

"How do you know Isadore?" Knox asked.

"She tried to kill me and Merek," Seth said.

"Where is the Dragon Slayer?" Isadore asked, glancing around as she moved away from the table.

"Keeping an eye on things," Seth said. He looked to his cousin. "Trust me, you're better off without her."

"We were just meeting," Knox said.

Seth gave a weary nod, glancing at the crown. "We need to talk."

# CHAPTER SEVENTEEN

# Lizelle

Kendra found a shockingly beautiful woman waiting in her cell, dressed in a pale frock. She had ethereal white skin and a luminous face that seemed to have recently reached adulthood. Her silken hair hung long and straight, silver-white. Somehow her physique blended the lines of a fashion model with the athleticism of a track star.

The fairies escorting Kendra guided her forward through the opening into the cell. After the guards stepped back, the wall behind Kendra flowed together like liquid, leaving no seams to hint at a portal. The room lacked corners—the floor sloped into walls, which curved into the ceiling. Soft light radiated from all surfaces of the translucent enclosure.

"You must be Kendra," the young woman said.

"This is a prison cell?" Kendra asked, running a hand

along the smooth wall, which she found somewhat warm to the touch.

"We can't get out," the young woman said.

"Will we run out of air?" Kendra asked.

The young woman smiled disarmingly. "You won't suffocate. The walls allow oxygen to pass."

"Who are you?" Kendra asked. "Is this some trick of Ronodin's?"

The young woman raised her delicate eyebrows. "You are wise to expect deception. But I am a fellow captive. Do I not remind you of anyone?"

Only one possibility came to mind. "Are you a unicorn?" She was the same kind of perfect as Bracken.

"I'm related to someone you know," she said.

"Bracken? Are you his sister?"

"Which one?" the young woman asked.

"The warrior?" Kendra asked.

"Does Bracken speak of me so little that you cannot recall my name?"

"Bracken doesn't discuss his family much," Kendra said.

The young woman rolled her eyes and gave an exasperated sigh. "Lizelle. I am the former captain of the guard here at the palace."

"You used to command the fairies?" Kendra asked.

"The fairy soldiers, up until very recently," Lizelle said. "Don't blame them for their behavior. They must heed the crown. Nevertheless, it is especially frustrating to be detained by the same warriors I trained."

"Where is Bracken?" Kendra asked.

"Were you hoping to see him here?" Lizelle teased.

Kendra felt her face grow hot. "I'm worried about him."

"My brother put up a fight after Ronodin stole the crown," Lizelle said. "Bracken managed to rally the astrids, but in the end he was unwilling to harm the fairies under Ronodin's control, and he was captured. He's here at the palace, in one of the deepest cells."

"What about the other unicorns?" Kendra asked.

"Those who agreed to surrender were put out to pasture," Lizelle said. "They are tucked away in a far corner of the Fairy Realm, what has essentially become a unicorn preserve. The unicorns who resisted were captured and are now prisoners. I'm unsure about the fate of my mother. She has not passed out of this realm, yet none of us can reach her."

"How did Ronodin get the crown?" Kendra asked.

Lizelle looked at her with concern. "All in good time, Kendra. Why did you come here? That was brave and foolish. Bracken is furious."

"I heard Ronodin took control," Kendra said. "I wanted to help."

"You should have known you could not defeat him head-on," Lizelle said. "Not here, while he wears the crown."

"It may have been impulsive," Kendra said. "I hoped to help Ronodin see reason. The Fairy Queen has done so much for me. And Bracken . . ."

Lizelle grinned. "I'm used to Bracken drawing female attention."

Kendra wished she could shrink out of sight. "He's one of my best friends."

Lizelle nodded knowingly. "You're not wasting your time. By all signs, the feeling is mutual. But it will be difficult to aid him from this cell."

"Can you communicate with him?" Kendra asked.

"Only in brief bursts, and with great effort," Lizelle said. "Ronodin is attempting to shield his cell and mine from outside influences. Thankfully, the dark unicorn's nature runs contrary to the power of the crown. Despite his sophistication, Ronodin wields it clumsily."

"Let's hope he's not a quick learner," Kendra said.

"I think there is a ceiling to how far he can progress without yielding to the light," Lizelle said, "which would require undoing many of his actions."

"How did you know I was in the Fairy Realm?" Kendra asked.

*I sensed many of the conversations between Bracken and the astrids,* Lizelle communicated telepathically.

*Should we speak mentally?* Kendra asked.

"I am shielding our conversation," Lizelle said. "Ronodin is not adept enough to eavesdrop without my consent."

"Why would he put me in here with you?" Kendra asked.

"He must want you trained," Lizelle said.

"You can train me?"

"Have you agreed to help him with something?"

"No," Kendra said. "I asked for his help. I'm involved in the war against the dragons."

Lizelle nodded. "Interesting. He must want you to

become a more significant obstacle for the dragons. He probably intends to let you go."

"Do you think so?" Kendra asked.

"I see no other reason to let you consult with one of his greatest enemies," Lizelle said.

"Will you help me?" Kendra asked.

Lizelle held out a hand. "I can and I will, if you are a true friend to light. Will you let me search your mind?"

Staring at the proffered hand, Kendra hesitated. "How do I know this is safe?"

"Your fairykind status protects your mind from intrusion," Lizelle said. "You can grant access on whatever conditions you choose. For example, please grant me access on the condition that I am on your side, and only if my observations are to confirm you are an ally as well."

"And if you're not an ally?" Kendra asked.

"I won't be able to see anything," Lizelle said. "Nobody can force their way into your mind."

"Then I consent," Kendra said, taking Lizelle's hand.

Lizelle closed her eyes, and Kendra did likewise. Soothing feelings began to flow through her. Her body sagged. She wanted to lie down. Kendra was settling into a deeply relaxed state when Lizelle released her hand. The broken contact snapped Kendra back to alertness.

"You are clearly aligned with the light," Lizelle said. "I am happy to assist an earnest friend of my family."

"What can you teach me?" Kendra asked.

"I can see you have never been formally instructed regarding the nature and uses of your power," Lizelle said.

"You have learned a fair amount through trial and error. And there is much you do not yet understand."

"That sounds about right," Kendra said.

"I now comprehend why you shine so brightly," Lizelle said. "When Mother made you fairykind, she linked your power to one of our Source wells."

"I don't know what that means," Kendra said.

"What you call magic flows into your world from two primary fountainheads—light magic comes from the Source, dark magic from the Void. Both are portals to other planes of existence. Long ago, unknown forces cut off direct access to the Source. Only a handful of items bonded permanently to the Source provide ongoing access to its power. These items are Source wells. The Fairy Queen's crown is one. You are bonded to another."

"Which one?" Kendra asked.

"It is not my place to tell you," Lizelle said.

"Don't you draw from the Source?" Kendra asked. "You have light magic. And Bracken does too."

"All creatures who originate from the Source have their own light, their own magic," Lizelle said. "It is part of our nature, and, when spent, the power gradually replenishes. But Source wells can restore that power much more quickly and easily."

"That's why I can recharge magical items," Kendra said. "And why Raxtus shines brighter when I touch him."

"Because of your bond to a Source well, you have essentially become a Source well, like the crown, or the Everbloom."

"Can I run dry?" Kendra asked.

"Any well can run dry," Lizelle said. "But it would take extreme circumstances."

"Can my power help you?" Kendra asked.

"You could refresh me if I were spent," Lizelle said. "But more importantly, there are ways you could harness that power to help yourself."

"Why has nobody taught me yet?" Kendra asked.

"Why do we let birds force their own way out of the egg?" Lizelle responded. "Normally these abilities develop over time, to the extent that they should. But in times of extreme need, there can be value in helping them along."

"What can I do?" Kendra asked.

"You do not perceive the light you emanate," Lizelle said.

"I've heard that before," Kendra said. "I can't see it."

"But you can see in the dark," Lizelle said.

"Yes," Kendra replied.

"When you see in the dark, you are seeing by your own light, without perceiving the light itself. I can also see in the dark by my own light, and I can recognize my light, but I could see much farther by your light, if you stood near me."

"Is there an advantage to me being able to see my light?" Kendra asked.

"It might help you better understand the great power within you," Lizelle said. "But there would be a higher advantage if you could make your light visible to all, especially to beings of darkness. It could stun and repel them."

"Like when I had the Fairy Queen's crown in the Under

Realm," Kendra said. "How can I make my light visible to all?"

"I believe I can teach you," Lizelle said. "And I can set you on a path to develop other aspects of your gift. Now, you wanted to know how Ronodin gained my mother's crown."

"Yes," Kendra said.

Lizelle considered Kendra for a prolonged moment. "My mother trusted you with her crown, to rescue my brother. And you returned it. You came here despite grave danger in an attempt to help us. I have seen into your mind and have personally recognized that your good intentions are genuine. And so I will share with you a tale known to very few, even in our kingdom. You must promise never to repeat it."

"I promise," Kendra said.

"Not with allies," Lizelle said. "Not with your grandparents or your brother. This is my family's tale to tell."

"I understand," Kendra said.

Lizelle nodded. "Fair enough. I believe my mother and brother would approve. Probably my father too. First I will tell you how Ronodin acquired the crown. And then I will tell you why. After all you have risked and all you have done, you deserve to know."

"Thanks," Kendra said.

"I have not mentioned where my father is presently located," Lizelle said.

"True," Kendra replied. "Where is he?"

"None of us know, except that he left this realm," Lizelle said. "But we do know that he let Ronodin into our domain."

"I heard that," Kendra said.

Lizelle looked puzzled for a moment. "Oh, Father sent a fairy to you."

"Can you still see into my mind?" Kendra asked.

"No, but I remember what I saw," Lizelle said. "I have processed much of it, but not all. That information gives me hope."

"Why?" Kendra asked.

"Because if Father sent Gwendolyn to you, he was trying to make amends," Lizelle said. "The same is true of his actions to seal off access to Titan Valley. Perhaps he had reasons other than sabotage for granting Ronodin access to our realm, though it is hard to imagine what they might be."

"I can't think of any," Kendra said.

"Father attempted to warn us," Lizelle said. "He felt his presence in the Fairy Realm put us all at risk, that he had been tainted by his time in Zzyzx."

"He told me and Bracken something similar," Kendra said.

"We heard him without believing him," Lizelle said. "We thought he was being noble, trying to protect us from having to witness him diminished and recovering. None of us foresaw such a devastatingly treacherous act."

"Even with access to this realm, how did Ronodin get the crown?" Kendra asked.

"He came through with dragons," Lizelle said. "The attack force contained some of Celebrant's best, including Mephisto and Jeruwat. Many fairies and several unicorns perished. At least ten astrids as well. Ronodin stormed the palace like lightning and wrested the crown from Mother before Bracken or I could arrive. Many of our best warriors weren't present to defend her because they were with us, trying to expel the rest of the demons."

"Did the demons join Ronodin?" Kendra asked.

Lizelle shook her head. "No, he succeeded where we had failed. The demons departed peaceably after Ronodin took power."

"They must have owed him a favor," Kendra said.

"Or else it was part of a larger scheme," Lizelle said. "It hurt that I was not there to defend Mother. I don't know exactly how the transfer of power took place. The astrids guarding her were slain. Mother lost the crown to Ronodin without being banished or killed. Beyond that, I can only imagine."

"I'm sorry," Kendra said.

Lizelle tightened her jaw. "I have shared *how* Ronodin took the crown. You will have future dealings with my wayward cousin. He tends to hide his history. It is only right that you should know his past. Take my hand, and I shall endeavor to show you *why* he took the crown."

Kendra stepped forward and accepted Lizelle's hand . . .

# CHAPTER EIGHTEEN

# Vision

And she no longer stood in a cell.

Kendra observed two boys sword fighting with sticks in a field. One was blond, the other had dark hair, and they fenced much more adeptly than she would expect from youngsters. The battle ranged all over the meadow, the boys thrusting, parrying, slashing, leaping onto rocks, gaining and losing ground, pressing aggressive attacks, and defending as needed. They had trained stances and accomplished footwork. Though they clashed fiercely, neither gained a clear advantage.

"Ronodin and Bracken grew up together," Lizelle narrated. "Bracken was the youngest of my siblings, the only one born after Mother gained the crown. We were encouraged to use our human forms after that day, to make us more relatable to the fairies. Yorlin, Ronodin's father, died nobly in combat shortly after his only son was born. Since Yorlin was my father's brother, Ronodin was raised alongside us."

Kendra could recognize Bracken's and Ronodin's features in the two boys. After parrying a thrust, Ronodin grabbed Bracken's stick with his free hand and stabbed the blond boy in the chest.

"Unfair, cousin," Bracken protested. "If that had been a blade, you would have lost your fingers."

"But it wasn't a blade," Ronodin replied. "And now your mother has no son."

The scene changed. Older versions of Bracken and Ronodin now fought side by side against actual enemies, pristine white blades cleaving through trolls and demons. Powerful astrids supported the cousins, some flying, others on foot.

"Father commanded the armies of the Fairy Queen," the disembodied voice of Lizelle explained. "Bracken functioned as his assistant, the second in command, while Ronodin led the astrids. Ronodin distinguished himself for his prowess in battle and his acumen as a strategist."

"What did you do back then?" Kendra asked, as if interrupting a movie.

"My sisters and I were more involved with statecraft," Lizelle said. "We were trained to one day rule in Mother's stead. On occasion I lent my strength to skirmishes. Later, after Father fell, I replaced him as commander of the armies. I operated under authority from my mother until Ronodin usurped the throne and put my highest-ranking fairy in charge."

Kendra turned her attention back to the battle Lizelle was showing her. Bracken sidestepped the spear of an on-rushing troll, then lunged forward and cut him down with two precise slashes. Ronodin held off three demons at once until an astrid came to his aid, and Ronodin used the distraction to dispatch all three.

"Were you at this battle?" Kendra asked.

"I was not," Lizelle replied. "Nor are we there now."

"How can you show me what happened so vividly?" Kendra wondered.

"Unicorns can convey thoughts and memories," Lizelle said. "Ronodin used to share his mind with me, and Bracken still does."

Kendra winced as a glancing blow from a club knocked Bracken back a few paces.

"You need not worry," Lizelle said. "This happened in the past. Bracken survived."

Ronodin stabbed the club-wielding troll in the back.

"They make a good team," Kendra said.

"They were fearsome together," Lizelle said.

The scene changed. Ronodin sat trading stories with shepherds around a campfire. Kendra could not hear the conversation, but she saw high interest from all parties, the repartee interspersed with jokes and laughter.

"Ronodin seldom seemed content in the Fairy Realm," Lizelle said. "He frequently left our realm to interact with mortals. Learn their tales. Share their food."

"Is that bad?" Kendra asked.

"It can be . . . dangerous, over time," Lizelle said. "There is a reason the Fairy Realm stays isolated from humanity. Unicorns are eternal by nature; therefore, we hardly change while we interact with other eternal beings. Conversely, contact with mortals invites change. Especially prolonged contact. Even simple acts like eating mortal food draw us toward your temporal reality."

"Are the changes harmful?" Kendra asked.

"Not always," Lizelle said. "But Ronodin became fixated on the wrong things."

Kendra beheld Ronodin clad in courtly attire, interacting with other aristocratic unicorns and fairies in a throne room as glorious as a sunrise. Ronodin spoke animatedly, commanding attention. Those around him portrayed a spectrum of reactions ranging from fascination to discomfort.

"Unicorns are beings of purity," Lizelle explained. "Our virtue is the primary source of our power. But Ronodin began to see our purity as limiting. He argued that our spotlessness prohibited us from fully engaging with life. He believed that mortals had much to teach us about unexplored possibilities."

Kendra witnessed a smaller chamber, far from crowds. Ronodin looked dejected as he stood before the Fairy Queen and Fairy King. The Fairy Queen appeared to be scolding him.

"Mother warned Ronodin that only those unicorns who remained unsullied could dwell in the Fairy Realm. She stressed that these conditions were essential to keeping the Fairy Realm a paradise. Ronodin stopped publicly advocating his radical ideas, but he continued to nurture them in private and, if anything, increased the frequency of his excursions into mortality and even to darker realms."

Lightning flashed across a dark and tormented landscape. Leafless trees clung to life amidst contorted formations of stone. Black pools of tar emitted rancid fumes and fat, slow bubbles. Foul creatures slithered and scurried to take cover in scant gaps among misshapen crags.

"Long ago, the Demon King ruled the Unhallowed Province, similar to how the Fairy Queen ruled the Fairy Realm."

"Did the Unhallowed Province become the demon prison?" Kendra asked.

"No. The Unhallowed Province occupied a separate location and was mostly abandoned after the capture of the Demon King. The Unhallowed Province was where those with darkness in their hearts found fellowship."

In the scene, Ronodin now sat at a rickety table in a dim wine cellar beside an old man. The spindly guy stabbed his finger at a crumpled map and spoke with wide eyes and active hands.

"Ronodin became fascinated when he heard about the Rocheblot—an ancient mushroom deeply connected to the Void. One of the Demon King's prized possessions, it was an endless fountain of dark power."

"Like a Source well," Kendra said.

"The exact opposite," Lizelle agreed. "Dark instead of light. Ronodin decided that the Rocheblot would be the perfect trophy to give the Fairy King. The battle against the

Demon King had claimed Ronodin's father, and he knew that losing the Rocheblot would weaken Gorgrog."

Under an oily sky, Ronodin crept along the base of a dark chasm, the light of his white sword thinly illuminating the blackness around him. A rivulet of sludge oozed along the bottom of the chasm. Inky black frogs scurried to avoid the white radiance.

"Denizens of darkness could not enter the Fairy Realm," Lizelle said. "But the Unhallowed Province functioned differently. All were invited into the obscurity. Most unicorns could not visit the Unhallowed Province because the light they carried inside forbade it, yet Ronodin's light had already dimmed enough that he managed to cross the border."

Ronodin trudged into the mouth of a cave rimmed with dark lichen and drooping mushrooms with long, curly stems. The light of his blade dimmed to a faint sliver in a cloying press of blackness. The image reminded Kendra of the aggressive darkness in the presence of the Underking.

"From the depths of a pit within a forsaken cave, Ronodin recovered the Rocheblot and, after an exhausting journey, smuggled that unthinkable burden into the Fairy Realm."

Alone with the Fairy King, in a large, forested chamber beside a pristine pool, Ronodin unfolded a shroud to reveal a hideous fungus shaped like a putrid wheel of cheese with the center scooped out. The gap in the middle of the pulsating mushroom was so utterly dark it seemed a window into depths of night where stars had never shone. The Fairy King glared at the offering with a mix of perplexity and horror.

"Where did you find this abomination?" the Fairy King asked softly.

"In the Unhallowed Province," Ronodin said, barely containing his excitement. "It is called the Rocheblot."

"I know the name," the Fairy King said sadly.

"It belonged to the Demon King and contributed significantly to his power."

"Why would you bring this foulness here?" the Fairy King asked.

"As a gift for you," Ronodin said. "A trophy from the bleak territory of your foes. Keeping it weakens our enemies."

The Fairy King nodded. "I see the good intentions behind this misguided scheme. Did you wonder why such a precious treasure would be unguarded? Why you were able to take it without armies opposing you?"

"I used stealth rather than strength," Ronodin said.

"Your presence in that shadowed domain was as unmistakable as the dawn," the Fairy King said. "Our enemies must have let you take it. You brought something into this pristine realm they could not have forced here with their combined might. You stole property of the Demon King, giving him a valid grievance against us. Doing so has compromised the protections of our home. I fear what costs might be required to mend the breach."

Ronodin stiffened. "Let me repair the damage. What should I do?"

"Our best chance is if you return it swiftly," the Fairy King said. "Replace the Rocheblot exactly where you found it, and let me work out the discord with Gorgrog."

Ronodin furrowed his brow. "And let the demons win? We'll look like fools."

The Fairy King gestured at the Rocheblot. "I know you meant to help. There is no easy way to undo this mistake. Please, Ronodin, take this vile mushroom out of our realm and return it to their province."

Looking conflicted, Ronodin gave a slight bow. "I was trying to honor you."

"I am grateful for the attempt, son of my brother," the Fairy King said. "You must understand, until you return the Rocheblot, your life is forfeit. And our entire realm is made vulnerable."

"I will do as you say," Ronodin said, turning. "Should I stay away?"

"Let me resolve the matter with the Demon King before you return," the Fairy King said. "For all of our sakes."

Kendra watched Ronodin making his way across rough country, neither Fairy Realm nor Unhallowed Province. Ronodin climbed steep green mountains and hiked along stony ridges. He carried the enshrouded Rocheblot over one shoulder and used a tall golden halberd as a walking stick.

Lizelle resumed her narration. "On his way out of the Fairy Realm, Ronodin stole Eluxiter from the captain of the astrids. His illustrious polearm was one of the mightiest talismans in the Fairy Realm, sharing a direct connection to the Source. Ronodin needed the weapon for secret purposes of his own."

Kendra watched as Gorgrog, the Demon King, came striding across the Fairy Realm. He looked much as Kendra remembered him when they had fought outside of Zzyzx. Darkness gathered around the colossal humanoid, defying the brightness of the surrounding paradise. Wherever he stepped, vegetation withered and died. A thicket of contorted antlers forked up from a shaggy, bullish head. He carried a huge, elaborate sword, made jagged by numberless spikes and serrations. Corpses dragged across the desecrated ground behind him, affixed to his wide belt by black chains. A murky gem adorned his heavy crown.

The Fairy King marched away from the palace to meet the Demon King in a green field made splendid by wildflowers. Astrids joined the Fairy King on one side, stern-faced and bearing bright weapons. Lamassus, with the bodies of bulls and the heads of bearded men wearing tall hats, protected the opposite flank.

"You do not belong here, Gorgrog, king of demons," the Fairy King called.

"Nor do I enjoy the visit," the Demon King replied in a rich, rumbly voice with a sinister edge. He came to a halt. "And yet here I stand, for I have a grievance to settle."

"Speak your grievance," the Fairy King invited.

"One of your household trespassed in my kingdom and stole an object precious to me," the Demon King said.

"Speak his name," the Fairy King prompted.

"The unicorn Ronodin absconded with a mystical fungus known to some as the Rocheblot," the Demon King said. "I demand justice, or it is war between us, with your borders as vulnerable as our own."

"These were not my actions," the Fairy King proclaimed.

"Yet you seek to exact justice from me? Ronodin did not operate under my authority."

"And yet he is a member of your household and a leader of your forces," the Demon King said. "Deliver him to me with the fungus and I will be satisfied."

"Ronodin is not here," the Fairy King said. "I commanded him to return the Rocheblot to where he found it. Would that not remedy the injury?"

"All but the insult of the crime and the trespass," the Demon King said. "What assurance do I have the unicorn will do as you say?"

"I offer myself as collateral for my nephew," the Fairy King said.

At this an outcry arose from the astrids and the lamassus. Several astrids stepped forward volunteering to serve as collateral instead. The Fairy King waved away their protestations.

"I rule the demons, but you are not the sovereign here, lord of fairies," the Demon King replied. "I would prefer for the queen to remedy this lapse of justice."

"I speak for her on this matter," the Fairy King stated. "I am the defender of this land, and since I outrank Ronodin, I am more than sufficient collateral."

"So be it," the Demon King acknowledged. "If you come with me now, as collateral, I will free you and hold your kingdom under no further obligation after the Rocheblot is returned. But should Ronodin fail to make reparations, you are mine."

"The risk is too great!" the leader of the lamassus exclaimed.

"Send me instead, sire," the chief astrid insisted.

The Fairy King held up a hand for silence, his gaze fixed on Gorgrog. "I agree to your terms, king of plotters, provided that you and your allies vow not to interfere with Ronodin discharging his duty."

The Demon King gave a nod. "Neither myself nor any under my influence shall prevent Ronodin from returning the Rocheblot, under penalty of dissolving this arrangement."

"Done," the Fairy King said.

"We have an accord," the Demon King said, turning. "Come with me."

After signaling for his companions to stay behind, the Fairy King turned away from the shining palace and followed the Demon King along his trail of decay.

"The bargain was struck," Lizelle narrated. "Meanwhile, Ronodin was well on his way to fulfill his assignment from the king. Before entering the Unhallowed Province, he stopped at a familiar tavern for the night."

Ronodin was sitting at a bar sipping a drink when the spindly man from the wine cellar sidled up to him. "Hello, old friend," the man said. "I never expected to see you again, but chance is a fickle mistress. How is it you have come to this tavern tonight?"

Ronodin did not look away from his drink. "I'm on a grave errand."

"What urgency brings you to this part of the world?" the man asked quietly.

"I am returning that which you helped me procure," Ronodin muttered.

"Returning, did you say?" the man asked, astonished. "Removing the object may have been easy, but putting it back will not prove so simple. It was after I realized you were a unicorn that I knew you could claim such a dark prize. The denizens of the Unhallowed Province would have smiled upon your transgression. But they will resist the repentance."

"What do you mean?" Ronodin asked.

"Seek to replace what was taken, and the armies of darkness will oppose you. They will hedge up your way, block access to the cave. In their unholy province, outnumbered and outmaneuvered, you will fall, and they will steal what you are trying to return."

"I'm determined to succeed," Ronodin said.

"If you want success, destroy the item you took."

Ronodin shook his head. "That is grounds for a war. My people would suffer."

The spindly man shook his head. "Not if you disavow your people. Not if you renounce your kind and take sole responsibility. Under those conditions, the only plausible grievance would be with you. Instead of walking into a trap, you would deal a major blow to your foes. The price is that you would become an exile."

"The price is not the problem," Ronodin said. "I have a duty to perform."

"Have you access to a weapon of light?"

"I brought something to fight with, in case enemies tried to bar my way," Ronodin said.

"That's all it would take," the spindly man said. "Or maybe you could use your horns."

"Enough," Ronodin said. "I'm sure you mean to help, but this mission is mine to fulfill."

The spindly man raised his hands and moved away. "I mean to spare you suffering and humiliation. Inevitably, you must discharge your duty as you see fit. I wish you good fortune in your travels."

"Ronodin resisted deviating from the plan," Kendra said.

"In the moment, yes," Lizelle replied. "Some seeds, once planted, take time to germinate."

"The Demon King had promised not to oppose him," Kendra said. "The old man was lying."

"Ronodin broke his promise to the king," Lizelle replied. "He knew his orders, but the next day, after traveling to the edge of the Unhallowed Province, he turned aside. Ronodin didn't want to risk the shame of failing to return the Rocheblot. Instead, he thought he could penalize only himself for his error, and he expected to achieve a better outcome than the Fairy King had requested."

Near the top of a high slope beside the brooding sea, Ronodin dumped the Rocheblot from the shroud onto a stone altar surrounded by a semicircle of tall, crooked standing stones. With the fungus unveiled, the menhir darkened, and the unicorn horn in Ronodin's hand shone with a pearly radiance.

"I hereby renounce my kinship to the unicorns,"

Ronodin bellowed. "I disavow all connection to the Fairy Realm. I am a solitary rogue, operating on my own, and all consequences of this action are mine!"

Ronodin began to stab the mushroom with his horn. Instead of purifying the fungus, the horn became first gray, then black.

"In the last undisguised memories we have from Ronodin, we see him seek to destroy the Rocheblot with each of his three horns. Willfully blind to his connection to the rest of us, he seemed to believe he alone would be to blame. He would have been wrong even without the deal struck by the Fairy King, but of course the agreement made the consequences more dire."

Panting, weary, his three horns cast aside, Ronodin lifted the golden halberd Eluxiter and brought it down on the fungus. In that instant, everything went black.

"Eluxiter was destroyed, as was the Rocheblot," Lizelle narrated sadly. "Ronodin survived, though we understand he was grievously injured."

"What happened to the Fairy King?" Kendra whispered.

The blackness dispersed, the vision over. Lizelle released Kendra's hand, and she was back in the bare cell with the pale, translucent walls.

"Bound by the accord, Father was chained to the belt of the Demon King," Lizelle said. "Under orders from the Fairy Queen, the astrids tried to rescue him. After they failed, Mother stripped them of their power, and they all were confined to their owl shape. As you might imagine, Ronodin was banished from the Fairy Realm, though he never attempted to return until now. When Archadius captured and imprisoned the Demon King, Father went with his captor to Zzyzx. For most practical purposes, the demon prison became the new Unhallowed Province, and Father was trapped there until you and your brother rescued him."

"What a tragedy," Kendra said.

"Father paid an unthinkable price for Ronodin's mistake," Lizelle said. "And somehow Ronodin remains bitter against us."

"He must hate himself," Kendra said.

"I can't imagine what he thinks or feels," Lizelle said. "He decided he knew better than everyone. He fancied that he could betray the virtues that made him a unicorn without losing his way. His heart and mind are foreign to me."

"Bracken must have been devastated," Kendra said.

"Bracken was never the same," Lizelle said. "Neither was Mother. She dismissed all males from leadership positions. She closed her borders tighter than ever and quit all involvement in politics. She looked outside our borders to nurture and beautify, but remained aloof from conflict. The first time we sallied forth to battle since Father was taken captive was at Zzyzx."

"I had no idea," Kendra said.

"Now you do," Lizelle replied.

"And Ronodin still thinks he knows best," Kendra said.

Lizelle sighed. "Some things never change."

# CHAPTER NINETEEN

# Wounded

T his is a most curious wound," Dagny said.

Seth rested on a fancy dining-room table in a spacious, fifth-floor penthouse apartment adjoining Crossroads Plaza, his wounded leg extended before him. Dagny leaned over the injury, studying the slit along his outer thigh. Doren had escorted Tess to bed, but Newel and Knox lingered nearby. Isadore had hastily fled after Seth arrived.

"It's from the Unforgiving Blade," Seth said.

"The wound is neither deep nor wide," Dagny said. "It's a long, narrow slice, as if from the light touch of a keen edge, identical to the corresponding tear in your pants. I would usually apply some antiseptic and forget about it. But the edges of the slit are black, as if barely charred. How long did you say it has been bleeding like this?"

"A couple hours," Seth said. "I told you, the scratch will never heal."

"It is unusual that it hasn't begun to clot," Dagny said. "If what you say is true, and the wound never heals, you could slowly bleed out. Or it could get infected. But even if the skin never knits back together, I suspect we can halt the bleeding with pressure."

Knox leaned over the slice. "Weird," he said, peering through Dagny's magnifying glass. "The blackness along the edges is so even. Almost like a cattle brand."

"Sounds about right," Seth said with a sigh. "I have to keep moving, though. I have too much to do."

"I've dressed injuries for years," Dagny said. "I'll coat the slit with surgical glue. My own special recipe. It contains a powerful antiseptic, and it should fill any gap through which blood could escape."

"How long does the glue last?" Seth asked.

"For at least a few days—longer, if it stays wrapped," Dagny said. "I'll give you extra glue to apply as needed."

"How bad does it hurt?" Knox asked, poking just below the cut.

Seth winced a little. "You know the sharp pain when you first slice yourself?"

"Sure," Knox said.

"It's still the same," Seth said. "Hasn't faded at all."

Knox scrunched his face. "Will it stay like that for good?"

"That's how the Unforgiving Blade is advertised," Seth said. "The wounds never mend."

"How did it happen?" Knox asked.

"I was flying and I crashed," Seth said. "It was an accident."

"Why not sheath it?" Knox asked.

"No sheath can hold the blade," Seth said. "It's my burden to carry it."

"Why do you have another sword?" Knox asked.

Seth glanced at Dagny, then at Newel. "Can we trust her?"

"I think so," Newel said. "But fair warning—she's a dragon."

Seth started, scooting away from Dagny a little. "Really?"

"I don't blame you for being jumpy about dragons," Dagny said. "But maybe I should be the careful one. I can smell dragon blood on you."

"Celebrant imprisoned me at Soaring Cliffs," Seth said. "I fought my way free."

"Impressive," Dagny said. "I no longer sympathize with my kind. I prefer a human shape."

Seth turned and motioned Newel closer. "How long have you known her?"

"Since earlier today," Newel said. "She seems like a good egg."

Seth nodded. "How did you learn she was a dragon?"

"She told us," Knox said.

"Dumb move for a spy," Seth said.

"I'm no spy," Dagny said. "Just a woman with a colorful history and an excellent taphouse."

"My other sword is Vasilis," Seth said. "The Sword of Light and Darkness."

"You got it back?" Newel asked.

"Along with an assignment," Seth said.

"Two magic swords?" Knox asked. "Let me have one!"

Seth shook his head. "These swords make life complicated. I think you have enough on your hands with that crown. Where did you get it?"

Knox lowered his voice. "We were in her throne room when the dragons killed the Giant Queen. The crown fell off when Celebrant finished her. I grabbed it during our escape."

"Wasn't the crown huge?" Seth asked.

"It shrank when I touched it," Knox said.

"And you decided to wear it?" Seth asked.

"We were backed into a corner," Knox said. "The valley giants were going to kill us until I put on the crown."

"It really was an emergency," Newel confirmed. "And a surprise to the rest of us."

"The giants accepted you as their king?" Seth asked.

"For now," Knox said. "Runder, the leader of the valley giants, has already challenged me to a duel for the crown."

"When?"

"Next month," Knox said. "I have one moon cycle before the duel can take place."

"That's assuming the sky giants honor your claim to the crown," Dagny said. "They won't care what the valley giants think. If the sky giants label you a thief, they may crush you on the spot."

"Nobody has managed to crush me so far," Knox said.

Seth eyed the stone in the crown. "You seem confident. What's your plan?"

"Still working on it, cousin," Knox said. "What's yours?"

"I have a lot to do." Seth glanced at Dagny.

"I need to go make the surgical glue for your wound," Dagny said. "I'll run to Shangri-La for materials, then change your bandage when I return."

"All right," Seth said. "Thanks."

She hurried from the room.

"I think she was giving you space to talk," Knox said.

"Can you guys keep a secret?" Seth asked.

"For minutes at a time," Newel said.

Seth gave him a look. "This one is life and death."

"In that case, hours," Newel replied.

Seth chuckled and shook his head. "I guess I make jokes at inappropriate times too."

"Those are the most appropriate times," Newel said.

"The Singing Sisters have called in the favor I owe them," Seth said. "They sent Vasilis to me, which is how I escaped from the dungeons at Soaring Cliffs. I have to collect all of the fragments of the Ethergem."

"What's that?" Newel asked. "Sounds flashy."

"It's the power source that kept the kingdom of the sky giants in the air," Seth said. "The biggest piece was the Wizenstone. The smallest is the Ethershard, which I just failed to steal when I cut my leg. I also have to get the stones from the Dragon King's crown, the Demon King's crown, and the Giant Queen's crown."

"Wait, from my crown?" Knox asked.

"Just the stone," Seth said.

Knox gave an uncomfortable laugh. "Maybe when I'm done with it."

"What do you mean?" Seth asked.

"If I have a mangled crown, Runder won't acknowledge me as the Giant King," Knox said.

"Do you really want him to treat you like the Giant King?" Seth asked. "Why? So you can fight him?"

"I've defeated worse," Knox said, taking a step back from Seth. "Remember a certain demon named Remulon?"

"No," Seth said.

"He killed an underwater demon at Crescent Lagoon with Kendra's windbag," Newel said.

"And with a magic sword I could easily kill a giant," Knox said.

"Really?" Seth asked. "That's what you want? To hold on to the crown?"

"I'll lead the giants against the dragons," Knox said. "That won't happen without the right leader."

Seth looked at Newel. "Is this a joke?"

"I don't think so," Newel said.

"Knox, even if you win a duel, they'll challenge you again," Seth said.

"Not if I have the right magic sword," Knox replied.

Seth closed his eyes and rubbed them with one hand. "I should let you have the Unforgiving Blade just to teach you a lesson."

"At least I wouldn't cut myself with it," Knox said.

"You don't know what you're talking about," Seth said, trying not to lose his temper. "Keeping the crown would be the dumbest move you could make."

"Dumber than collecting pieces of a gem for the Singing Sisters?" Knox asked. "Aren't they witches? Why do they deserve something so powerful?"

"They'll kill me if I don't deliver the pieces," Seth said. "They told me we'll lose the dragon war if I don't."

"They'll tell you whatever it takes to make you obey," Knox said.

"They have always told me the truth," Seth said. "Patton trusted their advice."

"It's not always about you, Seth," Knox said. "Some of us have our own plans."

"What's your big plan?" Seth asked.

"I'm still working out the details. It's better than freeing the undead from the Blackwell and letting Celebrant conquer Wyrmroost."

Seth balled his hands into fists. Knox's words burrowed into his mind and painfully expanded, validating his worst suspicions about himself. His cousin was right. Seth had caused massive devastation. Why should anyone trust his judgment? He felt angry at his cousin for rubbing it in. He wanted to draw Vasilis and hack the stone out of the crown with no further argument, but he suppressed the urge.

"Knox isn't thinking clearly," Newel said, patting Seth's shoulder.

"Am I wrong?" Knox pressed.

Newel scratched the back of his head. "I'm no political

expert, but I'm pretty sure if you try to rule the giants, before long, one of them will be scraping you off the bottom of his boot."

"I'm no king, but I've messed up royally," Seth admitted. "I got Agad killed. Without my mistakes, the dragon war might never have started."

"And I'm supposed to give up one of our biggest advantages because some witches gave you orders?" Knox asked.

"Do you really think the giants will follow you?" Seth asked. "Honestly?"

"Not until I'm established," Knox said. "I'll have to claim the right by winning some duels."

Seth studied Knox. His cousin could be a jerk, but he had never seen him act suicidal. "It's the crown, isn't it?" Seth asked. "It's inflating your confidence. Sort of like a courage potion."

"I'm using common sense," Knox stressed. "This crown gives us a huge advantage. Finding it was a miracle. You aren't the only one who can save the day, Seth."

"Save the day?" Seth asked. "I thought we just covered that I started the war."

"I've heard about the cool stuff you've done," Knox said. "But your time is ending. Mine is just beginning."

"This is a side of you I haven't seen, Knox," Newel said, head cocked.

"I keep a lot hidden," Knox said. He tapped his temple with his forefinger. "I've got more going on in here than anyone suspects—ideas, plans, abilities. I let my enemies think they have me figured out, then I strike."

"Are we your enemies?" Seth asked hesitantly.

"I guess that's up to you," Knox said, folding his arms. "Supposedly I'm a friend to the giants. One of them gave me that title. But if they cross me, they'll learn how my enemies feel."

"How is that?" Newel asked.

"Shredded to bits," Knox said, his expression deadly serious.

"Knox," Seth said. "I have a really hard mission ahead. Since you already have the Giant Queen's crown, getting that stone should be the easiest part."

"It was the Giant Queen's crown," Knox corrected. "Past tense. Now it's King Knox's crown. If you want a shot at it, get in line."

"Be careful," Seth said. "Don't let the crown control you."

Knox laughed defiantly. "I don't hear the crown saying anything. You're the one trying to control me, trying to ruin our best advantage. How will you get the Dragon King's crown without winning the dragon war first? And isn't the Demon King locked away in a prison? Go get those before you come after me."

"I'll get what I need one step at a time," Seth said.

"Take step one somewhere else," Knox said. "Or you're going to have me to deal with. And a lot of angry giants. You think they're mad now? Try chopping up their crown! They'll hunt you across the world."

Knox lunged forward, grabbed the Unforgiving Blade off the table, and sprang back, pointing the weapon at Seth. He had a wild look in his eyes.

"What are you doing?" Seth cried.

"Keeping things even," Knox said. "Wouldn't want the guy with two magic swords attacking the guy with none."

"Knox, the fact that you can even hold that sword is a bad sign," Seth warned. "It means you're turning dark."

"You would know," Knox said. His eyes lingered on the sleek, dark blade. "It's about time I had a kingly weapon."

Seth could see Newel sneaking up behind Knox, but he kept his eyes on his cousin to avoid giving the satyr away.

"Knox, your goal should be to escape Titan Valley alive," Seth said. "Leave the crown behind. You're grabbing a tiger by the tail."

"Where would I leave it?" Knox asked. "Let me guess—with you?"

"Maybe you're right," Seth said, trying to calm Knox. "Maybe you are the best custodian for the crown and all of the most dangerous—"

Newel made a grab for Knox, who sensed the motion and whipped around, the tip of the Unforgiving Blade dragging across the satyr's arm and part of his chest. Stumbling back, Newel gave a muffled cry through gritted teeth and fell to the floor.

"What did you do?" Seth shouted, rolling off the table to his feet and drawing Vasilis. The blade shined a furious red.

"He attacked me," Knox said, eyes wide, leveling the Unforgiving Blade at Seth.

"He was trying to help you," Seth said. "Are you all right, Newel?"

"I'm not sure," Newel replied, his voice strained.

"He took a risk," Knox said.

"You stole my sword," Seth said, walking toward his cousin, Vasilis magnifying his anger. "Within ten seconds you slashed Newel with it. That wound will never heal."

Knox looked frightened. "Stay back, Seth." He held the Unforgiving Blade away from himself, the tip aimed at his cousin.

"What is going on?" Doren cried, entering the room.

"Stay back, Doren," Seth warned. "Knox cut Newel with the Unforgiving Blade."

"They're ganging up on me," Knox said. "They want my crown!"

"Nobody wants your crown," Doren said. "Do they?"

"I just need the stone from it," Seth said.

"How about we put the swords away?" Doren suggested. "We're in enough trouble without maiming each other."

"Yeah, Knox," Seth said. "Put the sword away."

"I might as well hand over the crown if I do," Knox said.

"Might as well," Seth agreed.

"I'm leaving," Knox said, moving toward the door. "I'm going to get my people to protect me."

"Your people?" Seth mocked. "The giants want you dead as soon as possible."

"At least they're not trying to take what's mine," Knox said, keeping his sword aimed at Seth as he stepped into the doorway.

"What do you think that challenge was?" Seth asked.

"They are going to take that crown one way or another. And you are not leaving with my sword."

"We were doing fine until you showed up," Knox accused.

"You were about to make friends with Isadore," Seth said, "who tried to kill me and Merek because she wanted that blade you're holding."

"Knox, drop the sword," Newel said from the floor.

Seth lowered his sword to his side. "Are you going to kill all of us, Knox?"

Knox looked uncertainly at Newel. "I didn't want to hurt anyone."

"Why not take the crown off your head and see if you think more clearly?" Seth invited.

"You'd like that," Knox said. "One step closer to you taking it."

Seth took a step away. "Just try taking it off. Not handing it over."

Knox reached his free hand toward the crown, then stopped. "This sword cuts through anything?" Knox asked.

"So far," Seth said.

"Will it cut through Vasilis?" Knox asked, lowering his free hand to his side.

"Want to find out?" Seth asked, raising his sword. Vasilis tugged him forward. Did that mean Vasilis could survive a clash with the dark blade? Or did the sword just always want a fight? Seth knew that if he lost Vasilis, his assignment from the Singing Sisters might become impossible. But he couldn't let Knox have the Unforgiving Blade!

"Seth, don't," Doren cautioned.

"Get Newel out of here, Doren," Seth said. "Stay clear."

"You don't want to do this, Seth," Doren said.

"The crown is getting hold of him," Seth said. "It has some kind of power that makes him overconfident and greedy."

"I'm out of here," Knox said, stepping through the doorway.

"I have wings, idiot," Seth replied. "You can't run from me. Either finish this here or I'll hunt you down."

Knox came back into the room. "Help Newel," he yelled. "I didn't mean to hurt him."

"I've got this," Seth assured Doren.

Doren crossed to Newel and carefully hoisted him to his feet. Blood trickled down his arm and reddened much of his torso. Leaning on Doren, Newel exited the room.

"Do you see what you did?" Seth asked. "That will never heal. You don't have to keep going in the wrong direction."

"Take notes, Seth," Knox said. "If you don't leave me alone, you're next."

"What?" Seth asked. "You're going to kill me over the crown?"

"You'll kill yourself trying to take it," Knox replied. "Leave me alone. Fly back to where you came from."

"Set down my sword," Seth said.

"This isn't your sword," Knox said. "You found it or stole it and probably killed somebody for it."

Seth spread his golden wings wide. "Final warning."

"All you've got are warnings," Knox said. "Your wings

look lame. Come over here and I'll chop them off and throw them in the—"

Folding his wings, trying not to get lost in his rage, Seth charged his cousin. Lashing out with Vasilis, he knocked the Unforgiving Blade from Knox's grasp with a single strike. The dark blade flew sideways, taking off a table leg and cutting through the floor, leaving only the hilt visible, pointing upward.

Seth stopped with the tip of Vasilis inches from Knox's chest. The crimson glare lit their faces with devilish hues.

"Guess we found something the Unforgiving Blade can't cut," Seth said.

"Are you going to kill me?" Knox asked, voice quavering.

"You're an amazing swordsman," Seth scoffed. "I don't see how any giant found the courage to challenge you."

"I'll never give you the crown," Knox said.

"Don't give it to me yet," Seth said. "Just take it off."

"No way."

"Humor me," Seth said. "You can keep holding it."

"You'll have to stab me first," Knox said.

"I want to," Seth said. "But it might be more fun to change you into one of the undead."

Knox blanched. "You can't do that."

Seth cocked his head. "Can't I?"

"You're a maniac," Knox said.

"I could cut you to pieces right now," Seth said. "I could rip that ridiculous crown off your stupid head, but I'm worried stealing it from you might fry your brain. What's so hard about taking it off? Ask yourself that."

Knox furrowed his brow. "It does seem hard, Seth. It really does."

"The crown is like a parasite wanting to stay hooked to you," Seth said.

Knox groaned. "You're tricking me."

"It's tricking you," Seth replied. "You stole my sword and slashed my friend. If I was your enemy, we wouldn't be talking."

Knox shuddered. "How do you know taking off the crown will change anything?"

"I'm guessing," Seth said. "I'm hoping."

Knox raised his hands to both sides of the crown. "This feels impossible."

"Doesn't that tell you something?" Seth asked.

Knox gave a nod.

"What would a Texan do?" Seth asked.

Swallowing hard, Knox squinted his eyes shut and lifted the crown. He opened his eyes, blinking several times.

"Oh, no," Knox said, staring at Seth with a frightened gaze.

"I know the feeling," Seth said, lowering his sword.

"What have I done?" Knox asked.

"You took off the crown," Seth said. "That was brave."

"What was I thinking?" Knox tossed the crown to the floor. "Take it. Burn it. Do whatever you want."

"I just need the stone," Seth said, retrieving the crown. "Let's go check on Newel."

# CHAPTER TWENTY

# Radiance

"Good, Kendra," Lizelle said. "Look inside. Feel around. Find the light."

Sitting cross-legged on the lukewarm floor of the cell, eyes closed, Kendra breathed deep and slow. She tried to search within herself the way Lizelle had described—just as she had searched before she slept, and again a few hours ago.

Kendra opened her eyes. "I feel calm. I feel present. But I can't find what you describe."

"You often draw on your power," Lizelle said. "Every time you understand or speak a fairy language. It happens when you see in the dark. And when you transmit magical energy."

"Those things feel automatic," Kendra said.

"You will achieve new results as you learn to consciously access your power," Lizelle said. "The energy within you is integrated into your essence. You routinely draw from it. You just need to make the process more deliberate."

"I'm trying, Lizelle," Kendra said. "If I understood how to find my power, I would. It's like you're asking me to flex a muscle I'm not aware I have."

"You use this muscle all the time," Lizelle said.

"I fall asleep all the time," Kendra said, "but I can't do it on command."

"Not a bad analogy," Lizelle said. "You understand certain conditions that enable sleep to happen, but you have not yet achieved mastery over the process."

"I'm exhausted," Kendra said. "I don't know how else to try. I'm willing to keep making regular attempts. Hopefully I'll eventually have a breakthrough."

"Kendra, I wanted to lead you to discover some of these connections for yourself," Lizelle said. "Development tends to progress more evenly that way. But since this is an emergency, I can help you more directly, if you wish."

"Is it risky?" Kendra asked.

"A little," Lizelle said. "You will not be ready to handle all the possibilities this adjustment will make available. Discipline will be required to exercise the proper restraint. But it's also risky to leave your powers undeveloped considering the extreme threats you must face."

"I want the help," Kendra said.

Lizelle came and sat in front of Kendra. "Take my hands."

Kendra complied.

"Close your eyes," Lizelle said. "I want you to glimpse yourself as I see you."

Kendra shut her eyes and immediately beheld a young woman of extreme radiance, light pouring from her so brilliantly that it obscured her features. It took Kendra a moment to realize that she was looking at herself.

"That is how you appear if I don't make a special effort to offset the light," Lizelle said.

Kendra saw the radiant personage come into clear focus. Her duplicate remained luminous, but her features were now discernible.

"To see you clearly, I must exert considerable effort to filter your radiance," Lizelle said. "Only beings sensitive to magical energy see your brilliance. You have the potential to convert this energy into physical light, which would blind most mortals or beings of darkness."

Kendra saw her light become more intense than ever, and she closed her eyes against the dazzling glare. "That's too bright."

"It can't hurt your eyes, because you're only seeing this with your mind," Lizelle said. "Your physical eyes have been closed all along. Right now, you're closing your mind's eye."

Kendra peeked at the effulgence, but then closed her mind's eye again. "Whatever eyes I'm using, it's uncomfortable. I recently blinded a friend of mine with extreme brightness." Kendra wished she could know how Vanessa was faring.

"Then you know to be careful," Lizelle replied. "Pay attention as I demonstrate where this light originates."

The vision of herself ended, and Kendra became aware of her physical body, seated, eyes closed, holding Lizelle's hands. She saw nothing but suddenly felt a blazing source of power inside the center of her chest.

"Now do you feel it?" Lizelle asked.

"Are you doing that?"

"I'm highlighting what is already there. You're overflowing with magical energy all the time. You haven't seen your light, but you've seen by your light all along. You were benefiting from your own reservoir of magical energy without recognizing it."

"It's obvious now," Kendra said.

"Draw on the energy to shine bright," Lizelle said.

"How?"

"May I show you?"

"Yes."

"Like this." Kendra felt her power engage, and, even with her eyes closed, she could sense the sudden radiance in the room. She slit her eyes open a little and then closed them against the painful brilliance.

"Wow," Kendra said.

Her connection to the power broke and the light extinguished. "Now you do it," Lizelle encouraged.

Kendra connected to her power in the same way and the light returned.

"Good," Lizelle said. "You're a quick study. You can push to make it brighter. Keep your eyes closed, though."

Kendra drew more heavily from her power and felt the brightness intensify. "Can I blind myself?"

"In time, you may learn to transfigure your eyes so they can endure the brilliance," Lizelle said. "Until then, yes, it is possible to blind yourself. And you can blind your friends, too. Shine with caution."

"I'm scared to use this ability," Kendra said.

"Some hesitation is probably wise."

"Can I focus the light in a certain direction?"

"With time and practice, yes," Lizelle said.

"Can you show me?" Kendra asked.

"I don't know how," Lizelle said. "I showed you how to find your power and connect to it. Beaming light is a basic function. But by accessing your power in a similar way, you could eventually learn to turn a blade of grass into a sword, a leaf into a shield, or a twig into a spear."

"Really?"

"Not just that. You could also grant dumb animals the power of speech. Animate golems. Bestow wings. Create pocket dimensions. The possibilities are endless, though it will take time for your abilities to develop."

Lizelle released Kendra's hands.

"I still feel the power inside of me," Kendra said.

"But you can't see your own light," Lizelle replied.

"Why is that?" Kendra asked.

"You will see more as you gain deeper understanding of the light," Lizelle said. "Until you have greater mastery over your vision, seeing less is for the best."

"What should I practice?" Kendra asked.

"Use your power to generate physical light," Lizelle said.

"Try to control the amount of light and to direct where and how it shines."

"Is there a risk of blinding you?" Kendra asked.

"Me? No. Yourself? Definitely. Practice with your eyes closed until you gain greater control."

Kendra spent the next hour experimenting as Lizelle had described. She found it easy to produce a brilliant shine, but harder to emit a more measured quantity of light. It was even more difficult to emit light only from her hand. Once she called on her power to produce light, it tended to flood out in all directions.

She had managed to focus a beam of light directly ahead of her when Lizelle issued a warning: "We're about to have visitors."

A moment after Kendra extinguished her light, a wall of the cell flowed open like liquid, leaving an oval portal when the rippling ceased. To her surprise, Virgil entered, looking relieved when he saw her.

"Hello, Kendra," the satyr said with a little wave.

"Are you all right?" Kendra asked.

"I'm unharmed," he said with a small smile. "Who is your cellmate?"

"A unicorn named Lizelle," Kendra explained. He gave a little bow.

"Are you joining us?" Lizelle asked.

Virgil shook his head. "I'm here as a messenger."

"From Ronodin?" Kendra asked.

Virgil nodded. "If you want to bargain for release, you

are to come with me. Ronodin is willing to offer terms. If not, you will be placed in solitary confinement."

"Go," Lizelle urged. "Escape this realm, if you can."

"Any hints to the offer he will make?" Kendra asked Virgil.

"No idea," the satyr said.

"You should hear his terms," Lizelle insisted. "Solitary confinement will gain you little."

*If Ronodin is willing to release you, he has his own reasons,* Lizelle added telepathically. *Take care what you surrender in order to secure your release.*

*I'll be careful,* Kendra thought to the unicorn. "Thank you."

"Farewell," Lizelle said as Kendra exited. The wall streamed back together, again becoming smooth and solid.

Two fairy guards awaited, tall and lithe with wings like stained glass, armed with graceful spears. They marched Virgil and Kendra through winding halls until they reached an entrance blocked by a thin, folding partition fashioned from wood. The fairy warriors posted there stepped aside.

"Ronodin awaits," one of the willowy guards said. "Right this way. The satyr stays with us."

Kendra walked around the partition and through a zig-zagging bottleneck before pushing through a beaded curtain into a room saturated with mist. She could see only thirty feet in any direction and could not discern a ceiling or any wall besides the near one.

"Hello?" Kendra called into the murk, breathing the damp air.

"Kendra," Ronodin answered from out of view. "Isn't this an extraordinary chamber?"

He came into sight, riding a bicycle toward her. He hit the brakes a few paces away, then hopped off and propped it up with the kickstand.

"How big is this room?" Kendra asked.

"It extends for miles," Ronodin said, gesturing vaguely into the fog. "All of it misty. There are several enormous rooms like this throughout the palace. This one manifests various types of weather. I trust Lizelle was helpful?"

"What do you mean?" Kendra asked.

"She more fully connected you to your power, I presume?" Ronodin asked.

"Were you spying?"

"She is shielding the room, so I couldn't overhear, but I could recognize when you were glowing brightly. By the way, if you try to blind me, there will be no release."

"That's fair," Kendra said. "You're going to release me?"

"There was little sport in catching you," Ronodin said. "You came right to me. No thrill of the hunt. Next time make it more of a challenge."

"You wanted Lizelle to teach me?" Kendra asked.

"You will need all the power you can muster if you hope to give the dragons any kind of a fight," Ronodin said. "Would you care to hear the terms of your release?"

"Yes."

"I'm not open to bargaining on this," Ronodin said. "My proposition is more than generous."

"What are the terms?"

"I have three stipulations. First, you leave now. No delay. No farewell to Bracken. My fairies will escort you and the satyr to an exit immediately. Your job is to go through it."

"Virgil comes with me?"

"Hence my reference to a satyr."

"Second?"

"Your top priority must be to find the legendary Dragon Slayers. It's the only way you can cause significant trouble for the dragons. Do you have any leads?"

Kendra stared at Ronodin. "Sort of."

"Tell me," Ronodin said. "I don't want to send you back into the world unless you have a chance for success."

"I think some demons want to help me," Kendra said.

Ronodin raised his eyebrows. "You're open to their help?"

"It's an emergency," Kendra said.

"I'm impressed," Ronodin said. "The demons don't want to see the dragons on top. They're your strongest allies."

"A demon told me that since I destroyed their king, they expect me to take out Celebrant," Kendra said.

"That's how I would play it," Ronodin said. "You don't want the demons to maintain a vendetta against you. And you need to kill Celebrant anyhow. He is altering the nature of dragons in a way that is bad for everyone. Which demons are willing to help you?"

"I have three names," Kendra said. "Talizar, Batoosa, and Vez Radim."

"You have been busy," Ronodin said. "Those are some of

the biggest players outside of Zzyzx. Do you know where to find them?"

"Talizar is at Wyrmroost," Kendra said.

"He will be the easiest to access," Ronodin said. "I can send you through the fairy shrine to your fallen sanctuary. I expect Talizar will tell you much."

"Where do I find him there?"

Ronodin gave a delighted chuckle. "If only you could ask someone wise in the ways of shadowy beings."

"Do you know?" Kendra asked.

"The Moonlit Tower," Ronodin said. "It's only visible when the moon is in the sky. Go to the Pathless Forest northeast of Stormguard Castle. Watch out for lycanthropes there. Werebeasts. Talizar himself is one."

"Is it far from the fairy shrine?" Kendra asked.

"Yes," Ronodin said. "You'll want to fly. Too bad Raxtus fled."

"I'll figure it out," Kendra said.

"If all else fails, you have legs," Ronodin said. "And a satyr to keep you company. Though your satyr may want this pendant." He held up a thumb-sized ivory mask affixed to a leather cord.

"Jewelry?" Kendra asked.

"Your hunt for the Dragon Slayers will take you among mortals," Ronodin said. "In that environment, Virgil will look like a goat to most eyes. This will let him appear human."

"You'll just give it to me?" Kendra asked.

"If the dragons win in a landslide, we'll all suffer,"

Ronodin said, handing over the pendant. "I want you to make real trouble for them. The dragons have advantages enough."

Kendra pocketed the pendant. "If you want me to make trouble, can I have my weapons back? My bow and my sack?"

"Sure," Ronodin said with a dismissive wave. "They will be delivered when you exit."

"Third?" Kendra asked.

"Thanks for the reminder. I was about to release you with no further conditions."

"Really?"

"No. This is the most important one. You must swear by your power that when I call for your return, you will come back here."

Kendra scowled. "You're keeping me on a leash?"

"I don't give something for nothing," Ronodin said.

"What does it mean to swear by my power?"

"Your power is the collateral," Ronodin said. "If you fail to comply, I can strip you of your fairykind status."

"Would that mean you can summon me whenever you want?" Kendra asked.

"Yes, with this one stipulation: I promise not to summon you until the dragon war is decided. Either you will have defeated Celebrant, or the dragons will have destroyed the Sovereign Skull and begun their onslaught on humanity. And tell you what—if you're dead, I won't insist on your return."

"You're not really letting me go," Kendra said.

"Think of it as a work release program," Ronodin said. "You're still my captive, but you may go fight your war and help your friends and family."

Kendra frowned. Even if she won the war, she would still lose her freedom in the end. But at least she would have a chance to stop the dragons. "I'm not getting a better offer, am I?"

"Take it or leave it," Ronodin said.

Kendra sighed. "I'll take it."

"To be clear, you swear by your power to return when I call?" Ronodin checked.

"Yes," Kendra said.

Ronodin smiled. "Then we have a deal. I almost added a fourth condition."

"What?"

"That you name your firstborn son after me."

"Ouch."

"Should we add it in now?"

"We already have a deal. Maybe next time."

"I doubt there will be a next time," Ronodin said. "You will most likely perish. But at least you'll die doing what you love most—fighting for a hopeless cause."

"I heard about what happened between you and the Fairy King," Kendra said.

Ronodin covered his ears. "I feared as much. I don't want to go into that."

"You used to fight alongside Bracken," Kendra said.

"Nobody is perfect," Ronodin said.

"It doesn't have to be this way," Kendra said.

Ronodin closed his eyes and held up a hand for her to stop. "Please don't pretend you know my story because you glimpsed a skewed Viewmaster version. You might know some aspect of how I started down a certain path, but not how I walked it, nor who I became by doing so."

"It's never too late to change," Kendra said.

Ronodin gave her a death stare. "Is it too late for me to quit our bargain?"

"The deal is struck," Kendra said.

"I suppose so," Ronodin said. "But it might be more satisfying to feed you to piranhas."

"You're wearing the Fairy Queen's crown of light," Kendra said. "Is it comfortable?"

"For now," Ronodin replied, giving the crown a flick. "My soldiers will escort you to the appropriate gateway. Good luck against the dragons."

"Have fun here," Kendra replied.

Ronodin flipped up the kickstand and straddled his bike. "Always," he said, riding off into the fog.

# CHAPTER TWENTY-ONE

# Flight

Seth sat at a table with Knox and Doren, putting together a jigsaw puzzle that portrayed trolls unloading cargo from a docked ship. They had found the corners and had fitted most of the edge pieces to make a frame, along with having completed a few interior patches of the puzzle.

Hermo paced off to one side. The hermit troll had returned to the apartment in the night, greeting Seth enthusiastically before going to bed. They had spent part of the morning on the roof of the building making a game of tossing pebbles into chimneys. After Doren had found the puzzle in a cupboard, Seth and Knox had joined in solving it, but Hermo had refrained from participating, claiming the activity was beneath him.

"Hermo," Seth said, "help us find the missing edge pieces."

"Too easy," Hermo said.

"Prove it," Seth replied. "This is a thousand-piece puzzle."

The troll toddled over and without pause picked out the last two edge pieces from the jumble and put them in place. Hermo gave a huff. "Me do with eyes closed."

"Yeah, right," Knox said.

Hermo closed his eyes and began rapidly assembling pieces, filling in the image from the middle and expanding outward. "Easy."

"Okay, we get it," Knox said. "Save some for the rest of us."

Hermo opened his eyes and backed away from the table. "This for babies."

"How does he do that?" Knox muttered. "His eyes really looked shut."

"Finding stuff is easy for him," Seth said.

"We throw more rock at chimney?" Hermo suggested.

"After this," Seth said, scanning the pieces to see how he might build off the work Hermo had done.

Tess burst into the room and closed the door. "The sky giants are coming!"

"Are you sure?" Knox asked.

"I was downstairs with Newel," Tess said. "The news just came from Runder. A guard spotted them from the wall."

"How many?" Seth asked.

"At least forty," Tess said. "They're carrying weapons."

Seth nodded. After the confrontation with Knox the

night before, it had felt like a relief to do something just for fun, to delay hard choices for an hour or two.

"We have to leave," Seth said.

"You'll need the gem from my crown," Knox said.

Seth had hidden the crown in the room where he had slept, mindful that Knox might make another grab for it. Seth had not yet removed the jewel in case they needed the crown to bluff the giants again.

Seth nodded and looked to Doren. "Can Newel move?"

"He lost a lot of blood, but Dagny's glue has stopped the flow. To avoid getting slaughtered by giants, I'll get him on his feet."

"We need to leave without the valley giants noticing," Seth said. "They're holding us here at least as much as they're protecting us. Hermo, can you show us a route?"

"Sure," Hermo said. "On rooftops, then underground, then more rooftops. They smell you, though. Need to keep moving."

"Everyone gather what you need and go," Seth said. "Don't wait for me. I'll get the gem, then fly up and look around."

"How will you find us?" Knox asked.

"Where will you take them?" Seth asked Hermo.

Hermo folded his arms. "We go deep place under garrison by white tower with gold dome."

"I can find that," Seth said.

"You find tower," Hermo said. "Go in garrison. I find you."

"Is it deep enough that the giants won't smell us?" Doren asked.

"Hope so," Hermo said. "Goatman strong odors."

They could hear the valley giants shouting orders out on the street.

"Everybody move," Seth said. "If the sky giants get here before we leave, we're toast."

Seth ran into his bedroom. He picked up the Unforgiving Blade, then reached into the incision he had made in the side of his mattress and withdrew the Giant Queen's crown. He set the crown on the bed and carefully brought the edge of the Unforgiving Blade to the front of the crown. The blade sliced through the metal of the crown as though he were cutting butter.

"Careful," Calvin warned. "You don't want to nick the stone."

After a few cuts behind where the gem was set, the jewel fell out. Seth stuffed the gem into his satchel and hurried from the room. He ran downstairs to the bedroom where Newel was recovering. He found Dagny there, helping the satyr to his feet. Newel's chest and shoulder were wrapped, so Seth could not see the injury.

"Sorry we have to run," Seth apologized.

"Better to flee than get squashed," Newel said. "I've had worse injuries."

Seth stared at his friend. "But they weren't permanent. It was my fault. I'm so sorry."

Newel glanced at Dagny. "Her glue keeps the blood inside. You know that from your own scratch."

"Yours is deeper," Seth said. "And mine resulted from my own stupidity. I'm sorry I brought the Unforgiving Blade here."

"You're doing what you have to do," Newel said. "I couldn't stand aside while Knox threatened you."

"Actually, you could have," Seth said. "But you didn't."

"Knox feels terrible," Newel said, walking gingerly toward the door.

"I'm going to fly and scout the incoming giants," Seth said.

"Do you have the extra glue I gave you?" Dagny checked.

"Yes," Seth said.

"Keep it handy," Dagny said. "That wound will trouble you for the rest of your life. Untended, it will become fatal, either through blood loss or infection."

"That's an encouraging thought," Newel grumbled.

"Thanks for your help," Seth said, following the satyr out into the hall. Newel winced, taking care how he moved his upper body. Seth patted Newel on the shoulder. "Hermo needs you on the roof to start the escape. I'm going to run ahead. See you later."

"Don't let those giants shoot you down," Newel warned as Seth raced up the stairs. "They're watching the sky."

On the upper floor, Knox flagged down Seth. "Do you have the gem?"

"Yes," Seth said, walking past him.

"Did you take the crown too?" Knox asked.

"I left it on my bed," Seth said.

"I'm going to bring it," Knox said. "I'll hide the crown somewhere along the way. We don't want the giants to find it without the stone until after we're gone. And if I know where it's hidden, maybe we can use that as a bargaining chip."

"Good thinking," Seth said. "See you later." He dashed to a ladder and up through a square hatch in the ceiling.

Seth found Tess waiting on the rooftop. Fortunately, the flat roof had a parapet around the periphery and enough extra chimneys, water towers, and utility sheds that it was easy for the group to remain out of view from anyone on the street. "Do you have what you need?" he asked.

"Everything that makes sense to carry," Tess said. "I tried to warn the others they collected too much treasure. You're flying off?"

"To check on the sky giants," Seth said.

"I'm worried you'll disappear again," Tess said. "You keep getting lost."

"I'll be back," Seth said. "Unless I die."

"Don't die," Tess said. "We need you."

"I sometimes worry I create more problems than I solve," Seth said.

"You'll figure it out," Tess said, smiling up at Seth with such hope that it made his throat tighten. "I believe in you."

"Thanks," Seth said. "I'll make sure you guys are all right before I move on."

Having already lost so much time, Seth sprang into the air and flew low along the rooftops, away from Crossroads Plaza. He knew that promising he would return meant much less than actually showing up. He really wanted to keep his promise. He hoped he could.

After flying several blocks away from the valley giant encampment, Seth gained altitude and veered toward the nearest city wall. He expected that after he climbed high enough, the sky giants would come into view. The flying didn't strain his leg, though he felt the wound and was grateful for the bindings that held the glue in place.

"Watch out," Calvin warned from his pocket. "You're a target."

Looking down, Seth saw shorter, blockier giants than the valley giants hurling stones at him with slings. He seemed too high for the bombardment to reach him until a rock whizzed by inches from his head, compelling him to aggressively ascend.

"I see the sky giants," Calvin said. "To the northwest."

In the direction Calvin indicated, Seth saw a group of at least fifty sky giants marching toward Humburgh. Flying higher, Seth soared in their direction. Many of them carried shields and wore armor. All bore weapons. They advanced at a brisk pace, their long legs covering the distance of a football field every four or five strides.

"They're a lot bigger than the valley giants," Calvin commented.

"And they are heavily armed," Seth said.

"Seth," a familiar voice said from above and behind him.

Startled, Seth had to resist folding his wings into a dive as a defensive reflex. "Who said that?" he asked.

"Raxtus." The sound of the voice led Seth to identify a nearby shimmer in the air.

"You almost scared me to death," Seth said.

"Sneaking up on you is better than being seen," Raxtus said. "Dragons are unpopular around here lately."

Seth hadn't seen Raxtus since he left him behind with Merek and Kendra atop Beacon Hill. "Where is Kendra?"

"Bad news," Raxtus said. "Ronodin has her. Your friend Virgil too."

"Really?" Seth cried. "How?"

"I brought her to the Fairy Realm through the gateway at Obsidian Waste," Raxtus said. "She wanted to help Bracken and the Fairy Queen."

"You're sure she was captured?" Seth checked.

"A bunch of human-sized fairies apprehended her," Raxtus said. "I barely escaped. She asked me to find you. I didn't know you would make it so easy—flying around with those golden wings in broad daylight."

"What do you suggest we do?" Seth asked.

"She doesn't want a rescue attempt," Raxtus said. "Ronodin is too powerful in that realm right now. She wants us to fight the dragons."

"It's a complicated problem," Seth said, trimming his wings as a gust of wind made him wobble.

"I'm here to help," Raxtus said. "Warren, Tanu, and Vanessa are almost to Humburgh, coming across the plains, searching for your cousins."

"I already found them," Seth said. "They need help."

"Where are they?" Raxtus asked.

"In town," Seth said. "Knox established himself as the Giant King."

"What?" Raxtus exclaimed.

"He nabbed the crown after the Giant Queen died," Seth said. "Brought it to Humburgh. When some valley giants jumped him, he crowned himself king and they played along. Then their leader challenged him to a duel for the crown."

"Are the sky giants coming for the crown?" Raxtus asked.

"I assume so," Seth said. "I know news has been spreading. And they'll be furious when they find out I cut the gem out of the crown."

"Do you have a death wish?" Raxtus cried.

"Almost," Seth said. "I have to collect all of the pieces of the Ethergem, which includes the Wizenstone, the Ethershard, and the stones from the crowns of the Giant Queen, the Dragon King, and the Demon King."

"You're joking," Raxtus said.

"It's the mission the Singing Sisters require of me," Seth said. "They told me we won't win the war unless I succeed."

"Is that logical?" Raxtus asked.

"I believe them," Seth said. "I have two of the stones. And I know where to find the Ethershard."

"But Seth, think it through. My dad's crown? And Orogoro's crown?"

"I know it sounds like an impossible task," Seth said. "But if I can trash Celebrant's crown, hopefully it will weaken him."

"He would be weaker," Raxtus said. "A little. If you can pull it off."

"It's that or die trying," Seth said. "I'm committed."

"I'll help," Raxtus said. "First we need to rescue your cousins."

"Can you lead me to Tanu?"

"Sure," Raxtus said. "He, Warren, and Vanessa are a short distance outside the city."

"Off we go," Seth said.

"Not a moment too soon," Raxtus said. "The sky giants spotted you."

"Great," Calvin said. "They picked up their pace. A few are shooting arrows at us."

"Luckily they can't fly," Seth said. "Let's hurry."

# CHAPTER TWENTY-TWO

# Tower

A pair of warrior fairies lifted Kendra out of the little spring on the rocky mountainside and set her on the ground. One of them handed her the sack of gales and her bow. Two others brought Virgil through and placed him near her. A tiny white fairy statue stood beside a golden bowl where water bubbled out of the ground to trickle into a puddle and then drain off the lip of the rocky ledge, tributary to a larger flow of water. All four warrior fairies dived into the puddle and vanished even though it looked barely ankle deep.

The sun had just cleared the eastern peaks, bathing Wyrmroost with warm light and long shadows. Kendra could hear the rushing water of Split Veil Falls below her. Passing through the water from the Fairy Realm had left her a little damp, but not drenched.

Virgil nudged her. "We have company," the satyr said.

Following his gaze, Kendra looked down from the ledge where they stood to a broader area near the top of the waterfall. An ominous figure, cloaked and hooded, awaited beside a simple lean-to, branches propped against a boulder. A pair of astrids in their owl shape flanked the stranger, androgynous faces staring sedately.

The figure raised a hand in salutation. "Greetings, Kendra. May I have a word with you? I want to help."

*Is he safe?* Kendra communicated to the astrids.

*He means you no harm,* one of the astrids replied.

Virgil glanced over at Kendra. "Want me to approach first?" the satyr asked tensely. "How about I throw sand in his eyes and you run?"

"I think he's here to help," Kendra said.

"Do you know him?" Virgil asked.

"Let's find out," Kendra said, walking away from the shrine and climbing down toward the cloaked stranger. After stooping to pick up a stone, Virgil followed.

While Kendra descended to the top of Split Veil Falls, the man waited patiently, his face hidden in shadow. Virgil came up beside her, stone in hand.

"Who are you?" Kendra asked.

"I am called the Traveler," the man replied. "I'm here to aid you."

Kendra glanced at the lean-to. "How did you know I would come here?"

The Traveler indicated the astrids. "They knew. The

new sovereign of the Fairy Realm has abundant enemies. Many spies have eyes on him."

"Take your hood down," Kendra said. "I want to see your face."

"I prefer my anonymity," the Traveler said.

"You remind me of someone," Kendra said. "I want to see if I'm right."

He lowered his cowl. "I can see there is no fooling you."

Virgil dropped to one knee, head bowed. "Your majesty."

"Rise, my friend," the Fairy King said. "I no longer hold any office that requires obeisance."

"There is a difference between a criminal who steals a crown and a true king," Virgil said.

"I appreciate the sentiment," the Fairy King replied. "Please rise."

Virgil obeyed.

"It really is you," Kendra said. "You sent a fairy to warn me."

"I did," he said. "And recently I saw your brother."

"You gave him the wings!" Kendra exclaimed.

"I'm assisting where I can," the Fairy King said somberly. "Will you introduce me to your friend?"

"This is Virgil," Kendra said. "He lived in Humburgh, studying the Games. He helped us beat Humbuggle."

"My thanks, Virgil," the Fairy King said. "Kendra needs reliable comrades."

Virgil tossed his stone aside and gave a thumbs-up. "You can count on me."

"I have to ask," Kendra said. "Why did you let Ronodin into the Fairy Realm? Did he trick you?"

"I did not choose to let him in," the Fairy King said. "I was controlled in my sleep. Nyssa, the mother of all narco-blixes, bit me while I was inside of Zzyzx, chained to Gorgrog. I became aware of her connection to me only after I awoke from her control. I believe granting Ronodin access was the sole time she exerted her power over me."

"That wasn't your fault," Kendra said.

"It wasn't my deliberate choice," the Fairy King said. "But I knew I could have been compromised during those long years spent in darkness. I languished in a semiconscious daze much of that time. My ordeal probably tainted me in other ways I have not yet recognized. I should never have dwelt in a spotless realm unless I could be utterly purified. I tried to access the Source but found the way cut off. I endeavored to warn my family. I intended to leave but waited too long." His hands squeezed the folds of his cloak. "And now . . . I cannot undo the egregious damage I have caused. I've become a liability, so if I wish to help, it must be from afar."

"It's a tragic disaster," Kendra said. "But you tried hard not to cause it."

"A small consolation to those I have harmed," the Fairy King said. "You seek information from Talizar?"

"Those astrids really fill you in," Kendra said. "Maybe I can skip that step, if you know where I can find the legendary Dragon Slayers?"

"Unfortunately, I do not," the Fairy King said. "Are you uncomfortable soliciting information from a demon?"

"It isn't my first choice," Kendra said.

"Few have greater cause to despise the demons than I," the Fairy King said. "And yet, I have received occasional assistance from their kind over the years. Treading with care, I have profitably interacted with some."

"The dragon war isn't going well," Kendra said. "We've lost every battle so far. Even when we seem to win, we end up losing later."

"Pursuing the legendary Dragon Slayers is a sensible course of action," the Fairy King said. "I can help you make it to Talizar."

"Do you have extra wings?" Kendra asked.

"I had only two sets of astrid wings to give," the Fairy King said. "But I can ensure you have a ride." Raising his fingers to his lips, he gave a shrill whistle that was immediately answered by a whinny.

Kendra turned to find two winged horses flying toward them: a chestnut mare with white splotches and a dark brown horse with a black mane. "Glory!" Kendra exclaimed. "Noble!"

"You know flying horses?" Virgil asked.

"I helped them get their wings," Kendra replied.

"I should stop feeling surprised around you," Virgil said. "Anything is possible."

Glory landed near Kendra, who rushed forward to hug the neck of the mare and pet her. "It's so good to see you," Kendra said. "I'm glad you're safe. You too, Noble."

The dark brown horse tossed his head in acknowledgment. Glory nuzzled Kendra affectionately.

"The boundaries of Wyrmroost are compromised," the Fairy King said. "There is no limit to where these mounts can bear you. But start with the Moonlit Tower in the Pathless Forest. Though it is daytime, the moon is up, and the tower should be visible."

"Do you know the way there?" Kendra asked Glory.

The mare nodded her head and stamped a hoof.

"She loves to read maps," the Fairy King said. "Glory knows Wyrmroost as well as anyone."

Noble neighed.

"Noble, you know the best places to graze," the Fairy King acknowledged. "But have you been as diligent as Glory about the maps?"

After a brief pause, Noble shook his head and snorted.

"I appreciate the honesty," the Fairy King said. He narrowed his eyes at Kendra. "Would you like improved communication with these mounts?"

"Sure," Kendra said.

"I see you are more in touch with your power than when we last met," the Fairy King said.

"Lizelle helped me," Kendra replied.

"You would be hard-pressed to find a more able instructor," the Fairy King said. "Would you mind if I help guide you in an exercise with these Luvians?"

"I'd love that," Kendra replied.

"How would you Luvians like the power of speech?" the Fairy King asked.

Both flying horses nodded and stamped enthusiastically.

"May we have access to your minds?" the Fairy King asked.

Both horses made motions of consent.

"Touch each mount on the head or the neck," the Fairy King instructed Kendra.

Kendra stood between Noble and Glory, a hand on each of their necks, just behind their heads. The Fairy King rested a hand on Kendra's shoulder. She felt her connection to her power blossom, and she became strangely aware of the inner workings of Glory and Noble. She could sense their heartbeats, their breathing, their digestive processes. She also perceived diverse memories, along with their current thoughts and feelings. Her power projected into the horses, and she felt cocooned in light.

Then the Fairy King took his hand from Kendra's shoulder, and she removed her hands from the horses. "Did it work?" Kendra asked.

"Let Glory tell you," the Fairy King suggested.

"How am I supposed to . . . ?" Glory began. "Really? Just like that? After all this time?"

"We can talk," Noble said with relish.

"I've thought words since I was a foal," Glory said. "Yet I couldn't give them utterance. I never expected this day would come." She bowed to the Fairy King. "Thank you, your majesty."

"Thank Kendra," the Fairy King said. "It was done with her power. Bear her and Virgil safely wherever they care to go."

"They have our undying devotion," Noble said boldly.

"Thank you, Kendra," Glory said. "I finally feel like a true Luvian."

"Me too," Noble said. "I'm going to say so many things."

"Not all at once," the Fairy King said. "You know your destination. Best be off. No time to waste."

Kendra climbed onto Glory. "Come on, Virgil."

Virgil eyed Noble uneasily. "Satyrs don't usually . . ."

"Ride horses?" Noble finished.

"Ride any animal," Virgil said.

"We all learn new skills during emergencies," Kendra said.

"What if I fall off?" Virgil asked.

"Tuck and roll," Noble said.

"What if we're hundreds of feet in the air?" Virgil exclaimed.

"Don't fall off," Noble said.

"We won't let you fall," Glory encouraged.

Virgil came up beside Noble and placed his hands on the horse's back. Hopping on one hoof, the satyr awkwardly raised a furry leg.

"Get up there," Noble said, crouching a little.

Changing tactics, Virgil jumped with both hoofs and boosted himself up, leaning across the horse sideways. With some squirming, he got a leg over and managed to sit up. "It already feels high."

"Hold that thought," Noble said, springing forward, wings swishing down to launch horse and rider into the air.

"Thanks, your majesty," Kendra said.

"Call me the Traveler," the Fairy King responded.

"Thanks, Traveler," Glory said, lurching forward off the brink of the waterfall and into the sky.

For a terrible moment Kendra envisioned herself and Glory plummeting to their deaths. Instead, Glory soared forward, gradually rising as the mountainside fell away steeply beneath them. Within moments their shadow fluttered over the distant treetops below.

"I feel more at home in the sky," Glory said. "Running along the ground seems slow and jarring by comparison."

"You fly smoothly," Kendra complimented.

"It isn't just the wings," Glory explained. "My whole body becomes buoyant when I take to the sky. The wings let me maneuver, but the lift comes from my whole being."

"Do I weigh you down much?" Kendra asked.

"Minimally," Glory replied.

Kendra remembered soaring over Wyrmroost with Raxtus, who sometimes flew like a roller coaster, banking steeply, or turning loops, or twirling. Instead, Glory flew even and steady, but it was thrilling to soar so high, with the wind in her face and the sanctuary spread out beneath her like a living map. Glory moved into a fixed pace about a hundred yards behind Noble.

"The moon is peeking through the clouds," Glory commented.

Sure enough, scanning the horizon, Kendra found the faint white moon in a patch of sky between wispy clouds. It struck Kendra how diminished the moon looked in a blue, daytime sky compared to how dominant it appeared in the dark of night.

As they glided over jagged spines of rock and forested slopes, Kendra watched the sky for dragons. She noticed a couple of griffins swooping in the distance, and she briefly came close to an unusually large swan.

"How many dragons are still around?" Kendra asked.

"We stay on the lookout," Glory said. "I've been stabled with Thronis. For a time after the sanctuary fell, the dragons ran wild, but a few days later, most of them cleared out. Not all departed. We must remain cautious."

"Do the undead still hold Blackwell Keep?" Kendra asked, thinking of her grandparents.

"They continue to swarm the stronghold," Glory said.

"Can you outfly a dragon?" Kendra asked.

"I hope so," Glory replied. "I've never been tested."

Down below and to the left, Kendra saw Stormguard Castle, looking like a model from her present height. It wasn't long ago that she and Seth had freed the place from Humbuggle's curse. She was happy to see the castle intact—apparently it still enjoyed protection from the dragons. Kendra wondered what help King Hollorix and Queen Satilla might be willing to grant if she came knocking. Lockland and others were probably down there as well. But right now, her mission was to gather information from a demon. A stop at Stormguard Castle would cost too much time.

Beyond a range of steep hills, they flew low over a broad valley full of dense, tangled vegetation. The trees were not tall, but they looked tortured, with intertwining limbs. Kendra caught glimpses of filmy water choked with reeds and lily pads.

"Look up ahead," Glory suggested.

The Moonlit Tower was smaller and more ornate than Kendra expected. It poked four or five stories above the treetops, hexagonal, its entire pale surface carved with figures and faces. Something about the coloring of the structure mimicked the faint whiteness of the moon during the day, and the closer they flew, the more the tower appeared to be at least slightly transparent.

Noble landed on the flat roof of the tower, and Glory followed, hoofs clattering against stone. "The forest below is unsafe at any time, day or night," Glory said. "Better to remain above it if possible."

Virgil immediately dropped from Noble, but Kendra remained mounted. "How was your flight?" she asked.

"Scary at first," Virgil confessed. "I grew more accustomed to it as we went."

Kendra dismounted and crouched to study the smooth surface of the tower. The stone still looked semitransparent, as if it were somewhat misty, but it felt completely solid beneath her feet and when she poked it with a finger.

One side of the tower had a portion higher than the rest, with a narrow door. When the door opened, both horses started, and Kendra stood up straight.

A wolfman in a long, maroon smoking jacket emerged from the doorway, his fur dark and oily, his eyes a smoldering red. His hands and feet were more ratlike than wolflike, with wicked black claws.

"Kendra Sorenson," the wolfman said, showing a disturbing array of sharp, crooked teeth. "I wondered when you would find your way here. Your escorts are welcome to await you on the safety of my roof." He stepped aside and motioned toward the open door. "If you care to come inside, we can talk, and I offer the protection of my hospitality."

# CHAPTER TWENTY-THREE

# Diverging

Not far outside the Humburgh city wall, Raxtus and Seth landed beside Tanu, Warren, and Vanessa on a patch of ground charred by dragon fire. From where they stood, no giants were in view, neither on the walls of the city nor crossing the nearby plains.

"Seth," Tanu greeted joyfully, spreading his arms wide. "You're alive!"

"So far," Seth said. "How's Vanessa?"

"Blind," Vanessa said.

"Hey, Raxtus," Warren said, squinting. "I can't see you much better than Vanessa can." Vanessa swatted Warren in the chest with the back of her hand. "What? Too soon?"

"Sky giants are racing toward Humburgh," Seth said, pointing away from the city. "From that direction, not far out of view."

"We have to find Knox and Tess," Warren said.

"I already found them and the satyrs," Seth said. "There are a few things you should know. Knox got away from Terastios with the Giant Queen's crown and is technically now the Giant King."

"Knox? The Giant King?" Warren asked. "How does that even work? He's not a giant."

"Right, it makes him a big target, so he's on the run inside the city," Seth explained. "I destroyed the Wizenstone and I have the pieces. The Singing Sisters called in the favor I owe them. They put me on a quest to get all the parts of the Ethergem."

"The Ether-whatnow?" Warren asked.

"An ancient jewel," Vanessa said. "Incredibly powerful. The fragments are the feature stones in three of the monarchs' crowns."

"Yes, those three plus the Wizenstone and the Ethershard," Seth said. "First, we need to get Knox and Tess and the satyrs out of Humburgh. I know where they are."

"And I have a way to get all of us out of here," Tanu said. "Andromadus found the three of us yesterday and gave me a teleporter for as many of us as choose to depart Titan Valley. One use. One way."

"Andromadus was here?" Seth asked.

"Briefly," Tanu said. "He's globe-trotting nonstop, trying to help the scattered pockets of resistance. The forces aligned with Dragonwatch are falling back to the kingdom of Selona."

"Where is that?" Seth asked.

"Someplace in Europe," Warren said. "Very hush-hush. An entire country hidden from the nonmagical world by a distracter spell."

"I'd only heard rumors," Vanessa said.

"It's where the Fair Folk originated," Tanu said.

"Cool," Seth said. "I have to finish getting the other three Ethergem fragments. But first, I want to help you guys get Knox and Tess. We should hurry."

"Raxtus, can you fly me?" Tanu asked.

"Let's go," Raxtus said.

"Vanessa and I will hide just inside the walls, beyond that gap," Warren said, indicating the ragged opening where the city wall had collapsed inward.

"Right," Seth said, springing into the air, wings swooshing him upward. As he gained altitude, the sky giants came back into view, running hard. They were making good time. It would be a matter of minutes before they stormed Humburgh.

"Do you see the gold dome on the white tower?" Calvin asked.

"Got it," Seth said.

Seth flapped his wings hard, diving low enough that he skimmed rooftops and dodged chimneys as he raced toward the destination. The streets he flew over appeared deserted until he neared the designated tower, where a host of valley giants had gathered in the adjoining square. They congregated outside a squat building diagonal from the base of the white tower. Several of them huddled around a campfire preparing torches and lighting them.

Seth looked back at the barely visible shimmer of Raxtus carrying Tanu, and he motioned for them to stop on a nearby rooftop. Then Seth glided down and landed beside a covered well about ten paces from Runder, who wore his bronze helm and stood with his arms folded, conversing with a pair of other giants. The valley giants were less imposing than the sky giants. Even so, Seth was not much taller than their knees.

"What's happening, Runder?" Seth asked in Jiganti.

The giants swung around to face him. Several looked to their leader questioningly. Runder held up a hand for them to wait.

"Our king has tried to run away," Runder said.

"Isn't the king allowed to go wherever he wants?" Seth asked.

Runder snorted. "Not if he is trying to sneak away with the crown and avoid my challenge."

"He needs to show up to that duel in a month," Seth said. "Otherwise he gets to go wherever he wants."

"Not with the sky giants coming," Runder said. "A king stands and faces his adversaries."

"A king isn't questioned by his subjects," Seth countered.

Runder gave Seth a measuring stare, then spoke as if leveling with him. "That boy is no king. He is no giant. And the kid is certainly no giant king."

"But he has the crown," Seth said. "You have sworn fealty to him."

"A bit of fun," Runder said. "A pantomime."

"You wanted to duel somebody you thought you could easily beat for the crown," Seth said.

Runder grinned. "A valley giant has never worn it."

"Do you think the sky giants would let you keep it?" Seth asked. "You may look as silly to them as Knox does to you."

"But I would be the first valley giant to ever have worn it," Runder said with relish. Several of the other giants shouted exclamations of support. "And if we hurry, I can be wearing it when the blowhards arrive."

"If you betray your king by killing him unfairly," Seth said.

"Did that boy kill our queen fairly?" Runder asked.

"He didn't kill your queen," Seth said. "But he got the crown away from the dragons who did. It was a lot more than any giant managed to do. You should be thanking him."

"We'll thank him with a clean death," Runder said.

"How are you going to get him out?" Seth asked. "That building is mostly stone. It won't burn."

"Burning wouldn't help," Runder said. "He's gone too deep. We'll demolish it and dig him out."

"Before the sky giants arrive?" Seth asked.

"When they arrive, we'll work together," Runder said.

"Then you'll never wear the crown," Seth said.

Runder shrugged. "At least a human won't be desecrating it."

"Do you want me to teach you about desecration?" Seth

asked. He reached into his satchel and took out the stone from the Giant Queen's Crown. "Does this look familiar?"

Runder's face hardened. "You wouldn't have dared. This is a trick."

Seth swished the Unforgiving Blade through the air a few times. "Shoddy workmanship, if you ask me. Whoever claims that crown will wear the spoiled remnants. The power of the crown came from this jewel. It was once part of the Ethergem." Seth gave the stone a little toss, caught it, and returned it to the satchel.

"This is a pathetic ruse," Runder said, his voice thick with anger. "Your stone is made of glass."

"Your brain is made of garbage," Seth said. "You want the jewel back? Fight me for it. I challenge you to a duel."

"I have many mighty warriors waiting on my word to—"

"You were ready to fight my cousin," Seth interrupted. "Are you afraid of me? If I lose, you can take the stone off my corpse. If I win, order the rest of your giants to stand down."

"You want to fight me?" Runder asked, amused.

"I don't want to fight you," Seth said. "But I want to get my cousin and leave this burned-out sanctuary. If killing you makes that happen, let's stop wasting time."

Runder set down his club—a rough stone lashed to the fork of a formidable branch. He spat into one grubby palm, rubbed his hands together, and picked up the weapon. "You have a deal."

Seth spread his golden wings and drew Vasilis, which

flared a deep, bright red. "Fair warning—I can fly, and both of my swords have names."

"Enough talk," Runder bellowed. "Time to fight!"

"I'm right here," Seth said. "Come on. You like picking on little guys."

As the other giants shouted encouragement, Runder rushed forward, club held high in two hands. Seth knew that a direct hit by that weapon would pulverize him. The key would be to dodge the first swing. Vasilis burned hot in his hand, begging to attack, but he resisted until the club came sweeping down toward him. With a swish of his wings, Seth sprang diagonally forward. The head of the club crashed down slightly behind Seth, shattering paving stones. Flying low to the ground, Seth slashed Vasilis through Runder's mighty tree trunk of a leg, just above the knee, completely severing the lower portion from the upper.

Runder roared in anger and pain. Using his club like a cane, he pivoted to face Seth. Banking sharply, Vasilis trailing fiery light, Seth came back around toward the injured giant. Runder swung his club, and Seth swerved just enough to feel the breeze when it missed, then cleaved the giant's other meaty leg just above the knee.

Runder fell flat to the ground, face contorted in agony. Seth landed just out of reach. "Do you yield?" Seth asked.

"Never," Runder growled. "Come close enough to slay me, if you dare."

"You could still have two peg legs," Seth said. "We can stop here."

Runder heaved his club at Seth, who flew over it, landed

beside Runder, and stabbed the Unforgiving Blade into his side. The giant went rigid. Seth was ready to leap away in case the valley giant took a swipe at him, but Runder stayed paralyzed except for a series of twitchy jerks.

"No," Runder said, his voice choked and hoarse. "No . . . no . . ."

The surrounding giants edged forward in befuddlement. They looked confused and horrified.

Runder's convulsions became more severe, froth foaming from his lips. "No . . . please . . . stop."

Seth pulled out the blade and moved to better see the giant's face. Runder's wide eyes were bloodshot and staring, his features haggard and gaunt. Streaks of white had appeared in his hair and beard. His mouth hung open and his throat hitched as if he were striving to speak.

Seth heard the word "darkcraft" muttered among the giants as they moved away. One giant with an especially shaggy red beard charged forward. Wings flapping, Seth sprang away, but the red-bearded giant made no move to chase him. Instead, he decapitated Runder with a stone ax. The other giants scattered. Redbeard backed away, eyes on Seth as if viewing a ghost, then turned and ran.

Seth stared at the Unforgiving Blade. He remembered how the dragon Velrog had begged for death when that dark blade was inside of him. Runder may have been trying to articulate something similar before his comrade stepped up and ended his misery.

What did they feel when the blade was inside of them? The experience went beyond receiving a cut that never healed. The victims seemed to experience horrors much worse than death.

Raxtus dropped off Tanu near Seth, and the nearly invisible dragon landed just beyond them. The Samoan potion master held up the crossbow he had claimed from the Dragon Temple. "I was ready to join the fight. You handled that well. You are formidable with those swords. How did you get Vasilis back?"

"The Singing Sisters sent it to me when they assigned me to find the pieces of the Ethergem," Seth said. He glanced over at Runder's corpse, face contorted with concern. "I didn't want to kill the giant."

"He was a predator hunting your cousins," Tanu said. "You did the right thing."

Seth nodded, sheathing Vasilis. Without the sword in his hand, he felt drained. "I'm tired of killing. I don't want to fight anyone."

Tanu nodded. "I'm glad to hear it. I don't want you to kill anyone either. But we're in a war. Sometimes we do unpleasant things to defend what matters most."

"Where are your cousins?" Raxtus asked. "Those sky giants will be here soon."

"My hermit troll friend told me that if I go into that building, he'll find me," Seth said.

"Why don't I go get Warren and Vanessa while you guys retrieve the kids?" Raxtus asked.

"Good thinking, Raxtus," Seth said.

"Hurry," Tanu said. "We only get one shot with the teleporter. Everyone who is coming must be together."

Raxtus took flight.

"Come on," Tanu said, jogging to the stone structure. He tried the front door. "Locked."

"I've got it," Seth said, using his power to disengage two locking mechanisms.

The door swung open before Tanu grabbed the handle. Both he and Seth jumped back, startled, but they relaxed when they realized it was Knox.

"Are the giants really gone?" Knox asked.

"Told you," Hermo said.

"Hermo made us hurry," Tess added.

"He was right," Tanu said. "The sky giants are almost here."

Knox, Tess, and Hermo exited the building, followed by Newel leaning heavily on Doren, and finally Dagny.

"No deeper place than this," Hermo said, pointing back at the doorway. "We hide?"

"Tanu can get everyone out of here," Seth said. "You should all go with him."

"How?" Knox asked.

"Andromadus gave me a teleporter," Tanu said. "It will take us to a safe place, far away."

"Why don't we use those more often?" Knox asked.

"It's the first one I've seen," Tanu said. "Andromadus made it. Teleportation seems to be a strength of his."

"Are you coming?" Tess asked Seth.

"I have other duties," Seth said.

"Where are Warren and Vanessa?" Knox asked.

"Raxtus is getting them," Seth said. "Vanessa is blind."

"Permanently?" Tess asked.

"Apparently," Seth said.

Knox stared past Seth to the fallen giant. "Is that Runder?"

"Seth slayed him," Tanu said.

"He was trying to attack you guys," Seth said.

"I told you I could have beat him with a magic sword!" Knox exclaimed.

"The wings helped," Seth said. "Hermo, you should go with them."

"Me no need transport," Hermo said.

"You'll be safe with them," Seth said.

"Me no want them," Hermo said. "Me want lair. Maybe one friend."

"There will be great places for lairs where they're going," Seth said.

"Me stay," Hermo said. "Help you."

"It would mean lots of fighting, Hermo," Seth said. "Not much hiding."

"Me go then," Hermo said.

"With the giants invading Humburgh, nothing remains for me here," Dagny said. "Potion master, I'll make myself useful if I can join your group."

"This is the woman who bound our injuries," Seth said.

"I'm a dragon," Dagny said. "But I'm fully committed to my human shape."

"Can we take that risk?" Tanu asked.

"It's not a risk," Tess said. "She's good."

"I'll vouch for her," Doren said. "She's had ample chance to harm us if that were her game."

"I'll submit to whatever precautions you feel are necessary," Dagny said.

"All right," Tanu said. "But you have to understand, I can't promise—"

"The sky giants are in the city!" Raxtus called, whooshing over the nearest rooftops, Warren and Vanessa wobbling in his claws. Raxtus dropped his passengers near Seth and landed beyond the group, where he became visible, silvery scales flashing.

Tanu took out a clay sphere the size of a baseball covered in elaborate imprints. "How close are the giants?"

"Seven or eight blocks away," Raxtus said. "It's now or never."

Tanu looked at Seth. "You're sure you want to stay?"

"I have to stay," Seth said. "The Ethershard is nearby."

"I'll help Seth," Raxtus said.

Tanu looked at the dragon. "I'd really appreciate that."

"I'll help as well," Vanessa said. "I may seem sidelined, but my abilities can still be useful from Selona."

"We need to see if we can heal you," Warren said.

"Don't forget who I am," Vanessa said. "I bit three giants at Terastios while they slept. Two died in the dragon attack, but my connection to the third remains."

"Can you control a sky giant?" Tanu asked.

"It will be a struggle," Vanessa said. "But I studied my marks and bit giants who were both weak in magic and slow-witted. I suspect I can take control. Where is the Ethershard?"

"In a town by Terastios where everything is sized to the sky giants," Seth said. "The birds, the cats, the bushes—everything."

"It's called Stratos," Vanessa said. "Where should I meet you?"

"There is a big oak just outside of the town wall," Seth said. "Meet there at sunset?"

"Is there more than one oak?" Vanessa asked.

"Not close to the wall," Calvin inserted. "Several elms, though."

"I'll be there," Vanessa said.

"Can you exert control over the giant all the way from Selona?" Warren asked.

"I'll work it out with Andromadus," Vanessa said. "My giant will be there."

"We'll be there too," Calvin said. "In fact, we could probably—"

The head and shoulders of a giant came into view above and behind the buildings across the square. The soldier had to be more than twice the height of the valley giants. Raxtus turned invisible.

"Everyone who is coming needs to touch me," Tanu instructed, holding up the clay sphere. Knox, Tess, Newel, Doren, Warren, Vanessa, Dagny, and Hermo huddled around Tanu, arms outstretched. "Make sure you're in contact!" Tanu shouted. "Take us to Selona!"

With a reddish flash, the group disappeared.

The first giant was clambering over a building to reach the square. Part of the roof collapsed, slowing him. The furious face of a towering female giant came into view, along with part of her enormous sword.

"Fly low at first," Raxtus advised. "This way."

Taking flight behind Raxtus, Seth sped away from the square. They rocketed along streets, staying beneath the rooftops, occasionally swooping around corners.

"We have to gain distance before we rise," Raxtus said.

"If we fly straight up, they'll take shots at us," Seth said.

"That's the problem," Raxtus replied.

When they reached a street that dead-ended against the city wall, Raxtus soared upward just high enough to clear the battlements. Then they zoomed away low across the plains.

# Chapter Twenty-Four

# Talizar

Each room inside the Moonlit Tower occupied an entire level, connected to other floors by a wrought-iron spiral staircase running up the center. The exception was the roof access granted by a narrow stairway along one wall. The tower did not taper, so each room was a hexagon of identical size.

Talizar led Kendra down the tight, steep staircase, descending through three rooms before stopping at the fourth. Heavy velvet drapes covered the windows. Extravagantly framed oil paintings adorned the walls. The plush furniture would have looked at home in an antique mansion. A white harpsicord painted with tiny flowers occupied one corner. Plentiful candelabras offered flickering light.

"Make yourself comfortable," Talizar said, indicating a

massive armchair. A tray holding cookies and a steaming mug awaited on the little table beside it.

"Thank you," Kendra said, removing a bolster and a tasseled pillow to make room to sit.

"Help yourself to gingersnaps and mint tea," Talizar said, standing with his shoulders slightly hunched and his hands behind his back.

"Is this what you eat?" Kendra asked.

"On rare occasions," Talizar answered. "My appetites are more . . . carnivorous."

"Are you going to sit?"

"I'd rather stand, thank you. Tell me why you have come."

"I need help finding the legendary Dragon Slayers," Kendra said.

The wolfman gave a toothy parody of a smile. "A worthy goal. I am glad to hear my gingersnaps will not be wasted."

Kendra tried a cookie. It was soft and flavorful, but gingersnaps were not her favorite. "Were you expecting me?"

"Ever since Jubaya marked you, I hoped you would approach me," Talizar said. "You are in a precarious position with the demons."

"I killed your king," Kendra said.

Talizar's eyes flashed, and he began to pace. "Exactly. Most of us expected Gorgrog to rule for another millennium. You threw our hierarchy into chaos. But the current conflict could offer you the chance to settle up with us."

"We have a common enemy," Kendra said.

"The dragons have muddied the waters for ages,"

Talizar said. "Never have they been so dangerous as under Celebrant. They have evolved into a force of nature with a will, as if a hurricane could actively seek vengeance."

"I'm trying to stop them," Kendra said.

Talizar came toward her, crouching, his muzzle a foot from her face. "And that is why we are willing to deal with you. A king for a king. Kill Celebrant, and the destruction of our monarch is forgiven."

"What if I capture him?" Kendra asked.

Backing away, Talizar gave a slow chuckle. "Do you think Celebrant is likely to submit to recapture? Can you envision him signing a treaty? Returning to a sanctuary?"

"Probably not," Kendra said.

"If you wish to quiet this storm of dragons, Celebrant must die," Talizar said. "Otherwise, the fight will continue until every last dragon has perished. Ideally, his son Tamryn will die as well. But first things first—we must sever the head of the snake."

Kendra tried a probative sip of the mint tea and found it too hot. "Easier said than done. The dragons are winning the war."

"We're aware," Talizar said. "You need Dragon Slayers. And I will help you, if you vow to slay Celebrant."

"Do I have to personally kill him?" Kendra asked.

"What a question!" Talizar exclaimed, stalking back and forth across the room. "Nobody cares who issues the killing stroke. I need a commitment that you will orchestrate the demise of the Dragon King, whether by Dragon Slayer, wizard, or your own hand. Pledge that you will stay on the task until Celebrant is dead, and you will have my assistance."

"What if things go bad for Celebrant and he surrenders?" Kendra asked. "What if he yields?"

"That will not happen," Talizar said. "And if he did, he would be playing you, and the same war would have to be fought again in the future."

Kendra considered the implications of making a promise to a demon. She already intended to slay Celebrant. The forces of good were at war with the dragons. Celebrant had tried to kill just about everyone she loved, and had enjoyed some success. He was a menace, an active threat to the safety of the world.

But could she guarantee Celebrant would die? No matter the circumstances? Would that make her a hit man? An assassin engaged by the demons?

The war was desperate. She needed guidance. Killing Celebrant was almost certainly necessary if they hoped to win. And it was probably impossible without help.

"Do you already know where I can find the legendary Dragon Slayers?" Kendra asked.

"I can lead you to one of them," Talizar said. "She is not far away."

"Here at Wyrmroost?"

"No, but she dwells in this part of the United States. She is like me."

"A werewolf?" Kendra asked.

"No more information until you pledge to see the task

through to completion," Talizar said. "Kendra, you are not the only person capable of fulfilling this assignment. If you would rather endure the enmity of the demons, be my guest."

Celebrant had killed Agad. He would have killed her and several members of her family had Andromadus not intervened. Celebrant had overthrown the dragon sanctuaries and intended to achieve world domination.

"I'll destroy him," Kendra said.

Talizar pounced toward her, making her fumble her second gingersnap. "That's what I needed to hear! Excellent. A king for a king."

"Deal."

"Magdalena is not a werewolf," Talizar said. "But if my instincts are correct, she has become a lycanthrope."

"Meaning a were-something?"

"She seldom retains a human form these days," Talizar said. He crossed to a low table and lapped a drink from a fancy golden bowl.

"You're a werewolf, right?"

Talizar looked up at her, the fur under his jaws matted with liquid. "First and foremost, I am a demon. I am a werewolf as well."

"Do you sometimes revert to a human shape?" Kendra asked.

"Why would I choose an inferior form?" Talizar asked.

"To blend in?" Kendra tried.

Talizar shook his head. "This is now my permanent

shape. Long ago, I resisted this form, succumbing only when the moon was bright."

"The full moon makes a difference?" Kendra asked.

"All lycanthropes are influenced by the moon," Talizar said. "Most resist the transformations at first. The beast wants control, you see, and that tends to frighten the rational mind. We don't want to terrorize our friends and family. But some of us see benefits when it comes to our enemies."

Kendra shivered. "How long did you resist?"

"For a time," Talizar said. "But when the moon is full, no lycanthrope can withstand the pull. I awakened afterward as if from a coma, guilty for having hunted. Life was never the same after that first kill. Resistance wears down. The transformation happens whether the moon is full or gibbous. Most of us are eventually consumed by the beast. After enough time passes, most lycanthropes never revert, and rational thought dwindles to a faint memory."

"You sound rational now," Kendra said.

"A few of us overcome those primal urges," Talizar said. "Instead of seeking to suppress our feral side, we learn to work with it, and we evolve into a true hybrid of man and beast, a predator with an intellect."

"How many lycanthropes become demons?" Kendra asked.

"Very few," Talizar said.

"And you think Magdalena is a lycanthrope?" Kendra asked.

"Such is my suspicion," Talizar said. "I have a great deal

of experience mentoring lycanthropes. I currently work with hundreds here at Wyrmroost, helping them transition to the highest state of which they are capable."

"Has Magdalena become wild?" Kendra asked.

"Assuming I'm right, the power the beast wields over her waxes and wanes," Talizar said. "When she loses her identity, the beast reigns. When she remembers her long history, she reasserts dominance."

"What kind of beast is she?" Kendra asked.

"If I am correct, she is one of a kind," Talizar said. "A wereyeti."

Kendra remembered what she knew from reading *Legend of the Dragon Slayer*. "She has the fang."

"And sometimes it rules her," Talizar said. He returned to his bowl and lapped up more of the liquid.

Kendra lifted her mug of mint tea and blew across the surface. Taking a small sip, she found the temperature barely tolerable. She would have sweetened it a little if she had sugar, but it tasted decent, and she loved the smell. "So I'm looking for a yeti?"

"Some might say a sasquatch," Talizar said, wetness dripping from his muzzle.

"No way," Kendra replied. "I'm looking for Bigfoot?"

"Whatever else influenced that legend, Magdalena is part of it," Talizar said.

"Where will I be looking?" Kendra asked.

"I recommend you start your search in Coeur d'Alene, Idaho," Talizar said.

"Are you sure about this?" Kendra asked.

"I'm not positive," Talizar said. "I've never seen her. But I've conducted extensive research. The topic is of great personal interest. Go to the Couer d'Alene Resort and search the lakeshore for an older man with a metal detector. His name is Sal Greenbaum, and you must convince him you are legitimately interested in learning about the sasquatch. If Sal believes you, he will help."

"What if he doesn't believe me?" Kendra asked.

"You will have a lot of ground to cover," Talizar said. "You're searching for a needle in a vast field of haystacks."

"What about the other legendary Dragon Slayers?" Kendra asked.

"I don't know their exact locations," Talizar said. "In anticipation of this offensive by the dragons, we have been searching earnestly for months. You should visit Batoosa next. He believes Gerwin hides in his part of the world."

"Which is where?" Kendra asked.

"Peru," Talizar replied. "The Starlit Shrine, in the mountains south of Machu Pichu."

"That's convenient," Kendra said.

"Did you expect this to be easy?" Talizar asked, pacing again. "At least you have winged mounts."

"How will I locate the Starlit Shrine?" Kendra asked.

"Southeast of Salcantay, the tallest mountain in the region, you will find a deep valley shielded by a potent distracter spell. Thanks to the mark Jubaya gave you and your commitment to slaying Celebrant, the spell over the valley will work in reverse for you, summoning rather than distracting. At the bottom of the valley, you will find Batoosa and his shrine."

"If Magdalena has turned wild, how can I reach her human side?" Kendra asked.

"It will be a challenge," Talizar said. "She may wish to fight, but you must do the opposite. Calm her. Soothe her. Help her recall her identity. Do not approach her by moonlight."

"How do I calm her?" Kendra asked.

"That depends," Talizar said.

"Aren't you the expert?" Kendra challenged.

"Effective methods vary," Talizar said. "Speak softly. Move slowly. Show no fear. The right music can help. Items from their former life. Favorite foods. With Magdalena, the yeti fang she carries is instrumental in her transformation. To separate it from her could distance Magdalena from her bestial nature. But taking it could also enrage her."

"She's lived a long time," Kendra said. "Is there any chance she has mastered her condition by now?"

Talizar chuckled darkly. "You are new to life. For most of us, a long life simply provides more time to accumulate damage. Magdalena is likely coping in ways that work for her."

"Is there anything else you can tell me?" Kendra asked.

"Trust her strength," Talizar said. "Once you wake her, Magdalena will be a powerful ally. To defeat Celebrant, you will need all the might you can gather. That tea should be cool enough for you now."

Kendra tried a sip and found he was right. She ate another cookie.

"When you are finished with the refreshments, I will see you out," Talizar said. "Should you encounter your brother, please give him my regards."

"You know Seth?" Kendra asked.

"We have interacted in the past," Talizar said. "Between the two of you, I did not suspect you would visit my tower before he did."

"Seth has plenty of his own problems," Kendra said. "The last thing he needs is to get mixed up with more demons."

Talizar spread his arms, palms outward. "We're here for those who need us."

# CHAPTER TWENTY-FIVE

# Second Try

The embers of the sunset dwindled on the horizon as Seth waited beside Raxtus on the bough of a gigantic oak tree. It was the same tree where Seth had roosted before his first attempt to steal the Ethershard. Raxtus stretched languidly in the dying light, neck and tail elongating.

"I can't believe the scale of this place," Raxtus murmured. "I'm not a big dragon, but around here I feel like an insect."

"How do you think I feel?" Calvin asked. "The insects in this town could eat me for breakfast and still want seconds."

"I've had interactions with giants," Seth said. "I just hadn't pictured a place with giant trees, giant horses, giant crops—I guess it makes sense. The giants should have a homeland somewhere."

"You tried to steal the Ethershard once before," Raxtus said.

Seth picked at the chunky ridges of the oak bark. "The Ethershard is out in the open. It could have been easy! There is a flaming cauldron in the middle of the town square, and the shard is in the fire. But it was a disaster. I tried a surprise attack in the dark and made it to the cauldron ahead of the guards. When I touched the flames, I was teleported into a cage. Since I was flying fast, I crashed into the bars and cut my leg with the Unforgiving Blade. Fortunately, the blade could hack through the bars, so I escaped, but just barely."

"What's your plan now?" Raxtus asked.

"I'm working on it," Seth said. "Raxtus, are you sure you want to help me? This will get personal for you, since Celebrant is your dad, and the stone in his crown is on my list."

"Celebrant may have sired me," Raxtus said, "but he has never been my dad. My stepmom treated me better than he did. The only time he ever included me was when he was trying to use me, which felt even worse than being ignored."

"That's terrible," Seth said.

"He already wants me dead," Raxtus said. "I betrayed him when I rescued Kendra from Skyhold. I've been hunted ever since. All dragons loyal to Celebrant consider me an enemy. Why not finally live up to expectations?"

"I'm glad to have your help," Seth said.

"Look," Calvin said quietly. "A giant is coming this way."

"I was starting to worry she wouldn't show up," Seth said.

"Be quiet until we're sure it's her," Raxtus whispered, fading into invisibility.

The broad-shouldered sky giant sauntered toward the tree, taller than most of his kind, more muscular as well. He had dark hair and a closely trimmed beard and wore a broadsword sheathed across his back. His lumpy nose made Seth suspect he had joined many brawls. The giant paused under the oak tree, folded his arms, and leaned against the trunk. Seth had felt out of reach high in the branches of the colossal tree, but this giant would be able to climb to him in no time.

"You still here?" the massive figure mumbled.

"We're here," Seth called down.

Placing his hands on his hips, the giant twisted at the waist, first one way, then the other, and then sat down, back to the trunk. "Sorry for the delay. I intended to be here right at sunset, but gaining mastery over Moro took longer than expected." It was strange to know that the low, rumbly voice was speaking words dictated by Vanessa.

"You have control now?" Seth checked.

"He won't shake my hold until I release him," Vanessa said. "It's nice to see again."

"Have you ever inhabited somebody this big?" Seth asked.

"Not nearly," Vanessa said. "It's thrilling."

"He was asleep this early?" Seth asked.

"I started working on him this afternoon," Vanessa said. "My first job was to make him drowsy."

"I never knew you could put people to sleep," Seth said.

"I can help the process along," Vanessa said. "After I lulled him, Moro dozed off about an hour ago. Then it was an extended, steady push to get control."

"Did he resist?" Seth asked.

"If a target becomes conscious of my attempt to inhabit him, I will fail," Vanessa said. "But that didn't happen with him. Moro had considerable self-possession, so it took time to infiltrate his faculties and hijack them."

"Are you actually at Selona?" Seth asked.

"No," Vanessa said. "We made it there safely, though. Andromadus approves of your mission. Especially the part about taking the jewel from Celebrant's crown. Andromadus hopes losing the jewel can harm Celebrant's hold over the dragons."

"Where are you?" Seth asked.

"Here at Titan Valley," Vanessa said. "Andromadus used magic to send me and Warren back until I help you with the Ethershard. I tried to access the giant from Selona, but it was too far away for me to feel comfortable about the connection. I'm in a cave not far from Terastios with Warren watching over my actual body."

"Amazing," Raxtus said.

"What's the plan?" Vanessa asked.

"The Ethershard is in a flaming cauldron in the town square," Seth said. "If I go into the flames, I get teleported into a cage. So I want to hack the cauldron apart with the Unforgiving Blade until the flames die."

"And you need enough time to do that," Vanessa said.

"What good is a sword that cuts through anything if you don't use it?" Seth reasoned. "Having you will help a lot. The more time you can buy me, the better."

"I'm the first diversion," Raxtus said. "The giants are paranoid about dragons since the invasion, so I want to act like I'm going after the Ethershard, then lead away any guards who give chase."

"Don't get caught," Vanessa warned.

"I know," Raxtus said. "I'm the size of a bird compared to a sky giant. Given the chance, they would crush me."

Vanessa held out her thick-fingered hands, clenching and unclenching the fists, muscles writhing in her forearms. "I expect they could."

"They won't catch me," Raxtus said. "But I'll let them get close enough to keep them interested. I'm confident I can dodge whatever they shoot or throw at me."

"Be ready for anything," Vanessa said. "There could be hidden guards. Somebody might toss a net. Or any number of other tricks and traps."

"Maybe Vanessa should enter first," Seth said. "Just talk to the guards. Then after Raxtus makes his move, she can keep the remaining guards busy while I attack the cauldron."

"Remember that you don't have to worry about my safety," Vanessa said. "Even if Moro gets captured or killed, I'm safe far away."

"We don't want him to die, though," Seth said.

"I pick my targets with care," Vanessa said. "Moro is a lowlife even by the standards of giants. He likes killing folks smaller than him. Even so, I'll give him every chance to live."

"Good enough for me," Seth said. "When should we strike?"

"After our failed attempt to get the shard, they will be hypervigilant," Calvin said.

"Let's hold off for a while," Vanessa said. "Make our move later in the night, when more of the town is drooling on their pillows. For now, I'll pretend to doze."

"I hate waiting," Raxtus said. "Especially with a big task looming. There is no peace."

Seth yawned. "If it means the giants will be slower to wake up, I'll find a way to handle the suspense."

By the time Seth took flight beside Raxtus, midnight had come and gone. Clouds in the sky hid the moon and most of the stars. Nothing hindered their approach to the bell tower. From the belfry, Seth counted six giant soldiers in leather armor guarding the cauldron. The cage Seth ruined had already been repaired or replaced. The cauldron was positioned where Seth remembered it, on the raised platform, multicolored flames blazing, flanked by two huge iron statues with heads like vultures.

"They doubled the guards," Calvin whispered.

"I was a little worried they might have relocated everything," Seth replied softly.

"Our big advantage is the square being open to the sky," Raxtus whispered. "If you can get your hands on the Ethershard, you can escape through flight."

"My wings saved me last time," Seth replied. "I just have to avoid getting hit. One strike from a weapon and I'm a goner."

"Here comes Vanessa," Calvin whispered.

Inhabiting the strapping body of Moro, Vanessa ambled into the square. A guard wielding a halberd stepped away from his post and approached her.

"Heritage Square is now closed from sunset to sunrise," the guard said. "Surely you heard the news, Moro."

"I'm here to lend my sword to the cause," Moro said.

The guard called over his shoulder. "He wants to help keep watch."

The guard closest to the cauldron wore a helmet with horns and seemed to be the captain. "If Moro wants to help, he can do it from outside the square," the captain answered. "We want to keep lines of sight open and follow established protocols."

"You want me on a side street?" Moro asked, sounding offended. "Guarding what?"

"Ready to lend aid if needed," the captain replied. "The recent intruder escaped and could make another attempt to steal the Ethershard."

"Lend aid from a side street?" Moro asked, insulted. "Will the thief be driving a wagon?"

"Vanessa is playing this up," Seth whispered. "Maybe you should go for it while they're already distracted."

"Yeah?" Raxtus asked. "Now?"

Seth gave a nod.

Dwindling into a faint distortion, Raxtus flew away from the belfry toward the far side of the square. The plan was for him to approach from the direction opposite Seth's.

Down below, Vanessa continued her complaints. "Are you guaranteeing me that you six can protect the shard without aid? Wasn't the idea of placing it in the center of town to let everyone help keep it safe? Are you comfortable with me putting you on trial should you fail in this duty?"

Raxtus became visible and streaked down toward the cauldron. It took a moment for one of the guards to spot him.

"Dragon!" a guard cried in alarm.

To their credit, the other guards quickly readied their weapons and rushed to impede access to the cauldron. Raxtus came close to one of the female guards, dodging a thrust from her spear and then wheeling away from her. Another guard fired a crossbow, and the huge bolt pinged off the dragon's scales, making Raxtus spiral before righting himself.

"Was it a dragon last time?" the heaviest guard called.

"No, a little fellow with golden wings," the captain answered.

Three of the guards chased Raxtus, throwing knives and hand axes. Two others took up positions on either side of the cauldron, facing outward. The captain roved the area around the platform, sword in hand, eyes alert.

"Where do you need me?" Vanessa asked.

"Go sound the alarm," the captain said.

"For one baby dragon?" Vanessa asked.

The captain stalked about, head pivoting to look in all directions at once. "That dragon could be a prelude to a larger attack. Sound the alarm to bring reinforcements."

"Where is the alarm?" Vanessa asked.

"Are you addled?" the captain asked. "The bell by the cages."

"Right," Vanessa said, hurrying over toward the cages. When she reached the bell, Vanessa realized she was only a few paces from the cauldron. "Is that another dragon?" she called, pointing up into the night.

"Where?" one of the guards flanking the cauldron asked as she and her comrade turned to stare in the direction Vanessa had indicated.

With the guards facing away from her, Vanessa charged forward, grabbed the female guard, and thrust her into the flames of the cauldron. The female guard vanished and reappeared inside the largest cage, and an alarm started blaring. As the other guard turned, Vanessa lowered her shoulder and rammed him into the flames as well. The largest cage now held two occupants.

"Traitor!" the captain shouted, closing on Vanessa.

Vanessa reached over her shoulder and drew her broadsword, then met the captain's blade with her own. As their swords clashed, Seth sprang from the belfry and swooped down toward the cauldron. From what Seth could see of their combat, Vanessa and the captain looked evenly matched. "Return to me!" the captain shouted as they fought. The giants who were chasing Raxtus had passed out of sight, and Seth doubted whether they could hear the command over the alarm.

After landing on the platform, Seth raced to one of the three cabriole legs supporting the cauldron and slashed it with the Unforgiving Blade. With the iron leg severed, the cauldron tipped in Seth's direction. He dove sideways, wings swishing, and barely avoided being steamrolled. After recovering, Seth started hacking at the bulging body of the cauldron. After several deep cuts, the flames flickered out.

Looking up, Seth saw the sword of the captain embedded in Vanessa's ribs, and she had him in a headlock. The captain staggered around, trying to shake her loose. Two of the guards that had chased Raxtus were dashing back toward the cauldron. Some new soldiers came racing toward the square from a side street, apparently summoned by the alarm.

Seth didn't see the Ethershard inside the cauldron, so he took out half of the Wizenstone and moved it around until the hemisphere flashed and vibrated. Smaller than Seth had expected, the Ethershard had fallen free from the cauldron and slid almost to the edge of the platform.

The captain hurled Vanessa to the ground and picked up her broadsword. Seth took flight, skimming low across the planks of platform toward the Ethershard. The broadsword came flying through the air and swished past him as his wings pulled him into an evasive swerve. The huge blade swiped the Ethershard as it clattered past, knocking the little stone off the platform.

"Get the shard!" the captain shouted, indicating where it had fallen.

The oncoming guards sprinted toward the shard, and the captain pelted forward as well. Seth flew off the edge of the platform and landed in the dirt, pain shooting from the slice in his leg, eyes frantically hunting for the shard while he moved the Wizenstone hemisphere in different directions.

"There it is!" Calvin cried, pointing.

The hemisphere flashed in multiple colors, and Seth saw where the Ethershard had landed half-buried in dirt. With guards closing in from two directions, Seth ran forward and slid to his knees. His fingers closed around the Ethershard and he sprang into the air, wings flapping hard. He weaved to avoid a thrown spear, then again to dodge a poleax. Suddenly animated, the iron statues with heads like vultures came toward him, arms extended, but they were earthbound, and too slow. Eyes on the few misty stars peeking through the clouds, Seth passed out of reach and kept climbing, tuning out the furious giants yelling below him.

# CHAPTER TWENTY-SIX

# Bernice

From the sky, Kendra saw that Lake Coeur d'Alene extended long and narrow, with numerous bends and inlets lacing the erratic coastline. The Coeur d'Alene Resort rose above the edge of the lake, surrounded by a marina providing moorage for hundreds of private boats.

"We can land above those rocks," Kendra said, pointing out a hill opposite the marina.

"It's not very close to the beach," Glory replied.

"If we land right on the busy shore, I worry about freaking out the nonmagical bystanders," Kendra said.

"When we're airborne, what do the mortals see?" Virgil asked.

"I don't know," Kendra said. "Definitely not a satyr on a flying horse. Maybe a bird?"

"What's the trouble with a bird landing on the beach?" Noble asked.

"They'll see me like a normal person," Kendra said. "How can a normal person explain she was riding a gigantic bird? And who knows how they'll see Virgil? I don't want to test how far the illusion can stretch."

Gliding down smoothly, the horses landed on the side of the hill overlooking the water, trotting to a stop. Kendra and Virgil dismounted.

"We'll find a shady spot and graze," Glory said.

"Unless you need us," Noble said, tossing his mane. "Call out if there is trouble."

Virgil slipped the pendant over his head. "This will make me look like a person to the mortals?"

"Yes," Kendra said. "Otherwise, it will look like I'm leading around a goat."

"What if you can't find the guy Talizar told you about?" Glory asked.

"We'll need a place to spend the night," Kendra said.

"An inn?" Virgil asked.

"We would need money," Kendra said.

"I have coins from Humburgh," Virgil said. "I know people here wouldn't recognize our currency, but my most valuable coins are made of silver or gold."

"In my country, people pay with US dollars or credit cards," Kendra said. "Not many places will change gold into usable cash."

"At worst we can camp," Noble said. "Go find your contact while daylight remains."

Kendra picked her way down the hill. She and Virgil came out near a military memorial with a large bell and several flagpoles. Long rows of boats sat idle in the marina. Kendra noticed statues of coyotes placed periodically along the docks, presumably to scare away birds.

They walked around the resort to the public beach on the far side. Though some people were heading to their cars carrying towels and coolers, the beach remained fairly crowded. Out on a pier, a line of people waited to rent kayaks as workers distributed life vests. A tall clock tower revealed the time to be almost four-thirty. Kendra and Virgil walked along the beach, behind where people lounged and waded.

"I've never experienced a mortal community," Virgil said, eyes on the cars pulling out of the parking lot. "Your technology is astounding."

"Yeah, but no magic," Kendra said.

"It looks like magic to me," Virgil said, watching a pickup truck. "That huge building is an inn?"

"A resort," Kendra said. "A big, fancy inn where people go on vacation. Let's scan the beach for a guy with a metal detector."

"Right," Virgil said. "A rod with a disc at the end used for divining metal. And you don't think mortals have magic?"

"We're good at harnessing certain elements," Kendra said. "Electricity. Fossil fuels."

"Look how fast that boat is going," Virgil said, gesturing at the lake.

"Dragons are faster," Kendra said. "I guess some of our machines are impressive."

"I'd love a boat that fast," Virgil said.

Kendra peered up the shoreline for anyone operating a metal detector. No candidates were in view. What if he only came out in the morning? Or on certain days?

Virgil laid a hand on Kendra's shoulder. "Over there," he said, indicating the direction with a jerk of his chin.

Kendra looked away from the beach at a shady park with large, widely spaced trees. An older man in cargo shorts, a faded yellow Hawaiian shirt, and a wide-brimmed camping hat was roaming the lawn, a metal detector slowly swaying in his grasp.

"Good eyes," Kendra said. "Could be our guy."

"Maybe you should approach him alone," Virgil said. "A solitary teenage girl will seem less intimidating."

"Sure," Kendra said. "Keep an eye on me in case he gets creepy."

"Will do," Virgil said.

Kendra left the satyr behind. As she neared the man with the metal detector, Kendra waved at him and flashed a smile. "Hello."

The man paused, took off his unfashionable sunglasses, and gave Kendra a nod. "Did you lose something? You wouldn't believe how many wedding rings I've helped folks recover."

"I'm all right," Kendra said. "Have you found anything good today?"

"This and that," the man said. His slight accent made Kendra think of New York. "Another day, another handful of bottle caps."

"What's the most interesting thing you've ever found?" Kendra asked.

He shrugged his rounded shoulders. "That depends on what you find interesting."

"Any treasure?" Kendra asked.

"Not the kind you probably mean," the man said. "No strongboxes filled with gold and pearls. I once found a bayonet."

"Any cell phones?" Kendra asked.

"Is that the kind of treasure you mean? Plenty of cell phones. Keys and change, of course. The occasional railroad spike."

"What's the best time of day to hunt for stuff?" Kendra asked.

"Early in the morning," the man said. "Or in the evening, after people leave. It's surprising how much gets lost."

"Do you ever find huge footprints?" Kendra asked.

The man changed his stance and looked a little wary. "With a metal detector?"

"As you look around."

"Why would I see huge footprints?"

"Sasquatches," Kendra said.

The man frowned. "Did somebody put you up to this?"

"Up to what?" Kendra asked.

"Teasing me about Bigfoot," the man said.

"I'm interested in Bigfoot," Kendra said. "I'm looking for a man named Sal. Are you Sal?"

"You found me," Sal said. "Who told you I know about sasquatches?"

"I have a special interest in Bigfoot," Kendra said. "I ask a lot of questions. I heard you're a person with answers."

"So you came and found me," Sal said.

Kendra nodded. "What can you tell me?"

"Why do you want to know?" Sal asked.

"Because I believe Bigfoot is real," Kendra said. "Lots of people disagree."

"It's wise to stay open-minded," Sal said. "Don't ever let anyone tell you otherwise. 'There are more things in heaven and earth, Horatio, than are dreamt of in your philosophy.' The world is a stranger, more interesting place than many are willing to see."

"I agree. I'm Kendra."

"Nice to meet you," Sal said. "Do you want to sit and talk for a few minutes?"

"That would be perfect," Kendra said with a big smile.

Sal walked over to a nearby picnic table, set down his metal detector, and took a seat. Kendra sat across from him.

"Have you had an experience that sparked your belief in Bigfoot?" Sal asked.

"Sort of," Kendra said. "I've seen some things others don't believe in."

"Hmmm," Sal said. "Such anomalies do exist. Why sasquatches?"

"I have a friend who convinced me that a sasquatch lives in this part of the country."

"Near here?" Sal asked.

"Yes," Kendra said.

"Who is the friend?" Sal asked.

"Just a guy I know," Kendra said.

"Is it the guy watching us?"

"Who?"

"Looks like he could be your dad," Sal said. "Or an uncle?"

Kendra looked around and spotted Virgil at the edge of the park, looking away from her. "He's not who told me about sasquatch. That's Uncle Virgil. He's just making sure I'm safe."

"The father in me approves," Sal said. "Are you a reporter?"

"No."

"Do you have a YouTube channel?"

"Nope," Kendra said. "I'm just curious."

"Well, that is refreshing," Sal said. "I have a lot of hobbies. Investigating cryptids is one of them."

"Cryptids?"

"Creatures of folklore," Sal said. "Lake monsters, chupacabras, elusive hairy hominids."

"Like the sasquatch," Kendra said.

"Many cultures report some version of Bigfoot," Sal said. "Call him a sasquatch, a yeti, a yeren, a yowie, or a skunk ape—there seems to be a huge, mysterious personage who has appeared in diverse places over the years. You never mentioned what you saw."

"It sounds silly," Kendra said. "I don't often talk about it. I guess you could say I've seen winged cryptids."

"You've seen the Mothman?" Sal asked, eyebrows raised.

"Think smaller," Kendra said. "Fairies."

"You're serious?" Sal asked.

"Nobody ever believes me," Kendra said.

"I know how that feels," Sal said. "I've seen some odd-ness in the backcountry I can't explain. I take fishing trips. Stand still long enough and you notice things others miss." He wiggled the metal detector. "I enjoy finding what most people ignore."

"What have you seen?" Kendra asked eagerly.

"More than once, I've been in remote forests, with the hair on the back of my neck standing up straight, aware I was being watched, maybe even hunted. I've glimpsed in-explicable lights in the sky, moving in unnatural ways. I've heard strange chanting on the wind, and I've been woken by unearthly cries in the night. Most of what I've experienced, I've learned to keep to myself, so others won't judge me."

"I know what you mean," Kendra said. "It kind of cheap-ens what happened when people don't believe you."

"What did you do, Kendra, when you saw fairies?" Sal asked. "Did you tell all your friends? Did you catch one in a bottle?"

"I was just excited," Kendra said. "I didn't want to spoil anything for them. But I tried to see them when I could."

"Did they stay around?"

"I still know some places where I can usually spot them," Kendra said.

Sal gave a slow nod. "That's very interesting. Kendra, my experience happened by accident. I was tracking an elk up a steep slope, getting drawn into unknown country. Had I dropped dead from a heart attack, nobody would have ever found me. I started climbing a tree to get my bearings, and for a moment I found myself face-to-face with something much larger than me, hairy as an ape, but with intelligence in the eyes. It was brief, Kendra. The creature dropped through the branches and was gone in a flash. But for a crystal-clear moment I saw the sasquatch up close, and it saw me."

"Wow," Kendra said.

"I've kept my eyes open ever since," Sal said. "Even went looking on purpose a few times. Never had another sure sighting."

"Were you scared?" Kendra asked.

"I have no doubt the creature could have crushed me on a whim," Sal said. "Funny thing was, I saw something in the creature's eyes, during that fraction of a second when our gazes met, right before the sasquatch dropped to the ground and tore out of there."

"What was it?" Kendra prompted.

"Intelligence, maybe?" Sal shrugged, squinted eyes studying the shadows of leaves shifting on the grass. "Recognition? Definitely surprise."

"It was no dumb beast," Kendra added.

"Whatever it was, I felt kinship and even respect for it. Not fear."

Kendra waited until it was clear he was done speaking. "That's amazing."

Sal seemed to be awakening from a trance. "Look, kid, I generally discourage people from looking for Bigfoot because I don't want to scare the creature away from these parts. I hardly tell the full version of my experience to anyone. But I read something different in you."

"This matters to me," Kendra said.

Sal sniffed and nodded. "You'd be surprised how many people have a story to tell like mine, if you know how to let them talk. A few years ago, I met a woman with more knowledge than anyone on this subject. How well can you keep a secret?"

"I'm an expert," Kendra said.

"Most people don't like to talk if it's going to be broadcasted," Sal said. "I'd rather understand sasquatches than expose them. If they wanted to be found, they would have shown themselves long ago."

"I'm not trying to lead anybody to this information," Kendra said. "It's just for me. I promise."

"Fair enough," Sal said. "Some of what I know isn't mine to share. I can point you in the right direction. Follow the interstate toward Montana. Past the exit for the mission you'll find the Canyon Grill. They have a hokey little shrine to Bigfoot in the lobby. Ask for Bernice. If you can get her to talk, you'll learn as much as anyone knows about the topic."

"Bernice?" Kendra checked. "At the Canyon Grill."

"Tell her Sal likes you," Sal said. "Don't harass her. If she doesn't want to share, leave her alone."

"I'll be on my best behavior," Kendra said.

"Well, you look too young to be a reporter," Sal said. "I better get back to my other hobby."

"Thanks for the information," Kendra said.

She got up and walked away from the table. When she glanced back, Sal had resumed scouring the ground with his metal detector. Kendra didn't see Virgil, so she headed back toward the hill. The satyr caught up to her in the parking lot.

"I thought you ditched me," Kendra said.

"I was watching from afar," Virgil said. "Looked like you had a good talk."

"We have a new stop," Kendra said. "Another expert."

"Good," Virgil said. "Do I look human to you?"

Kendra glanced down at his goat legs. "You're still a satyr in my eyes."

"The rest of the mortals don't look twice at me," Virgil said, touching the pendant. "It must be working."

Kendra and Virgil found the horses grazing not far from where they had left them. "Back so soon?" Noble asked around a mouthful of grass.

"We have another stop," Kendra said. "We need to follow the interstate toward Montana past the mission until we find the Canyon Grill."

"I don't know what most of that means," Glory said.

"The biggest road with the most cars," Kendra said. "I saw it before we landed. We follow that east."

"Let's go see more of the wide world," Glory said.

"Are you hungry?" Virgil asked Kendra. "I have some provisions."

"I'm fine now, thanks. Maybe after this next meeting."

Glory surged into the sky with Noble as her wingman. The horse banked as Kendra pointed out the freeway, and soon they soared several hundred feet above the cars and trucks, overlooking an expanse of lake and trees. When

Kendra saw the mission, she had the horses fly lower, examining any building that might be a restaurant. Off the interstate farther east, she finally spotted a sign for the Canyon Grill. The winged horses landed on a quiet dirt road screened from the restaurant by some trees.

"I might go inside alone again," Kendra said. "I think you were right that my age puts people at ease."

"I'll go in after a few minutes," Virgil said. "To keep an eye on you."

Kendra gave a nod. She picked her way through the trees, crossed the gravel parking lot, and entered the front door of the log building. A homespun Bigfoot shrine immediately caught her attention. The featured attraction was a seven-foot statue of a sasquatch crudely carved from wood and wearing a wooly hat with earflaps. She also noticed the plaster cast of a huge footprint, a dozen sasquatch-themed postcards, several blurry photographs of a hairy humanoid, a handful of apelike figurines, and a sketched wanted poster offering a reward for the capture of Bigfoot. Christmas lights fringed the whole area, completing the kitschy vibe.

The eatery was not busy, with a few patrons at tables. There was no hostess, so Kendra entered and approached a server as the young man walked away from a table. His rolled-up sleeves revealed tattoos on his slim forearms.

"Excuse me," Kendra said. "I'm looking for Bernice."

"She just got in," the server said. "Should I tell her who's looking for her?"

"She doesn't know me," Kendra said. "I'm a friend of her friend Sal."

He gave a little chuckle. "You his granddaughter or something?"

"Something," Kendra said.

The server disappeared into the back. Kendra lingered by the entrance. After a minute or two, a woman emerged from the door to the kitchen. She wore a blue and black flannel shirt and blue jeans. Her graying hair was up in a messy bun, and her Converse sneakers lacked laces and socks.

"Is Sal making friends with teenage girls?" the woman asked.

"Lucky me. I'm Kendra. Are you Bernice?"

"What can I do for you?" Bernice asked.

"I need to find a sasquatch," Kendra said.

Bernice smirked. "We've got a lot of memorabilia right behind you. Or I could sell you a T-shirt."

Kendra glanced over her shoulder at the shrine. Virgil had entered and was crouched studying one of the figurines.

"I'm serious," Kendra said. "There is a sasquatch in this area, and I need to find her."

"Her?" Bernice asked.

"I'm pretty sure she's female and is actually a yeti," Kendra said. "Can you help me?"

"Why would I know squat about a yeti?" Bernice asked. "That stuff up front is for fun, kiddo. Do you want a table?"

"Sal said you know more about sasquatches than any-one," Kendra said.

"Maybe more than anyone Sal knows," Bernice said. "His social circle has a small diameter. Is this for your school newspaper?"

"It's for me," Kendra said. "I've had some experiences that have me convinced there is a yeti nearby."

"You may not be wrong," Bernice said. "There have been rumors about such things for years. But I find it odd that after all this time, nobody has produced concrete evidence."

"I think you know more than you're telling me," Kendra said.

"Whatever I know, I don't want to get mixed up in searching for sasquatches," Bernice said. "Or abominable snowpersons. If they exist, we ought to let them have a little peace. They have no obligation to satisfy our curiosity. Look, I'm just starting a shift. I'm sorry if you were hoping for more, but I'm afraid you've reached a dead end."

Kendra knew her window of opportunity was closing. She needed to hint at everything she knew about Magdalena, in case it sparked something. "What if the yeti needs our help? What if she's actually a woman who has forgotten who she is?"

Bernice paled. "A woman? Says who?"

Kendra saw that she had struck a chord. "It might sound silly, but I have a message for her from her family."

Bernice gave a slow nod. "You're serious."

"Her name is Magdalena," Kendra said. "I need to find her."

"Okay, girlie," Bernice said. "Let's talk. Have you eaten?"

"No," Kendra said. "What about your shift?"

"Come with me," Bernice said. "I own the place, and we're not busy."

# CHAPTER TWENTY-SEVEN

# Muster

Seth awoke to the smell of the sea. Disoriented for a moment, he then recalled spotting the freighter the night before, a boat heading from New Zealand toward Australia. It was a container ship—long, flat, and piled high with rectangular steel boxes. Seth and Raxtus had found a place toward the stern where the containers were stacked seven high, sheltered from view by a subsequent row piled eight above the deck.

The svelte dragon lay beside Seth, eyes closed, head and tail curled toward his body, the morning light refracting off his silver-white scales. Calvin lay beside the tip of the dragon's tail, a hat over his face, bundled in a handkerchief. The waves were choppy, noticeably rocking the ship. Seth unfolded his wings from around himself and stretched.

One of the dragon's eyelids slid upward. "Is it morning already?"

"We were up late last night," Seth said.

"We would have been up later if we hadn't found this ship," Calvin said.

"I like traveling in my sleep," Raxtus said.

"It's slow compared to flight," Seth said. "But better than nothing."

"I'm starving," Calvin said.

"Back at Humburgh, I put some crackers and cheese in my satchel," Seth said, rummaging in his bag. "Some kiwis, too, though I wish I had a knife and a spoon."

"Cut the kiwi with the Unforgiving Blade," Calvin said. "That will teach it."

"Are you hungry, Raxtus?" Seth asked.

"I'm content," Raxtus said. "Dragons aren't like humans. We don't require three meals a day. Once or twice a week is usually enough, though we eat serious helpings on those occasions. Right now, I have something on my mind other than food."

"What?" Seth asked, passing Calvin part of a cracker and a fragment of cheese.

"Father is calling a muster," Raxtus said.

"What does that mean?" Seth asked.

"I feel the call like a growing weight on my mind," Raxtus said. "I sensed it last night and tried to ignore it. But the summons rings unmistakably clear this morning."

"Summoning you where?" Calvin asked.

Raxtus closed his eyes. "The Carpathian Mountains,

in the Czech Republic. I can visualize the location in my mind." Raxtus opened his eyes. "Father is calling dragons everywhere to join him in preparation for the final assault. Only dragons with a conflicting assignment from Father are exempt."

"Are all dragons compelled to answer the call?" Seth asked.

"A handful of isolationists will resist," Raxtus said. "But all will hear the call and feel the tug."

"Doesn't Celebrant know you're on our side?" Calvin asked. "He's giving away his position to you."

"The call to muster is a general broadcast," Raxtus said. "It reaches all of our kind. He would rather assemble a vast horde of dragons than worry about the few who might betray the summons."

"I could find him anyhow," Seth said. "The Wizenstone will lead me to his crown."

"Are we going after Celebrant next?" Calvin asked. "Or the Demon King?"

"I'm not sure which will be more difficult," Seth said.

"We did well at Titan Valley," Calvin said. "But Titan Valley was smashed. The giants were reeling from the dragon attack."

"Father will be surrounded by the full might of his army," Raxtus said.

"Same with Orogoro," Seth said. "The majority of the demons are imprisoned with him."

"Can we isolate Celebrant?" Calvin asked. "There must be a way to lure him from the group."

"Would he meet with you, Raxtus?" Seth asked. "If you send him a message?"

Raxtus started laughing. "Not under most circumstances. He's much too busy to bother with me. His attention is on the victory he has craved for hundreds of years. But there is one way I could get close to him." Raxtus laughed again, harder.

"How?"

"I could challenge him to combat," Raxtus said. "For the crown."

"Could you beat him?" Seth asked.

Raxtus laughed some more. Seth glanced at Calvin, who gave a little shrug. Was the dragon going crazy? Regaining his composure, Raxtus cleared his throat. "Not a chance. Father would demolish me in a duel. But I don't need to beat him. I just have to get close enough to steal the crown off his head."

"How?" Seth asked.

"I'm fast, I'm durable, and I can turn nearly invisible," Raxtus said.

"You could be killed," Seth said.

"You or I could have gotten killed back at Stratos, too," Raxtus said. "If any dragons catch me, they will try to slay me. If Father gets his claws on me, I'm a goner. But if you want the crown before the war ends, this gives us a chance."

"Do you think he'll accept your challenge?" Seth asked.

"He won't want to postpone the fight. He'll relish the chance to eliminate me, to show what happens to those who cross him."

Seth gazed at the churning wake behind the ship. He hated to put Raxtus in danger. But how else was he supposed to access Celebrant? Raxtus had his own score to settle with his father.

"Honestly, this makes me uncomfortable," Seth said.

"If I fail, it will be a story," Raxtus said. "I'll have joined a small club of dragons who challenged a king. If I succeed, I will be infamous. Arguably the most villainous traitor to dragons since Archadius became the first wizard. You know what? Better infamous than pathetic."

"Really?" Seth asked.

Raxtus swiveled his head toward Seth, staring him in the eyes. "I'm against this war. It's bad for dragonkind, bad for humankind—bad for everyone. I heard how the crown influenced Knox. My father's crown may be affecting him in a similar way. What if taking the crown helps him see reason? Stealing his crown could reduce his credibility as a leader. I can't think of any other way I could strike a blow that might actually matter. I have to do this."

"Europe is far from here," Seth said.

Raxtus elongated his neck and extended his wings. "Then we had better get started."

# CHAPTER TWENTY-EIGHT

# Magdalena

Kendra sat across from Bernice at a wobbly card table in a back room. Mops and brooms leaned in a corner beside worn cabinets full of cleaning supplies. A hanging lamp with a tin shade provided light. A savory plate of chicken wings sat in front of Kendra, with blue cheese and ranch dressing in little plastic cups. A loaded baked potato awaited on a second plate, alongside a buttery heap of steamed broccoli.

"I joke about Bigfoot all the time," Bernice said. "I curate the silly shrine. It's a way to hide my interest in plain sight. I seldom share my actual feelings on the subject. And nobody knows the whole story. But you found me, and you know the local sasquatch is actually a human woman. Nobody besides me knows that, and I've never told a soul."

"How did you find out?" Kendra asked.

"It's quite a story," Bernice said. "I've been married

twice. It didn't take either time. I lived more adventurously after that. About fifteen years ago, I was hiking in the backcountry with my boyfriend, a fella named Ted. We both loved the outdoors, and we were spending five days hiking and fishing, sleeping under the stars. Imagine our surprise when we came across a mother grizzly leading her two cubs across a meadow."

"Aren't they dangerous around their young?" Kendra asked.

"They sure can be," Bernice said.

"What did you do?" Kendra asked.

"I froze, and Ted gave a shout or two to establish our presence. After a tense pause, the bruin shepherded her cubs away over a rise. Once she was out of sight, we hoofed it in the other direction. We were relieved the bear didn't seem to want anything to do with us. We never expected a grizzly, but we were traveling with bear spray, so Ted got it out just in case.

"Hiking fast, we had gone maybe two hundred yards before we heard crashing behind us. We turn and this huge mama grizzly is racing toward us like a freight train, full charge, much faster than a human could run, maybe forty yards away when we first spotted her."

"She got the cubs clear, then came back," Kendra said.

"That's what I figure. I've always heard to make yourself big, so I raised my arms and gave a shout while Ted fumbled with the bear spray. That mama bear could not have cared less what I was doing. She devoured the ground between us in no time. Ted hollered at me to get down, so I curled up like a fetus, head tucked low, hands on the back of my neck. Ted fired a blast of the spray at the last second, and then the bear was on him."

"Oh no," Kendra said.

Bernice shuddered. "I watched out of the corner of my eye as he tried to get down and curl up. That bear bit him on the shoulder and started working him over with her claws. He sprang up and tried to fight, probably trying to protect me, which enraged the bear. She got hold of his neck and shook him around like a toy."

Kendra winced.

"It was gruesome. I won't overdo the description. I knew he was extremely dead. After the bear dropped him, she lumbered over to me and bit me on the arm. I tried not to scream from the pain. Her teeth made punctures. I still have faint scars. Fortunately, the bear didn't latch on. Then I heard the roar."

"Right in your ear?" Kendra asked.

"The roar didn't come from any bear," Bernice said. "No bear could have produced that sound. I felt vibrations in the ground, and I had to cover my ears. The bear gave an odd cry, and I glanced up to see the grizzly bear hefted into the air by a larger creature and then hurled against a tree. The bear looked stunned, and when the sasquatch roared again, it scurried away. Can you imagine a grizzly bear scurrying?"

"I can now," Kendra said.

"If I thought I was dead with the bear attacking, now I was certain. Breathing hard, the sasquatch approached and stood over me, considerably taller than the grizzly, with broad shoulders and heavy limbs. I stayed down and lowered my gaze to the shaggy, clawed feet. When the creature lifted me up, I had to bite my lip to keep my screams in. The light gray fur was long and coarse, and the sasquatch was immensely strong. I was petrified. If you're right that she's a yeti, the light coloring would fit. Anyhow, she carried me a long way to a paved road, set me down, and ran off into the wild."

"I'm sorry about Ted," Kendra said.

"I led authorities back to the same clearing where the attack happened," Bernice said. "But there were no remains. None were ever found."

"The yeti saved you," Kendra said.

"That she did," Bernice said. "I wish she had gotten there earlier. I really liked Ted. Given some time, he might have become my third husband."

"Was that the last time you saw the yeti?" Kendra asked.

Bernice's eyes widened and she shook her head. "No, that was just the beginning. I became a bit obsessed with the yeti after that. I never told the authorities about her. I described the bear attack without mentioning a sasquatch. I didn't want to bring trouble her way. But I desperately wanted to find her again. Took me three years. Now I see her regularly."

"Really?" Kendra asked.

"Really and truly," Bernice said. "I bring her food. I have some friends who are hunters. They save certain parts of their kills for me. She also loves beef ribs."

"How do you know where to find her?" Kendra asked.

"We have developed a rapport," Bernice said. "I'm fascinated by her, and she seems to appreciate that I'm familiar. Of course, she also likes the treats I bring."

"She has learned to trust you," Kendra said.

"I've only seen her human form twice," Bernice said softly.

"Did she talk to you?" Kendra asked.

Bernice shook her head. "Both of those times I caught her sleeping. The first time, I had no idea why I had found a young woman napping on a bed of crushed evergreen boughs. I was startled by her native beauty, despite her filthy and unkempt state. I wondered if the sasquatch had rescued another human, and I resolved to wake her up. Before I could reach her, the woman began to swell. Bestial features deformed her face, and the rags she wore disappeared into her fur. Once the transformation was complete, she awoke, with no trace of humanity remaining."

"She reverts to her human form in her sleep?" Kendra asked.

"Not as a rule," Bernice said. "I know she also sleeps in yeti form. But the two times I came upon her as a human, she changed back into a yeti before waking."

"Can you take me to her?" Kendra asked.

"I wouldn't share so much if I weren't willing to try," Bernice said. "I've never attempted this with anyone. I'm not sure how the yeti will react when she detects a new scent. But you have a message from her family?"

"I've met her brother," Kendra said. "This yeti stuff is part of an ancient curse. She needs to remember who she is.

Hopefully that will give her more control over the changes. When you saw her human form, I assume there was no moon."

"It was in the daytime on both occasions," Bernice said. "She sleeps more often during the day than at night."

"She's like a werewolf," Kendra said. "We won't want to approach while the moon is out."

"Then our soonest chance is tomorrow afternoon," Bernice said. "Moon is up in the morning right now. Do you live nearby?"

"I'm not from around here," Kendra said.

"Do you have a car?" Bernice asked.

Kendra cringed and winced. "Not even that."

"How are you getting around?" Bernice asked. "Aren't you a little young to be on your own like this?"

"My Uncle Virgil is with me," Kendra said. "We're improvising how we get around."

"Is he a good person?" Bernice asked.

"He's great," Kendra said. "Kind. A little nerdy, if anything."

"Let me meet the guy," Bernice said. "If I get a good feeling about him, I'll invite you two to stay with me tonight. Does he need a meal?"

"I bet he'd love that," Kendra said.

"Then we'll get on bicycles tomorrow," Bernice said. "I have two, and I can borrow a third from a friend."

"Bicycles?" Kendra asked.

"You'll see," Bernice said with a smile.

They found the East Portal of the Route of the Hiawatha at the end of a winding road just over the Montana state line. Bernice parked her truck partway down the long parking lot. Virgil hopped out and began to unload the bicycles from the bed. Noble and Glory circled in the sky high above. Shielding her eyes from the afternoon sun, Kendra squinted up at the winged steeds.

Bernice followed her gaze. "Look at that. A pair of bald eagles."

Kendra felt glad to know how the flying horses appeared to mortal eyes. "Do you see many eagles around here?"

"Occasionally," Bernice said. Straddling his bike, Virgil walked it forward to get some momentum, then hopped onto the seat and started pedaling. He wobbled at first, then evened out as he picked up speed. "Looks like Virgil could use some practice."

"He never owned a bike," Kendra said. In fact, the satyr had secretly learned to ride a bike in the dark on Bernice's street the night before. She had a modest home in a town called Kellogg. Kendra had slept in the spare room and Virgil had crashed on the couch.

Bernice handed Kendra a bicycle helmet. "There's a headlamp on your handlebars and a spare on your helmet."

"Will I need the light?" Kendra asked.

"The Hiawatha Trail used to be a railroad," Bernice said. "This first tunnel is more than a mile long. You'll be grateful for the light—and for the jacket I loaned you. Might as well put it on now."

The afternoon was so warm that Kendra had a hard time imagining she could feel cold, but she followed the instructions. And though she could see in the dark, she knew it made sense to pretend to need the light as well.

Bernice strapped on her helmet and mounted her bike, and they were off. Kendra played with the gears until she liked the resistance. They caught up to Virgil and found the yawning mouth of a tunnel waiting to greet them. Bernice switched on her headlamp and Kendra did likewise.

Kendra led the way into the echoey darkness. The temperature plunged rapidly as the entrance shrank into a window of light behind them. Water dripped from the high ceiling and gurgled in the deep gutters cut along the sides of the trail. She biked carefully, trying to avoid puddles without slipping on the mud.

Before long, Kendra could see neither the entrance nor the exit. The long, dark tunnel seemed to stretch on forever. She wondered where all the water came from as it continued to weep down the walls and trickle from the roof. How much mountain was on top of her at this point? Her jacket could not repel the frigid air. As her hands began to grow numb, Kendra pedaled harder to generate heat.

Eventually the far end of the tunnel came into view, sides straight, top arched. They rode out into the blinding daylight. Both Virgil and Bernice had a brown stripe up their backs from cycling through the wet mud. The cold from the tunnel lingered even under the heat of the day.

Kendra took off her jacket, switched off the headlamp, and then followed Bernice along a path that trended downhill. She slowed on occasion to appreciate the dramatic vistas of hills thickly forested with evergreens.

"This is beautiful," Virgil called over to Kendra.

She nodded, barely remembering to turn her light back on as they entered the next tunnel. Darkness closed in, but this tunnel was not nearly as long or as cold as the first. More tunnels followed, along with astonishing panoramas. They crossed high trestle bridges, biking above the surrounding treetops. They passed bikers going at a more leisurely pace, some with young kids, and occasionally got passed by speedsters. When Kendra glanced at the sky, she could always spot Noble and Glory in view, though often at a considerable distance.

Kendra's attention was on a chipmunk when Bernice unexpectedly skidded to a halt. "This is where we make our own trail."

Following Bernice's lead, Kendra and Virgil walked their bikes uphill off the trail and stashed them against some trees. "We're on foot from here," Bernice said. "A couple of hours, if the sasquatch, I mean yeti, is where I expect. Get used to moving quietly so we don't spook her. Follow my lead. If she is awake, keep still and let her come to you. If she's asleep, I'll approach first."

"All right," Kendra said.

"There is a chance she'll retreat from your scent," Bernice said. "But we'll do our best to get the message to her."

Bernice led them on a pathless route. The trees pressed close, and the air was warm enough that Kendra began to sweat. She found the sappy tang of the evergreens refreshing.

"How do you communicate with the yeti?" Kendra asked.

"We haven't held conversations," Bernice said. "She has never made sounds beyond growls, snarls, or roars. I sometimes speak softly to her, like how a person might speak to a familiar dog. I don't really expect comprehension or responses."

"I hope she can understand, at least a little," Kendra said. "Otherwise, this becomes much harder."

"It might be wise to prepare for the worst," Bernice said.

As they paralleled a little trickle of a stream, Kendra imagined herself playing charades with Bigfoot. When they reached a soggy area where the water pooled, they cut up and over the shoulder of a hill and down to a scant path peppered with deer pellets. The path descended into a ravine, where they left the trail to climb a steep rise. At the top, Bernice raised a finger to her lips.

Crouching low, Kendra tensed up.

"Lately, she has inhabited the edge of a meadow on the far side of this little ridge," Bernice whispered. "Let's stay calm, especially if we see her. It's time to be extra slow and quiet."

Taking some deep breaths, Kendra tried to dispel her nervousness. What if the feral side of Magdalena's personality took over? What if the approach of two unfamiliar people sent her into a frenzy? Kendra tried to banish her worries. Such thoughts would make her telegraph tension and fear.

Easing over the ridgetop, Kendra immediately saw the yeti, surprisingly close, lying on her side with her broad, furry back facing them. The massive torso expanded and contracted with her breathing, long strands of pale fur subtly shifting with the movement.

Her stomach fluttering, Kendra looked to Bernice for advice on how to proceed.

"Asleep," Bernice mouthed. She held up a finger, then quietly unslung the military-style rucksack she was carrying and fished out large Ziploc bags crammed with raw meat. As she started opening the bags, the yeti stirred.

"It's me and two friends," Bernice said softly.

The yeti jerked, then leapt to her feet with alarming speed, confronting the three newcomers in a crouch. Kendra flinched away but held her ground and tried to project calmness. The yeti had enormous, claw-tipped hands and feet. If the creature stood up straight, Kendra estimated she would be at least the height of a basketball hoop.

The yeti motioned at Kendra and Virgil and gave a short, angry roar.

"They're friends," Bernice said, speaking with slow, exaggerated clarity. "They knew about you before they met me."

The yeti growled and chuffed as Bernice spoke.

"We're here to help you," Kendra said tentatively.

The yeti gave an angry snarl that showed her fearsome teeth.

"Your name is Magdalena," Kendra tried.

At the sound of the name, the yeti fell silent, and her posture relaxed.

"Yes," Kendra said. "You're Magdalena. I was just with your brother, Merek. Do you remember Merek?"

The yeti stared at Kendra with grave interest, then edged forward, sniffing. Holding still, Kendra glanced at Bernice, who stared earnestly and gave Kendra an encouraging nod. The yeti crept toward Kendra, who held out her hand flat as she might to a dog. Ignoring the proffered hand, the yeti grabbed Kendra's shoulders with her strong, oversized hands and leaned in to sniff Kendra's hair. Then the yeti sat back on her haunches and nodded vigorously at Kendra, breathing rapidly.

"Can you smell him?" Kendra asked. "Can you smell Merek on me?" How many days had it been since she was with Merek? Before the Fairy Realm.

The yeti clapped her hands once and nodded more.

"Merek needs you," Kendra said, keeping her voice even and calm. "Your family needs you. Konrad. Nadia. Merek. Gerwin. The dragons have declared war. And they are winning. The world needs you. Can you understand me? You are a legendary Dragon Slayer. You earned the yeti's fang. And your family needs you. Magdalena, do you understand?"

The yeti chuffed and stomped a foot. She shifted so she was sitting cross-legged, back erect, hands on her knees. Her breathing deepened, and her eyes slowly closed.

Kendra glanced at Bernice, who looked astonished.

The yeti opened her mouth wide, showing sharp teeth

and fangs. Kendra watched as the yeti began to shrink. Almost imperceptibly at first, her mass started to dwindle. Her shoulders narrowed, her limbs lost thickness. Her hands and feet shrank. The diminishing continued, hair retracting into her skin, arms and legs shortening. The yeti contracted into the shape of a young woman, sitting cross-legged, eyes closed, wearing a tattered brown dress. A large, yellowed fang hung from a cord around her neck.

"Magdalena?" Kendra tried.

The young woman swayed, then coughed several times. Her face scrunched and her eyes squinted against the late afternoon sun—green eyes that contrasted against the short, dark hair on her head. She didn't look much older than Kendra.

"You know Merek?" Magdalena asked, the words hesitant.

"Yes," Kendra said. "I left him a couple of days ago."

"You can speak," Bernice said, amazed.

"I remember you," Magdalena said. "You cared for me, though it feels like a dream. Thank you."

"You saved my life," Bernice said.

"I'm glad to hear that, though I don't recall," Magdalena said. "Your kindness left an impression." She looked at Virgil. "Who is the satyr?"

"I'm Virgil."

"He helped me get here," Kendra said.

"A satyr?" Bernice asked. "What was that about a dragon war? Who are you people?"

Kendra glanced at Bernice. "Yetis are just the beginning. There is a hidden world of magic all around us."

Kendra returned her gaze to Magdalena. "The dragons have destroyed all seven sanctuaries. Only Selona is left."

"Speaking of dragons, I sense one," Magdalena said, sniffing and cocking her head slightly. "Did you notice anything unusual on your way here?"

"I don't think—" Kendra began when the huge head of a dragon shot out from between two large evergreens and snatched Magdalena in its jaws. Her thrashing legs dangled out of the dragon's mouth, but the reptilian head rose up, chomped twice, and swallowed her.

The vast dragon was thundercloud gray, with glossy black horns. Bernice screamed. The dragon opened its jaws and snatched her up next, leaving behind part of one leg. The fierce head bobbed down again and gobbled her limb up as well.

"Close your eyes, Virgil!" Kendra cried, shutting her own and reaching for her power. Stunned and scared, resisting the paralyzing influence of the dragon fear, she blazed with all the brightness she could generate until a huge dragon claw grabbed her.

"Stop that shining," a calm, urbane voice invited, with a resonance like fifty gentlemen speaking in unison. "I have you and the satyr and will crush you both unless you extinguish that light." The dragon gave a squeeze that drove the breath from Kendra's lungs and made her bones creak.

"All right," Kendra said, dousing her light. "Don't hurt him!"

"That's better," the dragon said. "One more flash and I will squash you."

"You ate them!" Kendra shouted.

"Magdalena has slain many of my kind without remorse," the dragon said.

"Bernice never did anything to your kind!" Kendra yelled.

"Incorrect," the dragon said with a smile in his tone. "She fed me."

Kendra pushed with all her might against the constraining grip of his claws, but to no avail. Aware of the futility, she relaxed. "What happens now?"

"If killing you had been my aim, you would already be dead," the dragon said. "Your satyr friend too. But my father wants you alive."

"Your father?" Kendra asked.

"My name is Jeruwat," the dragon said. "I am the competent son."

"Your father is Celebrant?" Kendra asked.

"The one and only," Jeruwat said. "I have stalked this yeti for quite some time. Your approach provided just the distraction I needed. Thank you."

Wriggling in his iron grasp, Kendra screamed in frustration.

"I believe you know my half-brother, Raxtus," Jeruwat said. "I'll come for him soon."

The dragon released Kendra, turned, and sprang away, knocking aside a few trees in the process. An instant later he was completely out of sight, disappearing as quickly as he had come.

Kendra looked over to find Virgil seated ten yards away. The satyr appeared stunned.

A moment later, Noble and Glory landed between them.

"Oh, Kendra," Glory fussed. "We came as soon as we saw the dragon!"

"Shall I give chase?" Noble asked.

"No," Kendra said, fighting off shock, trying to hold back tears. "We've already lost enough today."

# CHAPTER TWENTY-NINE

# Duel

Rain pattered down outside the cave, dampening the moss at the entrance and splashing off the leaves of the vegetation beyond. Leaning against the wall of the cave, Seth carefully reapplied surgical glue to the festering slice on his leg. From his sheltered position, he watched the dismal day, waiting for Raxtus to return.

After three days of flying and foraging, Seth, Calvin, and Raxtus had reached the cave this morning. As their destination in the Czech Republic came within range, Raxtus had advised them to find a place to hide in the mountains of Slovakia while he looked for a dragon to take a message to Celebrant about his challenging the monarch. He had insisted it would be foolish for any of them to approach the muster unannounced.

"Do you think he'll find a dragon willing to be the messenger?" Calvin asked.

"If not, we'll have to come up with another plan," Seth said. "There should be plenty of dragons making their way there to choose from."

After some time, the rain eased off to a sprinkle, collecting on surfaces more than striking them. The air in front of the entrance shimmered, carving out a shape in the mist, and suddenly Raxtus appeared, silvery scales glossy with moisture. He shook to shed some water before entering the cave.

"Success?" Seth asked.

"I was lucky to find a young dragon who will deliver my message," Raxtus said. "She had bronze scales and was not much larger than I am. The two other dragons I tried to approach attempted to engage me in combat before I could explain my need. I was starting to worry that no dragons would honor a truce with me long enough to hear my request."

"What happened with the dragons who tried to fight?" Calvin asked.

"I gave them the slip," Raxtus said. "It was more annoying than difficult."

"What now?" Seth asked.

"We wait," Raxtus replied. "I designated a tree to be set aflame tonight if Father agrees to my terms."

"You really challenged Celebrant to a fight?" Seth asked.

"Don't remind me," Raxtus said. "But yes."

"How did the messenger dragon respond?" Calvin asked.

"Her name is Piza," Raxtus said. "She laughed at me.

She seemed eager to deliver the challenge. I think she felt my request was almost as good as having caught me herself."

"It's not a fight you could realistically win," Seth said.

"No conditions would give me a chance for victory," Raxtus said, "which is why perfect efficiency is needed. You must hide nearby, shade walking with all your skill. If I survive the attempt and get the crown to where you are hidden, you need to quickly cut the jewel out and go. I'll try to lead them away. It may be some time before we can meet up again."

"If your father agrees, the challenge happens tomorrow?" Calvin asked.

"Tomorrow at dusk," Raxtus said. "It's ideal lighting for my invisibility."

"For now, we have extra time on our hands," Seth said.

"I'll go steal you some food from the nearest village," Raxtus offered.

"You're sure we're in Slovakia?" Seth asked.

"The Slovak Republic," Raxtus said. "It used to be part of Czechoslovakia. You have to remember—I've been around for a long time, and I've always been an outcast. I spent my time traveling, both within and outside the sanctuaries. I've had plenty of time to get acquainted with your world."

"I can help get the food," Seth said.

"You rest," Raxtus said. "This mission is almost as dangerous for you as it is for me. I'm not sure anyone has ever been chased by as many dragons as we will have on our tails. Today, we mustn't be noticed. You're sneaky, Seth, but I can turn almost invisible, and in a pinch I can become really small."

"I don't have a fairy form," Seth conceded.

"I'll get food, then set up surveillance on the tree," Raxtus said.

"How far are we from where they're mustering?" Calvin asked.

"Less than sixty miles," Raxtus said. "Close enough to get there without too much flying, but hopefully far enough that random patrols won't discover us."

"Around here they would measure that distance in kilometers," Seth said.

"Less than a hundred kilometers," Raxtus amended. "I'll be back with bread or something."

"I still have some figs," Seth said. "Meat would be good too. Or some cheese."

"I'll see what I can do," Raxtus said.

"I'll have whatever Seth is having," Calvin said. "And I wouldn't say no to pierogies."

"Any other orders?" Raxtus asked.

"If it's a wish list, I'd welcome some peanut butter," Seth asked. "Have you eaten?"

"I had a lamb yesterday," Raxtus said. "That will be my last meal before the duel. See you soon."

The dragon whooshed from the mouth of the cave and disappeared. The rain had stopped, but the sun remained hidden by leaden clouds.

"What's a pierogi?" Seth asked. "It sounds familiar."

"A stuffed dumpling," Calvin said. "The contents vary. Often potatoes or cheese."

"Did your mom make them?" Seth asked.

"Sometimes," Calvin said. "It's been a long time since I've had one. A giant one would feel like a dream come true."

"You don't have to be there when we go after the crown," Seth said. "You can hide somewhere safe, and I'll come back for you."

"After all this time, do you not know me yet?" Calvin asked.

"You're with me until we break the nipsie curse," Seth said. "What if we never break it?"

"Then you have a sidekick for life," Calvin said.

Raxtus brought back bread and cured meat but no pierogies. No cheese or peanut butter, either. The dragon left again, and he returned that evening to report that the designated tree had been set ablaze, confirming that the duel would occur the next day. After full night had fallen, Raxtus insisted he should leave again to scout. He took Calvin along, and Seth fell asleep before they returned.

The following morning, Seth awoke to find Raxtus sleeping at the cave entrance like a huge, scaly guard dog. Calvin was already awake and doing calisthenics. When Seth started unwrapping bread for breakfast, Raxtus stirred, slitting one eye open.

"How did it go last night?" Seth asked.

"Father has already gathered more than a thousand

dragons to him," Raxtus said. "I've never witnessed such a host in my lifetime."

"Were you seen?" Seth asked.

"Please," Raxtus said. "Give me some credit. I'm rarely identified if I'm alone and trying to hide."

"Hey," Calvin complained. "Not completely alone."

"You're small enough to be as stealthy as I am," Raxtus said.

"How did it go?" Seth asked.

"We scouted a place where you two can watch the duel," Raxtus said.

"We'll be close enough to watch?" Seth asked.

"You have to be able to see what happens," Raxtus said. "If I get killed, you need to flee and devise a new plan. If I get the crown, be ready with your sword. With the stone in the crown, Father will probably be able to track it. So you have to cut it free. If you remove the stone slowly, we both die."

"I'll be pretty close if I can see you," Seth said. "What if they smell me?"

"I piled herbs into your hiding place," Raxtus said. "It will be fragrant for you and should mask your scent. The timing will be important. My arrival will draw their attention. You should approach after I do. Calvin will guide you to the hiding spot. I worry Father may suspect something amiss with my challenge. One doesn't remain king of the dragons without anticipating deception at every turn. Everything depends on you remaining undetected."

"Does their camp have guards?" Seth asked, biting off a hunk of bread.

"Half-hearted sentries," Raxtus said. "Shrouded Valley is protected by spells that hide it from mortals. And who can bother a horde of dragons? Last night, no guards approached the place I chose for you to hide. Your vantage point lies farther from the battleground than where the dragons will gather to watch the fight."

"The duel is in the evening?" Seth asked.

"Yes," Raxtus said.

"My shade walking works best in full darkness," Seth said.

"But dragons see worst in the twilight," Raxtus said. "Our vision in the day is good, and at night we also see well, but those hours in between give us the most trouble."

"Sounds like you planned well," Seth said.

"Our lives depend on it," Raxtus said. "This will be a long shot. When I'm close enough to swipe the crown, Father will have an opportunity to get hold of me. If that happens, flee immediately."

"This is really brave of you," Seth said.

"Low risk, low reward," Raxtus said. "I've already been rejected by dragonkind. I want to help my real friends. And honestly, if Father can be stopped, it will be better for dragons as well, even if they don't yet realize it."

The day passed slowly for Seth. Raxtus wanted them to stay inside the cave, beyond the sight of any dragons flying to the muster, and Seth reluctantly agreed.

Now that he was rested from his flight to Europe, Seth

didn't want to be idle, held captive to his thoughts. Staring at the deep blackness of the Unforgiving Blade, Seth felt a pull similar to the irrational urge to jump he sometimes felt at the edge of a cliff. The blade seemed to promise nothingness, an end to thought, an end to existence, an end to pain and worry.

What if he died collecting the stone from Celebrant? Many of his problems would be over. He wouldn't have to face Kendra and his grandparents after having released the undead from the Blackwell. Nobody would have to pretend to accept him after all the harm he had caused. He wouldn't have to find a way to accept himself.

As the afternoon waned, Raxtus got ready to leave and instructed Seth to wait for half an hour before departing. Raxtus planned to take an indirect route so he could arrive from a different direction than the line Seth would use. Seth dug a stopwatch out of his satchel so he could leave at the precise time.

"Do you know how to get there?" Seth asked Calvin as the countdown expired.

"Raxtus mapped the whole route with me," Calvin said. "We'll stay low and approach the valley under the cover of trees."

"I won't miss this cave," Seth said. "I'd almost rather fight Celebrant myself than sit here another day."

"Careful what you wish for," Calvin said.

Connecting with his power, Seth made sure he was shade walking before he flew out of the cave mouth. Calvin traveled on his shoulder so he could murmur directions into

Seth's ear. It was not efficient flying. Ignoring the optimal air currents, Seth hugged the contours of the ground, often sinking into ravines and skirting the lower reaches of hills or mountains. For a good while he skimmed along a few feet above a small river, enjoying the sounds and smells of the running water.

After abandoning the river, Seth flew a dozen feet above a trail. The sun had set while they followed the water, and now the colors on the horizon were beginning to fade.

"We're getting close," Calvin warned quietly. "The battleground is just beyond that hill ahead of us. Our hiding place is on the far side of the hill, to the right of the summit. If you can't fly under the trees, we should walk the rest of it."

The hill was densely forested, but Seth knew his astrid wings were up to the task. He darted in low, ruffling the tops of bushes, staying beneath the thickest branches, and weaving among the trunks. Looking up through the limbs above, he glimpsed a few dragons flying high, apparently sentries. He confirmed that his shade walking was in full effect and zoomed up the hillside.

Before cresting the shoulder of the hill, Seth landed silently and proceeded on foot. He stepped quietly, doing his best to avoid twigs and bushes. Whispering, Calvin directed Seth until they found a little hollow on the far side of the hill. The scent of mint permeated the shallow cove, along with other aromas Seth couldn't name. He crawled forward to a spot with a good vantage of the valley below.

Celebrant paced at the bottom of the bowl,

platinum scales bright even in the waning glow of the sunset. Hundreds of dragons used the slopes surrounding the valley like the bleachers of an amphitheater. Some were nearly as large as Celebrant, but many were smaller, closer to the size of a school bus or even an elephant. Seth was positioned higher on the hill than any of the dragons by at least fifty yards.

Seth could not yet see Raxtus. He waited, watching the dragons below swish their tails, curl their necks, and fan their leathery wings. A few dragons nipped at one another, threatening with teeth and claws.

At length, Celebrant spoke, his powerful voice carrying. "Come forth, Raxtus the fatherless, and meet your fate."

Raxtus glided out from a far ridge and landed in the valley facing Celebrant, a little toy dragon by comparison. Seth had seen Celebrant defend his crown once before, but last time it was against a dragon more his size. Raxtus looked tiny and alone.

"I hereby challenge you for the crown!" Raxtus called, his voice barely audible.

Celebrant laughed richly. "As you wish. You are a criminal and a traitor." He looked around. "I must confess I am surprised you actually showed up, and that you came alone. Such a move seemed like it had to be theater. I am pleased that you volunteered for your execution, and that I get to administer the punishment."

Magical globes of light flared to life around the base of the valley, bathing the battleground in white light. The scales of both dragons, large and small, gleamed brightly.

"Prepare to defend yourself, if you can," Celebrant declared. "This contest begins now."

"Enough bluster," Raxtus called.

Roaring, Celebrant launched forward, and Raxtus dodged sideways, staying out of reach. Celebrant rounded to intercept the smaller dragon, but Raxtus made acrobatic maneuvers to evade his father. Sudden as a striking snake, Celebrant's head blurred forward, teeth clashing, barely missing Raxtus, who dipped and twirled. Then Raxtus turned invisible.

A large dragon landed behind Seth, slightly closer to the summit than where he and Calvin lay nestled. Seth glanced up to see the head of a maroon dragon with forked horns staring down at him.

"Why, hello," the dragon said in a soothing, masculine voice. "Did you suppose you could approach Celebrant's host unnoticed? Did you imagine all dragons incapable of sight, hearing, and smell? Tell me, are you a fan of dragon duels? Or a prospective saboteur, perhaps?"

"Just watching the fight," Seth said, aware that this dragon could unravel all of their plans.

"Then, by all means, enjoy the fight," the maroon dragon said. "I don't want to miss it either."

"This is absurd," Celebrant complained from the valley floor, rotating twice before pausing to sniff. "You lived like a fool; must you insist on dying like one as well?"

"You fight your way, and I'll fight mine," answered a faint voice.

Celebrant lunged in the direction of the words, jaws

snapping. And then, before his head retracted, his crown lifted off his horny head, shrinking as it streaked away from him. Raxtus was flying toward the opposite side of the valley from where Seth lay hiding. Seth wondered how many dragons had noticed the crown being taken. Might the confusion distract this maroon dragon?

"Thief!" Celebrant bellowed. "Raxtus! You traitorous slug! I'll desecrate your corpse!" The Dragon King exhaled a fountain of fire into the air.

The head of the maroon dragon came near to Seth. Still smooth and calm, his voice took on a threatening edge. "Perhaps the winged boy hiding on the hillside knows something of this betrayal. Where is the crown, young one?"

"Find Raxtus!" Celebrant raged, his voice echoing across the hills. "This duel is over. That shameful wretch never meant to fight me! He is stealing the crown!"

Most of the dragons surrounding the valley took flight, enlivening the air like a cloud of bats. Seth debated over whether to draw Vasilis or attack with the Unforgiving Blade. Vasilis would fill him with power and confidence, but it was also bright and might attract extra attention.

"Start speaking if you wish to live," the maroon dragon demanded.

"You're surrounded!" Calvin cried from behind the dragon, having slipped away unnoticed.

The maroon dragon turned its head toward the sound, momentarily exposing its neck. Seth lunged and stabbed the Unforgiving Blade into the scales behind the head. The maroon dragon went rigid for a moment, then shivered twice.

"You win," the dragon murmured in a thin voice. "Top of my head, please."

"What?" Seth asked.

"Take . . . the blade . . . out and I'll . . . expose . . . the top of my head," the dragon managed, each word a struggle. "I swear it."

Seth pulled out the Unforgiving Blade, and the maroon dragon laid his head on the ground, the top facing Seth. After a few deep slashes and a final stab, Seth was sure the dragon was dead.

A moment later, an invisible form plopped down beside Seth, matting a patch of brush. Celebrant's crown fell at Seth's feet, sized to fit the head of Raxtus. Two quick whacks of his dark blade freed the gem from its setting.

"I'm with you!" Calvin cried, climbing up Seth's pant leg.

Seth grabbed the stone and immediately took flight. Snatching the remains of the crown in his mouth, Raxtus zoomed off in another direction.

Seth scooped Calvin from his pant leg to his pocket. Shade walking with all his might, Seth flew swift and low, brushing the treetops rather than weaving among the trunks. Behind him, dragons snarled and roared. Lightning forked and flames bloomed amid the chaos of wings and claws. Hugging the terrain, Seth concentrated on speed.

Backward glances showed a tangled confusion of dragons. Many collided and snapped at one another. Some fell from the sky intertwined. Random strips of terrain were aflame. Only a few dragons were beginning to spread out and search beyond the perimeter of the valley. They clearly had not been prepared for something like this.

Seth continued to put distance between himself and his potential pursuers. The dragons were hunting one of their own. They didn't even know he had been there. And their search was expanding much more slowly than he was flying.

Before long, there were no dragons in sight.

# CHAPTER THIRTY

# Batoosa

Astride Glory, Kendra looked up at a snowcapped summit, amazed that they had reached the Andes. Their destination could not be far off. She and Virgil had successfully flown from northern-hemisphere summer to southern-hemisphere winter. The winged horses had tirelessly maintained aggressive speeds, allowing them to cover an enormous distance in only a couple of days. The longest pause came in Manta, Ecuador, when Virgil had bartered for coats using gold coins.

Although snow blanketed the highest peaks, much of the surrounding terrain looked untouched by winter. Astride Noble, Virgil wrestled with a map that fluttered in the wind of their flight.

"I believe that mountain is Salcantay," the satyr said.

"If so, the Starlit Shrine should be that way." He pointed to some of the lower country southeast of the mountain.

"Feels good to me," Kendra said. "Talizar told me I would feel drawn to the right valley, like the opposite of a distracter spell."

Noble and Glory veered to follow the line Virgil had indicated, losing some altitude as they went. Kendra eyed the terrain, hoping a conspicuous feature would call to her.

The long flight had given Kendra some time to mourn the abrupt deaths of Bernice and Magdalena. Kendra felt terrible to have led Bernice to her death, and to have put Magdalena off her guard at a time when Jeruwat could attack. She had been left paralyzed with grief after the dragon departed. There were no remains left. There was nobody she could think of to notify. Virgil had suggested they set off toward their next lead, and Kendra had consented.

Bernice's truck would eventually be found in the parking lot. Would anyone find the hidden bikes? Kendra wondered if anyone who had seen her with Bernice would suspect her of wrongdoing. How could she possibly explain that Bernice had been ingested by a dragon while leading new acquaintances to a yeti?

Having lost Magdalena, Kendra had already failed to gather the five legendary Dragon Slayers. Could one less Dragon Slayer make the difference in whether they won or lost the dragon war? What were their chances of stopping Celebrant now? Was she going to end up as Ronodin's servant for the rest of her life while he hid in his Fairy Realm from a world ruled by dragons?

Kendra shuddered. Jeruwat could have easily killed her and Virgil. They had been completely at his mercy. Only orders from Celebrant had spared her. She wondered what the Dragon King planned to do with her.

It seemed likely that Celebrant had mercenaries after the other Dragon Slayers as well. Kendra hoped she didn't get the next Dragon Slayer killed too.

Kendra's eyes lingered on a deep crevice in the ground. Supposedly she was searching for a valley, but for some reason, the crevice continued to draw her gaze.

"Glory, head for that fissure," Kendra said.

"What fissure?" Glory replied.

"Down there?" Kendra asked, pointing. "Don't you see the big crack in the ground?"

"I'll proceed in the direction you're pointing," Glory said. "I'm not sure what you mean."

"Where's the crack?" Virgil asked, apparently having overheard.

"Right above those trees?" Kendra asked, pointing repeatedly.

"I'm trying," Virgil said.

"It's hard to miss," Kendra said. "It runs at a diagonal to our course." She drew the slant in the air with her finger. "A skinny, deep canyon."

"I'll have to take your word for it," Virgil said. "I just can't see anything that . . . wait a minute . . . isn't the Starlit Shrine protected by a distracter spell?"

"That must be it," Kendra said. "Glory, keep heading in this direction."

They had practically reached the opening of the fissure when Glory cried out, "Here it is! Where did this come from?"

"How did I miss this before?" Noble replied.

"Fascinating," Virgil said.

"We must have crossed the threshold where the spell turns people away," Kendra said.

Drifting downward, Glory glided into the gap in the ground, plunging into ever-deepening shadow. The walls of the ravine widened somewhat, until the winged horses could descend in a spiral. The bottom of the chasm came into view, illuminated by silver lanterns on poles. Kendra saw four large wooden cottages, two on the far ends of the ravine floor, two toward the center. The cottages at the ends were built over pools of water, one of them simmering and steaming, the other still.

A few fairies scattered from the long grass where the winged horses landed, taking cover in flowering bushes. Above them, the sky was dark enough to let them see stars.

"Weird," Kendra said.

Virgil noticed her gaze. "The Starlit Shrine. This chasm is so deep that you can see the stars in the afternoon. I bet this place only gets sunlight for a limited interval of time each day."

"Accurate assessment," approved a raspy voice.

Startled, Kendra whirled to see a tall, emaciated demon emerging from the cottage over the simmering water, using a cane to hobble toward them. His brown tunic hung loose about his scrawny frame. His arms and legs looked fragile;

his taupe, noseless face was shriveled; and his feet flapped like diving flippers.

"Batoosa?" Kendra asked.

"You have found the Starlit Shrine," the demon said, smiling grotesquely. "Few visit me in these depths. You are the girl Kendra?"

"And this is my friend Virgil," Kendra said. "And our horses."

"Your mounts may graze here," Batoosa said, his eyes lingering on the steeds. "My fairies keep my home improbably green. The satyr may frolic as he pleases. Come."

Kendra glanced at Virgil, who motioned for her to go. "I'll frolic," he mouthed.

She dismounted and crossed to Batoosa, who had to be at least eight feet tall. He led her to the cottage above the steaming water. A ramp spanned part of the pool, granting access to the front porch.

"Hot springs?" Kendra asked.

"This is my winter abode," Batoosa said. "The warmest of the four."

The inside was cozy and rustic, though a little stuffy. The portraits of four demons hung prominently on the walls. One was clearly Batoosa. The others had similar features, though one was quite young, another in his prime, and the third looked overweight.

"Is that your family?" Kendra asked.

"They all depict me, my girl," Batoosa said. "I evolve with the seasons."

Kendra reconsidered the paintings. "You get young in the spring?"

"And fat with the harvest," Batoosa said. "I waste away in the winter. A familiar cycle. I crave meat unbearably during this season. I don't suppose either of your mounts is for sale?"

"No," Kendra said with a shudder.

He rubbed his long-fingered hands together. "I would pay an exorbitant sum."

"They're my friends," Kendra said. "We're riding them."

Batoosa bobbed his head. "I'll mind my manners. It actually doesn't matter how much I eat in the winter—I always waste away, and I'm always hungry. Except while in the act of eating, you see. Especially meat." A dark tongue slid across his withered lips.

"Who lives in the other houses?" Kendra asked.

Batoosa gave a small bow. "I do, depending on the season. My summer home stands over chilly water, making it my coldest abode. And so forth. Explain why you have come."

"I'm looking for the legendary Dragon Slayers," Kendra said.

"You have undertaken the task of slaying Celebrant," Batoosa said.

"That's the plan," Kendra said. "Everything went wrong when I tried to awaken Magdalena."

"You found her?" Batoosa asked.

"Yes."

"What happened?" Batoosa asked.

"We were ambushed by a dragon named Jeruwat," Kendra said.

"Celebrant's son," Batoosa said, leaning forward with interest.

"He ate Magdalena and our guide," Kendra said.

"They must have been absolutely delicious," Batoosa replied, flexing his long fingers, the knuckles oddly prominent. "I would rank Jeruwat as one of the most dangerous living predators. Individually speaking. We tried to recruit him, but it isn't in him to be a team player. He is pure dragon."

"Meaning what?" Kendra asked.

"He works alone," Batoosa said. "Doesn't obey anyone except his father. Celebrant uses him like an assassin. A fixer. Jeruwat handles the toughest assignments. I'm curious—how are you still alive?"

"He let us go."

"Did he, now?" Batoosa asked pensively.

"He had orders from his father."

"He didn't try to capture you?"

"He had me in his claws," Kendra said.

"That must have been dreadfully tempting for him," Batoosa sympathized. "Human flesh is a delicacy."

"Apparently Celebrant has other plans for me," Kendra said.

Batoosa nodded enthusiastically. "Doesn't that make you curious? Why would plans of a known enemy involve neither your death nor your capture? It strikes me as uncharacteristically generous."

"I guess it doesn't make much sense," Kendra admitted.

"How long after you found Magdalena did Jeruwat attack?" Batoosa questioned.

"Almost immediately."

"And what does that tell you?"

"Wait," Kendra said. "He was following us?"

"Or your position was otherwise compromised," Batoosa said.

"Could he still be following us?" Kendra asked.

"I see no other reason for him to have released you," Batoosa said.

Kendra squirmed. "How do I lose him?"

"Have you received any gifts lately?" Batoosa asked. "Perhaps from a dragon?"

Kendra shook her head. "Let's see . . . I have my clothes. My bow. My sack of gales. I've had them for a long time. Wait. No, please tell me I'm not that gullible."

"What?" Batoosa prodded.

"Ronodin gave me a pendant for Virgil so he would appear human to mortals. Virgil wears it around his neck. But why would Ronodin sabotage me? He released me so I could cause trouble for the dragons!"

Batoosa shrugged. "Ronodin is famous for simultaneous dealings with opposing sides. The dragons helped install him in the Fairy Realm. Might I examine the pendant?"

Kendra crossed to the cottage door, opened it, and called out, "Virgil, come here for a minute."

The satyr came running, his expression concerned.

"There isn't an emergency," Kendra clarified. "Not yet, anyhow."

The satyr tromped up the ramp to the porch and entered.

"There's a fine fellow," Batoosa said. "You know, during all my years, I've never tasted a satyr."

"Just eat a goat," Virgil said. "You'll get the gist."

"I'm not terribly fond of goat," Batoosa said, smacking his lips distastefully. "Any port in a storm, I suppose."

"He needs to see your pendant," Kendra prompted.

Virgil took it off and handed it over. Batoosa rubbed the pendant between his bony hands. He held the little mask dangling at the end of the cord close to one eye, then licked it.

"This does more than disguise the satyr," Batoosa said. "The pendant carries a tracking spell as well."

"Ronodin!" Kendra groaned in frustration. "How did I fall for this? I know he can't be trusted."

"He fooled you the same way he beguiles all who deal with him," Batoosa said. "He's cunning and he's useful. But loyal he is not."

"I could have prevented this," Kendra said numbly. "Bernice and Magdalena got killed because I accepted that pendant from him."

"Bernice and Magdalena were killed because we're at war with the dragons," Virgil said. "They died because of what Ronodin did. You were simply used."

"What else am I missing?" Kendra asked, fighting back hysteria. "Are the demons using me too?"

"Absolutely," Batoosa said. "To slay Celebrant."

"Sure, and what else?" Kendra asked.

Batoosa spread his hands. "Whatever you'll let us get away with. At present, destroying Celebrant would be a major coup."

"What should I do with the pendant?" Kendra asked.

"Use it as a decoy, obviously," Batoosa said. "Send it off in the wrong direction."

"That could work," Kendra said. "We would need someone to carry it."

"I have some vultures that I use as messengers in a pinch," Batoosa said. "I could send one of them to Venezuela with the pendant. That should suffice."

"What will it cost me?" Kendra asked.

"We demons want you to succeed against Celebrant," Batoosa said. "I helped you discover that the pendant is tracking you, and I'd be happy to divert Jeruwat."

"Thanks," Kendra said.

"As much as I would love to eat your horses, I know you need transportation," Batoosa said. "How else can I be of service?"

"Do you know where we can find other legendary Dragon Slayers?" Kendra asked.

"I can direct you to one of them," Batoosa said. "I have long studied Gerwin."

"He's the youngest, right?" Kendra checked.

"The youngest of the five ancient Dragon Slayers, yes," Batoosa said. "He inherited the phoenix feather, and his life cycle corresponds to that of a phoenix."

"He dies and is reborn?" Kendra asked.

"Yes," Batoosa said. "Unlike with his siblings, the

rebirth occurs regularly for Gerwin. He doesn't have to be killed in order to die. If he lives long enough, he spontaneously combusts and is reborn as an infant."

"Weird," Kendra said. "Does he remember who he was?"

"No," Batoosa said. "It takes time for him to awaken to his identity. During some lifetimes, he regains his identity as a legendary Dragon Slayer only minutes before death. I have learned the tides of his existence. He accumulates lifetimes, sometimes fighting dragons, other times baking bread, or building ships, or tending chickens."

"Where is he now?" Kendra asked.

"I could sell the answer to that question for an outsized reward," Batoosa said. "A great pile of exotic meat, at the very least. But I will tell you that your quarry lives in Chile, just south of here, in a town called Huasco, by the sea. His current name is Miguel Santiago Duran Fuentes. He has dark hair and dark eyes, but his skin is fairer than most in his town. His address is 521 Victoria. Find him before the dragons do."

"Any tips on how to help him remember his history?" Kendra asked.

"I have no sure answer," Batoosa said. "I would bombard him with details from his past."

"If I succeed, I look for the third demon?" Kendra asked.

"Seek out Vez Radim within the kingdom of Selona," Batoosa said. "He dwells inside Blackthorn Manor. He has information about another Dragon Slayer. A word of caution—do not enter the manor. Speak to him only from outside, under the sun. Vez Radim is less . . . civilized than some of us."

"Thanks for the warning," Kendra said, suppressing a shiver.

"You should leave now," Batoosa said, holding Virgil's pendant. With the back of his hand he wiped a bit of drool from the side of his mouth. "The scent of your horses remains intoxicating."

Kendra and Virgil headed toward the door. "One last question," Kendra asked. "How old is Gerwin?"

"Ten years old," Batoosa said. "Younger than is ideal for the slaying of dragons. But who knows? Perhaps he will prove to be a prodigy."

# CHAPTER THIRTY-ONE

# Homecoming

As he sped away to the west, Seth kept hoping Raxtus would catch up. He wanted confirmation that the dragon had survived, and he also missed the company. Over Germany, Seth flew higher, searching for the most favorable breezes, knowing it would make him more visible to Raxtus. By the time he crossed the English Channel, Seth had lost hope of Raxtus rejoining him. Fortunately, he hadn't encountered any hostile dragons, either.

"I think we actually got away," Calvin said.

"I can hardly believe it," Seth said. "There were so many dragons! And they were so angry!"

"Anger doesn't always lead to effective reactions," Calvin mused.

"I thought we were dead when that reddish dragon showed up," Seth said. "Good job distracting him."

"You slayed him," Calvin replied. "That's the hardest part. The Unforgiving Blade really gets the job done."

"I worry it works too well," Seth said softly.

"Where are we going now?"

"I've been puzzling about what to do," Seth said. "The Wizenstone could guide us to the Shoreless Isle, where we would find the entrance to the new demon prison. But we have no way to get inside. Accessing the Demon King might be the hardest part of this quest. Let alone escaping him."

"Don't forget you have allies," Calvin said.

"Yeah, but it's a pretty short list, and even shorter if we limit it to those who would know how to get into the demon prison."

"Do we approach Dragonwatch?"

"I don't know," Seth said. "How many people who belong to Dragonwatch really trust me? They know me as Ronodin's assistant who caused the fall of Wyrmroost and started the dragon war. Who would give that guy access to the demon prison?"

"You're making good points," Calvin said.

"The members of Dragonwatch fight to keep the demon prison closed," Seth said. "They're not going to help a known traitor with an evil sword get all the Ethergem fragments for himself. Besides, they're going to be fending off a major assault from Celebrant and his billion dragons."

"Then where do we go?" Calvin asked.

"I've burned too many bridges," Seth said. "I've racked my brain, and I can think of only one person with decent resources who might be willing to help me—the Sphinx."

"Wasn't he helping Ronodin?" Calvin asked.

"He'll work with anyone if he sees an advantage," Seth said. "And he spent most of his life learning how to get inside the demon prison. He is dangerous, but there may not be safe options."

"Do you know how to find him?" Calvin asked.

"No clue," Seth said. "I haven't seen him since the Phantom Isle. I do have one idea that won't leave me alone."

"Better than none."

"You haven't heard it yet."

"Even a bad idea gives us something to work with," Calvin reassured.

"Let's go back to Fablehaven," Seth said.

"I wouldn't mind checking in with my people," Calvin said. "But Fablehaven is on the other side of the Atlantic. How would going there help you find the Sphinx?"

"Muriel Taggert," Seth said. "She is a witch we imprisoned there. She worked with the Sphinx."

"I remember Muriel," Calvin said. "We nipsies steered clear of her."

"She was a lot more than I could handle when I was starting out," Seth said. "But I've learned a thing or two since then. I don't think she would want dragons to overrun the world, and I suspect she could contact the Sphinx."

"Where is she imprisoned?" Calvin asked.

"We buried her and left her bound to a demon," Seth said. "But I have a friend who could dig her up."

"Why would she help you?" Calvin asked.

"I'll probably have to set her free," Seth said. "With conditions."

"We're really scraping the bottom of the idea barrel," Calvin said.

"Do you know another way to contact the Sphinx?"

"Sometimes the bottom is all we have," Calvin said.

"Let's find a place to rest in Ireland," Seth said. "Then we'll do the big flight over the Atlantic."

"Think Raxtus will still catch up to us?" Calvin asked.

"If he were able to catch up to us, it would have happened by now," Seth said. "I hope he's all right."

"If anyone could have slipped away from that confusion, Raxtus would be my pick," Calvin said.

"We have to stay alert," Seth said. "If Celebrant catches any of us, we're dead."

"We're already a long way from his muster," Calvin said.

"And it will only get farther," Seth said. "Calvin, we're going home to Fablehaven."

In preparation for adventuring, Calvin had read a lot and studied many maps. His knowledge came in handy as they planned a route across the Atlantic. They considered taking a northerly route using Iceland as a resting spot, but in the end, Seth decided on the uninterrupted flight across to Newfoundland.

Seth struggled to find favorable winds, but he soon learned that if he kept his pace moderate, his wings remained reliably tireless, and he made good headway. He had never flown so far without land in sight and was enormously relieved when he touched down in the town of St. Anthony, hugging a little bay in Newfoundland.

Seth made camp on the outskirts of town and devoured the last of his food stores before falling asleep wrapped in his wings. The temperature remained warm in the night, and the next day he flew with renewed vigor. He went south before crossing more water to a landmass Calvin identified as Nova Scotia. From there, they stayed within sight of land for the rest of the trip. The closer they got to Connecticut, the hotter and muggier the air became. By the time Seth flew over the outer wall of Fablehaven, he desperately wanted a cold drink and an air-conditioned space.

It was a first to look down at the Fablehaven house from the air, a view dominated by shingles and the slanted tops of gables. His Grandma and Grandpa Larsen were probably in that house. Maybe his parents too.

Tears stung his eyes.

Home was down there.

And there was no going home right now.

Maybe ever.

Bad things happened around him. After he spent a day with his cousins and the satyrs, Newel had a crippling life-long injury. Then Seth had to disarm Knox to keep him from exploiting a weapon of great evil. A weapon Seth had brought among them.

Seth knew he had a mission to finish. He would deal with unsavory people and take some serious risks. Hopefully, he could undo some of the harm he had caused. If he survived, he would think about his next move after that.

Seth soared over the familiar yard and the huge barn. He missed swimming in that pool. Then he glided over treetops, glimpsing the grass tennis court where Newel and Doren played. Finally, he landed in the clearing beside the pond containing the Fairy Queen's shrine. The few satyrs in the clearing eyed Seth suspiciously, their focus on his gilded wings. Seth walked over to a gazebo attached to the boardwalk encompassing the pond and took a seat on a bench.

"Hugo!" Seth called. "I need your help!"

Though the air was hot and humid, at least the gazebo provided shade. The head of a naiad poked up from the pond, then dipped back under the water when Seth's eyes met hers. "Hugo!" one of the satyrs imitated plaintively, laughing. "Hugo!"

"Will he come?" Calvin asked.

"He always does," Seth said.

Seth looked at the little island in the middle of the pond. Technically, it was now a shrine to Ronodin. And Kendra was a prisoner in his realm. Seth would have to find a way to help her. But he could only tackle one impossible problem at a time.

"We could fly around and look for him," Calvin suggested.

"Waiting will probably be faster," Seth said. "I don't want to accidentally move away from him. Besides, I don't want to give anyone the chance to see that I'm here."

"How is your leg?" Calvin asked.

"The pain is the same as when I first sliced it," Seth said. "It doesn't diminish. I think I'm getting better at ignoring it, though. Hopefully someday I will be like those people who live near railroad tracks and stop hearing the train when it goes by."

They waited. Seth noticed with interest that he didn't see any fairies. Were they on strike? Had Ronodin given them specific orders? There had always been fairies in this area near the shrine.

Heavy footfalls summoned Seth's attention. He turned to see the sturdy golem loping toward him across the clearing, his powerful body an amalgamation of dirt and stone, with a few tufts of greenery.

"Seth!" Hugo called in a voice that sounded like a jovial landslide.

The sight of the golem brought Seth real cheer. He jumped up and came out of the gazebo to greet him. "Hugo! I missed you."

"You alive," the golem said. "Hugo glad. You back now?"

"Just for a little while," Seth said. "I'm in the middle of an adventure and I need your help."

"Hugo help Seth."

"Do you remember where the Forgotten Chapel used to be?" Seth asked.

"Yes," the golem said heavily.

"I have questions for Muriel the witch," Seth said. "Can you dig down to her?"

Hugo hesitated. "Witch bad."

"There's a war with the dragons, Hugo," Seth said. "If

we want to win, I need to get something from the Demon King, and I can't find him without the witch. Kendra is in trouble. Grandma and Grandpa Sorenson are trapped at Wyrmroost. The whole world is in danger. I have to talk to Muriel."

Hugo stared down at Seth with his big, empty sockets. "Hugo dig fast. Come." Hugo effortlessly picked up Seth and placed him on one stony shoulder. The golem took off at a bounding lope.

"Seth," Calvin said. "Would you mind if I visit my people while you do this?"

"How will you get there?" Seth asked.

"Are you kidding?" Calvin asked. "I know more birds at Fablehaven than anywhere. Whistling one up will be no problem."

"Hugo," Seth said, "I need to set down a nipsie passenger."

The golem came to a halt and lifted Seth to the ground. Seth placed Calvin on a stump.

"Don't you dare leave Fablehaven without me," Calvin said. "I'll fly back to you after I check in."

"I won't leave you," Seth said. "Let's go, Hugo."

The golem picked up Seth and was off again.

Fruit trees and blossoms flourished on the low hill that had replaced the Forgotten Chapel. Seth took a bite of a juicy peach, the Unforgiving Blade in his other hand, as

Hugo tunneled under the hill. The golem's huge hands manipulated dirt and stone like it was malleable, pushing the earth aside rather than removing it.

Seth tossed the peach pit into a bush, wiped his sticky hand on the grass, then dried it on his pant leg. He was just sitting down in the shade when Hugo emerged from the tunnel. "Found witch," the golem announced.

"Good job," Seth said, hopping to his feet. "Take me to her."

Hugo beckoned to Seth and then ducked into the tunnel. Seth followed him down the slanting path, watching as the golem made minor adjustments to the walls and ceiling—shaping here, compressing there. Pausing, Seth took a flashlight from his satchel. The temperature became cooler as they descended, and the rich smell of freshly excavated earth drenched the air.

Before long, Seth noticed hunks of decaying wood embedded in the surrounding dirt, remnants of the collapsed chapel. Up ahead, Hugo stepped to the side and motioned Seth forward. "Here," the golem said.

The tunnel ended at crisscrossing golden cords knotted to form a net. Behind the wall of cords, within a larger space beyond the tunnel, an old woman stood lashed to a demon by several other golden cords. The three-legged demon slumbered, dragonlike head slumped downward, but the witch glared at Seth, her wrinkled features smudged with filth.

"What's this?" the witch asked. "Do my eyes deceive me? Has my stalwart adventurer returned?"

"Hello, Muriel," Seth said.

"You've become a young man," Muriel said, sounding impressed. "Look how tall you have grown! Your aspect has darkened, young one. And look at those fine swords!"

"I'm a shadow charmer now," Seth said.

"Have you burrowed down here simply to relish my misery?" Muriel asked, spittle on her shriveled lips. "No, let me guess—you need my help. What have your grandparents done now?"

"We're at war with the dragons," Seth said. "All seven sanctuaries have fallen."

Muriel cackled. "I've been safer down here than anyone up there."

"At least we're not tied to giant demons," Seth said.

"Don't get too smug," Muriel chided. "We're all bound to darkness one way or another. It's as inescapable as casting a shadow. At least my demon is hibernating."

"Do you know how to contact the Sphinx?" Seth asked.

"Who is that?" Muriel replied.

Seth rolled his eyes. "You don't need to play dumb. He was the leader of the Knights of the Dawn and the Society of the Evening Star. He was caught after he helped open Zzyzx. Now he's one of the Eternals serving as the lock for the new demon prison. I need to reach him."

"And you decided to exhume me," Muriel said. "You must be desperate."

"I'm in a hurry," Seth said. "If you can reach him, maybe we can make a deal. If not, there are a million other options I can try."

Muriel tittered. "A million other options, he boasts. Yet he digs up an old enemy. Why not try the other options first?"

"If you can reach him quickly, you're the best option," Seth said.

"Aye, I can communicate with the Sphinx," Muriel said. "Will I, though, is the real question."

"What will it take?" Seth asked.

"There is only one thing I want, boy," Muriel said. "Set me free and you have a deal."

"How about we untie one knot?" Seth asked.

"No, no," Muriel said with a chuckle. "These knots were crafted by elevated fairies. They will not come loose. Cut me free or no deal."

"Have it your way," Seth said, turning around. "Hugo, can you fill in this tunnel?"

"Yes," the golem said.

Seth started walking away.

"Wait," Muriel called. "Can't we negotiate?"

Seth turned back to her. "I have to collect something from the new demon prison. If I let you out, will you contact the Sphinx and help me retrieve what I need?"

"I will," Muriel said.

"And will you leave Fablehaven, never to return?" Seth asked.

"Agreed," Muriel said.

"And will you make your new home wherever the Sphinx decides you should?" Seth asked.

"Too many stipulations," Muriel said.

"Enjoy your roommate," Seth said, turning and walking up the tunnel.

"Come back," Muriel called. "I consent."

Seth went back. "I don't have time to waste. Do you agree to all of it?"

"All of it," Muriel said. "I swear."

"This only works if I can get you out without disturbing the big guy," Seth said, nodding up to Bahumat's slumbering head.

"Simple," Muriel said. "Use the void sword to sever two horizontal strands and two vertical strands of the mesh. Then come through and cut the strings binding me to the demon. Do this, and Bahumat will remain asleep and imprisoned."

"And you will do me no harm," Seth said. "Ever."

"So many additions," Muriel complained. "You really have grown up."

"I just want to be clear," Seth said.

"If you end my incarceration, I will do no harm to you or your sister or any of the staff of Fablehaven. I will contact the Sphinx immediately on your behalf, assist you in procuring an item from the new demon prison, flee Fablehaven never to return, and make my new dwelling where the Sphinx suggests. If you add no more adjustments to the agreement, I solemnly vow to all this by my power. Clear enough?"

When Seth used the Unforgiving Blade to cut the first golden strand, he heard a sound like the tolling of a distant bell, and the severed strand took on a dull, copper color.

The same happened with the next three strands. Having sliced two vertical and two horizontal strands, Seth found he could slip through the resulting gap in the mesh. He approached Muriel, aware of her foul stench. Five cords lashed her to the demon. Each chimed then grew dull as he cut it. When he sliced the final cord, the demon stirred.

Seth held his breath, sword ready, still and silent. Muriel remained motionless as well.

After the demon settled back to sleep, Muriel took tentative steps away from Bahumat, her smile revealing inflamed gums and missing teeth. "This is a good bargain. You have shortened my sentence, Seth Sorenson, and you now merit my assistance."

Not ready to talk, Seth jabbed his sword at the gap in the mesh. Muriel slipped through, and Seth followed.

"Would you close up this tunnel behind us?" Seth asked the golem.

Hugo gave a nod, and Seth followed Muriel toward the light.

# CHAPTER THIRTY-TWO

# Miguel

The village of Huasco was located on the coast of Chile, just south of the delta where a modest river emptied into the sea. The water nourished a rare strip of greenery in the otherwise desolate Atacama Desert. Most of the terrain around Huasco looked as dry and lifeless as the moon.

Kendra and Virgil landed on a beach north of town. The gray sand shone like a mirror when it was freshly moistened by the waves. Late in the afternoon, the temperature was cool, and no beachgoers lingered. Kendra might have had difficulty imagining such a long, ideal expanse of beach this empty, but she had flown over many quiet, beautiful beaches during her journey south from Peru.

"You should probably go into town alone," Virgil said. "Having a goat along seems conspicuous."

"I'm sorry we had to get rid of your pendant," Kendra said.

"It was for the best," Virgil said. "I wish I hadn't been so trusting of that gift."

"I made the same mistake," Kendra said heavily.

"We'll keep watch over Kendra," Noble assured them. "When we're in flight, the mortals see birds."

"You stay near Kendra, and I'll scout the surrounding area," Glory said. "We can't have another surprise dragon attack."

"At least this terrain leaves few places to hide," Noble said.

"I'll keep riding with Noble," Virgil said. "Kendra, if you need me, I won't be far away."

"I wish I spoke better Spanish," Kendra said. "I had a little in school."

"What can you say?" Virgil asked.

"Juan tiene el pelo rubio," Kendra said.

"Which means?" Virgil asked.

"John has blond hair," Kendra said. "My accent is terrible, and my vocabulary is really limited. I know a bunch of fairy languages fluently. But only one human language."

"Can Gerwin see magical creatures?" Glory asked. "A flying horse might help your credibility."

"Maybe," Kendra said. "I don't know whether he sees through mortal eyes or magical eyes. I wish I had some milk to give him to be sure."

"You'll find a way to convince him," Virgil said. "I have faith in you."

"How do I look?" Kendra asked.

"Presentable," Virgil said. "Fairly clean for how much we've been traveling. Your clothes are neither fancy nor worn out."

"Not what I would want to wear on a date," Kendra muttered. "But it might be about right for this assignment. Wish me luck."

"We'll never be far," Virgil said.

Kendra started up the beach toward the little town. The sand ended at a white lighthouse with a rounded top and a big anchor out front. Shy to approach anyone with her limited Spanish, Kendra followed the broad walkway parallel to the coast until she reached a major intersection. Here at least she saw a sign for a street called Craig. The stop sign looked the same as in the United States except with the word "PARE" instead of "STOP."

Kendra wandered over to a tall white church topped by a large cross. The building reminded Kendra of the prow of a ship. Turning in a circle, she saw palm trees and houses and the ocean. Kendra approached a middle-aged woman who looked pleasant.

"Hola," Kendra said. "No hablo mucho español."

"Yo tampoco," the woman responded. "Hablo castellano."

Unsure how the woman had responded, Kendra tried, "Dónde está calle Victoria?"

The woman thought for a moment, then said a lot of words Kendra couldn't follow while motioning away from the sea. Kendra nodded politely and finished with a "gracias."

Deciding to ask for clarification as she went, Kendra set out in the general direction the woman had described. Most of the houses were single story, roofed with corrugated aluminum. Some were painted brightly, while others had dull gray cinderblock walls. Those with small yards often had little gates, and sometimes a few shrubs. She saw almost no grass. The street signs were painted on walls at corners, names like "A. Prat" or "La Torre" stenciled on white arrows with black backgrounds.

The farther Kendra went from the sea, the simpler the houses became. A few people pointed her in the right direction as she asked. She noticed little neighborhood shops adjoining some of the houses. They seemed to be convenience stores, selling items like bread, soda, and ice cream bars. After crossing train tracks, she approached a man who indicated Victoria was close and showed her exactly which road to follow.

When she felt alone, Kendra would look up to see Virgil astride Noble, circling above. She wondered if anyone would notice the bird consistently orbiting the gringa. No matter how much Kendra checked the sky, she never caught a glimpse of Glory.

Kendra estimated it was an hour before sunset when she found the road labeled Victoria. The neighborhood street looked to be only a few blocks long, and the street numbers surrounding her were in the 500s. The desired number was a tidy, lime-green house with a couple of small palms in the tiny, gated yard.

Kendra let herself through the gate and knocked on the door. A moment later a young boy opened it and looked up at her curiously. He wore a striped shirt and blue shorts.

"Miguel?" Kendra asked.

She heard the word "hermano" in the boy's reply and remembered that it meant "brother."

"Dónde está Miguel?" Kendra asked in her kindest voice.

She could not understand the reply, but thought she heard "fútbol," which she knew meant "soccer."

Kendra pointed to herself. "Yo hablo Miguel, por favor."

The boy said something else she didn't understand, but he came out of the house and waved for her to follow. Relieved, Kendra walked beside the kid, who she assumed must be Miguel's younger brother, maybe eight or nine years old.

He led her up a couple of streets to a patch of empty ground where a pack of kids were playing soccer with a peeling, dusty ball. Stacked rocks marked the goals, and the kids played with skill, dribbling and passing adroitly. Most of the boys looked roughly twelve or thirteen, but the youngest was one of the most adept players, skillfully advancing the ball past taller kids, using clever fakes to throw off the other team. Kendra watched him draw off defenders near the goal, then sneak a pass to an open teammate for a score.

"Miguel?" Kendra called after the goal.

The boys paused and stared at her, especially the shortest.

"Miguel Santiago Duran Fuentes?" she tried.

Some of the boys oohed teasingly, and Miguel looked embarrassed but trotted over to Kendra, giving his brother a significant glance.

"Quién es ella?" Miguel asked his brother.

"No sé," his brother said.

"No hablo mucho español," Kendra admitted.

"I speak a little English," Miguel said.

"That's a relief," Kendra said. She looked at his brother. "Do you speak it too?"

The little boy looked to his brother.

"I'm the only one in my family who speaks English," Miguel said as the game resumed without him.

"How did you learn?" Kendra asked.

"Movies, songs," Miguel said. "It comes easy to me. I don't have many chances to speak, though. It's easier to listen."

"Your English is better than my Spanish," Kendra said.

"How do you know me?" Miguel asked.

"That is kind of a long story," Kendra said.

The little brother asked something in Spanish. Miguel answered and waved him away. The little brother wandered off. "He wanted to know what we are saying."

"What did you tell him?"

"I said you want my autograph. Then I told him to go home. What is the long story?"

"How much do you know about your history?" Kendra asked.

"I know I'm adopted," Miguel said. "That's why I have these hazel eyes."

Kendra considered what she should say next. "Have you ever seen anything . . . supernatural?"

"Like a ghost?"

"That sort of thing."

"No. But my uncle saw a spirit at the cemetery. A lady all in black."

Kendra turned and pointed up to where Noble soared above them. "What do you see up there?"

"The bird?"

"Yeah," Kendra said, disappointed.

"Is it a supernatural bird?"

"Sort of," Kendra said. "Have you ever felt different from other kids?"

"I'm very different," Miguel said with a smile. "I'm better at soccer than everyone my age. I get the best grades without studying. I know English like a pro. Do you want to be my girlfriend or something?"

"I may be a little old for that," Kendra said.

"I'm just kidding," Miguel said. "Unless you change your mind."

"What if I told you that I know one of your brothers?" Kendra asked.

"I'd be like, duh, Arturo brought you here," Miguel said.

"I mean one of your biological brothers," Kendra said. "From the same mother as you."

"I'd be surprised," Miguel said. "My mom and dad don't know where I came from. I showed up on their doorstep. My birth parents are long gone. I'm like Batman."

"Your brother's name is Merek," Kendra said. "Does that ring a bell?"

"My parents raised me since I was a baby," Miguel said. "I don't remember anybody else. But I really have a brother named Merek?"

"Yes."

"Where is he?" Miguel asked.

"I last saw him in Australia," Kendra said.

"Is he a kangaroo? Maybe he rides kangaroos? Or herds them?"

"He's older than you," Kendra said.

"Are you part of my birth family?" Miguel asked.

"No," Kendra said.

"Good. Or that part about being my girlfriend would be weird."

"Do you really want a girlfriend? You seem a little young."

"Only if she is taller than me," Miguel said. "And speaks English. And is wearing those shoes you have on."

"You're a charmer," Kendra said.

Miguel shrugged. "I have lots of skills." He looked over his shoulder at the kids playing soccer. "Anything else? My team is dying without me."

"What if I told you I need your help killing some dragons?" Kendra asked.

"If dragons play soccer to the death, I'm your man," Miguel said.

Kendra didn't know how hard to push. He hadn't seen Noble's true form. The name Merek meant nothing to him. And he treated talk of dragons like a joke.

"Have you ever wondered if you lived before this life?" Kendra asked.

"You should ask the Mormons about that," Miguel said. "They wear white shirts with little black tags."

"What if you had a previous life?" Kendra asked. "Can you imagine that?"

"I can imagine winning the World Cup," he said, spreading his arms wide. He glanced back at the game. "I should go play."

"I need to give you a nickname," Kendra said.

"How about Ace?" Miguel proposed.

"I thought maybe Gerwin," Kendra said, watching his eyes.

"Kind of weird, but go ahead, if you want," Miguel said. "Should I give you a nickname? How about Angel?"

"Sure," Kendra said with a smile.

"Are you here on vacation?"

"Yeah, for a little while," Kendra said.

"Nice to meet you, Angel," Miguel said. He returned to his friends. They teasingly shoved him and pointed at Kendra. She couldn't understand the words, but from the body language, she wouldn't be surprised if he was claiming her as his girlfriend.

Kendra realized she would look like a stalker if she

lingered too long, so she walked away from the dusty field where they were playing. What else could she try? Miguel only knew his current life and he seemed to be enjoying it.

How was she supposed to awaken him to his long history? Could this shrimpy kid fight a dragon? Hopefully he had tools and techniques that would transcend his age.

She was on a tight timeline. Dragons were looking for Gerwin, and it was only a matter of time before they found him. How much patience could she afford? The dragon war would not pause to accommodate her delays.

Kendra sat down on some steps in front of a house, elbow on her knee, chin heavy in her hand. She had found a second legendary Dragon Slayer. And he was a ten-year-old Chilean kid who liked to play soccer and flirt.

Miguel had friends and family. She didn't want to ruin his life. But he was in grave danger already, whether he knew it or not. He was being hunted by dragons, and he was needed in the war. She could not let him meet the same fate as Magdalena. Once Miguel remembered his identity, he would thank her, right? Shaking her head in frustration, Kendra thought hard about what to try next.

# CHAPTER THIRTY-THREE

# Scheming

M uriel knelt outside the tunnel and stroked the grass with her palms. Crouching low, she sniffed a wild-flower without plucking it. Leaning back, eyes narrowed, she breathed deeply, a small smile twisting her lips. At the base of the hill, Hugo patted down the ground he had filled in over the tunnel.

Seth stood near Muriel, the Unforgiving Blade in his hand. "When will you contact the Sphinx?"

"Patience, young Master Sorenson," Muriel said. "I have been caged for too long. Give an old woman a moment to enjoy the day."

"It's way too hot," Seth said.

"I have not felt warm in a great while," Muriel said, sitting cross-legged. "We had a deal. Allow me to reach out."

She placed her hands on her knees and serenely closed her eyes.

Seth watched her warily, half expecting a trick or some sort of attack. She held the pose long enough that he began to grow bored.

Finally, the witch opened her eyes abruptly and stood, shoulders stooped, crinkled limbs scrawny. "The Sphinx will meet you at the pond by the Fairy Queen's shrine," Muriel said.

"Wait, how?" Seth replied. "Is he already here? Visiting Grandpa Larsen or something? Or can he access the portal from the Fairy Realm? He probably can, if he's still working with Ronodin."

"I don't know his manner of conveyance," Muriel said.

"Hugo," Seth called. "We need to go back to the Fairy Queen's shrine."

The golem plodded over to Seth, grasped his torso, and lifted him to one shoulder.

"The witch too," Seth directed.

Hugo deposited Muriel on his other shoulder, then took off at a loping pace.

"Careful," Muriel said. "These old bones don't like to be rattled."

Hugo went no slower, but his gait smoothed out.

"How did you like being tied to a demon?" Seth asked.

"The conversation was lacking," Muriel said. "Bahumat is a being of immense rage. He stomped and roared for a season, testing his restraints. He tried to rattle me, but I ignored him. Eventually, the demon settled into hibernation. His constant malevolent presence remained palpable even in his sleep. Eventually I followed his example and became dormant. The road I chose to follow includes enduring discomfort."

"You were sleeping?" Seth asked.

"Not deeply enough to miss the approach of a golem excavating my prison," Muriel said.

"Did you have weird dreams?" Seth asked.

"I don't have nightmares," Muriel said. "I give them to other people."

"Nice line," Seth said. "You should write greeting cards."

When Hugo passed through the hedge into the clearing around the pond, Seth could see the Sphinx waiting for them in the tallest gazebo. Hugo stopped a few strides away from the boardwalk and lowered Seth to the ground, then set Muriel beside him.

The Sphinx exited the gazebo to greet them. His hair was buzzed down to stubble, and he wore a loose-fitting white shirt tucked into khaki slacks. Dark sunglasses hid his eyes, but he flashed a warm smile, and his easy stance seemed to welcome them to his private villa.

"Muriel," the Sphinx said. "I hope you don't take offense that you were the last person I expected to hear from."

"That puts us on equal footing," Muriel said. "Because this young scamp was the last person I expected to come to my rescue." She squinted at the Sphinx. "You're different."

"I'm an Eternal," the Sphinx said. "It's part of the compromise I made after the fiasco at the demon prison. Hello again, Seth. I understand you have been reunited with your memories."

"It's no picnic," Seth said.

"Ronodin had you confused for a time," the Sphinx said.

"You were part of that," Seth said.

"Ronodin is one of the most dangerous players in the world," the Sphinx said. "It pays to stay close to such individuals."

"You helped topple Wyrmroost," Seth said.

"It was time for the dragons to have their shot," the Sphinx said. "They suffered for a long time, caged and defanged, but after Zzyzx they started feeling their strength again. There was no stopping the war. The only question was how I would position myself."

"Do you still mean to help them?" Seth asked.

"Let's talk," the Sphinx said, backing into the gazebo.

Seth glanced up at Hugo. "I'm going to talk with these guys. If they try something shady, I might need you."

"Hugo watch," the golem said.

"It should have been you who came to my rescue," Muriel scolded the Sphinx as she entered the whitewashed structure.

"Circumstances never allowed it," the Sphinx said. He gestured for Muriel to sit down. After she settled on a bench, he sat as well, and Seth chose to stand. "Seth, this is your meeting, how can I be of service?"

"I've been given a task by the Singing Sisters," Seth said.

Muriel gasped. "You met the Sisters?"

"They're a pain," Seth said. "I keep owing them favors."

"Speak of the Sisters with respect," Muriel chided.

"The Singing Sisters are of considerable renown among witches," the Sphinx explained.

"Among anyone," Muriel corrected. "They protect the balance."

"Well, they ordered me to gather all the pieces of the Ethergem," Seth said.

"Interesting," the Sphinx said, drawing out the word. "A daunting task."

"Will you undertake the endeavor?" Muriel asked.

"I only need one more piece," Seth said.

At this the Sphinx sat up straighter. "The headstone in the Demon King's crown," he said. "That's why you want to talk to me."

"I have to get inside the new Zzyzx," Seth said.

The Sphinx motioned toward Seth. "Those are formidable swords. And impressive wings. You have diverse sponsors."

"The Singing Sisters told me that we can't win the dragon war unless I succeed," Seth said.

"Then it is probably true," the Sphinx said. "There are those who suspect the Sisters might be the Fates, or else that the Fates were modeled after them."

"The Sisters are our most gifted practitioners," Muriel said. "They stand at the summit of our art."

"What will they do with the pieces of the Ethergem?" Seth asked.

"Their reasons are their own," the Sphinx said. "If they didn't tell you, it's difficult to guess."

"Could they repair the Ethergem and use it?" Seth asked.

"Unlikely," the Sphinx said. "The Ethergem was broken by Raglamar. You hold a piece of that legendary sword in your hand, reforged into a smaller weapon. What Raglamar cut cannot be repaired. Besides, the Ethergem originated from the Source, and the Sisters do not wield that type of power."

"Their reasons tend to be layered," Muriel said. "Even if you discover one of their purposes, you are missing a hundred others."

"But is this a good quest?" Seth asked.

"You're asking me?" The Sphinx sounded amused.

"I know you don't want somebody else to end the world," Seth said.

"You are . . . right about that," the Sphinx said.

"And I can guess you don't want a dragon apocalypse," Seth said.

"Neither do the Singing Sisters," the Sphinx said. "Patton knew that much. The Sisters desire balance, so if you're the underdog, they become a reliable source of assistance."

"How did you get here today?" Seth asked.

"That's a good question." The Sphinx removed his sunglasses and ran a hand over his scalp. "How do you think?"

"Are you still working with Ronodin?" Seth asked.

The Sphinx smiled and looked over his shoulder at the shrine. "I see where your mind went. I wasn't part of Ronodin's latest power play. We've associated in the past, but I have no loyalty to him. Honestly, I think he made a stupid, greedy move invading the Fairy Realm. I don't see how he expects to hold what he took long term."

"He has Kendra," Seth said.

"I'm sorry to hear that," the Sphinx replied. "Ronodin nurtures grudges, and he has a peculiar interest in your sister."

"He's on my list," Seth said. "The Ethergem comes first. Muriel has already vowed to help me get Orogoro's stone."

"You failed to mention we were seeking the primary jewel from the Crown of Wrath," Muriel complained.

"And you failed to ask," Seth said.

Muriel opened her mouth to reply, then closed it. "You caught me in a desperate moment," she finally said.

Seth locked eyes with the Sphinx. "Will you help me break into the new demon prison?"

The Sphinx shook his head and grinned. "Kind of puts me in a tough spot, considering I'm one of the new Eternals."

Muriel cackled. "You have to die to open the lock!"

"Myself and others," the Sphinx said.

"Is the new demon prison fully locked?" Seth asked.

"It isn't," the Sphinx replied. "The artifacts have not all been rehidden, for example. But the prison is partially locked, and my life is already tied to the mechanism."

"You broke into Zzyzx when it was locked," Seth said. "Surely you can find a way inside. Aren't there weak points?"

The Sphinx held Seth's gaze. "I know one major weak point. Why would I assist you, Seth?"

"You helped start the dragon war," Seth said. "I'll forget about that."

The Sphinx nodded. "That would be convenient. It also happens that I think Celebrant needs to be derailed. The more success and power he acquires, the faster he forgets those who facilitated his freedom."

"Never deal with dragons," Muriel muttered.

"You have the feature stone from Celebrant's crown?" the Sphinx asked.

"I cut it out with the Unforgiving Blade," Seth said.

"Impressive," the Sphinx said. "I would love to hear the story someday."

"How much will the missing gem weaken Celebrant?" Seth asked.

"A little," the Sphinx said. "Not nearly enough. The Dragon King has too much momentum. Let's suppose I can get you inside the new Zzyzx. How would you intend to deal with Orogoro?"

"I'm still working on it," Seth said. "One impossible problem at a time."

"We cannot approach the Demon King without an airtight plan," the Sphinx said.

"We can't approach him at all without a way in," Seth replied. "I don't want to show you every card in my hand."

"He's lying," Muriel noted.

"But also quite capable," the Sphinx said. "He wasn't lying about amassing the other stones. Obtaining even one of them should not have been possible. Regarding the demon prison, why not solicit help from your friends and family? You still have many capable allies."

"I've burned some bridges," Seth said. "I don't think anyone in Dragonwatch would trust me entering Zzyzx, or want me to have all the pieces of the Ethergem. Besides, it's a horrible place, and my mission might end badly. Why would I want to draw friends into that?"

The Sphinx laughed openly. "But if Muriel and I get knocked off, no big deal, right?"

"It's not like losing a grandparent," Seth said.

"You've learned a lot," the Sphinx said. "You're more ruthless and candid than I remember. And you're less willing to risk the ones you love. You're floundering, but your head is somehow still above water. I like that. Great men tend to start out that way."

"Plenty of dead men too," Muriel said.

"Dead men too," the Sphinx echoed softly. "The way I arrived today could get you into the prison. I wondered if that was why you asked how I got here."

"If you didn't come here from the Fairy Realm, I don't know," Seth said.

The Sphinx pulled a familiar metal cylinder from his pocket, about the size and shape of a track baton. "Voilà."

"The Translocator," Seth said. "Where did you get it?"

"I'm seldom idle," the Sphinx said. "While Dragonwatch was trying to hide the keys to the demon prison, I was gathering weapons to resist the rise of the dragons."

"Do you have other artifacts?" Seth asked.

"The Chronometer and the Oculus are hidden again," the Sphinx said. "I'm not privy to the location. The Font of Immortality sustained damage and has not been restored, so I stopped paying attention to it. And I believe the wizards still have the Sands of Sanctity. But I helped hide the Translocator, so recovering it was fairly simple."

"You can travel instantly with that," Seth said.

"Anywhere I have already been," the Sphinx clarified. "As you know."

"Have you been inside the new demon prison?" Seth asked.

"Regrettably, no," the Sphinx said. "It was sealed up immediately after the demons transferred there, and we've been strengthening the lock ever since. Before the demons entered, it was the Fairy Realm, and I was not welcome there."

"Has anyone been inside the new prison?" Seth asked.

"Many of the inhabitants of the Fairy Realm once dwelled there," the Sphinx said. "But Ronodin has the Fairy Realm locked down. However, I know of one who escaped."

"Who?"

"Who do you think gave you those wings?" the Sphinx asked.

"He called himself the Traveler," Seth said.

"I know only two people who could bestow wings like that," the Sphinx said. "The Fairy Queen and the Fairy King. I understand the former queen is incarcerated. But I heard her consort escaped."

"The Traveler was the Fairy King," Seth mused. "That makes sense. I helped free him from Gorgrog. No wonder he did me such a huge favor."

"Now we have to figure out if he'll do you another one," the Sphinx said. "Because with the Translocator in his hands, you just might have a back door into the most secure prison on the planet."

# CHAPTER THIRTY-FOUR

# Gerwin

Kendra took a bite of her empanada. Ground beef and onions filled the bready pocket, along with part of a hard-boiled egg and one olive. "How did you get the money for this?"

"Better not to ask," Virgil replied with his mouth full. He sat beside her munching an empanada of his own.

"Nobody would trade with a goat," Kendra said.

"But goats can sneak around in the night and find loose change," Virgil said. "And leave a little gold or silver behind."

"Fair enough," Kendra said. The sun had risen. A passing child had told her she was on break from school, if Kendra had understood the Spanish correctly. It meant Miguel should be available all day.

Kendra and Virgil sat on a cement curb at the edge of

town. There was something surreal about eating breakfast at the threshold where a street abruptly ended, asphalt and curbing turning to dirt. The dry, rocky desert sloped away to the horizon, as if she had happened upon the outer limits of civilization.

"I have enough money for lunch and dinner," Virgil said.

"I want to be gone before the next meal," Kendra said. "Dragons are after Gerwin, and probably hunting Nadia and Konrad too. If we don't hurry, there may not be any Dragon Slayers left to gather."

"You think we can get that kid out of town before lunch?" Virgil asked.

"I can't wait around dropping hints and hoping he remembers his identity," Kendra said. "We have to take action. Trick him, maybe even kidnap him. You wait here where the town ends. I'm going to tell Miguel I need help catching my goat. You lead him out into the desert, and we'll force him onto the horses. Maybe flying through the air will open his eyes to the magical world. If not, going to Selona should jog his memory."

"It's an extreme solution," Virgil said. "But there are many lives at stake, including his."

Kendra looked up to Noble circling high above. "Can you flag down Noble and tell him the plan? Then he can relay it to Glory."

"Sure," Virgil said. "Good luck."

The morning warmed up as Kendra walked back to Victoria. She found Miguel and two other boys crouching on the edge of his street a few houses down from where he lived. The boys huddled close, fixated by something between them. Stepping softly, Kendra approached. The boys looked up startled when her shadow fell across them.

She could see they had a little matchbook and had lit a twig on fire. Miguel said something to the other boys in Spanish, and they relaxed.

"Are you a pyro?" Kendra asked.

"I don't know what that means," Miguel said.

"Do you like setting things on fire?" she clarified.

"Who doesn't?" Miguel said. "Do you care about these sticks?"

"Just don't burn yourselves," Kendra said.

"We won't," Miguel said. "There is dirt all around. The fire can't spread."

"How would you like to make some money?" Kendra asked.

Miguel perked up. "How much?"

Kendra held out some of the coins Virgil had given her.

Miguel raised his eyebrows. "Is it legal?"

"My goat got away," Kendra said. "I need help catching him."

"You have a goat?" Miguel asked, surprised.

"Goats are the best," Kendra said. "But he ran off."

"What's his name?"

"Virgil."

"Can my friends help?" Miguel asked. "Will you pay all of us?"

"It's a one-man job," Kendra said.

"Qué haces?" a gravelly voice asked from behind Kendra.

She turned to find a man behind her. He wore brown boots, and a blue shirt tucked into faded black jeans. He had fairer skin than most Chileans, and narrow features. Dark stubble roughened his jaw. He squinted down at the boys with a serious expression.

"Ellos están jugando," Kendra said.

The man smiled. "You're not a native speaker," he said in accented English.

Miguel and his friends frantically blew out the burning twig. One of the kids stomped it.

"I'm from America," Kendra said.

"This is America too," the man said.

"North America," Kendra clarified. "I'm from the U.S."

"You're teaching young boys to make fires?" he asked.

With the twig extinguished, Miguel stood up. "This guy is dangerous."

Kendra glanced at Miguel. "Do you know him?"

"No," Miguel said, one hand over his chest. "But something about him feels wrong."

"I caught you making mischief," the man said. "Now I'm the bad guy."

"They won't make more fires," Kendra said.

"You have to take the matches," the man said. "Leave a kid with matches and he'll burn down the house."

Kendra held out a hand to Miguel. "Can I have the matches?"

"Vaya," Miguel muttered urgently, and his friends ran

off. He stared up at the man as if expecting an attack. "Come to my house, Angel. This weirdo is a murderer or something."

"That's a big accusation," the man said, as if mildly offended. "Give the girl the matches."

Miguel handed Kendra the half-spent matchbook. "Happy?"

"No hard feelings," the man said. "How about I buy you two a soda?"

"We have sodas at my house," Miguel said, backing away. "Come on, Angel."

Kendra withdrew alongside Miguel.

The man followed them, keeping pace. "Don't run away. I need to practice my English."

"He's bad news for sure," Miguel said.

"I'm good news," the man said. "I'm a talent scout for Colo-Colo."

"Yeah, right," Miguel said. "And I star in lots of movies."

Kendra noticed that Miguel would not turn his back on the man, though he kept moving away. Kendra stayed with him. They were one house away from Miguel's.

"I know your parents aren't home," the man said.

Miguel stopped.

"Let's all go inside," the man said. "You can give me a soda."

"Who are you?" Kendra asked.

"I'm his uncle," the man said. "We play like this all the time. Knock it off, Miguel, you're scaring her."

"I don't know this guy," Miguel said, turning to run.

The man sprang forward and gripped Miguel by the upper arm, stopping his escape. "Enough games. Come with your uncle." Miguel tried to lurch away, but the man held him tightly.

"Let him go," Kendra said.

"This is family business," the man said, turning and dragging Miguel away.

"He's not my family," Miguel cried urgently. "He's a bad man! Can't you tell?"

The man gave Miguel a brusque shake, then heaved the thrashing boy over one shoulder and strode away briskly. Kendra ran to catch up. "Leave him alone or I'll—"

The man kicked backward as Kendra came within range, the heel of his boot clipping her side. Kendra crumpled, stunned, clutching the point of impact. The man strode on.

Suddenly Noble swooped into view, hoofs flailing, and struck the man in the head. He flopped to the street, dropping Miguel. The boy landed like a cat and ran off. The man staggered to his feet, one hand clamped to the gash in his scalp, trying to hold back the copious blood. He lunged sideways as Noble swung back around, barely avoiding another kick.

The man rushed to a low wall on the opposite side of the street, reached over, and produced a machete. Glaring, one eye gummed with blood, the man dodged and slashed as Noble made another pass, opening a long wound above the Luvian's foreleg. The horse whinnied in pain.

"Get away, Noble," Kendra cried, getting her breath back.

The man with the machete charged her, and Kendra ran. She heard his heavy footfalls gaining and was tackled from behind, skinning her knees and elbows on the asphalt. Noble whooshed above them, hooves swishing harmlessly above the prone man. The stranger yanked Kendra to her feet, the edge of his machete against her throat.

"Keep your distance or she's finished," the man called angrily, forcing her toward Miguel's lime-green house. Kendra let him guide her through the front door. He shoved her to a couch and pointed the machete at her. "No tricks."

Kendra glared up at him. "Who are you?"

"You're not very quick," the man said, losing his Spanish accent. The voice sounded more familiar.

"Jeruwat?" Kendra asked.

"I hate the human form," Jeruwat said, plucking at his shirt, a look of disgust on his face. He patted his bleeding scalp and frowned at the blood on his fingers. "It's pathetically fragile. But I can't use my true shape in a human community. There is too much ignorance and unbelief."

"At least Miguel got away," Kendra said.

"Did he?" Jeruwat asked with a smile. "Miguel!" he raged, raising his voice, his accent back. "I have your angel! Show yourself or she dies!" Jeruwat winked at Kendra. "Know your enemy," he whispered.

"Miguel, don't," Kendra cried. "It's a trap."

"Thanks," Jeruwat whispered, still grinning. "That's perfect."

"How did you find us?" Kendra asked.

"I tracked you as far as Batoosa," Jeruwat said. "Demons talk tough, but none of them want to die. He endured longer than I expected. In the end, he gave you up."

Kendra heard a back door slam open. "I'm here," Miguel called, his accent gone. "Try to catch me." His voice came from a neighboring room.

"Shut your eyes, Miguel!" she shouted. Closing her eyes, Kendra summoned her power and projected it as light.

Jeruwat cried out, and the machete clanged to the floor. Kendra doused her light and found Jeruwat on his knees, growling, hands over his eyes, blood streaming down his chin. Kendra raced by him and out the back door, where she joined Miguel.

"What was that flash?" Miguel asked.

"Quick," Kendra said, rushing behind the house. Miguel ran with her, looping back to the street. "Noble!" Kendra called.

The horse landed beside them. Kendra boosted Miguel up, then climbed behind him as the horse took to the sky.

"Are you all right?" Noble asked.

"Better than Jeruwat," Kendra said.

"We're on a flying horse," Miguel said.

"You can see it now!" Kendra said. "Noble, we have to find Virgil and Glory."

"Glory went to get Virgil," Noble said.

"We need to get away fast," Kendra said.

"No," Miguel said. "That man is a dragon."

"Are you sure?" Kendra asked.

"That nickname you gave me yesterday is my real name," Miguel said, his English perfect. "I'm Gerwin, son of Konrad. I can sniff out a dragon a mile away. We need a new strategy. Once we're outside Huasco, Jeruwat can assume his true form."

"Good point," Kendra said.

"Jeruwat is one of the deadliest dragons on record," Gerwin said. "I suspect he let us go on purpose. He wants to fight us outside the city so he can use his true shape. He'll hunt us down and kill us before we've traveled ten miles. Horse, head to the cemetery."

"So they can bury us easier?" Noble asked.

"I have weapons hidden there," Gerwin said. "They will give us a chance."

Noble was already over the desert, but he banked hard and descended toward a walled cemetery made colorful by faded blues, greens, yellows, and reds. Unlike the cemeteries Kendra had seen, most of the graves were aboveground in vaults and mausoleums. The diverse resting places bristled with crosses.

"Land there," Gerwin instructed, indicating a dusty path beside a tomb enclosed by a short picket fence. Noble landed roughly, favoring his left side. Kendra slid off the horse, and Gerwin dropped down beside her.

Kendra checked the wound above Noble's leg. "You have a deep cut."

"Everyone gets scratches in battle," Noble said valiantly.

A few other people were in the cemetery, but none were looking in Kendra's direction. Though the cemetery lacked trees and grass, there were many flowers in pots and vases. Miguel rushed over to a mausoleum that seemed to Kendra like a grim filing cabinet—four crypts high, three across. Kendra followed Miguel as he crouched at the rear of the mausoleum and produced a key.

"What are you doing?" Kendra asked.

"I hid my weapons here before I died last time," Gerwin said. He opened a little hatch at the base of the mausoleum and pulled out a seven-foot spear, the shaft made of smooth white wood, the head crafted from reddish metal, with tufts of red feather just behind it. Gerwin also removed a leather vest containing eight brightly plumed darts in tubular holders on the front. Before closing the hatch, he donned a blue hat with a brilliant red feather affixed to the side.

Gerwin stood. The vest hung almost to his knees, the hat nearly covered his eyes, and the spear looked out of scale for a kid his size.

"Can you use that stuff?" Kendra asked.

"We're about to find out," Gerwin said. "I wish I were taller and heavier."

Kendra heard hoofbeats and turned to find Glory landing, Virgil astride her. The satyr hopped down and tossed Kendra her bow. She fumbled the catch. After she picked up the bow, he handed her the sack of gales.

"I don't know how the dragon slipped by me," Glory said. "I was vigilant."

"He might have been in his human form," Gerwin said. "He's coming this way now."

"You can feel him?" Kendra asked.

"A humming in my bones," Gerwin said. "Even when in human form, they can't fully disguise the fear they project. Watch." He pointed across the cemetery with his lips. "He's about to come over the wall."

Exactly where Gerwin had indicated, a hand appeared, and Jeruwat hoisted himself over the wall, the machete in his other hand. He paused, straddling the top, and glared, then saluted with his machete.

"Shall we end this?" Gerwin called boldly.

"On the ground or in the sky, it's the same to me," Jeruwat said.

"His head isn't bleeding anymore," Gerwin said softly. "He must have gotten outside of town and changed into his dragon form. That would have healed him."

"This cemetery is on the edge of Huasco," Virgil cautioned. "If we run in the wrong direction, he could chase us down as a dragon."

Kendra raised her bow, aimed at Jeruwat, pulled back the string, and said, "Fifty."

A swarm of arrows leaped from her bow. Jeruwat pitched forward off the wall into the cemetery, disappearing behind a tomb just before the arrows arrived. About half rebounded off the top of the wall, and half sailed over it.

"He's coming," Gerwin said. "Let's take this to the sky."

"Really?" Kendra asked.

"I like a big target," Gerwin said.

"Fine with me," Noble agreed.

Virgil mounted Noble. Kendra pushed Gerwin onto Glory and then climbed up. The horse surged into the air and flew upward as Jeruwat ran toward them brandishing his machete. The attacker shrank behind them as they rose. Keeping an eye on him, Kendra saw him sprinting across the cemetery toward the desert.

"Don't stray too far from the town," Gerwin instructed. "If things go sour, we'll return to Huasco."

"What's the plan?" Kendra asked.

"These darts are fletched using parts of my phoenix feather," Gerwin said. "They seek out and target weak spots of their own accord. On dragons it is often the eyes."

"The darts are made from the feather in your hat?" Kendra asked.

"Everything I use grows back," Gerwin said. "Your arrows won't be much use against his dragon form."

"I also have a sack that blows wind," Kendra said.

"That could help, but it might blow us around, too," Gerwin said. "Use it if we land. Or as a last resort."

Kendra slung the bow over her shoulder and readied the sack of gales. All she had to do was loosen the drawstring to widen the mouth and a mighty wind would gush out.

"What can I do?" Glory asked.

"Dodge his breath weapons," Gerwin said. "Keep us above him if you can. Here he comes!"

The dark gray dragon rose from the edge of town, malevolent eyes burning. Kendra felt a smothering wave of dragon fear threatening to paralyze her. Tightening her grip on Glory with her knees, she grimly steeled herself against the panic.

"He's thinking like a dragon," Gerwin said, twirling his spear.

"What do you mean?" Kendra asked with an effort.

"He's angry," Gerwin said. "We made this harder than he expected. We hurt him. And right now, we look like easy prey. To him, these horses are flying appetizers. Ten minutes ago, I was Miguel—a kid who could have only beaten him at soccer. But now I'm a professional Dragon Slayer." Gerwin took two darts from the holders on his vest. "And I've never lost one on one."

He threw one dart, then the other. Flaring red, they streaked down toward the dragon like bottle rockets. Jeruwat swerved to avoid them, but the darts adjusted, impacting against his eyes with searing flashes. The dragon's jaws widened, spewing fire as his head whipped back and forth.

"He forgot who he is hunting," Gerwin said, throwing a third dart. "Take us lower, gallant steed."

Curving back toward Jeruwat, Glory dove. Gerwin gripped his spear in two hands, pointing the tip down at the dragon.

The third dart struck Jeruwat in the muzzle, perhaps hitting a nostril. The dragon roared in fury and frustration.

"Dive," Gerwin urged. "Like we're jousting the top of his head."

Glory tilted forward, and suddenly they were almost in a free fall. Kendra squeezed with her knees and clutched Glory's mane. Gerwin shifted his grip to hold the spear in one hand. The head of the dragon approached quickly.

With a grunt, Gerwin flung the shaft downward. The spear entered the top of Jeruwat's head and burst out below his jaw.

The dragon blurred past and the ground rose implacably to meet them. Glory pulled up from her dive, leveling out perhaps twenty feet above the parched terrain. Wings still extended, head and neck hanging limp, Jeruwat plunged toward the earth in a steepening dive. He landed in a crumpled tumble, plowing a shallow trough in the sun-baked landscape.

"One down, lots to go," Gerwin said brightly. "I need that spear back."

# CHAPTER THIRTY-FIVE

# Traveler

"Here we go," the Sphinx said, sitting up from where he had reclined on a bench inside a gazebo. "How long have you been there?"

Seth, Muriel, and the Sphinx had spent the night in separate gazebos around the pond. The Sphinx told them the night before about a method he had used to summon astrids back when he was in charge of the Knights of the Dawn. Before they went to bed, he played a tune on a piccolo, and now, the following morning, an astrid roosted atop the Sphinx's gazebo, staring down at him blandly.

"It worked," Seth said, leaving his gazebo and crossing the boardwalk to join the Sphinx. Seth waved at Hugo and the golem waved back. Hugo had left in the night to catch up on chores, but in the morning Seth had found the reliable golem watching and waiting.

*What is wanted?* the astrid asked in a mellow voice Seth heard in his mind.

"Can you hear it?" the Sphinx asked.

"Yes," Seth said.

"I can't anymore," the Sphinx said. "At least my call was received."

"The astrid wonders what we want," Seth said.

The Sphinx gestured at the astrid. "Have the conversation."

"I need to talk to the Fairy King," Seth said.

*Why are you with the Sphinx?* the astrid asked.

"He's helping with my mission," Seth said.

*His majesty is with another of my kind and wishes to know how he can be of service.*

"The Fairy King is with an astrid," Seth shared. "We can talk to him."

"Convey no details through the astrids," the Sphinx murmured. "I have the Translocator. Ask where he is."

"Where is the king?" Seth inquired. "We have the Translocator and might be able to talk to him in private."

The astrid paused. *His majesty is currently at Wyrmroost, in the abode of Thronis.*

"Wyrmroost," Seth relayed. "With Thronis."

"At the giant's home?" the Sphinx asked.

Seth gave a nod.

"I've been there," the Sphinx said. "I could take you with me, but I think it's better if I fetch the Fairy King and we converse here." The Sphinx took out a platinum cylinder and twisted it until the jewels aligned. Then he vanished.

"The Sphinx is going to get him," Seth said.

The astrid waited in silence.

"Could the Sphinx want private time with the Fairy King?" Muriel asked. "What if he means to double-cross you? Have you thought down that road?"

The astrid ruffled its feathers.

A moment later, the Sphinx reappeared with a man wearing a hooded cloak. Seth recognized him as both the Traveler and the Fairy King.

"Hello, Seth," the Fairy King said, giving Muriel a glance. "You're keeping strange company."

"I have a strange assignment," Seth said. "You gave me these wings. I didn't have my memories at the time, but I should have realized you were the Fairy King."

"I was once the Fairy King. Ronodin stripped my consort of her crown and subsequently assumed my title. Now I am the Traveler. No other names are relevant. Tell me about your assignment."

Seth described the mission he had received from the Singing Sisters to acquire the Ethergem and rehearsed what he had accomplished so far.

"How did you deal with the iron golems guarding the Ethershard?" the Traveler asked.

"The ones with vulture heads?" Seth checked. "I flew away."

The Traveler gave a nod. "Then they pursue you still. Some of my people helped create that enchantment. The golems will never stop while you possess the Ethershard. They will cross oceans, mountains, deserts—always taking the shortest route to you."

"Are they fast?" Seth asked.

"Not especially," the Traveler said. "But they are inexhaustible and relentless. Take care if you remain in one place too long."

"I will," Seth said.

"If I understand correctly, you lack only the stone from the Demon King's crown," the Traveler said.

"Which is why Seth sought me out," the Sphinx said, holding up the Translocator.

"That device can go anywhere the wielder has visited," the Traveler verified.

"Exactly right," the Sphinx replied.

"You need access to the new demon prison," the Traveler said thoughtfully. "I occupied that space back when it was the Fairy Realm. So I could get you inside."

"The Singing Sisters told me we can't win the dragon war unless I do this," Seth said.

The Traveler walked over to the edge of the gazebo, placed his hands on the rail, and looked out over the pond. "Please leave me alone with Seth." He did not watch as the Sphinx and Muriel withdrew.

"We're alone," Seth said.

"Yes, we are," the Traveler agreed. "How does it feel having your memories restored?"

"Painful," Seth said.

"What hurts?" the Traveler asked.

"I've always made more mistakes than average," Seth said. "But after I lost my memories, I made some really huge ones. By the time I realized Ronodin was my enemy, I'd freed the undead at Blackwell Keep and started the dragon war. I betrayed everything I had been trying to protect."

"Nothing aches like regret," the Traveler said with a sigh. He turned away from the pond and faced Seth.

"Now I don't know if I can trust myself," Seth said.

"I understand the feeling," the Traveler said. "A narcoblix used me in my sleep to grant Ronodin access to the Fairy Realm."

"A narcoblix controlled you?" Seth asked.

"She accessed me at my weakest, chained to Gorgrog," the Traveler said. "I suspect it was Nyssa, the originator of all narcoblixes."

"Have you broken her hold on you?" Seth asked.

"No," the Traveler said. "Thronis agreed to watch over me while I slept to keep me from causing more harm."

"I sometimes forget you were chained to Gorgrog for all those years," Seth said. "I can't imagine how well you must know suffering."

"Living in a mortal world involves pain," the Traveler said. "Entropy presides here. Everything moves toward dissolution and death. But physical damage is the lesser problem. The damage to our hearts is far more difficult to repair. We experience loss, disappointments, failure, mistakes. People deliberately harm us. Other wounds are self-inflicted. With experience we learn that we cannot harm another without also harming ourselves."

"I know what you mean," Seth said. "At least I've never been chained to a demon."

"Are you sure?" the Traveler asked. "Have you ever been tricked by a demon? Has evil lured you into behavior you regret? Has folly left you wounded, perhaps even doubting your value? There are many types of chains."

"It all seems so hopeless," Seth said.

"And that is why we need rescuers, Seth," the Traveler said. "I lacked the power to break my chains. You and Kendra liberated me. And now I can help you. In a world where damage is inevitable, nothing is more precious than a healer. I have discovered that we cannot help another without also helping ourselves."

"I definitely need help," Seth said, head bowed.

Sitting down, the Traveler nodded wearily. "When we leave issues unresolved, they invariably resurface. In life, if you fail a test, you're sure to face it again, in one form or another. Ever since I was freed from Gorgrog, I have avoided even thinking about the demons. I now recognize that the tides of life are sweeping me back toward them."

"I'm sorry," Seth said. "That has to be the last place you want to go."

"Accurate," the Traveler said. "Left to myself, I would never visit the demon prison. While there, I feared I would never escape, and going back could make that true. But there is much I would sacrifice to prevent dragons from overrunning the world. And I would do anything to remove Ronodin from the Fairy Realm."

"If you help me get the jewel from the Demon King's

crown, I promise to help you overthrow Ronodin," Seth said.

"A generous offer," the Traveler said.

"I have to stop Ronodin anyhow," Seth said. "He has my sister."

The Traveler shook his head. "He has released Kendra. That would not have happened unless he retained some claim on her. I last saw her at Wyrmroost. She is pursuing help from the legendary Dragon Slayers."

"At least she's not locked up," Seth said.

"You can't possibly understand the horrors that await in the demon prison," the Traveler said.

"I'm committed," Seth said. "I have to finish this quest, and I'm trying to repair what I can. This won't be the first time I've risked my life."

"If this endeavor goes wrong, death will be the least of your concerns," the Traveler said somberly. "There are entities within the prison who will not allow a clean death. They will feed on your agony as they subject you to a prolonged and excruciating parody of life."

Seth nodded grimly. "Can we succeed?"

"We won't be able to take the crown by force," the Traveler said. "Not inside their forsaken stronghold. All will depend on negotiation. I'm willing to try if you're determined."

"It's why I sought you out," Seth said.

"The Translocator and I are your passport in," the Traveler said. "I suppose the Sphinx will want to join us. What about the witch?"

"Muriel promised to help," Seth said.

"How much do you trust the Sphinx?" the Traveler asked.

"Not at all," Seth said. "He takes care of himself. He wants to come out on top no matter what else happens. But I trust he would prefer living in a comfortable world to a nightmare."

"Sounds about right to me," the Traveler said. "And the witch?"

"She's a witch," Seth said. "I don't trust her, either. But she promised to help if I freed her, and I think she'll hold to that."

"I'd rather bring scoundrels into the demon prison than innocents," the Traveler said. "But placing faith in a scoundrel is folly. We must tread carefully. Let me see what I can ascertain from the others." He raised his voice. "You may now join us!"

Muriel scuttled over excitedly. The Sphinx followed with one hand in a pocket.

"I have decided to help Seth access the demon prison," the Traveler announced. "I'm curious how either of you would obtain the jewel from the crown of Orogoro?"

"I wouldn't dare attempt it," Muriel mumbled.

"It would take the right deal," the Sphinx said.

"I agree," the Traveler said. "Would either of you care to come with us?"

"If Seth insists," Muriel said. "I am bound by my oath."

"You may come as a protector," the Traveler said. "We seek to parley with the Demon King. You are accustomed to treating with their kind. You will make our intentions known and keep all other demons away."

"As you command," Muriel said.

"Swear it," the Traveler demanded.

"You have my word," Muriel said. "To find Orogoro, I should summon a guide after we arrive."

"Probably wise," the Traveler said. "What about you, Sphinx?"

The Sphinx held up the Translocator. "This is one of the world's most valuable artifacts. I'm responsible for it. I can't lend it to others."

"Then you will join us?" the Traveler asked.

"The more I consider this endeavor, the less advisable it seems," the Sphinx said. "We can't afford to lose the Translocator to the demons."

"Which is why Seth will hold the Translocator," the Traveler said. "And you will serve as his bodyguard. Seth will be ready to exit with the Translocator at the moment either of us deems it necessary."

"What if that traps us inside?" the Sphinx asked.

"Having entered, he could return for us," the Traveler said.

"It may not be wise to bring me," the Sphinx said. "My life force is part of the lock that holds the demons inside. Should they slay me, they move a step closer to freedom."

"How many other Eternals are bound to the lock?" the Traveler asked.

"At least three," the Sphinx said.

"I'm comfortable with the risk," the Traveler said.

"What do I get out of this?" the Sphinx asked.

"The satisfaction of helping to save the world," the Traveler said.

"I'm more interested in practical gratitude," the Sphinx said.

"Should my consort return to power, we shall absolve you from your role in opening Zzyzx," the Traveler said. "Those of the Fairy Realm still mourn their lost home."

"That is indeed generous," the Sphinx said with a bow. "I never expected to encounter you, your majesty, let alone perform a mission with you. Have you a strategy for negotiating with the Demon King?"

"I believe so." The Traveler's lips bent into a frown. "It can't go worse than last time."

# CHAPTER THIRTY-SIX

# Campfire

Virgil dropped another log on the fire, sending up a column of sparks. Kendra turned her head away from the spreading smoke. They were camped somewhere in northern Colombia, having selected a small, level clearing in a region with no signs of humanity. The sun had set about an hour ago.

By the wavering glow of the fire, Glory licked the cut above Noble's foreleg. They had halted multiple times as they flew north from Chile. During each pause, Glory tended Noble's wound, and at each subsequent stop, the wound looked better and had closed more. Now the cut had almost completely scabbed over, except for a small, wet opening toward the center.

"Is it weird to be in a ten-year-old body after spending so much time as an adult?" Kendra asked.

Gerwin sat on an overturned log near the fire snipping his red feather to fletch a new dart. "A little," he said. "Not as strange as you might guess. Eternals don't all survive the same way. Maybe because of my bond to the phoenix feather, my life happens in cycles. I live each lifetime much like a normal mortal. At a certain age, I feel my death and rebirth drawing near, so I select a family, hide my weapons, and leave myself on their doorstep. I've been ten years old many times."

"How long do you live if you're not killed?" Virgil asked.

"Sixty or seventy years," Gerwin said. "As my body weakens it yearns to regenerate."

"Do you just shrink down into a baby?" Kendra asked.

"I've never seen the process, because I die as it begins," Gerwin said. "I'm told my old body is consumed by fire and all that remains after is my baby form."

"How much warning do you have?" Virgil asked.

"Depends," Gerwin said. "Usually at least a day or two. Up to a week. Sometimes I have lived out a whole life without remembering my original identity. But I always remember when my death approaches."

"A whole life?" Kendra asked.

Gerwin nodded. "Farmer, banker, soldier, entrepreneur—I've done a lot over the years. Some lives I awaken in my teens. Sometimes in my thirties. And, on occasion, right before I die."

"What if you are killed?" Virgil asked.

"That frustrates the timing of my life cycles," Gerwin said. "But I'm always eventually reborn. My most confusing experience was when I died and left myself on a doorstep in

Italy, then regained my self-awareness more than forty years later at age fifteen in France."

"What happened in the meanwhile?" Kendra asked.

"Hard to guess," Gerwin said. "I never came to my senses, which means I never died naturally. I must have been killed, maybe several times. I could have gone off to war without regaining my identity and died on the battlefield. I picture incidents like a coyote finding a baby and running off with it. If I am reborn in the wilderness, I don't have much chance. I could experience many rebirths before I get lucky enough to survive one. A defenseless baby needs protection."

"The other legendary Dragon Slayers don't turn into babies," Kendra said.

"They are reborn in their own ways," Gerwin said. "They don't cycle like I do."

"What brought you to Chile?" Virgil asked.

"I like to explore the world," Gerwin said. "It has been a long time since we had a dragon war. Usually, when I become aware of my identity, there are no dragons to fight. If I don't have children of my own, I travel and I have adventures. I was in Chile fishing and exploring the Atacama when I felt death coming and identified a family I respected. It was a good choice. I had a wonderful childhood."

"What made you remember your identity?" Kendra asked.

"Jeruwat," Gerwin said. "At first I could just feel he was a bad man. I couldn't explain how, but I was sure. After he tried to take me, and I got away, it finally hit me. My history came flooding back. Interaction with a dragon is one of the surest ways to revive my memories. You mentioned knowing Merek. Have you seen any of my other siblings?"

"We found Magdalena," Kendra said.

"That's great!" Gerwin exclaimed. "She's a powerhouse! Where is she now?"

Kendra glanced at Virgil.

"Jeruwat got her," the satyr said. "Kendra had just soothed her back to her human form."

"She would have been vulnerable during that transition," Gerwin said. "Disoriented. Bad luck for us. She and Merek are the most efficient slayers."

"You did pretty well against Jeruwat," Kendra said.

Gerwin smiled. "I'm no slouch either." He stared off into the dark jungle.

"I'm so sorry we lost Magdalena," Kendra said.

"She'll be reborn," Gerwin consoled. "But she is the slowest of us to return after a death. It will probably take months. Losing her is a terrible blow. Makes me doubly glad we dispatched Jeruwat."

"I still haven't found Nadia or Konrad," Kendra said. "Merek is also searching. Hopefully he is having success. I haven't seen your brother since Titan Valley. He's got wings, so at least he can cover lots of ground."

"Merek with wings will be any dragon's nightmare," Gerwin said. "I doubt we'll find Father. None of us have seen him for a long time. Any leads on Nadia?"

Kendra shook her head. "We're supposed to talk to a demon named Vez Radim at Selona."

"Is the demon reliable?" Gerwin asked.

"He was recommended by the demon who led us to you," Kendra said. "Finding him is our best option."

"Do you know how to get to Selona?" Virgil asked Gerwin.

"I didn't yesterday," he said. "I do now. But I'm not allowed to bring the uninitiated."

"Really?" Kendra asked.

"Yes," Gerwin said with a grin. "But reviving me and helping kill Jeruwat was a sufficient initiation."

"Where is Selona?" Virgil asked.

"Inside of Poland," Gerwin said. "Unbeknownst to most."

"Colombia to Poland," Kendra said. "That will be a long flight."

"So was Idaho to Chile," Glory said.

"We'll have to cross the Atlantic," Kendra said.

"No big challenge," Glory said.

"Flying is easier than walking," Noble said.

"Then I guess we know our next stop," Kendra said.

Gerwin yawned. "First let's get some sleep."

"Do you think there are more dragons chasing us?" Virgil asked, glancing up into the night.

"Count on it," Gerwin said. "Now that I've resurfaced, I should feel them coming."

"Let's keep watch to be safe," Kendra said. "I'll take the first shift."

"What's our move if dragons show up?" Virgil asked.

Gerwin smiled and chuckled. "You two scatter. I'll add to my count. With Magdalena out and a new dragon war on the horizon, I might pull ahead of her."

CHAPTER THIRTY-SEVEN

# Prison

The Seven Kingdoms of the nipsies were located inside a hollow hill with the top removed. Seth had flown to the location while Hugo pulled the Traveler, the Sphinx, and Muriel in a big handcart. Seth knew that in the past, poisonous plants had guarded the entrance to the tunnel through the hillside, so he flew above the hill and fluttered down through the crater in the top. He landed gently on a bare patch of ground near the entrance.

Before him spread a miniature civilization. Precious metals and gemstones gleamed amid the complex architecture, embellishing domes and spires. Extending from a central pond, a maze of canals and aqueducts irrigated seven communities dense with castles, warehouses, factories, mills, cottages, museums, roadways, and bridges. Seth bent down close to a tiny shipyard, where workers less than half an inch tall unloaded cargo from a pair of docked ships. The closer he looked, the more details came into focus—streetlamps, curtained windows, a juggler performing on a street corner, a woman reading in a park, kids playing tag.

"Seth!" Calvin called, running over to him. "I was about to come find you!"

Taller than many of the houses, Calvin dashed through a nipsie neighborhood. As he jumped a canal, Seth better appreciated how much larger the Tiny Hero was than a typical nipsie.

"You really are a giant nipsie," Seth said.

Calvin came to a stop, looking up at him. "It's the spell they put on me so I could adventure in the wide world. I know I'm still tiny to you, but my people don't come up to my knees."

"How long will the spell last?" Seth asked.

"That depends on the casters," Calvin said. "Traditional magic doesn't come easily to nipsies, but we have our rituals and our gifts. My giant state is supposed to last until the casters reverse it. I reported to my leaders about our progress. They wanted me to convey their gratitude for your efforts."

"Seth Sorenson," came a squeaky voice magnified by a pearl-colored megaphone atop an eighteen-inch tower. "You honor us with your presence. Please wait a moment. One of our leaders wishes to address you."

"How did it go with the Sphinx?" Calvin asked.

"We figured out a way into the new demon prison," Seth said. "We'll leave from here. Did you tell them you found Serena?"

"They were happy to hear it," Calvin said. "Especially her family."

A diminutive delegation arrived at the tower. Seth waited politely as they got situated. "Seth Sorenson?" a new voice inquired.

"I hear you," Seth said, crouching toward the megaphone.

"I am Rebus, ruler of the Third Kingdom," the voice announced. "I speak for all when I express our gratitude for your heroic efforts. Even now we are at work on a commemorative monument next to the sculptures of our supreme gigantic overlords."

Seth regarded the foot-high statues of Newel and Doren situated between grandstands and reflected in a rectangular pool. A crew of sculptors actively chiseled away at a third hunk of marble, a few inches taller than the stone satyrs.

"I am flattered," Seth said. "I will try to help Calvin succeed."

"We stand ready to aid you in your hardships," Rebus pledged. "We know of the threat posed by the dragons, and we have readied our forces for war, refurbishing the weapons and armor of our forefathers. We are small, but we are determined to stand with you against this threat, as you have endured adversity for us."

"Calvin has taught me never to underestimate little people," Seth said. "Thank you for your efforts. I must now take Calvin on another mission."

"Our appreciation goes with you," Rebus said. Seth could hear cheering throughout the miniature community.

He wished he enjoyed the same popularity among people his own size as he did with the nipsies.

Seth placed Calvin in his pocket, then flew up through the open top of the hill. He landed near Hugo and the handcart.

"I have Calvin," Seth announced.

"Very well," the Sphinx said. "All is in readiness." He produced the Translocator. "The Traveler will hold the middle of the device while thinking of the destination. The rest of us must get a hand on the Translocator above or below his. Seth, once we're inside the demon prison, you will carry the device. If trouble gets out of hand, think of a safe place, twist the middle, and take as many of us with you as can come."

"The Traveler is joining us?" Calvin asked Seth.

"He used to be the Fairy King," Seth whispered.

"Really?" Calvin exclaimed. "No wonder he could bestow those wings."

"I cannot predict what to expect within this prison," the Traveler said. "It was once a domain of tremendous beauty, a living celebration of light and creation. The demons dwell there now, which means the realm has been desecrated. We are about to discover how thoroughly they have despoiled what was once sublime."

"Won't demons swarm us the moment we arrive?" Seth asked.

"We must make it clear that we seek to parley with their king," the Traveler said.

"How?" Seth asked.

"We demand to see Orogoro, and we commit no violence against them," the Sphinx said.

Muriel held up a shriveled frog speared on the end of a stick. "This totem solicits a truce," she said. "I would prefer the mummified head of a goblin, but we make do with what we have."

"Are you prepared to summon a guide after we enter the prison?" the Traveler asked.

"I am," Muriel said. "Though I cannot dictate how the demons will respond."

"They can be unpredictably vicious," the Traveler said. "We will do our best to make ourselves strategically valuable. We'll fight only if all else fails."

"If we resort to fighting, we won't last long," the Sphinx said.

"We don't want a brawl," the Traveler agreed. "I see no benefit to waiting." He held out a hand for the Translocator. The Sphinx passed it to him. "We all need to touch it?"

"Yes," the Sphinx said. "I haven't used it much with groups, but I believe if you hold the middle segment, and we grab the rest, we'll all be transported with you."

"What about Calvin?" Seth asked.

"Put his hand on it to be safe," the Sphinx replied.

Seth turned to Hugo. "Thanks for your help. I know you have chores here. Take good care of Grandma and Grandpa Larsen. I hope to see you soon."

"Stay safe," Hugo said, pulling Seth into a big, earthy hug. His feet dangling in the air, Seth returned the embrace as best he could.

All of them except Hugo gathered around the ornate cylinder. The Traveler clutched the central section. Muriel and the Sphinx put hands on the bottom segment, while Seth and Calvin touched the top. The Traveler twisted the device. For a moment, Seth felt like he was folding into himself, as if contracting to occupy a single point . . .

. . . and then the world changed, the light dimming. Misty swirls of deep purple and blue curled in a hazy sky, its glow punctuated by occasional pulses of brightness, as if from distant lightning. The temperature had plunged from hot to cool. The uneven landscape looked like a stormy sea turned to stone. Tortured trees surrounded them, dark and twisted with few leaves, contorted limbs reaching nakedly. Septic sap bled from decaying trunks. Mottled patches of grass clung at their shoes like flimsy tentacles, and withered weeds nipped at their ankles.

"Oh, my," the Traveler murmured despairingly.

"What?" Seth asked, scanning for threats.

"I know this place," the Traveler said grimly. "I remember these trees when they were solid and healthy. The demons did not raze our home—they perverted it."

Muriel spoke guttural words that Seth could not understand, then slammed the totem with the desiccated frog against the ground three times. A brief croak echoed, diminishing until it faded to nothing.

"Chazrah the Reaper, come forth and guide us to Orogoro!" Muriel cried. "Chazrah, I summon you to our side! Come, Chazrah, and conduct us to our destination!"

"I've visited some warped places," the Sphinx muttered. "This wins."

"Not everything has been utterly corrupted yet," the Traveler said, looking around. "Some of these trees tenaciously resist their doom. The land remembers kinder shapes and richer soil. Light resiliently flickers in the sky. This realm is dying, but not yet undead." He placed a hand over his chest. "I am humbled."

A hunched creature emerged from a grove, shuffling on two feet, spurs of bone projecting from a crooked back. He wore a gunnysack over his head and grasped with two muscular adult arms above two thin childlike arms. Gibbering and squealing, he drew closer.

"Away," Muriel spat at the figure. "Our business is with Orogoro and Chazrah the Reaper." She shook the frogstick. "Begone, and spread the word."

The deformed figure scuttled away. Seth noticed a pair of large, green eyes glaring from a pocket of deep shadow. He heard enormous footsteps pounding toward them. Bursts of unsettling laughter emanated from a different direction.

"Occupants of this prison," the Traveler called, his voice strangely magnified. "We have come to parley with the Demon King Orogoro. He has claim on whatever value we bring."

The eyes receded. The stomping ended. The laughter ceased.

"What now?" Seth whispered.

"We await our guide," Muriel rasped.

Studying the violet sky, Seth could find no evidence of sun, moon, or stars. "Is it day or night?" he whispered.

"Neither," the Sphinx answered softly. "We're outside of the reality you know, in a pocket dimension that operates according to other principles."

The Traveler lifted a finger to his lips. They waited in an oppressive silence, disrupted occasionally by distant hoots or screams.

"He comes," Muriel finally whispered. "Hail, Chazrah!" she shrieked, waving her frogstick. "Convey us to your king!"

A strange version of a centaur approached. From waist down, he was a huge panther, with a naked human torso projecting up from where the head should have been. Powerfully muscled, elaborately tattooed, Chazrah carried a shadowy scythe and had both eyes sewn shut.

"Who seeks audience with my king?" Chazrah asked, his tone aggressive.

"Once, I was the Fairy King, though now I am the Traveler. I bring with me the Sphinx, Muriel the witch, a promising young shadow charmer, and a tiny being called Calvin. We seek to parley with Orogoro."

"The boy bears the sword that slew Gorgrog," Chazrah accused, pointing with his scythe.

"The shadow charmer deserves all he carries," the Traveler said. "We have come to confer, not to fight."

Chazrah gave a nod. "You belong to Orogoro the king. I shall conduct you into his presence, that he may determine your fate."

"Very good," Muriel said with a satisfied titter. "Lead on."

Chazrah prowled past them and the Traveler fell into step behind him. Seth went next, followed by the Sphinx and Muriel. Chazrah advanced at a leisurely pace, never looking back.

"Eyes forward," the Traveler muttered. "Minds firm."

Seth could sense creatures creeping near on either side to watch the procession. He resisted the urge to look at them.

They edged across a dilapidated bridge over a fuming chasm. On the far side, weary groans issued from a dark cavity in the rocks. As they went on, the ground softened into a mire, and Seth squelched forward, wrenching a foot free from slurping muck with each step.

They reached a broad river of glutinous sludge. Chazrah signaled at an obese woman operating a crude crane. The jib swung toward them, a battered platform dangling from corroded chains. Wood creaked as they stepped onto the platform and were shuttled over the river, heat radiating up from the gelatinous flow.

Marching onward, Seth stayed close behind the Traveler. After they had plodded up a chalky slope that left their legs dusted with ashen powder, a towering curtain came into view ahead, like the wall of a black tent, so high they could not see the top. Stopping, Chazrah indicated the curtain with his scythe.

"Orogoro awaits," he said. "I go no farther."

Muriel handed Chazrah the frogstick, and he accepted

it with a derisive grunt. The Traveler led the group to the curtain. Reaching forward, he found a seam where the fabric could part.

Passing through the gap in the curtain, Seth found himself in a bright, beautiful garden. Shining crystals hung from graceful, silver-trunked trees. Fairies twinkled amid delicate blossoms. Sculpted hedges served as backdrops for meticulously pruned rosebushes. Beside a pool of clear water, a dryad plunked a soothing melody on a gilded harp. Peacocks strutted among flower beds, and parrots roosted in high branches.

The black curtain enclosed the spacious garden, reaching so high that only a small circle of lavender sky was visible at the top. The Traveler led the way forward. They crossed a brook on flat, oval stepping-stones, navigated a simple hedge maze, then followed a winding path through small, dense evergreens.

The path ended at a circular field of clover. A hunched figure sat in the center of the field, his shaggy form lumpy with muscle. Many times the size of a man, he had enormous, shovel-shaped antlers, like a moose. A crown of dark metal wreathed his head. One of his feet was a prosthetic wrought from iron and strapped to his shin. A dainty fairy perched upon his forefinger and seemed to have his attention.

Seth recognized the massive demon as Orogoro.

"You have found me," the demon said in a rumbling voice. He extended his hand and the fairy flew away. "Only great need would bring you here." Seizing a huge battle-ax from where it lay half-buried in clover, Orogoro used it to stand. An odor like a stockyard wafted from his dark fur. Seth stood not much taller than his knees. "I thought you would be most comfortable conferring in my oasis."

"How does this retreat exist?" the Traveler asked.

Orogoro hefted the battle-ax to his shoulder. "Soon after we entered the Fairy Realm, I took a liking to this area and commissioned draperies to shield it. I gathered what I wanted to preserve, including a pair of dryads captured in battle and the chrysalises of many unborn fairies. This has become a refuge for me. A sanctuary of contemplation."

"Can it survive?" the Traveler asked.

"There has been some attrition around the border," Orogoro replied. "I constrict the draperies as needed. Time will reveal how resilient the garden will be." Orogoro swung his ax down into the ground, the bit sinking deep. "Come forward."

The Traveler led them into the field of clover.

"An exiled king," Orogoro said. "A failed liberator. A competent witch. A miniscule adventurer. And a lad bearing the sword that slew my father. Quite an unusual group."

"These are tumultuous times," the Traveler said.

"Indeed," Orogoro remarked. "Why should I let any of you leave? Having come here uninvited, you belong to me now."

"We have a common enemy," the Traveler said. "We resist the dragons."

Orogoro pointed at the Sphinx. "This one resists dragons?"

"I plan to help stop them, yes," the Sphinx said.

Orogoro gave a derisive snort. "Unless they let you join them." The Demon King pointed at Muriel. "She resists dragons?"

"I promised the boy I would come," Muriel said. She got down on her knees. "It is an honor to bask in your presence."

"I would hear from the boy," Orogoro said. "How did you arrive here?"

Seth looked to the Traveler, who gave a little nod. "We used a device called the Translocator."

"I know of this object," Orogoro said. "Having been created to seal our prison, it does not transport demons out of here."

"Good planning," Seth said.

"And one less way for you to bargain," Orogoro said. "Why are you here?"

"I need the jewel from your crown," Seth said.

Orogoro paused, then looked to the Traveler. "Does he jest?"

"He is in earnest," the Traveler said. "As are we all."

"You expect me to relinquish the jewel in my crown?" Orogoro asked. "To you five? Here in my domain? How did you hope to succeed?"

The Traveler cleared his throat. "The Singing Sisters have declared that unless Seth obtains all fragments of the Ethergem, the dragons will prevail."

Widening his stance, Orogoro bowed his head and

closed his eyes. The others watched in silence. After a moment, the Demon King raised his head. "I see."

"The boy has collected the other fragments," the Traveler said. "Only your stone remains."

Orogoro cracked the knuckles of one hand. "This problem is yours to solve. On the day the dragons were employed to frustrate our escape, their keepers lost dominion. It became inevitable that the wyrms would overspill their bounds."

"Do you wish to see the dragons rule?" the Traveler asked.

Orogoro's eyes shone with rage. "Were it not for Celebrant, my father would have subjugated the world, and you would still be one of his ornaments."

"Yet here I stand," the Traveler said.

Orogoro gestured at Seth. "That sword may have dispatched my father, but it was Celebrant who made the assassination possible."

"We need the jewel to stop Celebrant," the Traveler said. "Is it necessary to your crown?"

A guffaw escaped Orogoro. "The jewel is a prisoner of the crown. A slave to it. The dark blade the boy carries shattered from Raglamar. Do you know where the rest of Raglamar went?"

"Enlighten us," the Traveler invited.

"Let me bedarken you instead," Orogoro countered. "Most of the remains of Raglamar were used to forge this headwear. My crown works against the jewel, not with it."

"Does this mean you will hand it over?" the Traveler asked.

"To harm Celebrant?" Orogoro mused. "Surrender the jewel and let you walk out of here unscathed? Not likely."

"What will it take?" the Traveler asked.

"If I am to lose something precious, I should gain something of value," Orogoro reasoned.

"Your enemy will suffer," the Traveler stated.

"I have no such assurance," Orogoro said. "The chances of victory would remain small."

"Those chances are preferable to impossibility," the Traveler noted.

"I ought to gain something of great value," Orogoro maintained.

The Traveler nodded. "We will deliver to you the current monarch of fairydom."

"You will present Ronodin?" Orogoro asked. A slow smile spread his lips. "Easier said than done. What would be my guarantee?"

"I will remain with you until then," the Traveler said.

"No," Seth insisted.

"This is my decision," the Traveler told Seth.

"Give him the witch," Seth said.

"He wants something of value," the Traveler replied.

"I do indeed," Orogoro said. "You were never the true monarch, and you are no longer a king. But you did adorn my father's belt. I will accept your terms with an extra provision."

"Speak," the Traveler said.

"I want to use the Unforgiving Blade to extract the jewel myself," Orogoro said. "I vow to return the weapon, but before I do, I will give the boy a wound to help him understand what he carries."

"Unnecessary," the Traveler said.

"Absolutely necessary," Orogoro boomed. "Or else we have no deal, and all of you shall remain with me, enduring exquisite torture until the end of your days."

"Seth has already been scratched by the blade," the Traveler asserted.

"Not by me," Orogoro said.

"It cannot be a mortal wound," the Traveler said.

"I will not kill or maim him," Orogoro said. "But he will never forget me."

"I'll do it," Seth said.

The Traveler sighed. "Very well. Orogoro, keep me until you receive Ronodin. The others go free."

"I would remain," Muriel spoke up, "if the Sphinx and the rest of you consent. I would prefer to dwell here and be tutored by the best."

"Fine with me," the Sphinx said.

"The witch may stay of her own accord," Orogoro said, adjusting his crown. "Meet my conditions, and the Sphinx will be free to go, along with the miniature adventurer. The lad as well, with his jewel and his new wound."

"Done," the Traveler said. He faced Seth. "Give him the blade."

Seth stepped forward and set down the Unforgiving Blade in front of Orogoro. The demon removed his crown and claimed the blade. It looked tiny in his massive hand. Closing one eye, Orogoro made a precise incision, and the dark jewel fell free, disappearing into the clover.

The demon crouched toward Seth. "Lie down and keep still," Orogoro demanded. "The wound will be fatal if you thrash."

Wings extended, Seth spread out on his back in the springy clover. He steeled himself to withstand whatever came. Where would the demon cut him? Seth gritted his teeth. He had been sliced by the blade before. He had endured so much. If this would help stop the dragons, he would endure this, too.

The tip of the blade entered his belly, sinking into him.

It was not a cut. He was being stabbed.

Not deep. Not much more than an inch.

But this was different from the slit on his leg.

The Unforgiving Blade was inside of him.

Endless darkness was inside of his body.

Seth went frigid to his core. He doubted whether he could move if he tried.

The darkness of the blade seeped into him. And he was also being drawn into the blade. His life force ebbed toward eternal night.

Seth saw the path to joining the undead. He would reach the end of the path before long, as a wraith or a revenant. No longer alive, incapable of death, his existence would continue, devoid of warmth, without sleep, without peace, without hope. On and on his misery would persist for ages uncounted. He witnessed the agonizing reality as clearly as if it were in the past.

And then Orogoro pulled out the blade.

Seth stared up at the demon uncomprehendingly. Was he still in the field of clover? Was life still happening around him? What had he experienced while the blade was in him? Visions. Horrible, indelible visions.

He had seen himself. Unable to die.

"Kill me," Seth pleaded.

"That is not part of our arrangement," Orogoro said, setting the blade down beside Seth. "Use this weapon judiciously."

Seth touched his belly. His fingers came away damp with blood.

"It's still in me," Seth murmured.

"And it always will be," Orogoro promised. "Get on your feet. Don't fret, lad. You won't die."

# CHAPTER THIRTY-EIGHT

# Vez Radim

Kendra crouched beside Gerwin on a grassy slope, peering over a splintered wooden fence at a distant crossroads. Virgil knelt beside her, and the horses drank at a puddle behind a thorny bush.

"That's Selona?" Kendra asked.

"Not quite," Gerwin whispered. "It's the gateway into Selona."

"Is the entrance guarded?" Kendra asked quietly.

"Only select individuals know the way into Selona," Gerwin whispered. "Long ago, our kingdom was part of the normal world. But as our people became the Fair Folk, mortals began to instinctively avoid our land, driven away by our magical natures. It was Father who spearheaded hiding Selona completely. He was more playful and silly than you would expect from a hero and a king. But he was very serious about keeping Selona concealed."

"Why?" Kendra asked.

"My dad always told me that too many important things are hidden in Selona," Gerwin said. "He never got overly specific, but I know the Sovereign Skull, the fabled skull of Abraxas, is housed at Fairview, and if that were all our kingdom hid, it would be plenty. The dragons would give anything to destroy the skull and regain the ability to attack mortal communities."

"The skull magnifies the impact of mortal unbelief?" Virgil asked.

"Yes," Gerwin said. "The skull turns mortal unbelief into a barrier that dragons cannot overcome."

"Do the dragons know the skull is at Selona?" Kendra asked.

"Let's hope not," Gerwin said. "And if they know, let's hope they never learn how to access Selona. We must ensure they don't discover how from us. That's why I'm being so careful."

"I don't see any dragons," Virgil said.

"I don't sense any either," Gerwin said. "But dragons can use spies. We must be hypervigilant. Do you see the signpost?"

Kendra could see the crossroads, but no sign. "Not at all."

"No signpost whatsoever," Virgil reported.

"It's *really* tall and obvious," Gerwin said.

"Not to me," Kendra replied.

"I give you permission to see the signpost," Gerwin said.

And there it was, in the middle of the crossroads, at least ten feet tall, wooden and colorful—the kind of signpost with names and arrows pointing all directions, with different mileages listed. "I see it now," Kendra said. "Are you sure it was visible before? Mind magic doesn't usually work on me."

"You're up against a really strong distracter spell," Gerwin said. "It works in various ways, affecting not only the mind but also the senses. It's the strongest distracter spell I've ever encountered, and I've been all over."

Kendra knew they were dealing with a distracter spell. The horses had strongly resisted coming in this direction about fifteen miles back. Gerwin had coaxed them patiently, granting lots of permission as they went.

"We're in Poland?" Kendra checked.

"For now, yes," Gerwin said. "But not for long."

"Selona is in a pocket dimension?" Virgil guessed.

"That's one way to understand it," Gerwin said. "Selona resides in a parallel dimension that overlays the mortal world. Selona occupies much of the same space as Poland, but exists on a different frequency."

"Does Selona have the same natural landmarks as Poland?" Kendra asked.

"Selona is markedly distinct," Gerwin said. "Imagine two entirely different maps covering the same area, both perfectly accurate. The sun shining on Poland is the same sun giving light to Selona. But nobody in Selona buys bread in Poland, and nobody in Poland can buy bread in Selona. Unless they know how to get from one map to the other."

"Which you're about to show us," Kendra said.

"I think the coast is clear," Gerwin said. "Noble, Glory, I give you permission to take us to the crossroads."

"That seems like a bad idea," Noble said.

"It's the spell, Noble," Glory said. "We'll try."

Gerwin and Kendra mounted Glory while Virgil climbed onto Noble. Gerwin pointed beyond the fence. "That way," he said. "I grant permission to see the crossroads and permission to take us there."

Glory sprang into the air with Noble beside her. It was a short flight. The horses landed near the signpost.

"Better now?" Gerwin asked.

"Much better, actually," Noble said.

"Like we've reached the eye of the storm," Glory said.

"It's a weight off my mind," Virgil added.

Kendra hadn't experienced the same mental aversions as the others, but she was glad their discomfort was gone. Gerwin dismounted and she did likewise. Virgil hopped down from Noble.

"No ordinary person can get within five miles of this crossroads," Gerwin said. "They'll always find a reason to turn aside, even if they're deliberately trying to get here." He dropped his voice to the quietest whisper. "If we walk around the signpost three times counterclockwise, we'll be in Selona."

Kendra studied the tall signpost:

FAIRVIEW—9

RYSALIA—14

HOLVENGARD—15

MERDALE—19

BRESKAN—21

FARCASTLE—37

VASTRA—55

FENLAY—62

Unfamiliar with the cities named, Kendra figured they pertained to Selona.

"We should hurry," Gerwin prompted, beginning to walk around the sign. "We don't want to risk exposing ourselves to prying eyes any longer than necessary."

Kendra, Virgil, Noble, and Glory followed Gerwin around the signpost. After their third revolution, Gerwin turned with a smile and took a deep breath. "It's good to be home."

"This feels like the Emperor's New Clothes," Kendra said. "Everything looks the exact same."

"Yes, it does," Gerwin agreed. "But we were in Poland, and now we are in Selona, at the exact geographic center of the kingdom. Interestingly, if you venture far enough in any direction—north, southeast, even across the desert— you will eventually come to grassy country with a road that leads right back to this signpost."

"The edges connect to the middle," Virgil concluded. "To get out do we circle the signpost in the opposite direction?"

"No," Gerwin said. "In Selona, this signpost is too easy to find. The ways out are different from the way in."

"Are we trapped here?" Kendra asked.

"No," Gerwin said with a chuckle. "There are more ways out than in. A convenient one is at the castle in Fairview."

"But for now, we want Blackthorn Manor," Kendra said.

"A phrase seldom heard," Gerwin said. "In the years after Father dispelled fear of the vampire, nobody wanted to take up residence in the manor. It fell into disrepair until a demon claimed it. These days, none go near it, and the demon generally does not leave."

"Vez Radim," Kendra said.

"If you say so," Gerwin said. "I never learned her name."

"Do you know how to get there?" Kendra asked.

"With Glory and Noble?" Gerwin asked. "Easy!"

Kendra rested a hand on the signpost. "Until the dragons find the entrance to Selona, is the kingdom safe?"

"Yes," Gerwin said. "That's why we took extra precautions."

"That's a relief," Virgil said.

"Never underestimate Celebrant," Kendra warned. "He's good at getting what he wants."

Gerwin swung up onto Glory. "It should take him time. Meanwhile, if we gather the rest of my siblings, we can attack Celebrant before he gets to Selona."

"I like the sound of that," Virgil said from astride Noble.

Kendra scrambled up behind Gerwin.

"Where do I go?" Glory asked.

Gerwin extended a hand with a chopping motion. "Head east."

Glory took a running start and sprang into the air. Wind in her face, Kendra rose to a soaring perspective of the gently rolling countryside. She saw a patchwork of cornfields and wheatfields. The sails of a few large windmills rotated slowly in the gentle breeze. Flocks of sheep and herds of cattle grazed in expansive pastures.

"This looks like a postcard," Kendra said.

"Selona is gorgeous," Gerwin said. "Definitely worth protecting. Glory, see the lake up ahead? Fly over it."

Beyond the lake, they glided over a river spanned by a wide wooden bridge leading to a bustling town on the far side. The air smelled clean, and Kendra could see a remarkable distance in all directions. To the north, foothills climbed to snowcapped mountains. They crossed over forested terrain, and Kendra noticed the derelict remnants of an abandoned town, mostly foundations and chimneys.

"See the upcoming river?" Gerwin said. "There's the manor."

The gothic mansion dominated the little island on which it stood. Overgrown with ivy and creeping vines, the melancholy structure supported a central tower and a roof crowded with gables and turrets. A stone bridge built over three arches granted access from the near shore.

Glory and Noble landed together on the bridge, halting a few paces away from the gate into the manor's courtyard.

"Batoosa warned me not to go inside," Kendra said as she slid off Glory, landing lightly. "We should talk to Vez Radim from outside."

"Should we enter the courtyard?" Virgil asked. "It looks to be getting plenty of sunlight."

Leaning with his whole body, Gerwin hauled the gate open. "It isn't locked."

"I've read about this place," Kendra said. "It's where your father killed the vampire."

"Well, it's where he found the coffin and the stake," Gerwin reminded her.

"Right," Kendra said.

"The battle was internal," Gerwin said. "Father had to overcome much to set foot here. Everyone thought the vampire still haunted the region. I suspect if he had fought the vampire, Father would have destroyed it. My father was a complicated man. He despised violence, but he was the best fighter I knew."

Kendra collected her bow. "Have you ever been here?" she asked.

"I've seen the manor," Gerwin said. "I've never entered the courtyard."

Kendra paused to consider how scrawny Gerwin looked. "Is it weird that up until a few days ago, your main concerns were school and playing soccer?"

"I never worried much about school," Gerwin said with a smile. "This isn't the first time I've regained my memories during my childhood. If we get the situation with the dragons under control, I'll return to the Duran family and reassure them I'm not dead."

"Are we going in?" Virgil asked, peeking hesitantly through the gate.

"As long as we stay in the sun," Kendra said. "I'll take the lead."

She walked through the gate into the enclosed yard. The manor comprised the other three walls of the courtyard, the dusty windows half-concealed by ivy. Four doors granted access from the courtyard into the manor, including a main door with a rounded top. Kendra positioned herself in the middle of the yard, away from the shadows along the perimeter.

"Vez Radim!" Kendra called. "I'm Kendra Sorenson. I have already visited Talizar and Batoosa. Jubaya suggested I visit you as well."

The main door swung inward.

"Please come inside," a polished female voice invited, seeming to emanate from a echoing chamber. "I have awaited your visit."

"I'd rather talk to you from here," Kendra said.

"Poor manners," the voice lamented.

"Batoosa suggested it would be safer," Kendra said.

"How dull," the voice responded.

Virgil took a jerky step toward the front door. Then another. And another. "Help," Virgil managed in a choked voice.

Kendra grabbed one arm to hold him back and Gerwin

grasped the other. His body rigid, Virgil lurched forward in little spasms.

"Vez Radim," Kendra shouted. "Knock it off!"

"I long for company," Vez Radim said.

Virgil went limp.

"I yearn to draw you in, Kendra," Vez Radim said. "I prefer conducting interviews face-to-face. And in private."

"If you want privacy, my friends can step away," Kendra said.

"That would be a start," Vez Radim said. "And perhaps you could step closer to the shadows. The glare of sunlight wearies me."

"Go back to the horses," Kendra whispered.

"Be careful," Virgil whispered. "I felt like a puppet."

Gerwin winked. "I'll be right outside the gate. If you need us, we'll be ready."

Kendra nodded, and Gerwin departed with Virgil. Kendra approached the steps leading to the recessed door, careful not to enter the shadow. Just beyond the gloomy doorway, she could barely discern a figure, shadowy and maybe translucent.

"Can you see me?" Kendra asked.

"Oh, yes," Vez Radim said. "You look flagrantly alive. Tell me, how does the sun feel upon your skin?"

"Warm," Kendra said. "Want to join me out here?"

"You have no idea," Vez Radim said. "But it would not be practical."

"Are you a vampire?" Kendra asked.

"Not exactly," Vez Radim replied. "Though vampires have dwelled here in the past. How may I be of service?"

"I'm looking for the legendary Dragon Slayers," Kendra said.

"Who can build a wall high enough to repel a storm?" Vez Radim mused. "How many guards would be sufficient to frustrate nature?"

"No wall can turn aside nature," Kendra said.

"Is this a fight you can win?" Vez Radim asked.

"Dragons forming an army is unnatural," Kendra said. "And Celebrant isn't a rainstorm. We're going to try."

"Like all demons, I would love to see Celebrant perish," Vez Radim said. "Won't you come inside? Dine with me? I'll be on my best behavior."

"This is as close as I'm coming," Kendra said. "Our need is urgent."

"Many demons agree," Vez Radim said. "What if Nadia does not wish to be found?"

"I'll try to change her mind," Kendra said.

"I have studied this matter for years," Vez Radim said. "There is a woman who visits the town of Greenvale and does not show her face. She lives outside of town but visits the Swamp Goose Inn on a regular schedule. Chances are good she will be there tonight."

"Could it be Nadia?" Kendra asked.

"The woman is my only suspect," Vez Radim said. "I know little about her. She keeps to herself. Enters and exits through the back. Deals only with the gremlins."

"Gremlins?" Kendra asked.

"The people of Greenvale fought the local gremlins for years," Vez Radim said. "At one point it looked like residents would have to abandon the town. Eventually the humans and gremlins made a treaty. It was decided that all one-story houses would leave a crawlspace beneath or an attic above for gremlin use. Any buildings with multiple stories leave a space between every level for gremlins to occupy. In return, the gremlins would not steal or commit acts of violence or mischief against humans. They would also keep vermin away and protect local livestock."

"I've never seen a gremlin," Kendra said.

"If you wish to improve your chances," Vez Radim suggested, "ask the gremlins of the Swamp Goose Inn about the Rag Lady. If they like you, they may arrange an introduction."

"Is that all you know?" Kendra asked.

"On this subject, yes," Vez Radim said.

"Can you tell me where Konrad might be?" Kendra asked.

"He vanished long ago," Vez Radim said. "Many have sought him, including his children. None have found him."

"Thanks for the help," Kendra said, backing away.

"Thank me by slaying Celebrant."

# CHAPTER THIRTY-NINE

# Delivery

Seth could feel his vitality slipping away. Cold emanated from the wound in his belly out to his extremities. The process of becoming undead was in motion. He was doomed.

"Seth!" the Sphinx insisted. "Hold the Translocator."

Orogoro loomed over Seth against a peculiar background of black curtains. The Traveler stood off to one side. And the face of the Sphinx entered his field of view, peering down at him.

"I'll handle the middle segment," the Sphinx said, displaying the Translocator. "I'll get us out. Hold the Unforgiving Blade in one hand and the bottom of the Translocator with the other."

Seth scowled groggily. Wasn't it enough that his life force was draining away? Did everyone have to keep bothering him? He wanted to pull the covers over his head and go to sleep.

The Sphinx put the hilt of a sword in Seth's hand. Then the Sphinx grabbed his other hand and put it on the Translocator. The moment the Sphinx let go of Seth's hand, it fell limply from the device.

"You have to focus," the Sphinx said. "No matter how much it hurts, you must cling to the Translocator to get out of here."

"Your mission is not over, Seth," the Traveler said, his voice ringing clearer than the Sphinx's. "Trust me, you'll find no rest here. You have the strength to see this through."

"People are depending on us, Seth," Calvin urged. "Get us out of here."

The Sphinx put Seth's hand back on the Translocator. Seth squeezed it, and everything around him changed.

He was inside a gazebo, stretched out on whitewashed planks, the Sphinx crouching over him. They were back at the Fairy Queen's shrine at Fablehaven. The hot day contrasted sharply with the climate of the demon prison.

"You did it," the Sphinx said. "I can't believe we got away with the jewel from the Demon King's crown. Let me see your stomach."

The tacky fabric clung to Seth's abdomen as the Sphinx peeled the shirt away from the wound. "How is it?" Seth asked.

"Not a big wound," the Sphinx said. "But the blood keeps coming."

"I have medical glue in my satchel," Seth said. "The

kind that covers wounds." Did treating the wound matter? If he was becoming a wraith, who cared if he lost some blood?

"You're shivering," the Sphinx said, rummaging in Seth's satchel.

"I'm cold," Seth said. "I feel the blade inside of me like a void."

"The blade isn't there anymore," the Sphinx said. "It's in your hand."

"I see the blade in my hand," Seth replied, teeth chattering. "And I also feel it inside my gut. Taking it out made no difference. Somehow the blade is still there."

The Sphinx gently smeared something on his stomach. "The blade is out. And this glue is amazing. It's holding the blood inside. Your injury might be permanent, the discomfort may continue, but the damage isn't increasing."

"It feels like the wound is pulling me away from life," Seth muttered. "Am I joining the undead?"

"You have started in that direction," the Sphinx said. "But you're not getting any closer."

"The light inside of me is fading," Seth said.

"Do you feel the blade stabbing deeper into your innards?" the Sphinx asked. "Is it widening the incision?"

"No."

"The same is true of the summons to join the undead," the Sphinx said. "The initial call was made permanent. But it lacks power to advance the process."

"It feels like I will be undead soon," Seth said.

"But you won't without more wounds," the Sphinx assured him. "I know this process better than most."

"Is it daytime?" Seth asked.

"Yes," the Sphinx said.

"It looks shadowy," Seth said. "Like evening. Late evening."

"I'm sorry about your wound," the Sphinx said. "But you have a mission to finish. Can you get on your feet?"

Seth knew he had to take the stones to the Singing Sisters. Or die trying. "Did we bring the Demon King's jewel?" Seth asked.

"I have it," the Sphinx said.

"Put it in my satchel," Seth said, trying to sit up, then falling back.

"You're in bad shape," the Sphinx said. "You're shivering and sweating too."

"It's hard to think clearly," Seth said. "My mind feels hazy. I see . . . death coming. Not the restful kind."

"You're exhausted," the Sphinx said. "You've been through so much. I've never visited the Singing Sisters before. But I've been to Missouri, so I could teleport close to them. Do you want me to be your messenger? You're in no condition to travel."

Seth contemplated the suggestion. He was so tired. And he could hardly think. He desperately needed sleep. Did it matter who delivered the fragments?

"Put his satchel down," Calvin said. "Wait for permission. This is Seth's assignment."

"Seth, can you hear me?" the Sphinx said. "You fulfilled your mission. You gathered the pieces of the Ethergem. I'll deliver them for you. Should I take the Unforgiving Blade as well?"

"Seth, draw Vasilis," Calvin said.

Seth's hand fumbled to the hilt of his sheathed sword. The metal felt warm in his hand, almost alive, humming with power. As he pulled the blade from the scabbard, heat and vitality coursed into Seth. The day looked brighter. Sitting up with a grunt, he rolled to his knees, then staggered to his feet.

The Sphinx held the satchel in one hand, the Translocator in the other. Seth could still sense the Unforgiving Blade inside of his belly, but the pull toward night had faded to the background. Vasilis had never shone a darker red.

"What are you doing with my satchel?" Seth asked.

The Sphinx smiled uncomfortably. "I'm helping you finish your quest. Do you really want a sword in each hand? Doesn't leave room for much else. Would it help if I carry the Unforgiving Blade for you?"

"Why do you want it?" Seth asked, holding up the dark weapon.

"To ease your burdens," the Sphinx said, watching Seth warily. "And to protect the pieces of the Ethergem."

"Set down the satchel," Seth said.

"Seth, you've been traumatized," the Sphinx said. "You're not in your right mind."

"I'm going to finish what I started," Seth said. "I need the Translocator."

The Sphinx was holding the Translocator by the bottom

of the cylinder. Seth knew if the Sphinx grabbed the center and twisted, he could disappear.

"The Translocator stays with me," the Sphinx said.

"I thought you wanted to help," Seth said flatly.

In one motion, the Sphinx looped the satchel over his shoulder and reached for the Translocator with his newly freed hand. Seth lashed a wing at the Translocator, slapping it from the Sphinx's grasp with a ping of metal against metal. Holding Vasilis outward, Seth advanced to where the Translocator had fallen, forcing the Sphinx to retreat from the gazebo to the boardwalk.

"That was not friendly," the Sphinx said, shaking one hand as if it smarted.

"Neither was taking my satchel," Seth said.

"You're trying to steal my Translocator." The Sphinx glanced over his shoulder. "I could chuck your satchel in the pond. You won't see the pieces of the Ethergem again. Those naiads are loyal to Ronodin."

Seth held out the Unforgiving Blade. "Then I'll give you a taste of forever," Seth said.

"Don't be rash," the Sphinx said, a quaver in his voice.

"You wanted to be an Eternal," Seth said, moving toward him. "This blade could give you a present to keep you company through those long years. A wound that never sleeps. You'll learn more about the undead than you ever wanted to know."

The Sphinx set down the satchel and backed farther along the boardwalk, hands raised. "I was just trying to help. I don't know how this went sideways."

Eyes on the Sphinx, Seth paced forward to the satchel, crouched, set down the Unforgiving Blade, put the strap over his shoulder, picked up the Unforgiving Blade, and stood. Then he returned to the gazebo where the Translocator lay, not far from where the white planks were spattered with bright red blood.

Seth realized that to both hold and twist the Translocator, he would have to sheath Vasilis. He glanced at the Sphinx. "Back off," Seth said. "Get far away."

"Might be nice to have a friend right about now," the Sphinx said.

"He's got me," Calvin said.

"Back away," Seth said. "I won't ask again."

The Sphinx retreated to the next gazebo along the boardwalk, watching Seth with continued interest. Seth sheathed Vasilis, and immediately the day dimmed. His knees buckled, and it took effort not to fall flat. Icy despair rushed through him from the point where perfect night had entered his abdomen.

Seth heard footfalls.

The Sphinx was running toward him.

He could try to draw Vasilis again.

But wouldn't that lead to the same stalemate as before?

Pushing through mental fog, Seth groped for the Translocator. The Sphinx pounded closer. Awkwardly holding the bottom of the cylinder with the same hand gripping the Unforgiving Blade, Seth twisted the middle and thought of a cavern in Missouri.

His surroundings transformed.

Seth was now kneeling beside a pool of water in a subterranean chamber. The Translocator fell from his hand, clanging against the stone floor. A few torches were burning, reference points in the blackness.

"Intruder!" a voice shrieked.

"Trespasser!" another voice cried.

"Wait, it's the boy!" a third voice observed.

"That is no way to enter an abode!" the first voice complained.

"We can't have minions appearing at will!" the second voice griped.

"Pay attention," the third voice insisted. "He's badly hurt!"

Dropping the Unforgiving Blade, Seth slumped forward to his hands and knees. Dizzy and exhausted as he was, the voices seemed to come from far away. Where was he? Why was the room so dark? His dimmed vision seemed to be getting worse. How black would it get when he fully became a wraith?

Seth heard feet flapping against the stone floor surrounding him, accompanied by sporadic grunts and growls.

"No, don't kill him," the first voice instructed.

"Let's find out how his quest is proceeding," the second voice suggested.

"He's been stabbed by the Unforgiving Blade," the third voice shared in a hushed tone.

The voice was right—he had been stabbed. And the Sphinx had tried to take the Unforgiving Blade.

"Seth is hurt," Calvin said. "He was fulfilling the mission you gave him."

Seth realized he had reached the lair of the Singing Sisters. The voices must belong to the witches. The grunts were probably from the trolls who served them.

"Let him speak," the first voice said. "Can you answer us?" Seth recognized the speaker as Wilna.

"The boy is spent," the second voice whispered. Berna.

"He needs to recover," Orna said.

Seth's hand found the hilt of Vasilis.

"No," Orna said. "Don't draw it, not in this state. It will leave you more depleted, and you need your strength."

"I have them," Seth managed.

"The pieces of the Ethergem?" Berna asked.

"All of them," Seth mumbled.

"I told you," Orna said.

"In the satchel," Seth murmured.

"He's delirious," Berna said. "The boy can't possibly have them all."

"Use your senses," Wilna said. "I feel the presence of the fragments. I did not expect to see him again."

"I told you he might do it," Orna said.

"Rest, boy," Berna said. "We'll watch over you."

"I will too," Calvin said. "I made it. My hand wasn't on the Translocator, but I guess I'm small enough to be counted as a possession. You can rest."

Seth went limp on the cool stone, resting his cheek against his folded arms. Yes, he needed sleep. He might never wake up. And that might not be so bad.

🦎  🦎  🦎

"He's coming around," Orna said.

"About time," Wilna complained.

"He fulfilled the quest at great cost," Berna said.

"He deserves a break," Orna said.

"He is not done yet," Wilna cautioned.

Seth could still feel the Unforgiving Blade penetrating his belly. The same depth as before—just an inch or two. Cold radiated from the wound—piercing cold that made him wish he could go numb. The blade seemed to feed on him, a metaphysical vacuum draining his life away. Seth knew it was only a matter of time before he joined the undead.

But the witches were trying to talk to him.

"I can hear you," Seth said.

"Good!" Orna cheered. "We're pleased you brought the pieces of the Ethergem."

"Can you heal my wound?" Seth asked.

"Sadly, that is beyond our abilities," Berna said.

"Can you help me withstand it?" Seth said.

"We can try," Wilna said. "We made a concoction."

Seth squinted at the dim silhouettes of the witches, standing in a circle, arms conjoined at the wrists. "Has it gotten darker in here?" he asked.

"It is brighter than usual," Orna said. "You've been tainted by the Void."

"I'm afraid it's permanent," Seth said.

"Everyone in the mortal world gets contaminated by darkness," Wilna said. "Though your case is rather extreme."

A steaming bowl was set in front of Seth. Shifting, he noticed a thin blanket had been placed over him.

"Thank you, Gromlet," Orna said to the little troll shuffling away.

"Smell it first," Berna recommended.

Seth inhaled the warm vapors rising from the broth. He was still in the process of awakening, and the aroma hastened his alertness. Picking up the bowl, Seth tried a sip. The liquid was hot enough that he sipped carefully. As he drank, the scalding fluid provided a pleasant contrast against the frigidity spreading from the belly wound.

"My mind feels clearer," Seth said.

"If you hope to proceed, you must learn to see around the wounds from the Unforgiving Blade," Wilna said.

"Proceed where?" Seth asked.

"Onward," Orna said.

"You have paid your debt to us," Berna said. "We have three gifts for you."

"I'm turning into a wraith," Seth said.

"That process is arrested for now," Wilna said. "Resist despair. You still have much to accomplish."

"But my debt is now paid," Seth complained.

"Yes," Orna said. "But your life isn't over."

"Do your gifts have strings attached?" Seth asked.

"You be the judge," Wilna said. "They are freely given. You owe us nothing for them."

"We reward those who serve us well," Orna said. "Good help is hard to find."

"Do what you will with them," Berna said.

"What are they?" Seth asked.

"I give you Vasilis," Orna said. "The Sword of Light and Darkness is yours to keep for as long as you wish to bear it."

"Thanks," Seth said, surprised by the value of the offering.

"I give you the pieces of the Ethergem," Berna said. "Do with them what you will."

"You had me hunt down the fragments just to give them to me?" Seth asked.

"Yes," Berna said. "I freely bequeath them to you."

"Is Wilna giving me Witchprize?" Seth guessed.

"We're keeping the wraith," Wilna said. "Witchprize is your loss. My gift will be information."

"Okay," Seth said, trying to focus.

"The Wizenstone was used by Graulas anciently to seal off the Source," Wilna said. "When you cleaved the Wizenstone, you weakened the seal, allowing us to discern the Source's location."

"Where is it?" Seth asked.

"This information must be carefully guarded," Wilna said. "If the wrong person learned the whereabouts of the Source, the balance would be placed in extreme jeopardy."

"I get it," Seth said.

"You really don't," Wilna said. "At least you are trying. The Source is hidden in the desert outside Selona."

"I see," Seth said.

"Excuse me," Calvin said. "If you ladies know about Graulas and the Wizenstone, can you tell us how to break the nipsie curse?"

The witches cackled.

"The curse is tied to the fate of the Ethergem," Orna said. "You wish to break the curse?"

"With all my heart," Calvin said.

"And do you wish to defeat Celebrant?" Berna asked.

"It's why I did your tasks," Seth said.

"Then you must return the pieces of the Ethergem to the Source," Orna said.

Seth struggled to push away feelings of his impending undeath to process what he was being told. "Will that repair the Ethergem?" he asked.

Wilna laughed. "No. Nevertheless, you must take the pieces of the Ethergem to the Source if you want any chance of defeating Celebrant."

"The same must be done if you aspire to break the nipsie curse," Orna added.

"I can hardly think," Seth said. "I barely got these jewels to you. This was me stumbling across the finish line, tank empty. Maybe I could do more if I hadn't been stabbed."

"There is no one else to do this besides you," Wilna said.

"Anyone not stabbed in the gut might be a great start," Seth said. "Lots of people are fighting the dragons. Pick somebody."

"We've looked," Berna said.

"The only person who might be able to deliver the

necessary items in time is you," Orna said. "And your tiny friend is the perfect escort."

Seth groaned inwardly. He couldn't let Dragonwatch fall to the dragons. Not while he was alive. Not if there was a way of giving Kendra a chance to win. "How am I supposed to find it?"

"Travel to Selona and find a child without guile," Berna said. "While you slept, we placed a spell on the Ethershard. In the hands of an innocent, the shard will lead her to the Source."

"Her?" Seth asked. "Does it have to be a girl?"

The witches cackled uproariously.

"We have someone in mind," Berna said.

"We were trying to save you time," Wilna said.

The witches cackled again.

"I've been paying off a debt," Seth said. "And I'm finally done. Will this ever end?"

"You are under no obligation to continue," Orna replied.

"If I can give Kendra a way to stop Celebrant, I will," Seth said. "And I can't ignore a chance to break the nipsie curse."

Orna eyed her sisters. "I told you. We haven't seen anyone of this caliber since Patton."

"Tell none but the innocent about the Source," Berna warned.

"The secret of the Source must be kept," Wilna cautioned.

"How do I get to Selona?" Seth asked. "I've never been there, so I can't use the Translocator."

"Rizzle," Berna said.

"A river troll we have in our service," Wilna explained. "He spent some time in Selona."

"He's a little hard of hearing," Orna said. "Somewhat past his prime. But he could get you there using the Translocator."

"Not quite to Fairview," Berna said. "But you have wings."

"Even after a rest and your broth, I'm having a hard time focusing," Seth said.

"Use Vasilis when you must," Orna said. "The strength it provides might be your only hope. Just remember, when you put it away, you will be even more exhausted."

"Use the Sword of Light and Darkness as sparingly as you can," Wilna counseled. "Now and always."

Tossing aside the blanket, Seth rose unsteadily to his feet, then picked up the Translocator in one hand and the Unforgiving Blade in the other. He took a shuddering breath. He could see little more than the flames of the torches spaced around the cavern.

"What if I take a day or two to recover?" Seth asked. "I would have a better chance of making it."

"If there were more time, I might recommend it," Berna said.

"The attack on Selona draws nigh," Orna said.

Wilna spoke with quiet certainty. "If you wait much longer, the battle will be over."

# CHAPTER FORTY

# Nadia

Small farms occupied the high ground around Greenvale, with marshes inundating the lowlands. Roads meandered to stay above water, with many causeways and bridges through stretches of swamp made lush by cypresses and willows. Bordered by fens, the township was built on a raised parcel of land where ancient banyans competed with the buildings for dominance.

The Swamp Goose Inn looked to have been constructed from debris collected after a flood. The porch surrounding the three-story establishment rippled with warping, and the splintery roof sagged. A mangy dog with an eyepatch lay outside the entrance, occasionally nibbling at the scraps patrons donated when they departed.

Noble and Glory pulled up tufts of long grass among the aerial roots of a huge banyan tree. The light from the sunset was fading, and a lovely old woman moved along the porch of the inn, lighting lanterns. Behind the inn, where the ground became soggy, fireflies winked and bobbed in the twilight.

"How do we find a gremlin?" Kendra asked.

"We'll go inside the inn, but you manage the inquiries," Gerwin said. "As a child, I can probably go unrecognized, but if my identity leaked it would cause an unpleasant stir among the Fair Folk."

"Why?" Kendra asked.

"My siblings and I are famous in this kingdom. We come and go, vanishing for decades or centuries. Suffice it to say that I'm a weird novelty to them."

"We need to hurry," Kendra said. "Might not be a bad time to play the celebrity card."

"Trust me, it will slow us down if I am recognized," Gerwin said.

"Would my presence add or detract?" Virgil asked.

"The satyrs in this kingdom tend to be troublemakers," Gerwin said. "You are a different kind of satyr, but it might take time for anyone to figure that out."

Virgil heaved a sigh. "Satyrs are met with suspicion in most communities. Is it any wonder we keep to the woods? I'll stay back with Noble and Glory."

"There's plenty of grass," Noble said around a mouthful.

"I only eat grass in a pinch," Virgil said.

"I smell fruit trees not far off," Glory said.

Virgil sniffed the air. "I could go for some peaches."

"Come on, Kendra," Gerwin said, striding toward the inn.

"What's a swamp goose?" she wondered.

"You'll have to ask a local," Gerwin said.

"What do we know about gremlins?" Kendra asked.

"Gremlins are unpleasant creatures," Gerwin said. "You know how brownies mend and create? Gremlins do the opposite. In Greenvale, thanks to the treaty, gremlins and people generally ignore one another."

"So I need an excuse to seek them out," Kendra said.

"Tell the manager of the inn that you want to notify the gremlins about a lost item," Gerwin said.

"Report something I lost?" Kendra asked.

"Right," Gerwin said with a shrug. "Your favorite book. Your grandmother's brooch. Gremlins will find items for a fee."

They reached the swaybacked steps to the porch. The mangy dog lifted its head and gave a little whine. Gerwin crouched and rubbed the dog briskly with both hands as they went by. Kendra opened the door, and they entered the Swamp Goose Inn.

Inside, the inn was much more inviting. Wooden surfaces gleamed with polish. Diners sat at tables and along a bar. The patrons wore simple, homespun clothing, but they were so uniformly attractive that Kendra knew she was again among the Fair Folk.

Kendra approached a sturdy man at the end of the bar whose crisp white apron made him look official. "Welcome, miss," he said with a nod. "You're not from around here."

"Only my second time in Greenvale," Kendra said. "Could I talk to your gremlins?"

"Need a favor?" he asked.

"My grandma lost her favorite ring here," Kendra said. "I want to hire their services."

Scrunching his face, the man shook his head. "No rings currently in the lost items box. Who is your grandma?"

"Ruth Sorenson."

"I don't believe I've had the pleasure."

"She was passing through," Kendra said.

"You'll find a gremlin hatch at the top of those stairs," the man said, holding out a rag in the direction he meant.

"Thanks," Kendra said.

"Good luck," the man replied.

A thin, patterned carpet covered all but the edges of the stairs, clamped to each step by brass rods. Kendra and Gerwin hurried to the top, and Kendra promptly found a hatch in the landing, just shy of where the hall began.

"It's customary to knock," Gerwin suggested.

"How do I make a deal with gremlins?" Kendra asked.

"I'll handle it," Gerwin said.

Kendra rapped on the hatch.

"Wait a good minute before knocking again," Gerwin recommended. "Gremlins will use any excuse to get ornery."

After about forty seconds, the hatch swung open. Kendra flinched away from the little creature staring up at her, similar to how she might recoil from a rat in an alley. The gremlin was a humanoid just over a foot tall, with eyes and whiskers like a cat. He had tufts of black hair on his head, and green, bumpy skin like a toad.

"Why are you banging our hatch?" the gremlin snapped.

"I want to meet the Rag Lady," Gerwin said.

"What Rag Lady?" the gremlin replied sharply. "None of us know her."

Gerwin gave him a skeptical look. "How can you say who other gremlins know?"

"The same way I know you're wasting my time," the gremlin griped with a huff. "It's obvious."

"But I want to play a trick on her," Gerwin lamented.

At this the gremlin showed some interest. "Tricks can be rewarding. But not on the Rag Lady. We like her."

"You mean you would like her if you knew her," Gerwin corrected.

"Exactly," the gremlin said. "If we knew her, which we don't, we would like her. Hmmm, *like* is a strong word. It's hard to really like big clompers. But if we knew her, we might have an arrangement with her."

"The Rag Lady would like my trick," Gerwin said. "I'm her brother."

"You're not her brother," the gremlin bawled, waving Gerwin away. "You're too young. You're a little big clomper."

"I'm her youngest brother," Gerwin said. "I promise."

"Who's the other big clomper?" the gremlin asked, glancing at Kendra. "Is she just here to stink up the place?"

"I'm here to help with the trick," Kendra said.

The gremlin mashed his palm against his face. "I really want to do a trick." He peeked up at them from between his fingers. "It's illegal for gremlins to trick big clompers. But . . . big clompers can trick other big clompers."

"Especially when it's a brother," Gerwin said. "Where's your chief?"

The gremlin's jaw dropped. "The chief? You want to talk to the chief? As if the chief doesn't have a million more important issues to manage."

"More important than tricking the Rag Lady?" Gerwin asked. "You know, if she finds out you denied me, she'll quit your deal. But if you let me surprise her, she'll reward you."

The gremlin scratched one of the tufts of hair on his partially bald head. "A reward for a trick? You big clompers don't make sense."

"Fetch your chief," Gerwin said. "You don't want to miss this trick."

"I heard the chatter," said a new voice. "I'll take it from here, Scruntle."

"Chief!" Scruntle exclaimed. "It's all yours."

Scruntle disappeared into the hatch, and a new gremlin appeared, with a similar look, but he wore a pocket watch like a medallion and had whiter tufts of hair. "How will you guarantee the Rag Lady will reward us for the trick?" the chief asked.

"If she doesn't reward you, I will make the same deal with you that she struck, but twice what she offered," Gerwin said.

The chief waved him away. "Go climb a tree and hang there."

"Hey, no need to be rude," Gerwin said.

"You're a kid," the chief said. "You don't have the resources."

Gerwin lowered his voice. "Do you know who the Rag Lady really is?"

The chief lowered his voice in mimicry. "No. That is part of our deal. Go build a raft and sit on it."

"You're missing a choice opportunity," Gerwin warned.

"Go make a flag of your face and fly it," the gremlin said.

"What can I do to assure you?" Gerwin asked.

"I can't risk the deal we have with her," the gremlin said. "If the Rag Lady doesn't reward me for the trick, you're my indentured servant for ten years. And the girl for five."

"Sure," Gerwin said. "I'll make that deal. Because the Rag Lady is my sister and I know her."

"Spit on it?" the chief gremlin asked, staring up at Gerwin with one eye closed.

"Deal," Gerwin said, spitting on his palm. "Both eyes open, though. No getting out of it with a wink."

Opening both eyes wide, the chief spat on his palm and they shook. "Deal," the chief said. "You wait here."

He closed the hatch.

Gerwin looked at Kendra. "Easy."

"Indentured servants?" she asked.

"The stakes don't matter," Gerwin said confidently.

"What if the Rag Lady isn't your sister?" Kendra asked. "What if we got bad info?"

Gerwin's face fell. "That would be bad."

"Or what if she is your sister, but doesn't remember who she is?" Kendra asked.

Gerwin uncomfortably sucked on his bottom lip. "That might be problematic." Scratching his cheek, he regarded Kendra speculatively. "Have you ever made a flag of your face and flown it?"

"No."

Gerwin folded his arms. "There could be an upcoming scenario where we get a lot of practice."

Kendra and Gerwin waited in a bare room with a chair and two stools. Scruntle had helped them get settled. Five casks, three sacks, and two boxes were arranged neatly in the corner for the Rag Lady to claim. Kendra had asked how the woman would carry so much, and Scruntle had explained that she always arrived with a donkey hitched to a small cart.

Scruntle had left behind a lantern, which rested on the chair. Kendra paced while Gerwin perched on a stool.

"I'm worried the Rag Lady won't be your sister," Kendra said.

"We'd have to do some fast talking," Gerwin said. "Not so different from slaying a dragon—you charge in bravely and improvise as needed."

"Why is she hiding like this?" Kendra asked. "Did your sister ever live like a hermit before?"

"Nadia was reluctant to accept her role as a Dragon Slayer," Gerwin said. "She almost didn't join the family business. She wanted to live life on her own terms."

"Maybe she's hiding her face to avoid recognition," Kendra said.

"Or possibly she is embarrassed by her looks," Gerwin said.

"Give me a break," Kendra said. "You're all Fair Folk. You roll out of bed ready for a fashion shoot."

"Don't forget, her talisman is the gorgon's quill," Gerwin admonished.

"Meaning what?" Kendra asked.

"We have each been influenced by the talismans we carry," Gerwin said. "Gorgons are notoriously unattractive. Legend purports that some have been hideous enough to turn onlookers into stone."

"The quill destroyed her looks?" Kendra asked.

"It might explain hiding her face," Gerwin said.

Kendra paced steadily, trying to wear away time. "The Rag Lady comes after sunset?"

"Usually not long after sunset," Gerwin confirmed.

"The sun is down," Kendra said. "What if she doesn't show?"

"Relax," Gerwin said. "She'll come."

Kendra tried squatting on a stool. She lasted only a minute or two before she was pacing again.

Without warning, the door opened. A figure stood there, a little taller than Kendra, wearing a long, weathered coat and fingerless gloves. Shabby scarves and rags concealed her head. Mud spattered her scuffed boots.

"Who are you?" the woman asked, stepping back from the doorway. "What are you doing here?"

"Stay calm," Gerwin said. "We're looking for my sister Nadia."

"I'm sure I don't know anything about that," the Rag Lady mumbled.

Cocking his head, Gerwin squinted at the woman. "It's a good disguise. I can hardly even see your eyes. But I'm hard to fool."

The Rag Lady spoke in a clearer voice. "Gerwin? In front of a stranger? Really?"

Gerwin jerked a thumb at Kendra. "She saved my life from Jeruwat. Her name is Kendra."

The Rag Lady came inside and closed the door. "Jeruwat came after you? Is Celebrant trying to start a war?"

Gerwin gave an incredulous chuckle. "Have you heard no news, Nadia? Are you living under a rock?"

"Almost," Nadia said, folding her arms. "I live in solitude outside of town. I haven't held a conversation in years."

"While you were in your snail shell, the dragons declared war," Gerwin said. "And they're coming here next."

"Aren't most confined to sanctuaries?" Nadia asked. "What about Dragonwatch?"

"All seven sanctuaries have fallen," Gerwin said. "The remaining members of Dragonwatch have fled here. The skull is all that remains to hold the dragons at bay."

"This is another of your pranks," Nadia said in a firm voice. "Why can't you leave me in peace?"

"It isn't a prank," Kendra said. "Merek is helping us. Jeruwat already killed your sister."

"Magdalena?" Nadia asked.

"She was in the United States," Kendra said. "Near the Idaho-Montana border. Living as a yeti."

Nadia bowed her head. "I feel the truth of this. What does Agad intend to do?"

"Agad is dead," Kendra said. "Celebrant killed him."

"No," Nadia said, leaning back against the wall.

"The wizard died when Celebrant overthrew Wyrmroost," Kendra said. "I was there."

"Who is running Dragonwatch?" Nadia asked.

"A wizard named Andromadus," Kendra said. "He used to be the dragon Dromadus."

"A new wizard?" Nadia asked. "It has been ages since that happened."

"Celebrant has unified the dragons to destroy humanity," Kendra said. "Killing him is our only hope."

Heaving a sigh, Nadia moved the lantern from the chair to the floor and sat down. "Do the dragons know how to access Selona?"

"We don't think so," Gerwin said.

Nadia gave a nod. "If all the sanctuaries have fallen, the dragons will find their way here. Do we have the Harp? The Gauntlets? The Shield?"

"I don't know about the Gauntlets or Shield, but the Harp was destroyed," Kendra said.

"No!" Nadia exclaimed, aghast. "How?"

"The strings were cut by the Unforgiving Blade," Kendra said. "Titan Valley was under attack from the dragons. My brother did it to win the Wizenstone."

"Do we have the Wizenstone?" Nadia asked.

"My brother destroyed it with the Unforgiving Blade," Kendra said.

"I've missed a lot," Nadia said.

"Come with us to Fairview," Gerwin said. "Help us develop a counterattack."

Nadia raised a hand to her hidden face. "I can't participate. It's gotten worse. I would be more of a distraction than a help."

"Wear your rags," Gerwin said. "Or a mask."

"I would be flirting with disaster to go among men," Nadia said. "It's why I resorted to solitude."

"You've always come when the need was great," Gerwin said. "Our situation has never been more dire."

"Perhaps I could help from the fringes," Nadia said.

"Father is lost," Gerwin said. "Agad is down. Magdalena fell. Who knows how much of Dragonwatch was eliminated when the sanctuaries were overthrown? Time has gobbled our resources, and ease has softened our allies. We're vastly outnumbered."

"But my face," Nadia said.

"Let's see," Gerwin encouraged.

"Is it safe?" Kendra asked.

"As her brother, I have never been affected by it," Gerwin said. "And women tend to be immune to the worst effects."

"It might be instructive for me to gain an objective assessment," Nadia said, starting to unwind a long, tattered scarf from around her face. "I can glean only so much from mirrors."

Kendra averted her gaze. Did she want to see how Nadia appeared? Would she be deformed? Covered in boils? What constituted extreme ugliness? Nadia had used the quill to defend the world, and that very item had compromised her appearance.

Kendra braced herself as Nadia pulled the final rags away, revealing a face that provoked an involuntary gasp.

Nadia was divine.

Kendra had been dazzled by the flawless allure of the Fair Folk. She had seen the otherworldly appeal of Lizelle and even the Fairy Queen.

But Nadia redefined beauty. The young woman set a new standard. Kendra felt like she finally understood what women around the world were trying to imitate with the help of cosmetics and fashion—it was all a vain attempt to mimic some aspect of how Nadia looked naturally.

But Nadia's magnetism derived from more than the heavenly interplay of her features. She exuded the kind of warmth and understanding Kendra had been seeking her whole life. Somehow, Nadia's exquisite soul was both projecting virtue and awakening more goodness within Kendra than she knew she possessed. Standing in her presence was utterly absorbing.

"Yeah, it's worse, Nadia," Gerwin finally said. "I just want to stare at you for the rest of the day."

"Can you look away?" she asked.

The idea seemed ludicrous to Kendra. Why would anyone look away from such an irresistible, nurturing figure?

The rest of the world was a sad, lonely slog compared to the glory unveiled before her.

"I'm trying," Gerwin said.

"Do it," Nadia urged.

With a growl, Gerwin turned away from his sister. Panting, he stood with his back to her.

"What about you, Kendra?" Nadia asked, her voice preternaturally melodious.

Kendra staggered. The effect of Nadia's magnificence was multiplied as she gazed into her eyes. Kendra sank worshipfully to her knees.

Nadia turned away and began rewrapping her face.

Kendra blinked and looked around the room, confused. It felt as though she were waking from slumber, or at least from a trance. Why was she kneeling? Kendra stood up. She knew that Nadia had been gloriously beautiful, but strangely, she could no longer picture her face.

"You definitely pack an extra punch," Gerwin said.

"I feared as much," Nadia said.

Kendra turned and scowled at Gerwin. "You said the quill was making her ugly!"

"Opposite problem," Gerwin said with a smile.

"You have to watch what you believe with this prankster," Nadia said, turning to face them again, her countenance eclipsed behind dingy wrappings.

"Aren't gorgons ugly?" Kendra asked.

"Yes, but all gorgons were once sirens," Nadia said. "Similar to all imps once being fairies."

"Sirens lured sailors to their deaths," Kendra remembered.

"Gorgons leave men petrified with their foulness," Gerwin said. "Nadia can generate a similar effect with her good looks."

"It isn't so much the looks," Nadia said. "The quill is turning me into a walking, talking love potion. Beholding my face triggers the spell."

"I wasn't in love with you," Kendra said.

"It doesn't have to be romantic love," Nadia said.

Kendra nodded. "It was like basking in a beautiful sunset, or savoring a beloved piece of music. Or like seeing your best friend after a long absence."

"All of those things and more," Gerwin said. "You feel awed by her, and better about yourself, too. She fills you up with good feelings."

"It's incredible," Kendra said.

"And problematic," Nadia replied. Kendra noticed that her voice, while pleasant, no longer seemed as delightfully melodious.

"Men have fought wars over her," Gerwin said. "Killed for her. Died for her. Respectable men have committed crimes. Evil men have mended their ways."

"Let's not go into it," Nadia said. "I never wanted any of that."

"She doesn't encourage them," Gerwin said. "It isn't her fault. Or theirs either, really. They fall under her spell and can't help themselves."

"I don't want to enchant anyone," Nadia said. "I would undo the magic if I knew how."

"If the spell really takes hold, the effect is permanent," Gerwin said. "That mostly happens to lovestruck suitors."

"Much more of this topic and I will flee into the woods," Nadia said. "We have bigger problems."

"So you'll help us?" Gerwin asked.

"You know me well enough to guess the answer," Nadia said. "I'm going to need a good mask."

# CHAPTER FORTY-ONE

# Fairview

Standing in front of a full-length mirror in his sumptuous bedchamber, Knox squared his shoulders and adjusted his cape. His princely attire helped him blend in with the lords and ladies of Fairview, though he worried he looked a little like a sissy, and the hose made his legs seem skinny. Plucking at his sleeve, he tried to discern whether the material incorporated actual gold, or if it was just dyed with a metallic sheen.

Knocking as she entered, Tess skipped into the room. "You're up early," she said.

"The girls picked the time," Knox said.

"Are you going to meet those ladies from yesterday?" Tess asked.

"Not ladies," Knox said. "Girls."

"Compared to you, they're ladies," Tess said.

"I go into ninth grade next year," Knox explained. "In the normal world, those girls would be juniors or seniors." He smoothed a hand down the front of his shirt. "Sometimes famous guys date a few grades up."

Tess rolled her eyes. "In the normal world, those ladies would be in movies. You would never meet them."

Knox tossed his cape back and liked how it hung. "How do I look?"

"Like you're going to a costume party," Tess said.

"Around here, it isn't a costume," Knox said. He adjusted the medal pinned to his shirt, a platinum sunburst with a deep blue ribbon attached, a gift from King Russo, the current ruler of Selona.

He walked from his bedchamber to the living room he and Tess shared with Warren and Vanessa, enjoying the way his boots clacked against the stone tiles. He exited into a hall with tiled walls and an arched ceiling, then hurried down a winding stairwell into a shady courtyard. Two young women awaited him beneath a towering elm, both dressed as if they had been out riding, with slender swords at their hips. Their casual outfits made him feel overdressed and conspicuously unarmed. Knox determined that he would talk to somebody about getting a sword to wear around.

"Hello, Knox," Irisa said, gracefully crossing to him and crouching to give him a kiss on each cheek, her golden-brown curls swirling.

Next, Solange swept in and delivered two swift kisses of her own, smelling of honey and roses, her dark brown hair tied back. "Thanks for coming," she said.

Knox looked up at the smiling girls, who were at least three inches taller than him even with a boost from the thick heels of his boots. Why did the Fair Folk have to be so tall?

"Hi, Irisa," Knox said with a little bow. "Solange. It's good to see you again."

"It's Irina," she corrected. "We weren't going to miss the chance to hear rumors about the dragons."

"You were going to tell us more about Celebrant," Solange said eagerly, dark eyes expectant.

Knox wished the girls would head over to a bench so he wouldn't have to look up at them, but they remained standing, and he followed their lead. "You know I can't share anything from the meetings," Knox said.

"Yes, of course," Irina said. "You mustn't disclose anything shared in confidence behind closed doors."

"Unless you really want to," Solange suggested quietly.

"You have plenty of your own knowledge," Irina said.

"You were at the fall of Wyrmroost, Crescent Lagoon, and Titan Valley," Solange added.

"Well, I saved Crescent Lagoon," Knox said. "It fell after I left." These girls were incredibly attractive, even by Texas standards. He felt excited and flattered to have their devoted attention. They weren't princesses, but their fathers were important leaders. What did you call the daughter of a duke?

"What's it like to face a dragon up close?" Irina asked.

"They're savage and powerful," Knox said. "I've seen

them massacre sky giants. Be glad you have lived in a sheltered kingdom."

"It may not stay that way," Solange said. "I've heard Celebrant is gathering dragons near our borders."

"There are lots of rumors," Knox said, not wanting to overshare.

"Our forces have started training for combat," Irina said. "I've never seen a large army prepare to mobilize."

"We don't think the dragons know how to access Selona," Knox said. "But we want to be ready for anything."

"So many members of Dragonwatch have come here," Solange said. "Along with key refugees from fallen sanctuaries. Not to mention some of the Fair Folk who lived abroad. Most enter through secret ways Andromadus devises."

"Selona is one of the safest places left standing," Knox said.

"Our nation has seldom received outsiders," Solange said. "Won't it draw the dragons if everyone gathers here?"

"The people coming here can help defend Selona," Knox said. "You need all the help you can get resisting the dragons." He didn't want to mention the Sovereign Skull, which remained a secret to most.

"We've long protected ourselves," Irina said.

"From what?" Knox asked. "Who has attacked? You've been neutral."

"We needed to be neutral," Irina said. "Our duty is to maintain the balance. The last time the Fair Folk broke neutrality, those who fought were cursed."

"What was the curse?" Knox asked.

"They disappeared," Irina said.

"They were never seen again," Solange added. "But if we're attacked, we'll defend ourselves."

"If you had joined the fight earlier, the war might never have come here," Knox said.

"We follow King Russo," Irina said. "Otherwise, all order collapses."

"Heavy is the head that wears the crown," Knox said, looking up at Irina. "When I was king of the giants, it was hard to determine what would be best for my subjects."

"I can hardly believe you were one of the five monarchs," Irina said.

"We didn't get together very often," Knox said. "The Underking never asked me for advice."

The girls laughed.

"King Russo has never had to repel an attack," Solange said. "Historically, when great adversity loomed, King Konrad returned. Like during the dragon war."

"Did that mean two kings?" Knox asked.

"Konrad is the king emeritus," Solange said. "All other kings of the Fair Folk yield to him when he is present."

"There have been many kingdoms of Fair Folk over the years," Irina said. "During our apex, there were twelve."

"How many are there now?" Knox asked.

"Only two kingdoms and a few smaller communities," Irina said. "The main kingdom is Selona, of course. We're the motherland. Our other kingdom, at Stormguard Castle, was recently reclaimed by King Hollorix when he was freed from the enchantment of the Wizenstone."

"He sent some troops to help fortify us," Solange said.

"But with Wymroost fallen, he has problems of his own," Irina said.

"Look," Solange said, pointing skyward. "Merek!"

Golden wings glinting in the morning light, a sword clutched in one hand, Merek descended toward them.

"Is he coming this way?" Irina asked, flustered. Her eyes widened. "He's coming right at us!"

"I wondered if I would see him in my lifetime," Solange said, hands stroking her ponytail.

"You've seen him before now, right?" Knox asked. "He's been around for the past week."

"Not up close," Irina said.

"He's been in some meetings with us," Knox said. "He could lighten up. He gets too serious."

With a rush of air, Merek landed a few paces from Knox. "Hello, ladies," he greeted with a nod. "Sorry to interrupt." Then he focused on Knox. "Your cousin approaches Fairview."

"Seth?" Knox asked.

"Kendra," Merek said. "She isn't alone. Come with me to greet her."

"Yes," Knox said. He waved to the girls. "If you'll excuse me?"

"By all means," Irina said. "But catch us up later!"

Solange just stared at Merek shyly.

Merek turned to Knox. "Mind if I carry you?"

"Aren't I too heavy?" Knox asked.

"I can manage," Merek said, scooping him up, one

arm behind his knees, the other supporting his back. The Dragon Slayer sprang into the air and flew above the castle walls, then out to the main road through town. They landed in front of a donkey pulling a cart driven by a shabby figure wrapped in scarves. Resting in the back was the satyr Knox had met in Humburgh. To one side, a thin boy rode on a horse with wings tucked against its sides. Was it Noble, from Wyrmroost? On the other side, Kendra sat astride Glory.

"Merek!" the thin boy exclaimed. "You do have wings!"

"Gerwin," Merek greeted, setting Knox on his feet. "You look . . . young. And Nadia?"

The figure driving the cart gave a nod. "Is there someplace where we can speak privately?" she asked in a muffled voice.

"Sure, give us a lift," Merek said, climbing into the cart with the satyr and motioning for Knox to join them.

"Knox, I'm so glad you're all right," Kendra called out as he climbed into the cart, careful not to get splinters.

"Same," Knox said. "Why is your horse walking if it has wings?"

"Nadia refused to leave her donkey behind," Kendra said. "She joined us yesterday and rode through the night. How did you get here?"

Nadia flicked the reins, and the donkey started forward. The other horses kept pace alongside.

"Tanu, Seth, and some others found us," Knox said.

"I met them after they came here," Merek said.

"Is Seth here?" Kendra asked.

"He flew off with Raxtus on his own mission," Knox said.

"I'm glad Raxtus found him," Kendra said.

The conversation died. Knox settled back in the cart beside the drowsy-eyed satyr. As the castle gate approached, Merek flew ahead to secure entry.

Kendra sat down on a sofa, grateful to be off her feet. The others took up positions in the comfortable room. Virgil had expressed that he needed a nap before he participated in more conversations, and Merek had shown him to a bedroom across the hall.

"I can hardly believe three of us are together now," Merek said, looking around the room. "Since I parted ways with Kendra, I couldn't find clues about any of you. How did you do it, Kendra?"

"I got leads from the demons about all of your siblings," Kendra said.

Merek looked distressed. "What happened to Magdalena?"

Kendra slumped, at a loss for words.

"Magdalena was killed by Jeruwat," Gerwin said.

Merek's face fell. "How?"

Kendra fleshed out the details, including the treacherous gift from Ronodin and the battle with Jeruwat, interspersed with comments from Gerwin. Nadia listened quietly.

"It's a miracle you got Nadia and Gerwin back here," Merek said.

"And where have you been, elder brother?" Gerwin asked.

"Hunting where I could find leads," Merek said. "Every sage I consulted suggested Father was either dead or in Selona. And so I have been scouring Selona."

"Could Konrad have lost his memories?" Kendra asked.

"His pattern of rebirth didn't include memory loss," Gerwin said.

"He has been gone so long," Nadia said in frustration. "He always arrived before disaster struck. We never went and found him. He always gathered us. But he stopped appearing through the last few crises."

"Could he be dead?" Gerwin asked.

"He must be dead or otherwise incapacitated," Nadia said. "We're on our own."

"What other resources do we have against dragons?" Kendra asked.

"We have some wizards who can overpower them," Merek said. "The slayers we trained for the dragon war, like Banderbrux and Bronwyn, are no more. Most of the Dragon Slayers from the fallen preserves are missing or won't come. The Somber Knight is here, injured and recovering, and the three cyclopses that together form Mombatu joined us. Gerwin, you're not at full strength because of your age."

"Even at kid strength I'm worth more than some armies," Gerwin said.

"I hear the Fair Folk are prepping for battle," Knox said.

"They're undertrained and unprepared," Merek replied. "With their numbers and our leadership, I expect them to kill some dragons. But against Celebrant's full horde, I fear Fairview will end up like a sandcastle trying to resist the ocean."

"We still have time to prepare," Gerwin said.

"Maybe we can convince more giants to join us," Merek said. "A few have answered the call. Perhaps we can drum up other allies. Andromadus is a master of sneaking outsiders into our kingdom. Hopefully we have time to better prepare and equip our forces. Even with our best efforts, I worry our enemy will attack with overwhelming force."

"There is always a way," Nadia said. "We just have to find it."

"Before time runs out," Merek said. "Kendra, you look weary."

"Virgil had the right idea," she said, suppressing a yawn. "I could use a nap."

"At a time like this?" Knox exclaimed. "You can sleep after the dragons eat us!"

"I was up all night," Kendra said. "I love Glory, but it's hard to get good sleep on horseback."

"Nothing like traveling at the speed of a donkey cart," Gerwin said with a glance at Nadia.

"Let me show you to a room, Kendra," Merek said, rising. "Thank you for finding my siblings and bringing news. I'm sure others will want to see you, but it can wait until you get some rest."

"Even just a few minutes would help," Kendra said.

Merek led her out the door and across the hall. "This suite I've been using has three bedchambers. The satyr is occupying one. You are welcome to use the other until we find more suitable accommodations."

"Right now, a bare patch of floor would be more than enough," Kendra said gratefully.

Merek motioned to a doorway.

Kendra went into the room and closed the door. She felt the relief of being alone and unscrutinized. No more having to seem alert and polite while secretly wanting to collapse and sleep. A moment later, she realized a call was emanating from the unicorn horn she always carried with her.

Startled into higher alertness, she gripped the horn and reached out with her mind.

*Bracken?*

*Kendra! There you are. I've been trying to contact you. I escaped!*

*From Ronodin?*

*Lizelle helped me. Three astrids sacrificed their lives. Lizelle and I are outside the Fairy Realm and we're coming to you.*

*I'm in Selona. At Fairview Castle.*

*We just found out. I was able to reach Andromadus. He keeps an astrid nearby. He's going to help us access Selona.*

*This is good news. Is Ronodin still running the Fairy Realm?*

*For now. I'll deal with him after we handle the dragons.*

*I don't see a way out of this one! The situation in Selona is such a mess.*

*I'll help you clean it up,* Bracken communicated. *I better go. See you soon!*

*Okay*, Kendra conveyed. *Travel safely.*

The horn went inert in her hands.

Kendra could hardly believe the good news! Suddenly she wasn't tired at all. Bracken was safe! And he was coming to her! That meant extra help. But it might take some time. Kendra knew she should clear her mind and rest while she could before Bracken arrived.

Kendra crossed to the bed and was surprised to find an envelope on the quilt with her name on it. She didn't recognize the penmanship. Who could have left a message? Nobody knew she was coming here today.

Curious, she opened the envelope and removed a folded letter.

Skipping to the bottom, she saw it was from Virgil. Going back to the top, she read:

*Dear Kendra,*

*I hope this letter finds you before it becomes irrelevant. Merek seemed to think you would rest here after your meeting with the others.*

*Humbuggle's Games have fascinated me since childhood. For long years, my studies of the Games were met with derision. What satyr could be regarded as a serious scholar? Most dismissed my efforts as a form of compulsive fanaticism. Eventually, Dante found value in the reliability of my predictions. For the first time in memory, I was respected (and regularly compensated for my work).*

*But I yearned to accomplish more! I had theories*

*about how to approach the Games and no way to test them. No competitor would rely on a satyr for strategy, and it was never in my nature to participate directly.*

*Then Seth came knocking, and so began the most fulfilling period of my life. I wish we could have puzzled over those mysteries forever, unraveling layer after layer of the Games, uncovering secrets, making more headway than any other competitors against an unsolvable problem.*

*And then the unthinkable happened. Seth cleaved the Wizenstone in half. He succeeded. We succeeded. And my life promptly lost all purpose. Be careful what you wish for!*

*The Games I had loved were no more. The designer I admired had to flee. The city I called home lost all protection.*

*I became withdrawn and directionless. You showed up with Merek, and at least you needed my help. It was something instead of nothing.*

*You may recall, after visiting Humbuggle's manor, while you and I were looking for your cousins in Humburgh, you were searching the establishments on one side of Haymarket Street, and I was checking the other side. Imagine my surprise when I was scoping out a tavern and Humbuggle approached me on the sly.*

*It turns out that right after Celebrant took Seth prisoner, Humbuggle made a deal with Celebrant. Humbuggle has prospered for so long by consistently aligning himself with the winning side. That will* inevitably be the dragons for many years to come. Humbuggle wanted to strike a bargain with me.

You have to understand, Humbuggle has been my hero since childhood. And I had only just learned that, disguised as Dante, he was the mentor who first appreciated my work. In return for some help, Humbuggle proposed a joint venture in which I would play a key role. And I agreed.

My assignment was to discover the entrance to Selona. He told me your group would end up there sooner or later.

The information will seal Humbuggle's alliance with the dragons. The arrangement will set us up to develop a new series of Games, sponsored by Celebrant.

Make no mistake, you're not going to stop the dragons. Titan Valley had much better defenses than Selona. The sooner you realize the dragons will win, the better your chance for survival. I realize my actions will feel like a betrayal to you. It wasn't personal. Hopefully this letter proves I care. I didn't have to leave it, and Humbuggle would cut my throat if he knew about it.

I am off to tell Humbuggle and the dragons how to enter Selona.

If it wasn't me, someone else would have uncovered the secret before long.

They will be coming soon.

It will be an attack like the world has never known. I suggest you all flee. Take anyone and anything you treasure and escape to the farthest corner of the planet. Please hurry. There is little time.

I must go now. Don't waste time trying to stop me. I have a foolproof way to get clear and share the info about the crossroads with Humbuggle. It's time for you to do damage control. Warn who you need to warn and get everyone with a brain to abandon this castle and live.

Sorry for the inconvenience.

Yours truly,

Virgil

# CHAPTER FORTY-TWO

# Mission

Seth stood on a muddy riverbank beside a wrinkly troll. Despite a clear sky, the sun overhead seemed distant and dim.

"If that don't beat all," the troll said, looking around. "This is where I grew up. Have you ever seen a homier river?"

"Everything is kind of dim," Seth said.

"Yes, I know, perfect for a swim," the troll said. "I once buried my brother on that sandbar over there while he was sleeping. He woke up so mad! Your magic stick worked like a charm."

"Now I grab the middle," Seth said.

"I don't see no fiddle," the troll replied.

Seth helped the troll shift his grip to the top of the

cylinder. Then Seth took hold of the center segment and twisted.

They were back in the echoey darkness where the Singing Sisters lived.

"Thanks," Seth said, removing the troll's hand from the Translocator. He twisted the center of the cylinder again and returned to the riverbank. Seth steadied himself as he stashed the Translocator in his satchel, then dropped to one knee on the firm mud. He could feel his life force slithering into the permanent void in his belly. "I don't think I can fly without the sword, Calvin."

"Then draw Vasilis," the Tiny Hero said.

Seth gripped the hilt of the sword and pulled it from the scabbard. The day brightened, and vitality rushed into him. He rose to a crouch, then sprang into the sky.

"Feeling better?" Calvin asked.

"Night and day," Seth said. "I hope it can last."

"Based on the directions they shared, Fairview Castle should be off to the west," Calvin said.

"Is the sun coming up or going down?" Seth asked.

"Up," Calvin said.

Seth veered away from the rising light. Climbing, he found a favorable breeze and increased his speed. Ahead, the forest gave way to farmland. "If all we do is go west, we could miss our destination. We need better directions. Vasilis won't sustain me forever. I can't waste time."

"Fairview is the capital," Calvin said. "We're looking for the biggest city with the grandest castle. Anyone should be able to point us in the right direction."

As they came over the patchwork of cultivated fields, Seth dove lower, then sailed above a road, paralleling it. When a wagon came into view, Seth dipped within earshot.

"Which way to Fairview?" he called.

"Is that Merek?" the driver called up to him, shading his eyes with one hand. "Don't you know?"

"I'm Merek's friend from out of town," Seth yelled.

"That way," the farmer said, pointing northwest. "You'll pass over a mill."

"Thanks," Seth called, rising and increasing his speed. He saw a distant town to the north, and a smaller one to the south, but neither had a major castle.

"How are we going to find an innocent to carry the Ethershard?" Calvin asked.

"If all else fails, trial and error," Seth said. "First we have to get there."

Seth gained altitude. Hayfields went by below. A swift, narrow stream turned a waterwheel attached to a stone mill-house. Goatherds paused amid their flocks to point up at him.

Before long, a majestic castle rose into view, with square towers anchoring the outer wall and a bouquet of conical towers in the center, their spires topped by pennants. A sprawling town surrounded the castle, spilling across a wide river with two major bridges. Seth focused on the castle, sacrificing some altitude to increase the speed of his approach.

As Seth soared over the outskirts of Fairview, he noticed

a man with golden wings flying toward him. "Greetings, Seth!"

"Merek!" Seth called. "I wondered if you might be around. A farmer mistook me for you."

Merek swung around to fly alongside Seth. "Are you planning an attack?" the Dragon Slayer asked.

At first Seth didn't understand the question. Then he glanced at Vasilis, drawn and blazing. "Vasilis is keeping me awake," Seth said. "The Demon King stabbed me in the gut with the Unforgiving Blade. I still feel its shadow drawing the life out of me."

Merek winced. "I'm sorry."

"I'm here to carry out a final mission," Seth said.

"If so, you better hurry," Merek said. "The dragons have learned the way into Selona."

"That's bad news," Seth replied. "They're gathered nearby. Thousands of them."

"Our scouts have reported as much," Merek said. "We're currently holding a war council."

"The nipsies stand ready to lend aid," Calvin called from Seth's pocket.

"Maybe Andromadus can bring them here," Merek said. "Good to see you, Calvin. All assistance is appreciated."

"Is Serena with you?" Calvin asked.

"She is back at the meeting," Merek said. "She'll be glad to see you."

"The Singing Sisters believe my final mission can give you a chance for victory," Seth said.

"That would be welcome," Merek said.

"Shouldn't you be at the meeting?" Seth asked.

"I was," Merek said. "Our guards are on high alert. We're expecting the dragons at any moment. They notified me when you were sighted. Your sister is with us."

"Kendra is here?" Seth asked.

"She arrived this morning," Merek said. "She brought two of my siblings with her—Gerwin and Nadia."

"Where are we going?" Seth asked. They were flying toward the castle.

"That balcony, with the guards on it," Merek said, pointing. "The war council lies beyond."

They landed, and a guard opened a filigreed door, warily eyeing Seth's swords. Merek led Seth into a spacious room where many tables had been arranged so the participants were facing one another. Seth saw several people he knew. Trask, one of his favorite Knights of the Dawn, conversed with a white-bearded dwarf. Lomo and Lockland, Fair Folk from Wyrmroost, gave Seth a wave. Lord Dalgorel hunched over a parchment making notes. Warren and Vanessa sat at the same long table where Tanu hurriedly mixed potions. A group of wizards wore embroidered robes, and there were many Fair Folk in fancy clothes and uniforms.

The moment Seth's eyes found Kendra, he ignored everyone else. She sat beside their cousin Knox and a younger kid.

"This is Seth Sorenson," Merek announced to the room. "Forgive his drawn blades. The dark weapon can't be sheathed, and the other is keeping him on his feet."

"That's Vasilis!" one of the Fair Folk exclaimed.

"And a portion of Raglamar," a female wizard said in awe.

"This is an auspicious time for such storied blades to come into our midst," another of the Fair Folk remarked.

Seth heard the comments without paying much attention. He felt strained, his eyes sore, as if he needed sleep. The assistance from Vasilis was starting to wear thin. His heart hammered faster than normal.

"Seth!" Kendra said, rising. "I've been so worried about you."

He hurried over to Kendra, carefully set the Unforgiving Blade on her table, then rummaged in his satchel with his one free hand. "Sorry to interrupt," Seth said to the assemblage. "I'm on a mission from the Singing Sisters that could help you against the dragons." He pulled out the Ethershard, pinching the crystalline fragment between his thumb and forefinger.

"What is that?" Kendra asked.

"Hold out the shard," Seth said, giving it to her. "It will glow when you point it in the right direction." Kendra let the fragment rest on her palm. "In your hands it should work like a compass."

Kendra swiveled from side to side.

"All the way around," Seth prompted.

Arm extended, Kendra turned in a circle with no result.

"Try high and low," Seth said.

Kendra turned, raising and lowering the shard. "Like this?"

"It should work in the hands of an innocent person,"

Seth said. His eyes went from the Ethershard to her face. "The Kendra I knew was without guile."

Kendra locked eyes with him. "I've done some hard things while you've been gone. I stormed the Under Realm alone. I vowed to kill Celebrant. I'm not the same Kendra you left behind at Stormguard Castle."

"Yes," Seth said, slowly nodding his head. "I see that now. I left a lot of disasters for you to tackle alone. I'm sorry." Seth turned to Merek. "I need someone else."

"Somebody more innocent?" Kendra asked.

"Tess," Knox said. "The cloak of innocence worked on her."

"Until I shot the revenants," Kendra muttered.

"That messed up the cloak's protection, but it was your mistake," Knox said. "I bet Tess is still innocent."

"Is Tess here?" Seth said.

"Probably climbing trees in the courtyard," Knox said. "We could go find her."

"Seth's barely standing," Calvin said. "Only Vasilis is keeping him awake. Bring her to him."

One of the Fair Folk cleared his throat. "We have a defense to plan."

"Sorry," Seth said. "Kendra, Knox, can we talk outside the room?"

Kendra started toward the door. Seth picked up the Unforgiving Blade and followed Knox. They exited into a hallway. Seth could feel his heartbeat in his throat and in his hands, the pace accelerating.

The guards outside the door moved away to give them space. Warren joined them as well.

"I'll go find Tess and bring her," Knox said.

"Looks like you're in deep," Warren said.

"I'm just trying to finish this mission," Seth said.

"What is your mission?" Kendra asked.

"Part of my assignment is to keep it a secret," Seth said. Kendra rested a hand on his arm. "You don't look well."

"Remember when I stabbed Velrog with the Unforgiving Blade?" Seth asked, speaking hurriedly. "How it was game over?" He steadied himself against the wall. "Well, the Demon King took the Unforgiving Blade and stabbed me in the stomach."

"But you still have it," Kendra said.

"He gave it back," Seth explained. "But it feels like the blade is always inside of me, sucking my life away, turning me into one of the undead."

"That pain is with you now?" Kendra asked.

"It's permanent," Seth said. "Maybe I can learn to live with it—if I can survive the constant pull toward becoming undead. Right now, I'm on the brink of collapsing. Except I can't. Time is running out. Vasilis is keeping me on my feet, but it's meant to be used sparingly."

"Put down Vasilis and rest," Kendra said. "At least until Knox gets back with Tess."

Seth struggled to connect his thoughts. His breathing was ragged. Maybe a break was what he needed before one last burst of effort. "All right. But if you can't wake me up when Tess gets here, put Vasilis back in my hand."

"I will," Kendra said.

Seth set down the Unforgiving Blade. Then he sheathed Vasilis. The moment the blade was covered, gravity seemed to increase threefold, and the hall became almost completely dark. Seth crumpled, delirious, and spread out on the stone floor, taking comfort in the cool, hard surface beneath his cheek.

Without Vasilis to buoy him, there was no ignoring the summons of the undead. Sucking air through his teeth, he endured the soul-withering sensation, trying to rest.

The next thing Seth knew, Vasilis was in his hand, and Tanu knelt beside him. "How long was I out?" Seth asked.

"Maybe fifteen minutes," Kendra said. "Not long."

"You looked dead," Knox said. "We could barely see you breathing."

"Tess?" Seth asked, sitting up.

"The crystal glows when she points it to the west," Warren said.

"Then she's the one I need," Seth said, rising to his feet, Vasilis in hand. The Unforgiving Blade remained where he had set it.

"Drink this," Tanu said, handing Seth a cup. "You may find it restorative."

Seth guzzled the cold drink. It tasted like water with a faint hint of fruit, and it was surprisingly refreshing. He turned to Tess.

"I've been on a long journey," Seth said. "Will you help me finish it?"

"Yes," she said. "Using the crystal."

"It only works for you," Seth said.

"Will it be dangerous?" Tess asked.

"Probably," Seth said.

"I'll protect you," Tess replied.

"Would you like some company?" Warren asked.

"I wish," Seth said, retrieving the Unforgiving Blade. "But only Tess and I are supposed to go."

"And me?" Calvin asked.

"And Calvin," Seth amended.

"I told Serena to offer the help of the nipsies to Andromadus," Calvin said. "I'm not leaving you now."

"We should go," Seth said. "While I still feel functional." He turned to Kendra. "Supposedly my mission will help your battle."

"We need all the help we can get," Warren murmured. "Dragons have been sighted outside of Selona approaching the crossroads."

"What's your plan?" Seth asked.

"We'll go after Celebrant," Kendra said. "Hopefully, without his leadership, the dragon attack will fizzle."

"The wizards will concentrate on shielding Fairview," Warren said. "And Andromadus will prepare an escape as a last resort."

"Hold out for as long as you can," Seth said. "When I finish this mission, I'll come back. I mean, if you want the help of a half-dead wraith person."

"We will always need your help," Kendra said, sharing a glance with Calvin. "Just try to come back from this mission alive."

Seth gave a nod. "How can Tess and I leave without interrupting the meeting again?"

"This way," Warren said, leading them down the hall and into another room with a balcony.

As Seth stepped outside, he looked at Tess and realized the logistical problem. "I have to hold both of these swords," he said. "How will I carry Tess?"

"She could ride Glory?" Kendra proposed.

"What?" Seth asked.

"My winged horse," Kendra said. "She can talk. It would kind of be like having an extra person. Is that allowed?"

"I'm not sure I have another choice," Seth said.

Kendra rushed onto the balcony. "Glory! I need you! Come quickly."

It was not long before Seth heard a neigh in the distance. A chestnut mare with white splotches flew into view and alighted beside them. "What's wrong?" the horse asked.

"Tess needs a ride to go on a mission with my brother," Kendra said. "It's urgent."

"Then let's not delay," Glory said, stamping a hoof.

"The crystal Tess holds will show us where to go," Seth said. "Tess, we want whatever direction makes the crystal brightest. I'll be right behind you."

"You could ride too," Glory offered.

"I think flying will help keep me alert," Seth said.

Warren boosted Tess onto Glory.

"Good luck, Seth," Kendra called.

Seth waved with Vasilis. "Don't step on any dragon tails."

Glory leaped from the balcony, wings fanned wide, and soared upward. Seth sprang into the sky behind the mare. Vasilis flared brighter. Seth suddenly realized the vitality from the sword flowed better when he was in motion. It was a weapon of action.

"Am I going too fast?" Glory called back.

"The faster the better," Seth replied.

The horse picked up speed, and, with effort, Seth matched her. Soaring westward, they flew over fewer farms and drier terrain. Seth noticed a large settlement to the south. After the landscape turned to desert, they passed over a dusty fortress surrounded by sun-beaten tents.

As they glided over empty country, weariness began to overtake Seth again. His eyes itched with exhaustion. It was hard to scratch an itch with a sword in each hand. He thought about sheathing Vasilis and draping himself over the back of the horse. But how would he carry the Unforgiving Blade?

Seth squeezed the hilt of Vasilis. He found more energy welling from the sword as he committed to his mission with determination. He had to make it to the Source. Who knew what he would do there? But he had to arrive.

Parched gulches traversed the arid desert, winding among sculpted buttes and mesas. Some of the fanciful rock formations would probably have drawn tourists if they weren't so remote. Seth soared above a sandstone maze and a simmering green pond.

Seth noticed they were descending, as if preparing to land, though the upcoming stretch of desert was nondescript, with no landmarks that might conceal the Source. Did Glory need a rest? Seth could feel his heart rate rising. His head ached. And they were about to land in the middle of nowhere for no apparent reason. Maybe Tess had to go to the bathroom?

Glory touched down on hard-packed dirt and trotted to a halt. Seth landed beside the horse.

"What's the problem?" Seth asked.

"We're here," Tess said, holding out the brightly shining Ethershard.

Seth looked in the direction she was indicating and beheld a white dome big enough to contain multiple tennis courts. His jaw dropped. "Where did that come from?"

"I just saw it too," Glory said. "Must have been a distracter spell."

"Makes sense," Seth said. "Let me search for an entrance."

Seth flew in a complete circle around the dome and found the smooth surface uninterrupted by doors, windows, or ventilation shafts. Seth landed beside Glory again.

"I don't see a way in," Seth said, holding up the Unforgiving Blade. "But this cuts through anything. Shall we hack our way in?"

"I'll go no closer," Glory said. "My heart has misgivings about treading here. You two go ahead."

Tess slid off Glory and dropped to the ground. They stood about ten paces from the nearest portion of the dome.

"No time to waste," Seth said, striding forward. He tapped the dome with the hilt of Vasilis to make sure it was solid, then slashed it with the Unforgiving Blade. The black blade cut cleanly through the pale surface. A few more slices, and a thick section of the dome fell inward, creating an opening.

Seth glanced at the crystal glowing intensely in Tess's hand. "This place is called the Source," he said. "It's a big secret."

Tess nodded eagerly. "Should we have a look?"

Ducking and stepping, Tess passed through the carved opening, then beckoned for Seth to join her.

CHAPTER FORTY-THREE

# Source

Stepping into the dome revitalized Seth. He had expected the atmosphere inside of a sealed structure to
be stale and hot. Instead, it was the freshest, cleanest air he
had ever breathed. Which made more sense once he beheld
that the dome housed a verdant garden.

A sword in each hand, Seth watched Tess crouch to sniff
an orchid. She stood, and for a moment, they took in the
lush greenery together. Then Tess held out the Ethershard
and pivoted until finding the maximum glow. "This way,"
she said, leading them forward.

Strangely, the indoor garden seemed brighter to Seth
than the direct sunlight beating down on the desert outside. Could his normal vision be returning? Shouldn't the
solid dome block all sunlight? Looking around the enclosed
paradise of fruit trees, ferns, watermelons, pumpkins, other

vegetables, shrubs, and flowering vines, Seth could identify no sources of light.

How was everything so vivid and bright? The garden existed in higher definition than the rest of reality, as if he had needed glasses his whole life and he was finally wearing the perfect prescription. Seth paused to stare at some shockingly red blossoms before Tess urged him on. The color spectrum was richer here, with nuances of hue more crisp and distinct than he had ever seen.

Glancing at the Unforgiving Blade, Seth noticed a dark aura around the edges, a dim corona of shadow. He moved the blade closer to his eyes, then held it at arm's length. He had never noticed a gloomy halo like that before.

"The crystal is pointing at a lake," Tess called from up ahead. "Or maybe at something in the lake."

Seth caught up to his cousin. The body of water was more a pool than a lake, not much bigger than a basketball court. The water inside was abnormally clear and startlingly deep. Seth gazed down into an endless tunnel of pristine water, evenly lit until shrinking out of view.

"After all this time, a couple of kids found us," a friendly male voice said from the far side of the pool.

Startled, Seth looked up to see a man with a close-cropped beard tromping around the pool toward them from the far side. His feet were bare, and he wore beige pants rolled up almost to the knees. His shirt was unbuttoned enough to show a portion of his moderately hairy chest.

"Is this the Source?" Seth asked.

"So the secret is out," the man said.

"Hardly anyone knows," Seth said. "You live here?"

"I've been sealed here for centuries," the man said, coming closer. "A powerful spell raised a magical barrier around the Source and trapped me inside." The man stopped a few paces away.

"No tunneling out?" Seth asked.

The man shook his head. "This whole area was enclosed within an invisible wall of energy. The barrier flashed red if you struck it. Nothing I tried could penetrate the barrier, aboveground or below. I gave up trying to escape. Then, not long ago, something changed. Without explanation, the wall of energy disappeared. Only the dome remained."

"Seth cut through the dome," Tess said.

"I noticed," the man replied.

"Why didn't the dome collapse with the rest of the barrier?" Seth asked.

"The dome was added later," the man explained. "And it was connected to other magic. The rest of the barrier was generated by some object of enormous power."

"Graulas sealed off the Source with the Wizenstone," Seth said. "I had a history lesson in Humburgh."

"Ah," the man replied, taking a step closer. "Yes, that explains it. The biggest portion of the Ethergem. If you're right, Graulas had it in his possession for a good while before he took action against the Source. Did something happen to the Wizenstone?"

"I cut it in half," Seth said.

The man held out a hand to shake. "Then you were the person who made this place accessible."

"Is he safe?" Tess asked.

"I mean you no harm," the man said, holding up both hands innocently. "I know I look ragged, but I was once a friend to many. I am Konrad. I was once a defender of Selona."

Seth stared. "Merek's dad?"

"Do you know my son?" Konrad asked. "Is he well?"

"Yes," Seth said. "I saw Merek earlier today. But Celebrant and his dragons are attacking Selona."

"Truly?" Konrad asked. "No dragon was more ambitious than Celebrant. Did his sanctuary fall?"

"They've all fallen," Seth said. "Celebrant has thousands of dragons under his command."

"Those are sobering numbers," Konrad said.

"The dragons just gained access to Selona," Seth said. "They're after the skull of Abraxas."

"I can slay dragons," Konrad said. "But not several at once. And nobody could stop a thousand. What brings you to the Source?"

"The Singing Sisters told me that coming here would be the only way to give my friends a chance to beat the dragons," Seth said.

"You run errands for the Sisters?" Konrad asked curiously.

"I've run a couple," Seth said. "It's not my day job. My grandpa was the caretaker of a preserve called Fablehaven. Normally I try to protect the preserves. I used to really trust my instincts, but I end up making such a mess sometimes that I barely know what to think anymore."

"Seth is still remembering who he is," Tess said.

"I lost my memories, and I even ended up serving the Underking for a time," Seth said. "Now I'm trying to figure out if I can really help anyone."

"Never let your mistakes define you," Konrad said. "What do the Singing Sisters want you to accomplish here?"

"I brought the pieces of the Ethergem," Seth said. "They didn't explain more."

Konrad nodded pensively. "All the pieces of the Ethergem?"

"I collected them all," Seth said.

Konrad raised his eyebrows. "Then you accomplished a feat I would have considered impossible."

"What can I do with the pieces?" Seth asked.

"We will investigate the possibilities," Konrad said.

"I'm Tess, Seth's cousin," Tess said. "I made the crystal glow when it pointed the right way."

"The Ethershard would only show the way in the hands of an innocent," Seth said.

"Innocence is a valuable commodity," Konrad said. "You seem strained. Are you injured?"

Seth indicated his belly with the tip of the Unforgiving Blade. "The Demon King stabbed me with this dark weapon. And it also cut my leg."

"An offspring of Raglamar," Konrad said somberly. "You bear a grievous wound."

"I feel a little better inside this dome," Seth said.

"Naturally," Konrad said. "You are at the Source. Look

around you. Breathing this air and basking in this light invigorates."

"Where is the actual Source?" Seth asked.

Konrad pointed at the pool. "You're looking at it."

"I pictured the actual Source brighter, like I'd have to squint to look at it," Seth said.

"This is pure light," Konrad said. "True light doesn't blind. It reveals."

"Everything is sharper and more vivid," Seth agreed.

"Pure light casts no shadows," Konrad pointed out.

As Seth looked around, he realized Konrad was right. He had no shadow. In the surrounding garden, no trunk, branch, or leaf made a shadow. It was part of what made everything so vivid. He had seen the phenomenon without naming it. "Weird."

Konrad shook his head slightly. "Even after all these years, I'm not sure if the light passes through solids or if it somehow comes from all directions."

"I think the light is thick, like syrup," Tess said. "It seeps around everything."

"Maybe," Konrad said with a nod.

"I want to give the good guys a chance to save Selona," Seth said. "Time is running out. What should I do?"

"Have you heard my story?" Konrad asked.

"Merek hit the essentials," Seth said.

"How much do you know about my last battle?" Konrad asked.

"Against that guy called the Dragon?" Seth asked.

"The warlord was an actual dragon in human form," Konrad said.

"Really?" Seth asked.

Konrad nodded. "That day of triumph earned me the enmity of several dragons and started me on the path to becoming a Dragon Slayer. I yearned to be a teller of tales more than I wanted to be a killer of monsters. But I am forever grateful I won the heart of the princess."

"Where is the princess?" Tess asked excitedly.

"Princess Lilianna, my wife, has departed from this world," Konrad said. "She took the best of me with her, I'm afraid."

"Merek mentioned that you're one of the undying," Seth said.

"Left alone, I would never perish," Konrad said. "Even if you struck me down with those swords, I would return. My wife, however, did not make the same choice I did. Lilianna lived an abnormally long life, but when she died, it was permanent."

"I'm sorry," Tess said.

"My wife got what she chose," Konrad said. "Lilianna never wanted to live forever. At least not in this mortal place. Living without her has taught me that I do not want to live forever either. Not here."

"How did she die?" Seth asked.

"The Dragon King Merazog killed her," Konrad said. "Merazog understood the only way to really hurt me. I slew him for it, but the damage was done."

"That's terrible," Tess said.

Konrad gave a nod of acknowledgment. He rubbed his knees. "I had a sacred trust to keep certain aspects of my story secret until somebody else learned about the Source. With you here, the time has come to share the complete version."

"All right," Seth said.

"While hunting the phoenix, I discovered this oasis," Konrad said, his gaze faraway. "The phoenix was alive and nesting here. And I found someone else as well."

"Who?" Tess asked.

"The Alderfairy," Konrad said. "The original Fairy Queen. The renowned mother of all fairies. She had set aside her crown to serve as guardian of the Source. You have to understand, I was barely alive when I found this oasis. Dehydrated and malnourished, I crawled to the brink of the pond in desperation. The Alderfairy appeared as I reached for what I believed to be water."

"It isn't water?" Tess asked.

"It's a substance called aether," Konrad said. "The Alderfairy explained the consequences of drinking aether from the Source. One sip and I would join the undying."

"That was why the Dragon couldn't kill you in the duel," Seth said.

"I had no guarantee that a taste of the aether would render death harmless to me," Konrad explained. "Only the word of the Alderfairy. My donkey, Rozeltine, drank too, and I almost tested the magic by killing him, but I couldn't bring myself to do it. I pretended he died, though, to avoid giving away too much. Until the Dragon bested me, I had never died. When he buried his sword in my chest, I was worried that my death meant the destruction of my kingdom. It was a great relief when I came back. In the end, the Source worked as promised."

"Everyone thought the feather brought you back to life," Seth said.

"The phoenix feather has great power," Konrad said. "With encouragement from the Alderfairy, I dipped all of my talismans in the Source. Contact with the aether heightened their power. But I survived the Dragon because I could not remain dead."

"How does it feel to die?" Seth asked. "Is there relief?"

"It's much like falling asleep," Konrad said. "I'm not sure I really know, because I've never stayed dead. After my battle with the Dragon, I had new problems to face."

"Where to bury him?" Tess asked.

"Well, I left the Dragon's body with his army," Konrad said. "I had decisions to make relevant to the Source. I didn't want to live forever without my family. But I had given an oath to the Alderfairy never to divulge what I had found. The balance of light and dark magic in the world depended on keeping the Source hidden."

"Did you keep the secret?" Seth asked.

"I never revealed I had found the Source," Konrad said. "I told my wife and kids that I had found a magical fountain that could prolong our lives. I explained that by drinking from it, we would become undying. I elaborated that washing in liquid from the fountain would renew our youth.

My wife chose to only wash with the fluid. As my children reached adulthood, they each elected to drink."

"How did they get the fluid if you kept the Source a secret?" Seth asked.

"Were they blindfolded?" Tess wondered.

"I got permission from the Alderfairy to fill my water-skin in the Source," Konrad said. "I brought the aether to them."

"Were there conditions?" Seth asked.

Konrad pointed at him. "You know something about fairies. There were indeed provisions. The Source must remain in balance with the Void. Before any of us could drink the aether, the Alderfairy demanded we pledge to serve as agents of balance. We agreed. Our primary function has been to keep dragons from overrunning the world."

"Have you slayed a lot of dragons?" Tess asked.

"I slew some," Konrad said. "Gerwin, Magdalena, Nadia, and especially Merek killed many more than I dispatched. Some of my children helped train other Dragon Slayers. But time created a new problem. We tried to conceal our pro-longed youth, but as the years went by, the people of Selona realized that while they aged, my family did not."

"What did you do?" Tess asked.

"I returned to the Alderfairy and made a new deal," Konrad said. "I wanted to share some of the benefits of the Source with my people. In return, my people would help the Alderfairy keep the balance. I dunked baskets of seeds in the Source. Then I watered crops and orchards with aether, car-ried to my kingdom in barrels hauled by me and Rozeltine.

All who partook of those crops and that fruit became the first generation of Fair Folk."

"The Fair Folk don't live forever," Seth said.

"No," Konrad said. "They received other effects. The crops they consumed did lengthen their lifespans, increased their physical beauty, and gave most of them a magical ability or two. All who partook of my special harvest vowed to serve as agents of balance, which is why they were called the Fair Folk."

"Did you grow more crops over the years?" Seth asked.

"No, that original harvest sufficed," Konrad said. "The attributes of the Fair Folk were passed down to their children through heredity. The orchards I planted continued to yield fruit, but experience taught that consuming additional fruit had little effect."

Seth pointed at the pool. "If I drink from the Source, will I live forever?"

"You would become undying," Konrad said. "Not quite immortal, but as close as you can get in this world."

"That is the last thing I want," Seth said.

Konrad studied him. "You've been hurt."

Seth choked back the reflexive laugh before it could turn to a sob. "You have no idea. And it doesn't matter. I just want to help my sister. I want to give Selona a chance against the dragons. What should I do?"

Konrad approached Seth and placed a hand on his shoulder. "Start by setting down the swords. You won't need them here."

"Without Vasilis, I'll collapse," Seth said, crouching to lay the Unforgiving Blade on the ground.

"That may be true outside this dome," Konrad agreed. "Not in here."

Seth sheathed Vasilis. Konrad was right. Sheathing it did not diminish his strength.

"You've reached the Source and you need healing," Konrad said. "Shall we find out what is possible?"

"Can it heal me?" Seth asked.

"I've seen the Source work wonders," Konrad said. "In my experience, it heals no two people the exact same way."

Seth peered down into the pool. "How deep is it?"

"That's undefinable," Konrad said. "This is a conduit into numberless realms of light."

"Does anything ever come through?" Seth asked.

"Besides magical energy from loftier spheres?" Konrad asked. "Very rarely. I have never witnessed such an event."

"I came through," a melodic voice said from behind Seth. "Long ago, when the world was young."

# CHAPTER FORTY-FOUR

# Alderfairy

Seth twisted to find a fairy coming toward him, perhaps three inches tall, elaborate wings rippling with variegated colors. At first her dress and wings looked like a smoldering sunset, but then green became dominant, followed by a sparkling blue.

"Where did you come from?" Seth asked, realizing belatedly that Konrad had dropped to one knee with his head bowed. Tess and Seth followed his example and knelt as well.

"I came from one of the eternal realms of light connected to the Source," the fairy said. "It is a place that would be difficult for you to comprehend from your present perspective. The entities that do not naturally pertain to this world had to come from somewhere. I have been in your world since it was young, and I have remained trapped here with Konrad since the barrier appeared. You may rise."

"Are you the Alderfairy?" Tess asked.

"That title suffices," the Alderfairy replied. "I am the original fairy, mother to all the others."

"I hoped you would favor us with your presence," Konrad said respectfully. "This boy Seth has been gravely injured. And he has brought the pieces of the Ethergem."

"This place is so pristine," Seth said. "I'm not sure I belong here."

"How does it compare to the Void?" the Alderfairy wondered.

Seth glanced at the Unforgiving Blade upon the grass, the only darkness in sight. Did she ask him because he was a shadow charmer?

"You are the only person to set foot here who has also been to the Void," the Alderfairy said.

"When was I at the Void?" Seth asked, gazing into the glassy pool. "I didn't even know the Void was an actual place."

The Alderfairy smiled. "For the Source to exist in your world, there must also be a Void. It is a place where the darkness has more substance. A location where darkness smothers light."

Seth remembered pushing through oppressive darkness as he crawled backward across a tile floor. "The lair of the Underking!" Seth exclaimed. "On the Phantom Isle!"

"That kind of darkness is hard to forget once you have

felt it," the Alderfairy said. "The Underking guards the Void."

"The darkness there was suffocating," Seth said. "The opposite of here."

"And now you are in a place of light and truth," the Alderfairy said. "I am wondering when our other visitor will make himself known."

"That would be me, I suppose," Calvin said sheepishly, poking his head out of Seth's pocket. "I intended no disrespect."

"And why are you here, giant of the nipsies?" the Alderfairy asked.

"Seth slew Graulas, making him the chosen one to break the nipsie curse," Calvin said. "I vowed to assist him."

"You have worthy goals," the Alderfairy said. "To resolve the nipsie curse, you must return the Ethergem to the sky giants."

"But the gem was broken by Raglamar," Seth said. "Whatever that sword cuts can't be repaired."

"I have heard that boast before," the Alderfairy said. "There is some truth to it. But the claim ignores the fundamentals of magic in this world. Raglamar was forged here, and anything with a beginning must have an end. Also, any attempt to produce a permanent effect in this world inevitably unravels. And any magic that can be done can also be undone."

"Can the Unforgiving Blade be destroyed?" Seth asked.

"Certainly," the Alderfairy said. "One who is guiltless need only place the blade into the Source."

Seth looked at his cousin. "Tess is an innocent."

"The Singing Sisters are masters of their trade," the Alderfairy said. "It is no coincidence that you arrived with your purehearted cousin."

Seth looked at the Alderfairy, scared to hope for too much. "What would happen to the wounds inflicted by the Unforgiving Blade if it were destroyed?"

"They will become regular wounds," the Alderfairy said. "Wounds that could potentially heal."

"Where would we be without healing?" Konrad said. "When I chose to become undying, I didn't understand all of the costs. Most were discovered through experience."

"I bet it gets exhausting," Seth said.

"The nature of a mortal world brings unique opportunities for development and change," Konrad said. "Even as one of the undying, I can only postpone my ending. This world itself will not endure forever, nor will the sun that warms it. To live in a mortal world is to sustain damage. Such environments are separate from the immortal realms of light and the eternal domains of darkness. Anyone born into this world becomes subject to entropy, deception, sickness, and death."

"That's depressing," Seth said.

"Challenges give us something to push against, a way to try our strength," Konrad said. "Challenges can also break us. After enough time here, our bodies sustain damage and die. The immortal spirit within can be harmed as well."

"I've felt that," Seth said.

"I have persisted in this world for a long time," Konrad

said. "That means I have absorbed significant damage. My body is undying, but what about my spirit? I lost the woman who became my reason for living. I have witnessed horrors I cannot forget. I have heard humans keen with pain like wild animals until their voices grew hoarse. I have felt my insides sicken with the realization of intimate betrayal. And I have perpetrated my own wrongs. I've damaged relationships, taken others for granted, maimed and killed on the field of battle. The only thing worse than enduring pain is knowing you have dealt it to others."

"Hurting others is the hardest part," Seth said. "Feeling like the world is worse off because I'm in it."

"My father was a cobbler," Konrad said. "I failed at his trade and two others. Nobody else was willing to take me on. And I couldn't blame them—I was a frustrating combination of lazy and headstrong. I couldn't figure out how to provide for myself, yet I dreamed of making a grand impact on the world. Then the king called for a hero. A volunteer was needed to perform an impossible task—or die trying. My whole life until that point had been a story of failure. Someone had to be willing to risk all they had for the good of the kingdom. That suddenly looked easy to me. I had nothing. I desperately wanted to leave my old self behind. So I decided to try."

"That was bold," Seth said.

"And simple," Konrad replied. "It changed everything for me."

"We're in the middle of an emergency," Seth said. "I

know you're trying to help me. But maybe we should move on to fixing the Ethergem."

Konrad gestured toward Seth's stomach. "The Source cannot heal you against your will."

"I've done things that can't be reversed," Seth said. "I got people killed. I got Agad killed. I started the dragon war. I freed the undead from the Blackwell at Wyrmroost and made it possible for Celebrant to overthrow the preserve. Sure, I had lost my memories, and yes, Ronodin tricked me, but I still made fatal mistakes. I don't deserve forgiveness."

Konrad regarded Seth for a long moment.

"Nobody in need of forgiveness deserves it," Konrad said. "Not one person. We all make foolish mistakes that we cannot fix. Though we may not deserve forgiveness, we all have a right to it. Just for having the courage to live in this difficult world, where fallible people do imperfect things. The supply of forgiveness is unlimited."

"The name of the Unforgiving Blade is no accident," the Alderfairy said. "Some wounds close only with forgiveness."

"And remain open forever without it," Konrad added.

Tears stung Seth's eyes. "How do I find forgiveness?"

"Just claim it," Konrad said. "Own your mistakes, then leave them behind as you keep trying. Also, you'll find that the more you forgive others, the easier it gets to forgive yourself."

"I'll try," Seth said.

"That's the best any of us can do," Konrad said, glancing at the Alderfairy.

"Tess," the Alderfairy said. "Would you kindly place the black sword into the Source?"

"Won't it harm her?" Seth whispered.

"I could not touch it," Konrad said. "Neither could the Alderfairy. Nor any dedicated servant of light. This girl is innocent, allowing her to cross certain lines without penalty."

Tess picked up the Unforgiving Blade and, holding it away from herself, walked over to the Source and tossed it in. A dark stain appeared in the aether around the blade, spreading outward. The light around the stain intensified, and the darkness withdrew, until the blade was again visible, now infused with brilliant luminosity. In a flash, the blade vanished.

Seth's hand went to the stab wound in his belly. It felt different. He no longer perceived the blade inside of him. His life had stopped draining into the emptiness. But a murky taint remained, beckoning him to join the undead.

"My wounds have changed," Seth said.

"All injuries delivered by that accursed blade are now regular wounds of this world," the Alderfairy said. "Everything cut by the Unforgiving Blade can now be mended."

"The blade is gone?" Seth asked.

"In the utter destruction of this fragment, Raglamar has been completely unmade," the Alderfairy said. "Meaning, to keep the balance, it can eventually be reforged, or an equivalent talisman of dark power can be created. But that will be a problem for another day."

"What about those I killed with the Unforgiving Blade?" Seth asked.

"Anything dead stays dead," the Alderfairy said. "But all remaining wounds have the chance to mend."

Seth felt relieved for Newell. Then he frowned. "I still feel darkness inside."

"The damage to your nature can also be repaired," the Alderfairy said. "But it will be more difficult than stitching a cut. You have a decision to make. Are you willing to renounce all darkness?"

Seth considered how much of his power derived from darkness. "Would I still be a shadow charmer?"

"No," the Alderfairy said. "The darkness within you would be expunged."

"You might find it rejuvenating," Konrad suggested.

Seth rubbed his brow. What use would he be without his shadow-charming abilities? He had come to rely on them. Then again, much of the trouble he had caused resulted from his ties to darkness.

"Renouncing darkness won't make me undying, right?" Seth checked.

"Not if you refrain from drinking the aether," Konrad said. "Immerse yourself in the Source, and that should purge the darkness without extending your lifespan. Be careful to keep your mouth closed."

"Will it heal my injuries?" Seth asked.

"This world can be debilitating," Konrad said. "But better, higher, purer realms exist. The Source is proof of that. It connects to them. This will benefit you. The aether works a little differently on everyone, depending on who they are and what they really want."

"Do you formally renounce darkness?" the Fairy Queen asked. "Will you serve the cause of light and strive to keep the balance?"

Seth thought about Graulas inviting him to become a shadow charmer. He considered the champions of darkness he had met, like Ronodin, the Underking, and the Demon King, then compared them to those who favored the light, like Bracken, the Fairy King, and his own family. Seth reflected about how he felt in the presence of the Void, contrasted with how he felt here beside the Source. He contemplated the misery of the undead, remembering how the Unforgiving Blade had felt inside of him. "Yes. I renounce darkness. I'll fight for the light. I'll help keep the balance."

"That is what I needed to hear," the Alderfairy said. "I have high hopes for you if you mean those words."

Seth glanced at the pool. "Do I jump in? Cannonball?"

"Keep hold of my hand," Konrad said. "I'll pull you out. If you go in untethered, we may never see you again."

The Alderfairy raised her tiny hands, palms outward. "Enter the Source with my blessing," she instructed.

Seth sat down on the edge and dipped his feet in. Warm tingles traveled up his legs. Keeping hold of Konrad's hand, he scooted off the edge, sinking completely into the aether. For a moment, time slowed, and Seth experienced overwhelming bliss. Not a single care or fear could trouble his mind. He was forgiven and deeply loved. Whether he lived or died, everything was going to be fine.

Konrad's hand sank below the surface with him, then hoisted him out. Seth scrambled away from the edge of the Source, aware that he was strangely dry for having just been immersed in fluid. A profound peace lingered. Tears blurred his vision.

"How do you feel?" Konrad asked.

Seth gave a little laugh. "I can't believe it. I feel amazing. People could get addicted. I never thought I'd feel this way again. I feel . . . alive. Like I've been in a deep sleep for a long time and I finally woke up. Almost . . . joyful."

"It happened," the Alderfairy said. "He made the full transition."

"What do you mean?" Seth asked, unable to suppress a smile.

"You must have been sincere," Konrad said. "Often exposure to the Source simply burns away the darkness. Which is marvelous. But occasionally, the darkness is replaced with light."

"Is that why I feel so good?" Seth asked.

"You'll find it's contagious," Konrad said. "You're no longer a shadow charmer, Seth. You're something much more unusual. You're a shadow healer."

# CHAPTER FORTY-FIVE

# Dragon Storm

Murky clouds massed on the horizon, laced with sickly streaks of green and yellow, like a fading bruise. Kendra stared at the strange sky from where she stood outside the main gate in the city wall, and Andromadus paused to look as well.

"An unnatural storm," the wizard said. "Apparently Celebrant has a flair for the dramatic."

"It's caused by the dragons?" Kendra asked. "Does that mean Celebrant has reached Selona?"

"At least some dragons have arrived," Andromadus said.

"All the more reason to get started," Serena called up from where she stood nearby.

"Agreed," Andromadus said. He waved a hand, and the air in front of Serena began to shimmer. Serena dashed into the shimmer and vanished.

"Is bringing a tiny army worth this effort?" Knox asked.

"It isn't much effort," Andromadus said. "The difficulty of teleportation increases with the mass of the subject. Opening a gateway for their entire army should be no harder than translocating a single person your size."

The shimmer flickered, and, with Serena at the forefront, the nipsie legions began marching out of the portal. Being around Calvin and Serena had helped Kendra forget that regular nipsies were the size of grains of rice. In groups they hauled war engines—catapults that could fit inside a shot glass, ballistae that could rest atop a quarter. The multitude looked more like a colony of ants than a military force.

Knox leaned toward Andromadus and spoke softly. "They're going to help us fight dragons? Their whole civilization could be destroyed by a hungry raccoon!"

Andromadus answered quietly. "We put out a call for aid. Few have responded. Many have expressed that any attempt to resist Celebrant's full host is doomed to failure. Some of them denied assistance despite knowing we protect the skull of Abraxas. And yet this tiny force has volunteered eagerly. They are small enough to remain beneath the notice of the dragons. Perhaps they can find a way to prove useful."

"The nipsies are no less suited to fight dragons than we are," Kendra said. "The city wall is about fifteen feet high. How many dragons will that stop? How many will rethink their attack because of your size, Knox?"

"At least some of our humans have killed dragons before," Knox said.

"The nipsies are standing with us," Andromadus said. "Which is more than many of our larger allies can claim."

The nipsies fanned out after coming through the portal, inching forward in various directions. "That's everyone," Serena called as the final columns paraded out of the portal.

Andromadus waved a hand and the shimmer vanished. "Stay off the road," the wizard warned the nipsies. "This is a high traffic area and there is danger of being crushed."

"We'll deploy intelligently," Serena assured him.

Kendra watched the nipsie forces disappear into the grass at either side of the road. Raising her gaze, she saw the eight sky giants who had arrived earlier, lined up before the city wall with broad shields and heavy armor. It made Kendra sad to consider how much more effective one giant would be against the dragons than the entire nipsie civilization. There was a real chance the upcoming battle could push the nipsies to extinction. Hopefully some had stayed behind at Fablehaven.

"Here comes Merek," Knox observed.

Against the backdrop of brooding storm clouds, Kendra noticed light glinting off golden wings in the distance. Merek had gone to scout the crossroads to see if dragons were coming through yet. His prompt return was not a good sign.

"Any updates from Bracken?" Kendra asked.

"He will be here soon," Andromadus said. "I created two extra portals into Selona. Bracken has reported reaching the entrance nearest to Fairview."

"Why not just zap him here like the nipsies?" Knox asked.

"I'm conserving my strength for the upcoming siege," Andromadus said. "Bracken escaped the Fairy Realm to a preserve in Ukraine, which placed him and his sister a reasonable distance from the portal near Krakow."

"The portals were made for the refugees," Kendra explained to Knox. "Agents of Dragonwatch and other allies who escaped fallen preserves. There were too many to teleport in one by one, and it was too dangerous to have a lot of traffic at the crossroads."

"What if bad guys start sneaking through the portals?" Knox asked.

"They are being watched," Andromadus said. "I can collapse them at any time."

Merek arrowed toward them at top speed. He looked flustered when he landed, but his voice remained steady. "Dragons are pouring through at the crossroads. The attack is imminent. We should withdraw to battle positions."

"I'll wait here for Bracken," Kendra said.

"I saw him on my way here," Merek said. "He's close. I'm surprised we can't see him yet."

"Kendra, we need to fall back behind the city wall," Andromadus said. "We will raise the magical barrier immediately after Bracken and his sister enter."

Kendra knew the barrier was the most important element protecting the town, an invisible force field that would cover them like a dome, so she followed orders, even though it greatly reduced her line of sight. After passing beyond the gate, Kendra considered ascending the wall for a better view, but she decided she would rather be on the road when Bracken entered Fairview.

The rising wind gusted through the open gate, heralding the oncoming storm. Kendra heard the quick, patterned hoofbeats of a horse at full gallop. The drumming increased in volume as a unicorn with a male rider raced into view at a pace much faster than any racehorse could attain.

After Bracken rode through the gate, Andromadus gave a signal, and several wizards began chanting, a few with arms upraised, others clutching staffs. The gate closed. Bracken sprang from the back of the unicorn, sliding to a stop in front of Kendra.

Bracken's concerned gaze searched Kendra's face as if taking full measure of what he had missed. With a sudden smile, he pulled her into an embrace, tilting back until she stood on her tiptoes.

When he released her, Kendra staggered a little. "You're here."

"Sorry it took so long," Bracken said. "You're hard to catch up with. At least I made it ahead of the dragons."

The unicorn Bracken had been riding melted into human shape, and Lizelle gave Kendra a hug. "It's good to see you again, Kendra."

"How did you escape?" Kendra asked.

"Ronodin's control is slipping," Bracken said.

"He keeps offending the fairies," Lizelle said. "And the crown is unwieldy for him. The more he tries to channel its power, the faster his limitations are revealed."

"Ronodin will eventually undo himself," Bracken said. "Now, how do we stop thousands of dragons? Is there a plan for defending Selona?"

"A caravan of Fair Folk went north to a large cave system," Kendra said. "We'll make sure some stragglers are visible to the dragons. Six separate groups are traveling to other fortified locations. We're hoping these groups will draw dragons away from the city."

"That might help a little," Bracken said.

"We know we can't face them on open ground," Kendra continued. "We have squads of Fair Folk under the strongest bridge in Fairview and taking up positions in the sturdiest buildings around town. We want Celebrant to wonder where the skull is hidden. If the dragons have to get close to kill, it will give us a chance to strike back."

"Better than open ground, maybe, but that is still poor shelter against dragons," Bracken said. "Many will die. It won't take long."

"Where is the skull?" Lizelle asked.

Kendra leaned close. "In the deepest chamber of the castle's dungeon, below many halls much too narrow for dragons. Hundreds of the best Fair Folk soldiers are positioned down where the dragons will be forced to take human form. The Somber Knight, Vanessa, and others await in the room with the skull."

"Why Vanessa?" Bracken asked.

"We picked up a dragon named Dagny who pledged herself to Dragonwatch," Kendra said. "Dagny prefers her human form, but she agreed to drink a sleeping potion and let Vanessa control her dragon shape."

"Ordinarily a dragon would be too powerful for a narcoblix to control," Bracken said.

"But this is voluntary," Kendra said.

"A good idea," Lizelle said.

"What else?" Bracken asked.

"The rest of the Fair Folk are stationed on the walls and in the castle," Kendra said. "Opportunities for ambushes abound among the alleys of the town and the corridors of the castle. We have a decent amount of giant crossbows and some catapults. Wizards have raised magical barriers."

"The castle had none built in?" Bracken asked.

"No," Kendra said. "There has been peace here for a long time."

"We're facing Celebrant's full horde," Bracken said.

"At least two thousand dragons," Kendra said.

Bracken laced his fingers behind his head and whistled. "Without the Dragon Slayers, ten strong dragons would have a good chance of taking this castle. With the Dragon Slayers, thirty should be able to do it. Celebrant and his elite guards could probably handle the job themselves. But two thousand? The magical shields will last only minutes against such an onslaught. Especially if the shields have to be broad enough to cover the whole town."

"Then we'll fall back to the castle," Kendra said. "It will be shielded separately."

"Even the castle barriers won't last forever," Bracken said.

"What about fighting them in the dungeon halls?" Kendra asked.

"It's a good idea under the circumstances," Lizelle said. "But if the dragons are smart and use a little patience, they can collapse underground hallways and clear passages with their breath weapons."

"Celebrant is about as clever as they come," Bracken said.

"Our main hope is taking him out," Kendra said. "And his son, Tamryn. Merek and Gerwin will target them."

"It's nice to know we have two legendary Dragon Slayers on the front line," Bracken said. "But how will they access the Dragon King?"

"Merek has wings," Kendra said. "And Gerwin will be riding the winged horse Noble."

"It's a bold gambit," Lizelle said.

"I see the merit," Bracken conceded. "But Dragon Slayers operate much better when they can isolate their targets. I worry for their safety flying into a sky crowded with dragons to hunt the biggest game on the planet."

"If we slay Celebrant and Tamryn, the nature of the war could change," Kendra said.

"The dragons would not hold together as such a cohesive unit without Celebrant," Bracken said. "But that wouldn't save Selona. The dragons will burn this country to cinders if their leader dies here."

"And they will finish their intended task," Lizelle said. "After they destroy the Sovereign Skull, who knows what they will do? It would depend on how much Celebrant's successor shares his grudges and goals."

"Does Andromadus have an escape plan for you?" Bracken asked.

"He thinks he can get a good number of us away if it comes to it," Kendra said.

Bracken considered Kendra somberly. "I care about you."

Mouth dry, Kendra nodded.

"I need you to be ready to flee," Bracken said.

"We have to win," Kendra said. "Too much depends on it. Do you have your horns?"

"I didn't manage to escape with them," Bracken said. "Lizelle has her third horn."

"Here is your first," Kendra said, handing over his smallest horn. "Better than nothing?"

"Much better than nothing," Bracken said. "I wish I had stored all of them with you."

"Seth is on a secret mission from the Singing Sisters," Kendra said. "They told him it could give us a chance."

"The Sisters are wise," Bracken said. "Did they mention how much of a chance?"

"Dragons!" a voice called from the top of the wall.

A moment later, diverse voices took up the cry, until the clamor bordered on panic.

"Silence!" Andromadus boomed in an enormous voice. "Dragons thrive on fear. Make your final preparations. If you were given courage potions, take them now."

"Fair Folk can usually avoid paralysis from dragon fear," Bracken said. "Not all of them, but a majority."

"Kendra," Knox said, approaching. "Should we climb the wall so we can see?"

Bracken gave Kendra a wry smile. "It will be a sight none have ever witnessed—this many dragons attacking at once."

"None have encountered a quarter this many," Lizelle said.

They started toward the stairs.

"Ready for battle?" Bracken asked, clapping Knox on the back.

"I took my courage potion, so I'm feeling pretty good," Knox said.

"Lizelle, this is my cousin Knox," Kendra said.

"I'm the former Giant King," Knox said casually.

"It's an honor to meet you," Lizelle said.

The top of the wall was nearly ten feet wide. After climbing the stairs, Kendra advanced to a crenellation in the parapet and stared out at the foreboding clouds. Odd shades of lightning flickered and flashed, mostly greens and blues.

Kendra gasped.

Ahead of the clouds, the sky was thick with dragons.

Talking about thousands of dragons was one thing. Seeing them was another. The dragon storm heading their way made the assault on Titan Valley look like a gentle sprinkle.

"We are so dead," Knox moaned.

"Lizelle, stay with Kendra and Knox," Bracken said. "Take your true form and run them to the castle when the time is right."

"Where are you going?" Kendra asked.

"I have an observation to share with Andromadus," Bracken said. "And I want to find out where I can be most useful."

"What's the observation?" Kendra asked.

Bracken gestured at the sky. "Why would dragons summon a storm? Rough air makes flying problematic."

"Good question," Kendra said.

"Notice the storm is staying behind the dragons," Bracken said. "It isn't coming with them."

"Does it give them a tailwind?" Knox asked.

"Sure, but they don't need help flying here," Bracken said. "It's a short trip."

"Then why make the storm?" Kendra asked.

"The dragons know we have wizards here," Bracken said. "Celebrant probably realizes the greatest threat to his attack would be weather magic. That storm they made is meant to preempt what we might do. If we send a storm at them, they will try to use theirs to blow ours back. I want to make sure Andromadus has considered every atmospheric advantage we can create."

"Go!" Knox urged, waving Bracken away. "We need all the help we can get."

Bracken ran along the top of the wall to where Andromadus stood consulting with three other wizards.

Bracken spoke animatedly, gesturing toward the distant clouds.

Merek landed beside Kendra. The town had gone quiet as everyone moved to positions with a view of the oncoming dragons.

"The scale of this attack is unprecedented," Merek said.

"Dragons came to our aid at Zzyzx," Kendra said. "There must be a hundred times that many heading our way now. But this time they're not here to help."

"You're going to fly into that?" Knox asked Merek.

"It doesn't appear to be a great idea," Merek said. "I just hope I last long enough to reach Celebrant."

"Gerwin should be here soon with Noble," Kendra said.

"Two flying Dragon Slayers against two thousand dragons," Merek said. "Not the odds I would choose."

"How will you even get close to Celebrant?" Knox asked. "Won't the dragons blast you out of the sky before you reach him?"

"We have a secret strategy," Merek said. "Only Gerwin and I know the specifics. And one other person. We can't risk the idea leaking."

"Can you tell us now?" Knox asked.

"You'll see soon enough," Merek said.

Bracken returned. "Kendra, I'm heading to a tower in the middle of town. See, over there? The one with six enormous crankbows. While others reload, Andromadus wants me to aim them."

"Won't you be a target up there?" Kendra asked.

"A target launching spear-sized arrows every five

seconds or so," Bracken said. "It will be better than trying to fight dragons from the ground." He gazed out past the battlements. "There are too many dragons for the magical shield to hold out long."

"I'll watch over her," Lizelle assured him. "We need Kendra here."

"Try to stay out of harm's way," Bracken said to Kendra, giving her hand a squeeze, his eyes lingering on hers for a moment. A trumpet sounded, and he took off at a sprint.

"Did you consider asking for physical aid from the demons?" Merek called over to Kendra.

"Andromadus looked into it," Kendra said. "The demons would join the battle only if we released a bunch of their friends from the prison to help, including Orogoro and Brogo. The price was too high—we didn't want to start a new apocalypse to slow the current one."

"They're closing in fast," Knox announced.

Kendra looked out at the dragons. She could now distinguish differences in shape and color. They were organized in clusters, like squadrons of bombers ready to demolish a city.

"I'm going to shine at them," Kendra told Lizelle. "Want to boost me?"

"Focus your brightness outward, like a lighthouse lantern," Lizelle said. "It should cast a glare into their eyes."

"I'll hit them with all I have," Kendra said.

"I'll be careful not to look back at you," Merek said. "The disturbance should help me reach Celebrant."

The invisible barrier shielding the battlements flashed

temporarily into view right above them with a flat burst of blue energy. Kendra flinched away from the strobe and heard an electric crackle. A moment later, Raxtus appeared outside the invisible barrier, hovering just beyond the wall, having approached unseen.

"A shield!" Raxtus exclaimed. "I should have realized. Good thing my scales are durable. It was impossible to see— you should put up a sign."

Startled murmurs passed along the top of the wall at the sight of the glittering dragon.

"Where should I fight?" Raxtus asked.

"This dragon is an ally," Merek shouted. "Can we bring him inside?"

"Through the main gate," Andromadus called. "I have a wizard on it for just such an emergency. Chuntao can make a breach in the barrier and temporarily open the gate."

Merek zoomed away. After a pause, the main gate opened, and Raxtus flew through. The undersized dragon perched on the wall beside Kendra, the defenders along the parapet pushing away to make room.

"How did you get here?" Kendra asked.

"Seth and I stole Father's crown," Raxtus said. "The dragons chased me, but I eventually gave them the slip. Seth was so far ahead of me that I decided to return to the muster instead of trying to find him. When the drag-ons started sneaking into Selona at the crossroads, I came through invisibly, right under their noses. Outflying them here was no great feat."

"I'm so glad you're safe," Kendra said.

"Are you serious about fighting?" Merek asked.

"Whatever I can do," Raxtus said.

"Gerwin and I are hunting your father," Merek said. "I have wings, but Gerwin had been planning to ride a flying horse."

"You want me to carry a Dragon Slayer into battle against my father?" Raxtus asked. "Is it my birthday or something?"

"Is that a yes?" Merek checked.

"I have unfinished business with Celebrant," Raxtus said. "It's a definite yes."

"Excellent," Merek said, turning to Kendra. "I don't want to overemphasize the peril, but this is probably a one-way trip for Gerwin and me. Noble would almost certainly have perished too. But this dragon is wily. He might survive."

"Those dragons are almost here," Knox said. "If this shield doesn't hold, we're going to be roasted alive."

"The shield felt solid to me," Raxtus mentioned.

Andromadus came along the top of the wall, followed by Gerwin astride Noble. "It's almost time," the wizard said.

"Change of plans," Merek announced. "Raxtus will carry Gerwin into battle."

"Wait!" Noble said. "This was my moment."

Merek pointed at the dragons. "Fly into that swarm and you will die."

"In the best way ever," Noble replied.

"You'll have plenty of chances for bravery today,"

Kendra said. "There are others who could use your help, especially if we have to make a quick escape."

Gerwin slipped off Noble and crossed to Raxtus. "Your back looks spiny."

"I'll carry you in my claws," Raxtus said.

"I never expected you to fully turn against your father," Andromadus said.

"I never expected my father to put his ambitions above the good of dragonkind," Raxtus said.

"We have to eliminate him," Andromadus said. "Slaying Celebrant will move all dragons onto a better path."

"I hear you," Raxtus said. "He won't see me coming."

"I'm going to improve the endeavor," Andromadus said. "As soon as we spot the Dragon King, I'll teleport you, Gerwin, and Merek near him."

Raxtus stared at the wizard. "That could give us a real chance."

"We're about to find out," Andromadus replied.

"I can provide a distraction," Kendra said.

"She can shine more blindingly than anyone I have seen," Lizelle added.

"Once we engage them, back off with the light," Merek said. "It should leave them dazzled, and that will allow us to maneuver without getting blinded as well."

The lead dragons were now close enough for the group to distinguish features—horns and frills, whiskers and wattles, scales of every shade. Many had their mouths agape, baring nightmare rows of razor teeth. The dragons spread wide, curling around Fairview to attack from all directions. Squadrons of dragons broke off from the main body, chasing down the decoy forces Andromadus had sent abroad.

"There," Raxtus said. "High and to the right, near the top of the formation, several ranks back. Father is flying near Tamryn."

"I see him," Andromadus confirmed. "Kendra?"

Lizelle rested a hand on Kendra's shoulder. Kendra effortlessly found her power and, holding up one hand, projected a cone of blazing light from her palm. She could feel the extra energy and control Lizelle lent to the effort. Swinging her arm, Kendra swept the glaring light across the oncoming horde, then deliberately spotlighted the area where Celebrant was flying for a prolonged moment.

"Enough," Andromadus said.

Kendra lowered her hand and extinguished her light. The formerly organized dragons had broken ranks and now flew in disarray. Glancing over her shoulder, Kendra saw that Raxtus, Gerwin, and Merek were gone. She followed Lizelle's gaze to the sky.

In the vicinity of Celebrant, a huge orange dragon turned to ash beside the golden gleam of Merek's wings. Kendra could not find Raxtus, but she saw fiery darts streaking toward Celebrant. The Dragon King turned away from the darts, curling his head into his chest, and other dragons moved to block them. A dragon that got hit in the wing spiraled out of the sky. The darts that impacted against Celebrant did no visible harm.

"His scales are too tough," Andromadus murmured. "They need to hit the eyes."

Merek streaked toward Celebrant while his head was tucked away, and a second volley of flaming darts took flight. Just before Merek reached Celebrant, a silver dragon nearly the size of the Dragon King intercepted the Dragon Slayer.

"Tamryn," Lizelle muttered.

Tamryn spewed fire, but Merek got in close, and the son of Celebrant dissolved into a cloud of ash. Celebrant had reset in the air, and even as fiery darts rocketed toward his head, the Dragon King unleashed a searing exhalation of pure white energy that evaporated Merek. An instant later, flaming darts exploded against the side of Celebrant's head.

One eye maimed, the enraged Dragon King roared, his fury momentarily overpowering all other commotion. Raxtus became visible, caught in the jaws of a colossal black dragon that went hurtling toward the ground. Kendra watched anxiously, hoping Raxtus would shake free, but they crashed together. She could not tell what had happened to Gerwin.

"Obliterate them!" Celebrant bellowed, streaking toward the city wall. His jaws spread wide, and an intense column of white energy slammed against the invisible shield, making the entire wall shudder.

Kendra held up a hand, searching for her power, but Lizelle pulled her away from the battlements. "Time to fall back," Lizelle demanded.

Kendra, Lizelle, and Knox bounded down the stairs. Lizelle hit the ground first and immediately transformed into a sleek unicorn. Kendra climbed onto her back, and Knox scrambled up behind his cousin. The unicorn shot forward, accelerating to an incredible speed so smoothly that Kendra felt no fear of falling.

Looking over her shoulder, Kendra saw an incomprehensible barrage of fire, lightning, energy, acid, frost, and fluid forcing the magical shield to flex inward. The city wall quaked so violently that merlons toppled and great fissures opened from top to bottom. Amid the relentless bombardment of dragon breath, other dragons physically rammed the barrier, and, with a noise like the breaking of the world, the magical shield shattered.

The Fair Folk manning the city wall scattered. Many screamed as they fell, bodies on fire. Kendra fixed her gaze forward as a tide of dragons flowed into Fairview from all sides.

# CHAPTER FORTY-SIX

# Ethergem

D id you notice your wings?" Tess asked.

"What?" Seth replied.

"They turned white," she said.

Seth checked. Still metallic, they now gleamed like platinum. "You're right."

"You look happy," Tess said.

Seth smiled at her. "I can't remember the last time it felt natural to smile. When it just came easily. I feel way too good, considering dragons are about to attack Selona."

"Let's see what we can do with the pieces of the Ethergem," Konrad said.

Seth rummaged in his satchel, pulling out the fragments one by one. "Dragon King's jewel, Giant Queen's gem, half of the Wizenstone, Demon King's jewel, other half of the Wizenstone." He looked over at Tess. "She has the Ethershard."

Tess held it up.

"That's all of it," the Alderfairy said. "Graulas could have fully destroyed the Ethergem, but he put the fragments to work instead."

"Can it be repaired?" Seth asked.

"We'll find out soon," Konrad said. "I haven't told you how I came to be at the Source when the spell sealed it off."

"What were you doing?" Tess asked.

"I was delivering a message to the Alderfairy," Konrad said. "A message from the Singing Sisters."

"They were around back then?" Seth asked.

"The Sisters predate almost everyone," Konrad said. "Those who protect the balance tend to encounter them."

"What was the message?" Tess asked.

"'That which was broken by betrayal can be mended through sacrifice,'" the Alderfairy said.

"I didn't understand those words until you arrived with the pieces of the Ethergem," Konrad said. "I finally see my role in all of this."

"You don't have to do it, Konrad," the Alderfairy said.

"I know," Konrad replied. "But I feel it is time." He looked at Seth. "The thing about the Singing Sisters is they play the long game."

"They're why you got trapped here," Seth said.

"So I would be present when you arrived," Konrad said. "Among many other reasons, I'm sure."

"What sacrifice did they mean?" Tess asked.

"The one sacrifice I have withheld all of these millennia," Konrad said. "My life." He looked at the Alderfairy. "Will it be enough?"

The Alderfairy fluttered her wings. "To voluntarily move on after so long, when you have the option to persist? Yes, it will be enough."

"That settles it," Konrad said.

"Wait," Seth said. "You're going to die?"

"The Source unnaturally prolonged my days," Konrad said. "Too many of those days have been spent without my wife. It's time to see if I can catch up to her." Konrad winked. "I'm going to return the gift the Source gave me, and maybe help Selona one last time."

"You have been my most reliable servant," the Alderfairy said. "I am sorry to see you depart."

"Perhaps we will meet again," Konrad said. "For now, you have a new servant to train."

"Indeed," the Alderfairy said. "Seth, should you survive the conflict in Selona, as one who has pledged to help maintain the balance, I ask that you return to me."

"I will," Seth said.

"And now to the matter of the Ethergem," the Alderfairy said.

"What must I do?" Konrad asked.

"Gather the fragments," the Alderfairy said. "Hold your intent clear in your mind. With the pieces of the Ethergem in your grasp, descend into the Source. I will take care of the rest."

Konrad gathered the jewels into his hands. Tess added

the Ethershard last. "Seth, when you get the chance, please tell my children that I love them, and that I will forever be watching for them. Tess, it was my pleasure to meet you. Thank you for leading Seth here."

"I won't forget you," Tess said.

"Tess, when the Ethergem is mended, you will need to carry it for Seth," the Alderfairy said. "Your innocence will shield you. The gem is too much for most to handle."

"I will," Tess said.

"Just scoop it out of the aether when I tell you," the Alderfairy said.

Tess nodded somberly. "All right."

"Calvin, do you know where to take the Ethergem?" Konrad checked.

"To the sky giants," the nipsie said. "To break the curse."

"It's the top priority," Konrad said. "Before you return to Selona."

"We can do it quickly," Seth said. "I have a device called the Translocator."

"I noticed," Konrad said. "I'm familiar with the device. Remember—sky giants first, then Selona. Fight hard. Set things right."

"Got it," Seth said. "How can I ever thank you?"

"Save Selona," Konrad said.

Konrad walked to the brink of the Source, bouncing on his toes. He glanced at the Alderfairy. "It was a privilege to serve you. Seemed long while it lasted. Seems like a blink now."

"Any amount of time always feels brief at its end," the Alderfairy said.

Taking a deep breath, Konrad peered down into the Source. "One last adventure."

"It's the beginning of much more," the Alderfairy said. "You'll see."

"Do a cannonball," Tess requested.

"How?" Konrad asked.

"Legs folded up," Seth said, "so you make a splash."

Konrad shrugged and gave a little smile. "Sure. Why not?" His eyes swept the garden around him. "I'll miss this place."

"It's better where you're going," the Alderfairy said. "In almost every way."

"But this world has been home for so long," Konrad said. "I suppose we all have a last day."

He leaped forward, tucked his legs, and vanished into the aether.

The Alderfairy flashed brightly. Her eyes were closed, her tiny arms outstretched, palms down.

"Remove the gem from the aether, child," the Alderfairy intoned.

Tess knelt at the edge of the Source. Seth stayed by her, in case she toppled forward. Crouching, she reached down with both hands and lifted an oblong gem of the purest white from the aether.

"It is done," the Alderfairy said.

"What now?" Seth asked.

"Hurry to the sky giants," the Alderfairy said. "Time

grows short. Defend Selona. If you live, return to me. Tell no one about the Source."

"Tess," Seth said. "Can you put a hand on the Translocator while holding the gem?"

Tess cradled the Ethergem in one arm and placed her free hand on the top segment of the Translocator. Picturing a town square, Seth twisted the middle.

Seth shrank inward, then stood in the town square where he had stolen the Ethershard. It was night. Enormous buildings surrounded him.

"Why is it dark?" Tess asked.

"We're on the other side of the world," Seth said. He looked around. The three cages remained—large, medium, and small. The platform was still there. But the cauldron was gone. And there were no guards. The square was deserted.

"What now?" Tess asked.

"I brought back the Ethergem!" Seth yelled as loudly as he could, his voice small in the gigantic square.

There came no reply.

"Grab the Translocator again," Seth instructed.

Tess complied.

Seth twisted the center, and an instant later they were standing in the belfry above the square.

"You'll be safer up here," Seth said. "In case there is a misunderstanding."

Leaving his cousin in the tower with the Ethergem, Seth soared down to the bell affixed to the largest cage, noticing that his wings had more thrust than ever before. He seized the string attached to the clapper, which, in his hands, felt uncomfortably thick. Swaying from side to side, Seth began ringing the bell.

One strike was all the bell needed, and a familiar, magically enhanced alarm started blaring. Seth flew higher into the air and watched as befuddled giants rushed to the square. A giant wearing long underwear hustled to the bell and touched it gently, and the alarm ceased.

"I'm up here!" Seth called.

Half a dozen giants glared up at him, sleepy and annoyed.

"I brought the Ethergem back to you," Seth declared. "The whole thing."

"What are you talking about?" asked the giant who had silenced the alarm.

"I took the Ethershard," Seth said. "I'm sorry for the trouble. I did it so I could return with the entire Ethergem. Who can accept it?"

"Officially," Calvin prompted.

"Who can officially accept it?" Seth amended.

"This can't be true," one of the giants said, removing his nightcap to scratch the crown of his head.

"It's a trick," another asserted.

"Look, this isn't a trick," Seth said. "But I need you to hurry, or I might take back the offer. We're trying to fix an ancient wrong, and it's an emergency."

The giants huddled and conferred, and then two ran off in different directions.

The giant who had silenced the alarm called to Seth, "If this is true, you will be a legend. If you're lying, I will personally hunt you down and feast on your flesh."

"I'd be more of a light snack," Seth said. "But I hear what you're saying. Luckily, this isn't a lie or a trick. Do you have a name?"

"Ulnick," the giant replied.

"I'm Seth."

"We're fetching the appropriate parties," Ulnick said.

"Am I still speaking Jiganti?" Seth checked.

"Fluently," Ulnick confirmed.

"At least I kept that ability," Seth murmured.

He waited. Other giants began to gather. As the crowd surpassed fifty, two giants came to the forefront. One wore a pale green toga, and a laurel rested on his curly, white hair. "I am Dectus, acting governor of the sky giants."

The other prominent giant was an older woman wearing a loose robe sashed about her waist. "And I am Madam Ladonna. You claim to have retrieved the Ethergem?"

"Yes," Seth said.

"This is exceptionally difficult to believe," Dectus said.

"Many years ago, the Ethergem was irreparably sundered," Madam Ladonna stated.

"Well, I gathered all the pieces, destroyed what remained of Raglamar, and had some help fixing the Ethergem," Seth said:

"May we see the gem?" Dectus asked.

"First I need to clarify a couple of things," Seth said. "My name is Seth Sorenson. I'm the one who stole the Ethershard. I also took the gem from the Giant Queen's crown. I request a full pardon from that."

"If you indeed brought the Ethergem, you will be a giant friend until the end of cloud and sky," Dectus said.

"I did not come alone," Seth said. "A nipsie named Calvin helped me."

The mention of a nipsie caused murmuring among the assemblage.

"He would like to share some words," Seth said.

"Come closer," Madam Ladonna said. "We pledge to do you no harm until after these claims are sorted out. If you brought back the Ethergem, you have nothing to fear."

Seth flew down to Madam Ladonna's shoulder and held Calvin on his palm. "Is this close enough?" Seth asked.

"Ah, I see him, but only because my eyesight is superb," Madam Ladonna said. "Speak up, Calvin of the nipsies."

"I am here to apologize on behalf of my people," Calvin said. "We were tricked into stealing the Ethergem ages ago. As representatives of the nipsies, Seth and I have come to return what was lost."

"I see," Dectus said. "May we examine this alleged Ethergem?"

"One moment," Seth said. He flew up to the belfry, alighted beside Tess, and held out the Translocator. After a quick twist, they stood on the ground before Dectus and Madam Ladonna.

"I'm down here!" Seth called.

"We see you," Madam Ladonna said.

"Go ahead," Seth murmured to Tess.

His cousin placed the Ethergem on the ground, and they backed away.

Madam Ladonna gasped. She bent forward, scrutinized the Ethergem, then inspected it again through a lens. "Stay back," she commanded, motioning for the other giants to make space. "Unbelievably, they have done it! This is indeed the Ethergem, returned as if from the dead. Assemble the guards. Cordon off the area. We must handle this treasure with caution and care. Do you realize what this means? Do you comprehend the import? Stratos can be restored!"

The sky giants broke into spontaneous, uproarious cheering.

"Let me speak," Calvin requested.

Seth extended his arm with Calvin on his palm. "My nipsie friend has more to say!"

Madam Ladonna and Dectus hushed the crowd. "Say whatever you wish," Dectus invited. "This miracle defies my wildest imaginings."

"We nipsies were cursed for betraying you," Calvin called. "With the return of the Ethergem, will you accept our apology?"

"Absolutely," Dectus said. "Apology accepted."

At those words, Calvin immediately expanded. Surprised, Seth dropped him and shuffled back. Calvin shot up until Seth was not quite the height of his knees.

"There you are," Madam Ladonna said. "You grew." Calvin now came almost to her waist.

"Thank you very much," Calvin said. "We hate to meet you and run, but we are dealing with an emergency." Calvin bent toward Seth. "Translocator," he whispered.

Seth held out the Translocator. "What happened to you?"

Calvin shrugged. "My people made me a giant. Let's go."

"Tess, grab hold of the bottom," Seth said. "Calvin, you have the top?"

Envisioning his destination, Seth twisted the middle.

# CHAPTER FORTY-SEVEN

# Reinforcements

Hooves pummeling the cobblestones, Lizelle turned down another alley as dragon breath transformed the street she left behind into an inferno. Looking up, Kendra saw dragons crisscrossing the narrow slice of sky visible from the alleyway.

"Are we going to make it?" Knox asked.

"We will reach the castle," Lizelle confirmed.

"It feels like we keep backtracking," Knox said.

"To avoid dragons," Lizelle said. "Which is why we're going to survive. Keep your weapons handy."

Kendra clutched her bow and Knox carried the sack of gales. Despite her great haste, the unicorn galloped so smoothly that Kendra could hold her bow ready with both hands. They burst out of the alley onto a wide avenue and pelted toward the castle. Dragons wheeled overhead at various altitudes.

The thoroughfare was deserted except for some burning wagons and torched vegetable stands. The soldiers were learning quickly to fight from cover. Kendra leaned forward. If Lizelle maintained their current speed, they would reach the castle in less than thirty seconds.

Then a huge bronze dragon dropped down onto the avenue in front of them. Lizelle swerved toward a side street, but then veered away from the two spindly dragons flying toward them, mouths agape, fumigating the road with bright green gas.

"Poison," Lizelle murmured.

Knox used a gust of wind to push the gas away from them and disrupt the flight of the spindly dragons. Then Lizelle was charging the bronze dragon.

The dragon opened its mouth and expelled a searing burst of lightning that streaked over Kendra's shoulder, exploding thunderously somewhere behind her. Kendra pulled the bowstring to her cheek, whispered, "Thirty," and released. The dragon tucked its head, and the swarm of arrows rebounded off metallic scales.

With a battle cry, an enormous woman leaped from a rooftop near the bronze dragon and plunged a long spear through the base of its neck. The dragon hissed and snapped at the giant woman, who warded off the attack with a heavy sword. It took Kendra a moment to recognize the giant as Serena. Had Tanu given her a potion?

"Get to the castle, Kendra," Serena cried. "We'll cover you."

Soldiers in unfamiliar armor appeared on the roof Serena had jumped from. Each pair of soldiers carried a bulky crossbow between them, with a third infantryman operating the firing mechanism.

The javelin-length projectiles from the hefty crossbows pierced the bronze hide, and the dragon flew away shrieking, the spear still transfixing the base of the neck. More soldiers in heavy armor appeared on the street, bearing pikes and longbows.

"Ride, Kendra," one of them called.

"I think it's the nipsies," Kendra said. "They're our size."

"And Serena is a giant," Knox marveled.

"Cover us," Lizelle said, increasing her pace to top speed. "We're almost to the castle gate."

Seth appeared on the castle balcony he had departed from earlier in the day. Beside him, Tess peered over the balustrade, and Calvin, absurdly tall, filled the rest of the ledge.

They stared in stunned silence at the panoramic scene of destruction. The sky teemed with dragons. Wing to wing, reptilian squadrons strafed the city with fire and lightning. Black smoke billowed from burning rooftops. Pockets of Fair Folk held their ground, but most of the soldiers were retreating toward the castle.

A three-headed dragon feasted on one of the few knots

of defenders remaining atop the city wall. A white dragon exhaled frost onto a broad terrace, leaving several archers encrusted in ice. Armored by heavy granitic plates, a bulky dragon thundered down a side street, crushing the Fair Folk in its path.

Volleys of arrows bounced off scales or stuck like pins, doing little evident harm. Lance steady, an armored knight on a galloping horse charged a crouching dragon, only to be hurled backward by an incinerating torrent of flame. Swordsmen and pikemen dove into doorways to avoid a roiling jet of acid exhaled by a green dragon passing overhead.

Seth saw only minor victories against the dragons. The triclops Mombatu chased a two-headed dragon hobbled by a broken wing, pummeling the panicked creature with a massive club. A long harpoon launched from a tower pierced the side of a turquoise dragon with curved quills along its slender neck. The heavy body crashed ruinously beside a park, mowing down part of a long colonnade.

A graceful unicorn raced down the main avenue toward the castle gates. From the back of the elegant mount, Kendra fired clouds of arrows with her bow while Knox used the sack of gales to blow aside the dragons trying to chase them. After the unicorn darted through the castle gates, the pursuing dragons swung away. One breathed fire, only to have the conflagration blocked by a previously unseen barrier.

"The shields around the castle are still intact," Seth said. "But the barrier around the city is gone. This is a massacre. What should we do?"

"Fairview is burning," Tess said.

"If I'm going to die today, I'll go down fighting," Seth said.

One hand shading his eyes, Calvin spoke quietly. "Look beyond the wall."

Largely obscured by smoke and swooping dragons, a vast army was fighting on the plain beyond the city wall. The dragons attacking the distant troops were falling from the sky.

"Where did those soldiers come from?" Seth asked. "I thought most of the Fair Folk were defending from inside the city wall."

"You're right," Calvin said. "I would know my people anywhere. Those are the nipsies! It was the curse that made us small."

"All those tiny nipsies got big?" Tess asked.

"They're human-sized now," Calvin said. "Along with their weapons and armor and the war engines they brought. The nipsies increased my size when they made me their champion, so now I'm a giant."

A sudden westerly wind surged across the city, jostling the flight of the dragons. This was followed by a strong gust from the northeast, making several dragons collide in mid-air. A few crashed to the ground. Above the castle, dark tendrils of cloud swirled.

"Look," Tess said, pointing. "Our giant friend."

Thronis clung to the pinnacle of a neighboring tower, one arm holding a dark orb aloft. He was chanting, eyes reading the sky as the wind continued to rise, his toga snapping like a flag.

"Hold to the plan!" the mighty voice of Celebrant demanded over the clamor of battle. "Press the attack! Reserves, destroy this new army!"

"Time to join the fight," Seth muttered, drawing Vasilis, the blade a searing white. Clarity and certainty poured into Seth. He had to silence the Dragon King. "Tess, go inside."

"I'm going to help my people," Calvin said. He dangled his long body from the balcony and dropped to the court-yard below.

Seth sprang into the air, pushing upward with his wings. When the next gale rose from the west, Seth tucked his wings close and experienced little difficulty flying, though most of the dragons looked frantic, flipping and flailing, oversized wings dragging them like sails rather than working with the air currents.

A grin crept onto Seth's lips. Compared to the peren-nial storm, these were mild breezes. When the gust subsided, a smallish blue dragon careened from behind, snapping at Seth. With a slight maneuver and a swipe of Vasilis, Seth dodged the bite and lopped off the crown of its head.

Seth felt centered and calm despite the confusion around him. The more he relaxed, the better his wings steered. Vasilis eagerly tugged him toward the heights where Celebrant flew, surveying the battle.

During the next prolonged gust, a long Chinese dragon with a head like a lion corkscrewed toward Seth. Swerving adroitly, Seth avoided the head and multiple sets of claws, then hacked off the last ten feet of its tail. Sinuous body thrashing, the rudderless dragon plummeted to the ground like a kite with a cut string.

Upward Seth climbed, Vasilis humming in his grasp, flaring brighter the closer he got to Celebrant. As dragons breathed fire and lightning at him, his wings instinctively angled him out of danger. Whenever dragons got in close to attack, Seth gave them wounds to remember, opening up a gash on the neck or chopping off a wing. While gaining altitude, Seth killed four more by cleaving the head or spine.

Clouds streamed toward the castle at a supernatural rate. Down below, the army of enlarged nipsies knocked dragons from the sky with ballista projectiles and catapults that hurled clusters of spiked metal cubes. Once on the ground, lancers and pikemen swarmed the fallen dragons, the tips of their weapons piercing the stubborn scales, even as many attackers fell to fire and claw. As greater numbers of dragons moved to confront the vast army, greater numbers died.

Reinforcements from the nipsie army rushed into the city, aiding the beleaguered defenders. In many quarters the dragons sought shelter, surprised by arrows that sank deep and swords that parted their hides.

Celebrant saw Seth coming. The Dragon King hovered for a moment, as if undecided, then came flying straight at him, one eye seared shut, a few dark scuffs defacing his otherwise gleaming scales. Seth soared directly at Celebrant as fast as he could, Vasilis vibrating in anticipation.

"You choose death today," the Dragon King called.

"Yes, yours," Seth replied.

The Dragon King opened his jaws, and a quick swerve

allowed Seth to avoid a dazzling column of white energy. They fell into a pattern circling each other.

"I have a war to win," Celebrant declared.

"Don't worry, I'm here to fight," Seth called.

"Vasilis has been tested against me before to no avail," Celebrant warned.

"Vasilis is having an unusually good day," Seth said. "Konrad sends his regards. I'm here filling in. You have killed good people who were watching out for your kind."

Celebrant released another blinding exhalation of white energy. Seth dodged it adroitly, though a dragon some distance behind him was nearly cut in half by the blast. Roaring, Celebrant turned sharply and streaked directly at Seth. Holding Vasilis outstretched, Seth accelerated on a collision course with the Dragon King. An instant before Seth would have flown into Celebrant's gaping mouth, he dipped down enough to pass beneath the colossal dragon, the Dragon King's jaws clashing shut right above him.

"Raxtus says hi!" Seth yelled, his upraised sword opening Celebrant's underside lengthwise from the base of his neck to the start of his tail. The syrupy matter that dumped out could have kept Tanu busy making potions for months.

Celebrant's explosive roar of agony turned into a violent gurgle. "Impossible," the Dragon King gasped as he plunged from the sky. "Impossible!" His strangled gargling lasted until he struck the ground.

Vengeful dragons converged on Seth. Fire came from so many directions that Seth cocooned himself in his wings, spiraling downward hundreds of feet before swooping out of his dive.

Lightning flashed in the darkening clouds, and the wind became more violent. As the dragons floundered, Seth hunted them efficiently, Vasilis parting the toughest scales as though they were made of mist.

Below, dragons were landing to get out of the wind, only to be mobbed by the nipsie soldiers, led by the oversized figures of Calvin and Serena. Nadia had joined the fray, her face unmasked. Wherever she went, the fighters rallied, and dragons were paralyzed by her gaze.

"Hear me, former dragon brothers and sisters!" boomed the authoritative voice of Andromadus, magically magnified. "Celebrant has fallen, as has most of his guard. Tamryn has joined Jeruwat in death. This ill-advised battle is lost. The storm will only worsen, for none of your weather workers can match Thronis. Celebrant led you into a trap. We will shortly possess enough advantage to render dragonkind extinct."

The wind howled. More dragons hugged the ground than risked the sky, and the airborne dragons were struggling.

"Cease your attack and we will spare you," Andromadus continued. "Your king is dead. We will negotiate the terms of your surrender with your remaining leaders. Dragons are not meant to form armies or scheme together in castles! That nonsense is for humans! Dragons hunt. Dragons hoard. Dragons live independently.

"Land and rest your heads on the ground. This will be the token of your nonaggression. You will not be harmed if you submit. Those dragons who wish to live in the wild may do so if they take the appropriate pledges. Others can return to the sanctuaries. You need not perish. This war was Celebrant's folly, not yours. Survive. Preserve our kind. Live to breed and raise your young. This is your last chance."

Lightning forked across the sky, followed closely by a cannonade of thunder.

Seth found himself alone in the air. Looking down, he saw many dragons hunkered down across the city and the surrounding fields, bodies flat, heads on the ground, as if bowing. The dragons struggling to remain airborne were being hurled from the sky, flipping and twisting out of control. The nipsie army surrounded and dispatched noncooperative dragons who continued to fight on the ground. The turbulent wind was becoming too volatile even for Seth's skillful wings, so he took out the Translocator, twisted the middle, and returned to the balcony where he had first arrived.

Fairview continued to burn. Uniformed corpses lay crumpled in the streets among hulking carcasses of dragons. Tess was not in view, so he flew down to the main gate of the castle.

Sheathing Vasilis, Seth felt his hyperawareness relax, and a wave of fatigue made him slump. He waited as a procession of Fair Folk hurried through the gate bearing injured fighters on litters. One block down the main avenue, several soldiers wrestled to remove fallen debris, working to free people trapped beneath a collapsed building. Farther along the outer wall of the castle, Trask spoke with a stooping dragon, taking notes as they conversed.

Seth wandered into the crowded courtyard, where healers had gathered to perform triage for the wounded. He wanted to find his sister, but he saw no sign of her, and he had to dodge around those rushing to help the incapacitated. Seth found his way back to the streets beyond the gate, coughing and rubbing his eyes to combat the irritation from the smoke. He noticed that though the clouds above were darker than ever, the wind had died down. Then he heard his name called. Turning, Seth found Knox and Doren running up to him.

"Seth, you did it!" Doren cheered. "You were fabulous up there!"

"We thought you were doomed," Knox said. "Then you ripped Celebrant open like a piñata!"

"I was lucky to have Vasilis," Seth said. "The sword guided me."

"How many dragons did you get?" Doren asked.

"Plenty," Seth said.

"It had to be thirty," Knox said. "Probably more."

"I honestly lost count," Seth said. "There was hardly time to think."

"You lost count?" Knox exclaimed. "You have to keep track of these things! I saw at least thirty. I'm sure I missed some. Maybe we can find the number if we talk to enough witnesses."

Seth forced a smile. He knew Knox meant well. But all the killing in the sky had felt more like a necessary evil than something to celebrate. "Have you seen Kendra?"

"We were out looking for her," Doren said.

"I saw her race into the castle," Seth said. "On the unicorn."

"Right, I was with her, but then she went out again," Knox said.

"During the battle?" Seth exclaimed. "You let her leave?"

"Lizelle and I were watching you fight Celebrant," Knox said. "After you killed the Dragon King, we looked around for Kendra, but she was gone. Lizelle called to Kendra with her mind. I guess Kendra saw Warren being chased by an injured dragon and went to help him."

Panic started to claw at Seth. "That's all you know?"

"Lizelle ran ahead to find her," Knox said. "Doren and I followed behind but had no luck. Want to head out again together?"

"No need," Doren said. "Here they come."

Seth saw Lizelle, Kendra, and Bracken coming toward the castle. Bracken had a supportive arm around Kendra, and although she was limping, she was definitely alive. The tension inside of Seth loosened. He ran to his sister.

"Are you all right?" Seth asked.

"I probably sprained my ankle," Kendra said. "Along with a few cuts and scrapes."

"She was blinding a dragon who didn't appreciate it," Lizelle said.

"It was chasing Warren," Kendra said. "I stayed behind cover."

"Until the dragon knocked it over," Lizelle added. "You could have been crushed."

"Now you're a Dragon Slayer," Kendra told Lizelle.

"Only because you distracted him," Lizelle said.

"You're both very brave," Bracken said. "And it was risky."

"We saved Warren," Kendra said.

"I'm glad you survived," Bracken said. "The dragons didn't get me, so Kendra decided to give me a heart attack."

"I'm relieved too, Kendra," Seth said. "I was getting worried."

"Worried about your sibling?" Kendra asked. "I wonder what that feels like?"

"Did you see what Seth did?" Knox asked.

"You were amazing," Kendra said. "My heart was in my throat when you charged Celebrant. But you made it look easy."

"During emergencies, these wings have a mind of their own," Seth said.

"You look . . . happier," Kendra said, studying him. "Is it the victory? I haven't seen you like this in a long time. I'd hug you but . . . maybe I'll take a rain check."

Only then did Seth realize that most of his body was soaked in dragon blood. "I'm kind of messy."

"What about the wound in your stomach?" Kendra asked.

"I found the help I needed," Seth said. "I've been healed. We destroyed the Unforgiving Blade. Newel's injury should heal now too."

"Really?" Doren asked. "I have to go tell him. Do you mind?"

"Go," Seth encouraged the satyr.

"Who fixed you?" Kendra asked.

"I promised not to mention certain things," Seth said.

"The nipsies grew," Kendra said. "You guys must have broken the curse Calvin has been worried about."

"Yeah," Seth said.

"You look good," Kendra said. "Under the layer of blood, I mean."

"I feel good," Seth replied. "I'm not a shadow charmer anymore. I wrestled with darkness for so long. I'm not sure I ever understood the toll it was taking. I feel . . . unburdened."

"You made it back here at the right time," Bracken said. "We were about to be annihilated before the nipsie army sprouted up."

"Bracken, I hated that you were such an obvious target on that tower," Kendra said.

"I fought alongside brave men and women," Bracken said. "We hit several dragons." Leaning toward Seth, Bracken punched him lightly on the shoulder. "Nothing like this guy, though. You better watch out, Seth. They'll be writing songs about you before long."

Seth shook his head. "I'd rather not have my story told. Let's just call it even. I helped start this war, and I'm glad I could help finish it."

"You and the nipsies," Bracken said. "They fought like lions. After they appeared, I finally understood who they were."

"What do you mean?" Seth asked.

"They were the lost kingdoms of the Fair Folk," Bracken

said. "At least some of the kingdoms. I recognized their armor and dragon-fighting tools."

"The nipsies must be really old," Seth said.

"Maybe these are their descendants," Bracken said. "I'd love to uncover the whole story."

"You must be exhausted," Kendra said to her brother.

"I was," Seth said. "I'm too wound up now." He patted his jeans. "I keep looking for Calvin. Forgetting he isn't in my pocket anymore."

"You're going to need way bigger pockets," Knox said. "Maybe you can take a turn riding in his."

Bracken stared out at the city. "Many Fair Folk died today. And what remains of Fairview is littered with destruction." Bracken turned to Seth and Kendra. "But it could have been worse. We're lucky to be alive. The dragons could be rampaging across the globe. You two made the difference."

"And you with your weather idea," Kendra said.

"Andromadus didn't have weather workers strong enough to build a storm in time," Bracken said. "Especially since the dragons brought weather magic of their own. But after we discussed the potential opportunity, Andromadus remembered Thronis, who can summon a storm faster than anyone. They had spent some time together at Wyrmroost. Even so, it's amazing that Andromadus convinced him to come, and that he mustered enough power to transport him here."

They were strolling back toward the castle. At the gate, Lizelle excused herself. Seth, Kendra, and Bracken sat down together, backs against the castle wall. Knox paced in front of them.

"Did that battle make you guys hungry?" Knox asked.

"Not yet," Seth said. "Might be the smell of all this dragon blood."

"I'm really hungry," Knox said. "Like for eggs especially. Or actually, how great would a milkshake taste right now?"

"I could do a milkshake," Kendra said.

"I think all the best fast-food places got torched," Seth said.

"I know it's old-time technology here," Knox said. "But they have cows, right? Do they make ice cream? Where does chocolate syrup come from? Chocolate beans or something? If nothing else, they must have eggs."

Seth looked at Kendra seriously. "I'm sorry for the trouble I caused." Seth picked some drying blood off his sleeve. "For a while I thought there might not be a way back."

Kendra took his hand. "I know. I'm so happy you figured it out."

They sat together until Andromadus approached them, strolling beside Calvin and Serena, who were no longer gigantic. Wings folded, Raxtus walked with them.

Kendra scrambled to her feet and ran to Raxtus. "You made it!"

"They had to pry me from Herrigan's jaws," Raxtus said. "He had me tight."

"What about Gerwin?" Kendra asked.

"He got Herrigan through the throat with his spear as we fell," Raxtus said. "But the landing killed him. Poor kid. Snapped his neck, I think. He burned away. The fire came out of nowhere. Only ashes were left."

"He'll be back," Kendra said. "You're all right?"

"These scales of mine can take a beating," Raxtus said. "None of Herrigan's teeth pierced me. He just had me trapped. I outlived my dad. I can't believe he's dead."

"Sorry about that," Seth said.

"Don't be sorry," Raxtus said. "Father was the aggressor. I tried to kill him before you did. He was a power-hungry tyrant. His death was necessary. It's hard, though, too." Raxtus sighed. "Lots of conflicting feelings, now that he's actually gone."

Seth elbowed Calvin. "I look away and you change size."

"It's a theme for us today," Calvin replied, one arm around Serena.

"How are the nipsie troops?" Seth asked Calvin.

"They fought gallantly," Calvin said. "Thousands died. Tens of thousands survived. It was a day we have awaited for a long time."

"It's weird that you're my size now," Seth said. They were almost exactly the same height.

"Imagine being me," Calvin said. "I've felt out of scale all day."

"You almost outgrew the world for a while," Seth said. "You went from the Tiny Hero to the Giant Hero."

"And now we're just right," Serena said. "You did it, Seth. You were the hero our prophecy foretold: *The curse arose from the demon's blight; the lord who slays him will set it right. The slayer shall restore our pride, the Giant Hero at his side.*"

"Sounds like something Humbuggle would recite," Seth said.

"Our elders wish to thank you," Serena replied.

"They may have to wait for a little while," Seth said, turning to Andromadus, who had been listening contentedly. "Did the dragons surrender?"

"Against all odds, yes," Andromadus said. "Most of the dragons will return to sanctuaries. The others will follow sworn guidelines to live in the wild. Dragons in the wild will have protocols enabling them to return to preserves if they so choose. Those dwelling in sanctuaries will be able to petition to live in the wild. This flexibility should produce a more sustainable situation than we had before. There are still details to hammer out. Members of Dragonwatch are processing the remaining dragons. I will meet with them tomorrow. I expect I can do more for the good of dragonkind now than I ever could before."

"That is welcome news," Kendra said. "Dragonwatch needs to be more mindful of the dragons in its care."

"There will not be another Titan Valley situation," Andromadus said. "I will make sure of that."

Rain started to fall, gently at first, but the pattering droplets increased rapidly. They moved under the shelter of the gateway as the rainfall escalated into a downpour.

"Thronis is helping with the lingering fires," Andromadus explained.

"There you are!" Tess called, holding a half-eaten roll. "I was looking for you guys!"

"You found food?" Knox exclaimed.

"They have a huge kitchen here," Tess said. "Tons of

abandoned food. Everybody left it behind when the fighting started, I guess."

"You weathered the battle all right?" Seth asked.

"Eve kept me company," Tess said. "We watched through a window."

"Lord Dalgorel's daughter?" Seth asked.

"Yes," Tess said. "She's really nice. She showed me the kitchen. Want me to take you there?"

"I've got somewhere I need to go," Seth said. "Nothing shady," he added hastily to Kendra. "I just have a promise to fulfill. Speaking of which, I owe a favor to a lich in the Under Realm. Can you ask around about a guy named Toleron? Son of the Duke of Hester. His mom was named Ingrid. He's supposedly one of the Fair Folk in Selona. Or he was."

"What do you need to know about him?" Serena asked.

"Just a little about how he is doing," Seth said. "Or if he's dead, what his life was like. I'm trying to get to a place where I owe no favors."

"Will you be back soon?" Kendra asked.

"I think so," Seth said. "Don't worry. See if you can track down some eggs. Maybe some milkshakes. I'll catch up."

"All right," Knox said.

"Calvin?" Seth asked. "Want to come?"

Calvin smiled. "I hoped you would ask."

Seth produced the Translocator. Calvin laid a hand on the top, and Seth twisted the middle.

# CHAPTER FORTY-EIGHT

# Ronodin

Thank you for returning," the Alderfairy said. "I observed the battle from here. With the barriers around the Source unsealed, I can see abroad more clearly. There were many casualties."

Seth and Calvin stood a few paces from the Source, staring up at the little fairy, her wings fluttering.

"None of this could have happened without repairing the Ethergem," Calvin said. "You helped us break the nipsie curse. It meant everything to me and my people."

"More accurately, it was the curse of the Fair Folk," the Alderfairy said. "Previous generations brought it upon themselves when Humbuggle and Graulas beguiled them."

"Weren't they already nipsies when they stole the Ethergem?" Seth asked.

"There was no race of nipsies back then," the Alderfairy

said. "Few know the full story. Because of the curse, those of us who knew that the nipsies had once been Fair Folk were not able to talk about it. Ten kingdoms of the Fair Folk agreed to take action against the giants. Seven of those kingdoms sent delegates to be shrunken down by magic in order to steal the Ethergem. The members of this strike force were approximately the size of a human finger—roughly the height of Calvin when he traveled in Seth's pocket. After the demons shattered the Ethergem, the seven shrunken kingdoms were cursed to lose even more stature and become the nipsies. Their memories were erased. They were left with only a prophecy to guide them."

"What about the other three kingdoms who participated against the giants?" Calvin asked.

"They were punished in other ways," the Alderfairy said. "I can tell you now, because the curse is broken. The citizens of one of those kingdoms became the conscious trees of the Sentient Wood at Wyrmroost. Another kingdom became the singing fish of Luster Harbor at Isla del Dragón. And the last kingdom became the Wandering Stones of Titan Valley."

"They were all once Fair Folk?" Calvin asked.

"All of them," the Alderfairy said. "And because you broke the curse, they are Fair Folk once more."

"We've long awaited this day," Calvin said.

"The former nipsies made the difference against the dragons," Seth said. "My wings came in handy too. They seem to work better than ever since my bath in the Source."

"Those wings are a part of you in ways they were not

before," the Alderfairy said. "For example, if you wish to hide them, they will vanish entirely until you desire their return."

Seth found it took only a minor effort to make the wings disappear. He simply had never thought to make the attempt. With another small effort they returned. "They're retractable!" he exclaimed. "That's convenient. Speaking of new abilities, I have a question. What does it mean to be a shadow healer?"

"You have sampled the process of becoming undead," the Alderfairy said. "You walked a portion of that nightmarish road. Imagine following that path to completion and being stuck at the end in a grotesque parody of immortality."

"I can't think of anything worse," Seth said.

"A shadow healer has the power to release the undead from their tortured state," the Alderfairy said.

"I can cure them?" Seth asked.

"You can reverse the process if someone is still in transition to becoming undead," the Alderfairy said. "But you cannot restore life to those who have completed the transformation."

"Then what *can* I do for zombies and wraiths?" Seth asked.

"You will still hear the undead," the Alderfairy said. "And they can understand you. If any of the undead let you touch them, you can grant a release that brings the fulfillment and peace they have long craved. They can move on from their abominable existence."

"What if they don't want me to touch them?" Seth asked.

"Then you cannot heal them," the Alderfairy said simply.

"Can they feed on me?" Seth asked.

"If they voluntarily touch you, they will be delivered from their state," the Alderfairy said. "Enough theory. This art is best learned by doing. I summoned you here for a more urgent purpose."

"Tell us," Seth invited.

"A usurper now wears my crown," the Alderfairy said.

"Ronodin," Seth said.

"My Fairy Realm has been despoiled by demons," the Alderfairy said. "The realm Ronodin currently governs needs to be cleansed, beginning with his expulsion. Will you help me?"

"Yes," Seth said. "I have unfinished business of my own with Ronodin."

"And I will help Seth whenever he needs it," Calvin said.

Seth regarded Calvin. "I thought that would end when the curse was broken."

Calvin shook his head. "I placed no limit on my pledge. You'll have my help for any emergency."

"Thanks," Seth said.

"We need access to the new Fairy Realm," the Alderfairy said. "I have never been inside the former Demon Prison. If you have been there, you could take us with the Translocator."

"I've been inside," Seth said. "But only barely. Bracken has been all over that place. And he wants Ronodin ousted as much as any of us."

"You have my permission to bring Bracken here," the Alderfairy said. "Along with his sister, Lizelle. And your sister, the girl who briefly wore my crown. If they desire."

"All right," Seth said, happy he would be able to share this secret with Kendra. "Should I fetch them now?"

"Please," the Alderfairy said.

"I can wait here if it makes the traveling less cumbersome," Calvin said.

Seth gave a nod. "I'll be right back." He twisted the Translocator.

Seth seemed to fold into himself, and then he was back at the main gateway to the castle. Nobody he knew remained in view. Would they have ventured out to the streets? Or would they be inside the castle?

A short form detached from the shadows of the gateway and toddled over to Seth. "You made good fight," Hermo said.

"Hermo!" Seth exclaimed. "You're here! Are you all right?"

"Hermo always fine," the hermit troll said. "Hermo hide and watch."

"Are you going to make a lair around here?" Seth asked. "If not, I can relocate you wherever you want."

"You too busy," Hermo said. "You famous now. You kill big dragon."

"I'm not too busy for you," Seth said. "You're my friend."

"Still friends?" Hermo asked. "Even famous?"

"You were my friend at my lowest point," Seth said. "That's a true friend. I'll always be yours."

Hermo grunted. "You not dumb as look." He looked around and sniffed the air. "Me like this place. Old. Many stupid people. Many place to hide."

"You'll have to let me know where you hide," Seth said. "So I can find you to play some games."

Hermo grinned. "You want lose more games? You beat dragon. Me beat you. Me better than dragon."

"Maybe I'll beat you, too," Seth said.

"Me find place I like," Hermo said. "Then me find you."

"Could you do me a favor first?" Seth asked.

Hermo rolled his eyes and huffed. "What now?"

"I need to find Kendra and Bracken," Seth said.

"Easy," Hermo said. "This way."

Hermo led Seth into the castle. They climbed a set of stairs, then saw Kendra leaning against Bracken for support as they moved away down a corridor.

"Kendra," Seth called. "Wait up."

Seth glanced toward Hermo, but he was already gone without a trace. Kendra and Bracken were looking back expectantly, so Seth jogged to catch up.

"I can let you in on my secret!" Seth said. "I got permission to show you something incredible. And we can take back the Fairy Realm. Want to come with me?"

"Yes," Kendra said.

"Is that a good idea?" Bracken asked. "You're injured."

"Even hobbling, this will be worth it," Seth said. "Your sister is invited too, Bracken."

"Lizelle?" he asked.

Seth nodded.

Bracken bowed his head for a few seconds. "She will be here momentarily."

"He called her telepathically," Kendra explained.

"I know," Seth said. "I'm not new here."

"Where are we going?" Kendra asked.

"You'll see," Seth said, waggling the Translocator. "It won't take long."

Lizelle rounded a corner and came into view. "Is everything all right?"

"Seth wants to take us somewhere interesting," Bracken said.

"Everyone place a hand on the Translocator," Seth said, holding the middle. Once they complied, he twisted the device.

Their surroundings transformed into a beautiful garden. Calvin waited near the Alderfairy, a few steps from the pristine aether of the Source.

"A dome?" Kendra asked, looking around. "Is this a greenhouse?"

Bracken and Lizelle slowly turned in wonder, absorbing the new environment. Upon seeing the Alderfairy, they swiftly dropped into kneeling positions, heads bowed.

"Where are we?" Kendra asked.

*We're at the Source,* Bracken communicated to her. *She is the mother of all fairies. The original Fairy Queen.*

Bracing herself against Bracken's shoulder, Kendra got down on one knee.

"You may rise," the Alderfairy said. "Kendra, you are hurt."

"Just a sprain," Kendra said. Bracken arose and helped Kendra back to her feet.

"And a fractured bone," the Alderfairy said. "You may dip the afflicted ankle in the Source for relief."

"Do it," Seth encouraged.

Kneeling down, Bracken carefully unlaced and removed Kendra's shoe.

"I'm surprised you're allowing us here," Lizelle said. "The location of the Source is the most closely guarded secret in fairydom."

"It is the most closely guarded secret in the world," the Alderfairy corrected.

"By the way, guys, the Void is in the Under Realm," Seth said. "Guarded by the Underking."

"I remember that place," Kendra said as Bracken gingerly rolled down her sock and pulled it off. "The darkness was thick."

"Do not spread that fact casually," the Alderfairy said. "Agents of balance respect the secrets of both sides."

"I never thought I would see the Source," Lizelle said.

"I intend to invite your mother to take my place guarding the Source," the Alderfairy said.

"Why do you need a replacement?" Seth asked.

"The hour has arrived for me to reclaim my crown," the

Alderfairy said. "The Fairy Realm is in disarray. I must restore true order."

"You know Ronodin has the crown," Bracken said, helping Kendra to the brink of the Source.

"I'm aware," the Alderfairy said.

"The water is so clear," Kendra said. "I feel like I can see forever."

"Perhaps you can," the Alderfairy said. "Just dip your leg in the aether up to the shin."

Steadied by Bracken, Kendra immersed her foot as directed. "Oh, wow," Kendra gushed. "That tingles in a good way." She pulled out her foot.

"How does it feel now?" the Alderfairy asked.

Kendra tested her weight on it. She tapped her foot hesitantly, then stomped hard and jumped twice. "Like the injury never happened."

"How can we help you dispose of Ronodin?" Lizelle asked.

"He is out of his element in the Fairy Realm," the Alderfairy said. "He transformed into a creature of darkness long ago. Ronodin doesn't belong in a realm of light. A ruler should wear his crown. We will challenge Ronodin to don mine."

"Isn't he wearing it now?" Kendra asked.

"He has not worn it since the barrier around the Source fell," the Alderfairy said. "The increased light now associated with the crown would overwhelm him."

"How is he keeping control of the Fairy Realm?" Bracken asked.

"Mostly by bluffing," the Alderfairy said. "From what I can see, his act is wearing thin."

"I need Ronodin alive," Seth said.

"What do you mean?" Kendra asked.

"I made a deal with the Demon King that I would exchange Ronodin for Bracken's dad," Seth said.

"Orogoro has our father?" Lizelle asked, an edge of hysteria behind her words.

"Your dad made the deal," Seth said. "Not me. But I have an idea of how to get Ronodin where I need him."

"We're listening," Bracken said.

"You guys come at Ronodin from one direction," Seth said. "Chase him toward me. I'll take care of the rest."

"Ronodin is very dangerous," Bracken said.

"I'll make him think I'm going to help him escape," Seth said.

Bracken gave a nod. "Loan me the Translocator. I'll scout his location."

"Sure," Seth said, handing it over.

Bracken twisted the Translocator and vanished.

With a squawk, a phoenix glided into view, feathers blazing, smoke trailing. The bird wheeled around the inside of the dome before vanishing behind some trees.

"You have a phoenix?" Seth asked.

"She has nested here for ages," the Alderfairy said. "Sometimes she crosses into higher realms through the Source, but she always returns."

"I'm surprised she hasn't burned down the place," Kendra said.

"She is respectful of the vegetation," the Alderfairy said. "Her nest is composed of stone."

Kendra commented on the strange quality of the light, and Seth drew her attention to the lack of shadows. She was moving her hand around in an attempt to produce a shadow when Bracken reappeared.

"I found him," Bracken said. "He's in the Great Hall, playing several concurrent games of chess against multiple fairies. The fairies do not look amused. I can position Seth, then bring the rest of you."

"I'll need the Translocator back," Seth said.

Bracken gave a nod. "I'll return it after I shuttle the others."

"Lizelle," the Alderfairy said. "Would you mind guarding the Source while we are absent?"

She hesitated. "It would be an honor."

"We shall not tarry long," the Alderfairy said, nodding to Bracken.

Bracken faced Seth. "The Great Hall has a secret passage for escape in the adjoining lounge. Ronodin will try to flee there." Bracken held out the Translocator. Seth gripped the top, Bracken twisted the middle, and suddenly they inhabited a small, comfortable room adjacent to a larger one. Bracken put a finger to his lips, pointed at the doorway to the Great Hall, then twisted the Translocator and vanished.

Seth held still, listening. He could hear someone pacing in the other room. After a moment, Bracken reappeared and held out the Translocator. Seth touched it, Bracken twisted the middle, and they teleported to a hallway where

Kendra, Calvin, and the Alderfairy stood ready. Bracken handed Seth the Translocator. With a quick twist, Seth returned alone to the lounge.

Within a minute, Seth heard Bracken's voice. "Hello, Ronodin."

"Back already?" Ronodin asked, almost concealing that he was startled.

"I brought some friends," Bracken said. "Have you met the Alderfairy?"

At this Ronodin gave an exaggerated gasp. "Yeah, right. I suppose next you will produce Father Christmas?"

Seth stifled a snicker. Brilliant white light flashed from the Great Hall, and the voice of the Alderfairy was magnified to a staggering degree that overpowered both the ears and the mind. "Silence, defiler. Your pretended rule is over."

Seth could hear Ronodin shuffling toward the room where he waited.

"Where are you going?" the Alderfairy thundered.

Seth poked his head out, and Ronodin saw him. Seth waved Ronodin toward him and withdrew into the lounge.

He heard Ronodin running, and the dark unicorn came through the doorway clutching the Fairy Queen's crown in one hand.

"I owe you from before," Seth said, holding out the Translocator. "You want out? Now or never."

"You cannot escape me!" the Alderfairy bellowed.

Ronodin set down the crown and grabbed the offered end of the Translocator. Seth gave the middle a twist.

They now stood in a field of clover at the center of a

lovely garden enclosed by a curtain. Orogoro looked up from where he sat, then stood when he recognized Seth and Ronodin.

"Here is Ronodin," Seth said.

"What is this?" Ronodin asked.

"Business," Seth said.

"You ruined my crown," Orogoro accused. "It disintegrated."

"You shouldn't have stabbed me with the Unforgiving Blade," Seth countered, drawing Vasilis. "Destroying the Unforgiving Blade dissolved Raglamar."

"Including the portion used to forge my crown," Orogoro said.

"I had to mend the wound you gave me," Seth replied.

Orogoro snorted and narrowed his gaze. "You've changed."

"Adapt or die," Seth said. "I completed my part of the bargain. Ronodin is yours."

Ronodin lunged for the Translocator, but Seth slapped him away with a wing, then pointed Vasilis at him. "Don't try that again."

"Traveler!" Orogoro called. "You are free to go."

The former Fairy King walked into view from behind a hedge. Seth was relieved to see that he looked unharmed. The Traveler smiled at Seth. His gaze hardened when it shifted to Ronodin.

"I made great efforts to spare you this agony, nephew," the Traveler said. "But since you insisted on this road, I hope you can stomach the destination."

Ronodin laughed. "You brought me right where I want to be. Orogoro is an old friend."

"Am I?" Orogoro asked.

"Friend of a friend," Ronodin adjusted. He glanced at Seth. "Run along with uncle. I have a deal to negotiate."

"Make no mistake," Orogoro said. "You are my trophy now."

Ronodin looked as if he might say more, then turned and sprinted away.

"Do you need help with him?" Seth asked, flexing his wings.

Orogoro gave a brief chuckle. "I like when they run."

"Are we square?" Seth asked.

"All terms have been met," the Traveler said.

"I appreciate that you gave Celebrant an exceedingly public demise," Orogoro said. "You may go."

The Traveler placed a hand on the Translocator.

Seth twisted the middle.

And then they stood together in the small room adjoining the larger one.

Bracken and Kendra waited in the doorway. The Alderfairy hovered behind them, wearing her crown.

# CHAPTER FORTY-NINE

# Healer

Seth watched Kendra dig a little trench in the soft soil with the toe of her shoe. They sat together in a room of the fairy palace where a waterfall tumbled down a rocky face into a wide pool. Delicate fairies played on the surface of the water, wings ablur, until a naiad emerged and splashed them away.

Bracken entered the room with a warrior fairy, the partially armored woman slightly taller than him. "The Alderfairy is once again the undisputed Fairy Queen," the warrior fairy announced.

"Turns out Ronodin had almost no supporters among his subjects," Bracken said. "I'm not sure who to pity more— Ronodin, or the Demon King."

"I have a hunch Ronodin will get the worst of it," Seth said.

"If you'll excuse me," the warrior fairy said with a little bow.

"Thank you, Ila," Bracken said. The warrior fairy exited the room.

"How did your mom take not being the Fairy Queen anymore?" Kendra asked.

"Honestly?" Bracken replied. "She seemed relieved. Mother and Father are currently speaking with the Alderfairy."

"The fairies seem fine with the transition," Seth said.

"Almost every being in this realm wanted a revolution," Bracken said. "What is tragic is that nobody took action."

"Mind if I stare, Bracken?" the naiad called, raking one hand through her auburn tresses. "I missed you while you were imprisoned."

"Why didn't you come help me, Olette?" Bracken asked.

The naiad pouted. "Ronodin had the crown. What could we do?"

"What I did," Bracken said. "I resisted Ronodin."

"Some of us have allegiance to the crown," Olette said with a sniff. "If we all went rogue, there wouldn't be a Fairy Realm left." The naiad disappeared under the water.

"Have you gone rogue?" Seth asked.

"I suppose," Bracken said. "There are consequences when magical beings spend time with mortals. I've begun to see the Fairy Realm through new eyes. It seems ridiculous to honor a crown more than the person wearing it. I can't help seeing a disappointing lack of individuality here. Change is rare, making progress slow. Many of the risks you and Seth take are foreign to the unicorns and fairies I grew up with."

"You take plenty of risks," Kendra said.

"I do now," Bracken said. "That started with the mortal examples I observed. And that is why the naiads consider me a rebel."

"Is it why they flirt with you?" Kendra asked.

"Next question," Bracken said flatly.

"Speaking of risks, Kendra has a custom courage potion ready," Seth said. "We popped back to Tanu while you were talking with the Alderfairy."

"Good," Bracken said. "The three of us are a perfect res-cue team. Kendra provides the light. Seth brings the heal-ing. And I'm your backup."

"Grandma and Grandpa Sorenson have been trapped in Blackwell Keep for a long time," Kendra said.

"We may get there and find they already escaped," Seth said.

"I hope so," Kendra said. "But remember, they were sur-rounded by the undead."

"Why hasn't Andromadus teleported them to safety?" Seth wondered.

"The refuge where they hid is shielded against magic," Kendra said.

"Seth, are you sure you don't want to try shadow healing in a more controlled environment first?" Bracken asked.

"I made all the creatures of the Blackwell promise to do me no harm," Seth said. "Besides, we have the Translocator.

If the undead apply too much pressure, we can teleport away."

"Good thinking," Bracken said.

"I want to see what you can do," Kendra said, drinking the courage potion. "And I wouldn't miss helping Grandma and Grandpa."

Seth held up the Translocator. "Who twists it?"

"I've walked the hall that leads to the refuge," Kendra said.

Seth handed Kendra the Translocator. She gripped the middle, Bracken took hold of the top, and Seth squeezed the bottom. Kendra twisted, and darkness engulfed them. An unnatural chill made the air brittle. Seth could perceive a host of malevolent presences around him.

Seth slid Vasilis from the sheath. The blade blazed white, bringing a surge of vigor and confidence. Raising a hand, Kendra produced even brighter radiance, and suddenly the hallway of mortared stone held no secrets.

The shadowy forms of two wraiths were visible twenty paces down the hall ahead of them. From the other direction trudged a revenant, pale flesh pocked with sores, one foot dragging a manacle affixed to a rusty chain.

*I have returned*, Seth projected telepathically. He could sense that the undead throughout the castle were already aware of them. A clamor of overlapping voices answered his statement with complaints.

*Hungry.*

*Thirsty.*

*Cold.*

*Empty.*

*Help us.*

*Stop blabbering,* Seth thought sternly. *I need a single spokesperson. Everyone else hold still and keep quiet.* He looked down the hall at the lone revenant. *Who are you?*

*Who am I?* the revenant replied, the labored words coming slowly.

*What is your name?* Seth asked.

*Savaric,* the revenant answered.

*How have things gone since your release from the Blackwell?* Seth asked.

*Hungry,* Savaric replied. *Alone.*

Other voices interrupted.

*Belrab.*

*Belrab.*

*Speak to Belrab.*

Seth remembered he had negotiated the release of the undead from the Blackwell with a lich named Belrab. *Are you still here, Belrab?*

*You placed stringent limits on how far we could wander,* Belrab replied.

"What's happening?" Kendra asked.

"You can't hear any of it?" Seth asked.

"I only pick up some types of mental communication," Kendra said.

"I'm talking with them," Seth said. "I'll speak out loud as well as with my mind so you can follow. Belrab! I need to converse with you."

*You have immunity from harm, as we pledged,* Belrab

acknowledged. *But you brought two tempting specimens into our midst. They brim with vitality.*

"It won't go well if you attack them," Seth warned.

*We suffer more than ever,* Belrab confided. *After so much time locked away, we finally had a chance to devour the living. We tasted warmth. We fed, if only momentarily. Now, every rat in this castle is a husk. We need more. The little we sampled sharpened our appetites, but now there is nothing to sate us.*

Several other voices clamored their agreement.

"Undeath is not life," Seth said. "That state is a trap. It ends growth and progress. You are no longer living, but you are also unable to rest, unable to move on. I am here to help. I freed you from the Blackwell. I have now come to free you from the Void."

*The Void,* hushed voices repeated.

*None can accomplish what you claim,* Belrab accused.

"Let me show you," Seth said. "Savaric, would you like peace?"

*Hungry,* Savaric conveyed. *Alone.*

Seth slowly approached the revenant. "Would you like to finally feel satisfied? How about an end to feeling hungry and alone?"

The revenant took shambling steps toward Seth, one arm outstretched. Seth gripped the being's hand and felt energy flowing from himself into Savaric. The revenant locked eyes with him, and, for a moment, Seth detected a flicker of humanity in the clouded eyes and withered features. Surprise. Maybe even hope.

Savaric closed his papery eyelids. The revenant gave

Seth's fingers a squeeze, and his voice whispered through crumbling lips, "At last. It's over."

The revenant collapsed, its bony hand slipping from Seth's grasp. The corpse looked smaller, shriveled, like ancient remains an archeologist might discover. How had it been walking a moment before?

The castle was silent.

"Anyone else?" Seth asked.

*Trickery,* Belrab accused.

"There is no trick," Seth said. "I've glimpsed your pain. The Void has you trapped. I used to be a shadow charmer. Now I'm a shadow healer. Let me help you." Seth started toward the wraiths at the other end of the hall. "What about you two? Have you had enough? Want some rest?"

The wraiths advanced toward him. Seth touched one and then the other. No words were expressed, but Seth could sense relief as their forms melted away.

*He means to destroy us!* Belrab cried.

"No, this sword would destroy you," Seth said, swishing Vasilis through the air. "It would cut you down in your misery, bringing no peace. I'm offering something much better. I'll give you the completion you have wanted ever since you entered this state."

*Rise up,* Belrab declared. *Do not go quietly. Rise up and stop him!*

"Belrab's just afraid," Seth countered. "I'll give you three options. Come to me and I will release you. Return to the Blackwell. Or fight me and perish. It's one of the three. No way around it."

A figure stepped into the light. He was bald, somewhat stooped, and wore a cassock. His fleshy face looked healthy but was slightly transparent, making his skull faintly visible. The apparition strode a few inches above the floor.

"Come, show me your talent," the newcomer invited in a reasonable, sonorous voice. "Put me to rest, if you dare, if you can." He stopped walking and spread his arms wide, inviting contact.

Holding Vasilis ready just in case, Seth went to the lich and put a hand on his chest, over his heart. Seth's knees buckled somewhat as a surge of light energy flooded out of him.

The lich closed his eyes and licked his lips. *Yes, this is real, this is bliss and deliverance.* He opened his eyes. *Thank you.* He vanished like smoke.

"Anyone else?" Seth asked.

*Aaron vouches for him,* a telepathic voice stated.

*Deliverance,* another voice uttered with awe.

*Your offers appear genuine,* Belrab expressed. *Some of us would prefer not to exit this life yet. I will return to the Blackwell with any who care to join me. The rest of you may do as you will.*

The majority of voices begged for deliverance. A smaller faction spoke of returning to the Blackwell. Droves of the undead came into the hall from both directions. Seth had them take turns approaching to keep Bracken and Kendra from feeling overwhelmed. He felt an outflow of energy every time he laid one to rest, but his stamina never became depleted. Countless wraiths came to him, about a dozen revenants, and a few more liches. He could feel their gratitude as their suffering ended.

"Is that all?" Seth called when no more of the undead approached.

*The rest of us would prefer a return to the Blackwell,* Belrab conveyed.

"Your return must include a vow to remain there, trapped, and not to emerge," Seth said. "Each of you must promise, or empower Belrab to promise on your behalf."

Seth heard a general murmuring.

*All who remain have empowered me to speak for them,* Belrab expressed. *We will return to the Blackwell, imprisoned as before.*

"Starting immediately," Seth said.

*Immediately,* Belrab repeated.

"We're all set," Seth told Kendra and Bracken, no longer projecting his words to the undead. He sheathed Vasilis. "Those that are left agreed to return to the Blackwell."

"I can't believe you can talk to those creatures," Kendra said. "Even with a courage potion, it takes my best efforts not to become paralyzed."

"I can't hear them either, Kendra," Bracken said. "The minds of the undead are inscrutable to most."

"I could sense their relief when I freed them," Seth said. "If I were in their position, I would want that too."

"It was merciful," Bracken said. "I can't imagine choosing to persist in that state."

"And yet a bunch of them chose the Blackwell over release," Seth said.

"Some view death with such fear, they would go to any lengths to delay it," Bracken said.

"So much about death is unknown," Kendra said. "I sometimes worry dying will be the end."

Bracken nodded. "Death is a difficult test from a mortal perspective. Trust me, though, death is a transition, not an ending. Sometimes the timing is tragic. But under the right circumstances, death is a mercy."

"I plan to avoid it for a while," Seth said, looking up and down the corridor.

Kendra nodded. "We're close to the refuge." She stepped around the remains of revenants to proceed down the hall. "This way."

They reached a large, low room with a vaultlike metal door set into the stone wall. Beaming light, Kendra went to the middle of the room, waved her arms above her head, and called out, "Grandma! Grandpa! It's Seth, Kendra, and Bracken. We cleared the undead. You can open the refuge."

"Can they hear you?" Seth asked. "Or see you?"

Kendra looked at her brother. "I really hope so. I can't remember how they see out. I know they explained it once when we first got here."

With a resounding clang, the metal door edged open. "Kendra?" Grandma Sorenson's voice asked.

"Grandma!" Kendra cried. "It's us!"

The door opened further, and Grandma stepped out, hair matted, clutching a crossbow, followed by Grandpa Sorenson holding an ax. "Kendra!" Grandpa exclaimed. "How are you glowing so brightly?"

"I'm learning more about my abilities," she said. Kendra went to Grandma for a hug.

"Seth, you're back," Grandpa said.

"We were worried about you," Grandma said over Kendra's shoulder. "Did your sister find you?"

"We found each other," Seth said.

"Is it clear?" a dwarf asked, poking his head out of the refuge.

"The undead are either laid to rest or back in the Blackwell," Seth said.

"Laid to rest?" Grandpa asked. "What do you mean?"

"Seth has become a shadow healer," Bracken said. "His touch can release the undead from their fate."

"If they're willing," Seth added.

"Remarkable," Grandpa said, coming forward to hug Seth, ax still in hand. "I have heard rumors of such abilities in ancient texts, but I never took them seriously."

"I guess it's pretty rare," Seth said.

"It came in handy today," Grandma said, moving in for a hug of her own. "Good to see you, Bracken."

"We've come through quite a storm," Bracken said.

"What is happening with Celebrant?" Grandpa asked.

"Not much anymore," Seth said.

"All seven sanctuaries fell," Bracken reported. "Then, at the battle of Fairview, Seth slew Celebrant."

"What?" Grandpa asked, eyes wide. "You're kidding."

"With Vasilis," Kendra said.

Seth showed his wings for a moment. "I had some help."

"We've missed a lot," Grandma said, rubbing her eyes.

"Ronodin took over the Fairy Realm," Kendra said. "Then the Alderfairy reclaimed it. Seth and Calvin broke the nipsie curse, which restored the lost kingdoms of the Fair Folk."

"The nipsies were Fair Folk?" Grandpa asked.

"Seven of the lost kingdoms," Seth said.

Grandpa nodded slowly. "I suppose that makes sense. You have some stories to tell us."

"Hey, put those back," Grandma scolded.

Seth saw a pair of dwarfs hustling out of the refuge, one holding three stacked boxes, the other carrying a large cask. They froze under Grandma's scrutiny.

"Those supplies are for emergencies," Grandma said. "If you're hungry, feel free to eat, but leave the food stored here."

The dwarfs slunk back into the refuge.

"Were you all right in there?" Kendra asked.

"We had plenty of food and water," Grandma said.

"We could have lasted another month," Grandpa agreed.

"All we could see through our peephole were wraiths, revenants, and a lich milling around," Grandma said. "We worried for you kids and everyone else."

"The waiting was brutal," Grandpa said. "If this sanctuary has fallen, what will become of it?"

"Andromadus will reestablish the sanctuary," Kendra said. "The dragons surrendered, and Dragonwatch is working out how to move forward."

"Andromadus?" Grandma asked.

"The dragon Dromadus became a wizard," Kendra said. "And Agad died."

"Oh, no," Grandma said.

"What about your cousins?" Grandpa asked.

"Knox and Tess are fine," Seth said. "They've been really helpful. At least most of the time."

"We have a lot to catch up on," Grandpa said. "Where can we go?"

Seth held up the Translocator. "Pretty much anywhere we want."

# CHAPTER FIFTY

# New Beginnings

Kendra sat down at the end of the twin bed in the attic playroom. Bright and spacious, the long room featured shelves crammed with children's books, multiple toy chests, and a corner populated with stuffed animals. Beside the other bed, Seth kicked off his shoes. Since the house at Fablehaven was full of visitors, they had requested this room. At least they had beds—Knox and Tess were downstairs on the floor in sleeping bags, sharing a room with their parents.

"Can you believe we're back here?" Seth asked, flopping on top of the covers.

"Barely," Kendra said. "I'm just glad they didn't try to recruit us as caretakers for one of the reopened sanctuaries."

"Mom and Dad would have hunted down anyone who tried," Seth said. "Fortunately there were several good candidates from the kingdoms of lost Fair Folk. None of the other Fair Folk had ever been willing to take over those positions."

"I guess that is one advantage of getting the more daring Fair Folk back," Kendra said.

Seth looked around at the toys. "I flew over this house on my way to dig up Muriel. I honestly wondered if I would ever enter it again."

"It feels surreal to be back in this room," Kendra said. "There were a few times I doubted whether I would ever see Fablehaven again. It's good to know we'll always be welcome here."

"I can think of a few people who wouldn't be super welcome here," Seth said. "I never would have figured Virgil for a traitor."

"Maybe he wasn't a traitor," Kendra said. "I mean, he did risk his life for both of us, but he also idolized Humbuggle. He must have really wrestled with his loyalties."

"Virgil knows what he did," Seth said. "He couldn't make eye contact with me after they caught him. He pretended to be on our team! When you act like a friend, then betray that, you're a traitor. Newel and Doren mocked him nonstop."

"What did they say?"

Seth smiled. "'Never trust a satyr with manners.' 'Never trust a satyr who writes things down.' 'Never trust a satyr who feeds his mind before his belly.' They had a million of them. I hope Virgil rots in the Fairview dungeon."

"It's not the kind of dungeon you rot in," Kendra said.

"Pretty cushy by most standards. The prison may be soft, but the Fair Folk took his betrayal very personally. They tracked down Humbuggle and Virgil fast. Humbuggle didn't expect the dragons to fail. He and Virgil weren't far from the crossroads."

"Virgil got off easy," Seth said. "Humbuggle ended up in Zzyzx. Let's see him rhyme his way out of there."

"Do you think they'll track down the Sphinx?" Kendra asked.

"Even if they do, what is the charge?" Seth asked. "Sort of helping Ronodin? Almost taking the Unforgiving Blade from me?"

"He's hiding out as if there was a crime," Kendra said. "He must have rigged Mendigo to kidnap you."

"Can we prove it, though?" Seth asked. "He also helped me. Without the Translocator, I couldn't have done everything in time."

"I hate that the Sphinx dodges punishments," Kendra said.

"Only partially," Seth said. "Remember, he's no longer a shadow charmer. He's lost most of his clout. And his life is tied to the demon prison's lock."

Kendra took her bedside glass of water from a folded paper towel on the nightstand. Ice clinked as she sipped. Seth lay sprawled on his back, eyes closed. "Does it feel good to have settled your debts?" Kendra asked.

Seth opened one eye. "Almost settled. We found out that Toleron died."

"You learned more than that. He died about four

hundred years ago, in a duel, at the age of two hundred and thirty-four. He left behind two sons and a daughter. What more could the lich want?"

"I sent a wraith who refused healing to deliver that message to Ezabar in the Under Realm. Once I hear back, I will owe no more favors."

"I'm a little worried that I won't know what to do without nonstop emergencies," Kendra said.

"I have an idea," Seth said, rolling out of bed and crossing to the unicorn rocking horse. He petted the silky mane. "Hi, Bracky. Wanna go for a walk with me? I could feed you some carrots."

Kendra chucked a pillow at Seth. "Knock it off," she said. "It isn't like that."

"He promised to visit you soon," Seth said.

"So what?" Kendra said. "Lots of people visit Fablehaven."

"He's cool," Seth said. "You should date him."

"He's a magical creature," Kendra said.

Seth extended his wings. "So am I, kind of." He gave his wings a couple of gentle flaps. "I hope nobody holds it against me."

"Bracken doesn't see me as someone to date," Kendra said.

"I'm not so sure," Seth said. "You're almost a magical creature yourself. Most girls don't light up on command."

"Just drop it," Kendra said, blushing. "I can't think about this."

Seth went to the nightstand, then turned the light off

and on three times. Leaving it on, he climbed into bed. "Are you going to read?" Seth asked.

"We can turn off the light," Kendra said.

She heard a click against the window.

"What was that?" Kendra asked.

"Maybe the wind?" Seth suggested.

Another click followed.

"It's not windy outside," Kendra said. "And since when does the wind tap? A bird, maybe? Pecking?"

"Have you seen a lot of birds pecking windows?" Seth asked.

Then came a third sharp click against the glass.

"We're three floors up," Kendra said. "Is somebody tossing pebbles?"

Seth got out of bed and shuffled to the window, peeking through the curtains. "I'm going to open it."

Kendra frowned. "Is that a good idea?"

"It isn't a festival night," Seth said, undoing the latch and pushing the window open. "Wow. You may want to come look."

Kendra suspected that Seth was up to some silly trick, but she slid out of her cozy bed and padded over to the window. Leaning forward, she looked down at a figure who waved.

Kendra backed into the room. "It's Bracken!"

Seth smiled.

"Did you know he was coming?" Kendra asked, suddenly hyperaware of her T-shirt and sweatpants.

"There are better questions," Seth replied with a smirk. "Like, did I signal him with the light?"

Kendra leaned out the window again. "Hi!" she stage-whispered.

"Come down," Bracken whispered back. "I'll be outside the back door."

"Okay," Kendra replied. "Give me a second."

Pulling back into the room, she glared at Seth. "Next time, warn me."

"Would you have gone to sleep in a prom dress?" Seth teased.

"It wouldn't have been sweats," Kendra said. She rummaged for some clothes. "How long have you known he was coming?"

Seth made a zipper motion over his lips. "Nobody likes a squealer."

Kendra carried her shirt and her jeans down the stairs from the attic and ducked into a bathroom. Her hair was in pretty good shape. She changed quickly, thought about makeup, then decided it would look like she was trying too hard at this point.

Kendra stashed her T-shirt and sweats at the foot of the attic stairs, then descended to the ground floor. In the kitchen, she found Grandma, Vanessa, Warren, and Tanu playing cards at the table.

"I thought you were in bed," Grandma said.

"I just want to stretch my legs," Kendra said.

"Is that what they're calling it these days?" Grandma asked innocently.

Kendra felt her face growing warm. "What do you know?"

"Nothing," Warren said.

Vanessa smiled.

Kendra knew they were using braille playing cards. The Alderfairy had allowed Seth to transport two buckets of aether for use in healing. None of it was ingested, but anywhere the aether was ladled over an injury, the problem was cured. Except for Vanessa's eyes. Andromadus theorized that because she had been blinded by magical light powered by the Source rather than the Void, the Source couldn't reverse it. Warren had seemed more crushed by the news than Vanessa.

"Enjoy your stroll," Tanu said.

Kendra walked out the back door and into the yard. Bracken cleared his throat, and she whirled.

"Did everyone know you were coming except me?" Kendra asked, stepping closer to him.

"Isn't that how surprises work?" Bracken replied, eyes trained on her.

"I guess," Kendra said, sliding her hands over her pockets. "How are your parents?"

"They accepted their new duty," Bracken said. "They're at the Source now. Father bathed in the aether and seems incredibly rejuvenated. He looks forward to dwelling in an environment saturated with pure light. And Mother seems less careworn than I have seen her in centuries."

"That's good to hear," Kendra said. "They deserve happiness."

"I agree," Bracken said. "And so do I." He stood up a little straighter. "Notice anything different about me?"

Kendra narrowed her eyes. "Yeah, something has changed." She scanned him up and down. "I can't quite put my finger on it."

Bracken chuckled. "I'm no longer a unicorn."

"What?" Kendra asked.

"I've considered this choice for a long time," Bracken said.

"But why?"

"Blame it on too much time around mortals," Bracken said. "I'm not the first and I won't be the last."

"Is it permanent?" Kendra asked.

Bracken shrugged. "Theoretically I could reverse it, though I have no interest in that pursuit. I'm ready for a new path."

"What do you mean?" Kendra asked.

"Kendra, I'm mortal," Bracken said. "I'm no longer a semi-eternal being. You could argue this is my first day of life. In practical terms, I'm around seventeen. I have about as many years left as anyone our age."

Kendra stared at him. Bracken in the flesh was more present and compelling than before. Mortality had infused him with new appeal. "What happened to your horns?"

"They're still unicorn horns," Bracken said. "I just share no connection to them anymore."

"I don't know what to say."

"This wasn't meant to put pressure on you," Bracken explained hastily. "I didn't involve you in the decision because

I wanted it to be my own choice, regardless of what happens with . . . anything else."

"How do you feel?" Kendra asked, trying not to let her mind run wild with the possibilities.

"Different," Bracken said. "Everything seems more immediate. I feel cut off from the past and the future in a way that is difficult to describe. It also feels like anything is possible. Like I could change my entire destiny at any moment."

"That might be true," Kendra said, smiling.

Bracken stepped close, staring down at her. He gently took one of her hands.

His touch sent a thrill through her. "It shouldn't be scarier than fighting dragons," Kendra said, staring up at him.

"Possibly more exciting," Bracken mused.

Kendra turned away. "You've probably kissed a lot of nymphs."

He placed his hands on her shoulders from behind. "Fewer than you might guess."

"As a new mortal, I expect you'll want to date a lot," Kendra said. "Explore your options."

"Mortals have a finite number of days," Bracken said.

"Yes."

He turned her around. "Why would I waste any of them kissing someone besides you?"

His lips brushed hers.

Kendra leaned forward, shining brighter until she lit up the yard.

# Acknowledgments

Books take time and effort to write. They start as ideas in my mind, and it is a long process to translate those internal visions into words that readers can interpret. I have been blessed with some amazing people in my life who help me convey my stories.

I cannot overstate the help of my wife, Erlyn Mull. She gives each book of mine a thorough, professional edit. Thanks to her, what I turn in to my publisher is already in fighting shape, and we get to improve the text from there. People would have to watch my whole process from start to finish to understand what a vital role Erlyn plays and how many of her good ideas and adjustments elevate the story.

So many others contributed to the making of this story and series. Chris Schoebinger applied his unique creative genius to all stages of the project, including brainstorming, editing, marketing, and even driving my kids to school one busy morning. Emily Watts has edited all of my Fablehaven and Dragonwatch books. She has used her sharp memory and powers of observation to become an expert loremaster regarding this story world. This is the last book she edited before retirement. I will miss her experienced eye and brilliant mind improving my work.

Many friends lent insights or additional edits, including

Jason and Natalie Conforto, Monte Conforto, Pamela Mull, Cherie and Bryson Mull, Hamish Elliott, Marc Bienenfeld, Davis Mull, Lila Mull, Sadie Mull, Rose Mull, Clark Baker, Brock Baker, and Fiona Baker. Kerilyn Conforto Meyer helped me fix an important detail about Raxtus.

Once again Brandon Dorman illustrated the cover and the interiors for this book, and his quality contributions speak for themselves. I'm grateful I have been able to collaborate with him so many times. A large team at Shadow Mountain helped with various aspects of making this book available. I want to thank Ilise Levine, Troy Butcher, Callie Hansen, Haley Huffaker, Heidi Taylor Gordon, and Lisa Mangum.

Writing books and promoting them demands lots of hours. I'm thankful for my understanding family—Erlyn III, Ava, Anika, Sadie, Brock, Clark, Chase, Chet, Rose, Erlyn IV, Calvin, and Fiona.

And of course, thank you, dear reader, for taking this journey with me. Without fellow imaginers like you buying my books and telling others about them, I would not be able to do this as my job. Thank you for bringing the stories to life in your mind—that is why I share them. To connect with me online, try finding me on Instagram @writerbrandon and on Facebook or Twitter under my name.

# Note to Readers

Writing a novel is like climbing a mountain that does not yet exist, reaching for handholds that become tangible only as you curl your fingers around them, yearning for a towering summit that must be willed into reality before you can stand on it. Creating an entire series is an even grander and more daunting expedition.

Writing the Fablehaven and Dragonwatch series has been quite a climb. I spent ten years of my life producing these books, and now I'm finally done. I believe these were mountains worth climbing, and I am happy to leave them as part of the landscape so others can explore them.

I didn't want to write Dragonwatch unless it would build upon what Fablehaven started in a way that felt important. Now that I'm done, I feel like Dragonwatch is the second half of a single sweeping story, and that without these five books, the adventures of Kendra and Seth would be incomplete.

Will I write more books in this story world? Anything is possible. For now, I have found an end to the story of Kendra and Seth that feels right to me. Might I return to this story world someday? It all depends on whether I find ideas that excite me. The adventures of a young Patton Burgess could be fun, for example.

One of my favorite parts of this journey was exploring the origins of magic in Fablehaven. I particularly enjoyed working with Brandon Dorman to create an illustrated version of *Legend of the Dragon Slayer*. He did an amazing job helping me produce a book that feels like a genuine artifact from the Fablehaven universe.

I have many other books and series to write. Some of my favorite ideas have yet to be written. I can't wait to share them in the years to come.

COVID has made the last couple of years crazy for everyone. I love to share about my books by touring, and I love meeting my readers, but it has been nearly impossible to do that lately. If you thought this series was worth reading, please tell others about it. Many who read the Fablehaven books still don't know about Dragonwatch. When I sell books, publishers make it easy for me to keep telling stories.

Readers like you are some of my favorite people in the world. You understand how to augment reality with fantasy. Keep building your imagination by reading awesome stories and let me know about the best ones you find. I largely cope with life by making up stories and sharing them. I hope you find lots of ways to share what makes you unique.

# Reading Guide

1. Seth wielded two swords throughout much of the book. What are the pros and cons of each weapon? If you had the chance to battle using either Vasilis or the Unforgiving Blade, which would you choose? Why?

2. Calvin wanted to break the nipsie curse since book one of Dragonwatch. In what ways did Seth help Calvin succeed? In what ways did Calvin help Seth? Could one have succeeded without the other? Explain.

3. Five monarchs ruled the magical world when this series began. Which two crowns remain at the end? How might this new situation change the balance of power in the magical world?

4. Bracken chose to become mortal at the end of the story in part so he could be closer to Kendra. What other reasons did he have for making that choice? Do you agree with his decision? Why or why not?

5. If you could visit the Source, would you drink from it, bathe in it, or just look at it? Explain why.

6. Kendra spent much of this series away from her brother. In what ways did their time apart allow her to grow? In what ways could Seth have aided her? In what ways might he have made her job harder?

7. Do you think Virgil was ever a true friend to Seth or

Kendra? Why or why not? What were his reasons for the final choice he made? How do you think he felt about the way things turned out?

8. If you could experience being tiny or gigantic, which would you choose? Why? Calvin changed size throughout the story. If you could choose a permanent size for him, what would it be?

9. Vanessa lost her sight in the Dragon Temple. How does she proceed after the blindness occurred? As a narco-blix, what extra abilities does she possess to help her cope with the loss?

10. Earlier in this series, we received hints that there were other Fairy Queens before Bracken's mother held the position. How do you think Bracken's mother felt about surrendering the crown? Why? How might the Fairy Realm be different with the Alderfairy wearing the crown?

11. Konrad's history has layers to it. Why did he choose to share parts of the story rather than the whole tale? Do you think he was right to do so? Explain.

12. Who do you think was the most effective Dragon Slayer in the story? Why? Who was your favorite Dragon Slayer?

13. Sasquatches blur the line between reality and fantasy, because some people believe in them, while others don't. Do you think sasquatches are real? Why or why not? What other cryptids interest you?

14. What has Seth learned since the beginning of his adventure? What has Kendra learned over the same period? Do you think they are more capable adventurers than at the

start of Fablehaven? Do you expect them to seek adventure or avoid it in the future? Explain your answers.

15. After the fourth book of Dragonwatch was published, some people told Brandon Mull there was too much unfinished business for him to wrap up the story in one book. Should those people be sorry? Did you feel that way? If so, are you sorry? How sorry?